LAURA CHRISTEN
Rich. Gorgeous. And a step away from one of Washington's most powerful positions.

CATSY BRADEN
The Congresswoman's daughter serves as her press secretary by day. Her nights are another story . . .

PENELOPE KRIM
The high-powered columnist wants the inside story on Laura. And she'll do just about anything to get it . . .

JAKE ALBAN
Gray-eyed and gorgeous, he has a special interest in Laura's past. Especially since he's a part of it.

◆

"*Capitol Secrets* reads like a true insider's personal tour of the chambers of Washington power. Every character has a closetful of skeletons in this fast-paced and terrifically entertaining novel."
—Edward Stewart, author of *Deadly Rich* and *Privileged Lives*

CAPITOL SECRETS

MAUREEN DEAN

JOVE BOOKS, NEW YORK

This Jove Book contains the complete
text of the original hardcover edition.
It has been completely reset in a typeface
designed for easy reading and was printed
from new film.

CAPITOL SECRETS

A Jove Book / published by arrangement with
the author

PRINTING HISTORY
Jove edition / September 1992

ISBN: 0-515-10924-X

Jove Books are published by The Berkley Publishing Group,
200 Madison Avenue, New York, New York 10016.
The name "JOVE" and the "J" logo
are trademarks belonging to Jove Publications, Inc.

With love to Sara Magill Dean
With special thanks to Dick Lochte

Politicians should read science fiction, not westerns and detective stories.

ARTHUR C. CLARKE

CAPITOL SECRETS

1

♦

Washington, D.C.

♦

"A newspaper is the lowest thing there is!"
                                        MAYOR RICHARD J. DALEY

DR. PENELOPE KRIM's office at Empire Features Syndicate had floor-to-ceiling windows that looked down on Washington Channel and, in the near distance, the Potomac. To the right were at least three memorial bridges crossing the Tidal Basin, to the left the Capitol Yacht Club. Penelope rarely bothered to enjoy her view. It was enough that she rated an office with that kind of spectacular panorama. Usually she kept the blinds closed, the desk lamp casting a strangely homey soft light over all the glass and chrome furniture. And Penelope Krim.

Cradled near her ear was a telephone into which a source known only as "Jolly" was nattering about a visiting fireman from Moscow who'd been caught the night before in an amorous embrace with a lady of tender years. "His exact words when busted were, and I quote, 'Vun minute I am on my way to my apartment. The next I am in hotel room wit' young woo-man I do not know. I do not know vat comes over me.' Beautiful, huh?" Jolly chuckled.

"Not for me," Penelope snapped. "What else? Let's have it."

There was a plaintive whine from the other end of the line. "Russian diplomat caught in sex scandal with teenage girl? You can call it 'the dark side of glasnost.' "

"I said no! What else?" she asked, drumming her fingers.

1

"That's all I've got."

"So don't waste my bloody time," Penelope said, slamming down the phone so hard the thick glass top vibrated. Then, smiling to herself, she printed the words: "Vashensky and Lolita: Dark Side of Glasnost?" in a pink leather-covered-Fileofax that had been a gift from Mrs. Thatcher. She tossed the notebook into a drawer, locked it, and began rooting through a nearly empty box of candy turtles someone had sent over from a shop in the Watergate.

In the nest of brown wrappers she uncovered the final lurking glob of sweet bribery—a caramel and walnut and milk chocolate molded into a vaguely turtlelike shape, and, salivating, popped it into her voracious mouth. She felt good for the first time that day.

Smoothing the silk Forgotten Woman dress over her more than ample body, she walked swiftly to the door and threw it open. "Loo-eeze," she bellowed in the general vicinity of the Empire Features bullpen. "In here, please!"

She'd scarcely returned to her desk when Louise Dubin entered the room toting a bulging manila folder. Louise was of average height, thin, with an intelligent, scrubbed, post-schoolgirl face that some men found attractive. Penelope glared at her and mumbled threateningly, "I hope for your sake it's all there."

Not a day passed that Louise didn't curse the eagerness that had made her actually volunteer to serve as Penelope's assistant/whipping girl when Empire ponied up a sultan's ransom to bring her popular column of political musings under its syndicated umbrella. Biting her tongue, Louise carried the folder to Penelope's desk and gently deposited it next to the empty chocolate box. "Plane tickets . . . name of the limo drivers . . . notes and list of those attending the conference. Plus a timetable for the week . . . Oh, and Mr. Marsten would like to see you."

Horace Marsten was the National Editor of Empire. "Tell him I'm available," Penelope said.

Louise shrugged and left the room.

Penelope wandered to the window and jerked open the blinds. The late morning sun lasered through the window. Smiling again, she sat at the desk, her back to the light and glare. Five minutes later an obviously peeved Horace Marsten barreled into the office, briefly squinted at the glare, then raised a hand to shade his eyes, Indian style. There was nothing else even remotely Indian about him. He was an authentic WASP of sixty-one years, one of those aristocratic figures whose families have existed in the Georgetown area so long that they are labeled Cave Dwellers by the locals.

Horace Marsten was a few millimeters over five feet tall, with silver hair that he brushed forward over a balding pate. He was dressed like Hollywood's idea of a thirties news chief—blue shirt, rolled to the elbows, bright red suspenders, and pale yellow tie, somber trousers neatly pressed, breaking neatly over polished black shoes. Someone right out of *The Front Page*.

"What can I do for you, Horace?" she asked, liberally applying a layer of Lancôme lipstick.

"For starters, you can shut the bloody blinds."

"I like the light. Anything else?"

"Be at the Rayburn Building at two for the Christen press conference," he grumbled, slipping around her desk and shutting the blinds himself.

"I'd love to," she said, putting the lipstick away, "but I'm leaving at twelve-forty for the Caribbean. The President is addressing the Inter-American Economic Council meeting this week."

Marsten shook his head, causing a few strands of his combover to flutter. "A stringer can cover that. We need you here, to see how Laura Christen plans to do the impossible."

Penelope barely kept her fury under wraps. The story, to her way of thinking, was that Christen, a twelve-year congresswoman with nothing more to her credit than several million dollars, blonde hair, firm tits, and a dazzling smile, had suddenly decided *she* had the stuff to become the first woman Speaker of the House. The present Speaker, Lew Ronkowski, one of the most savvy and powerful politicians extant, was not about to relinquish the post. Christen's announced press conference was nothing more than a feeble effort to do a little self-promotion. It was definitely not a serious news story. But unless Penelope could convince the little asshole who paid her checks of that fact, there would be no luxuriating at the newly constructed Saint Croix Palace. No hobnobbing with the President and the First Lady at the Governor's Ball. No bronze beach boys proffering exotic fruit drinks on silver beaches.

"It's a non-event, Horace," she rasped. "Christen's a Beverly Hills Barbie Doll, for Christ's sake."

"A Barbie Doll who was a self-made millionairess by the time she was thirty."

Penelope had to admit that was true. Before entering politics, the Congresswoman had helped to create one of the country's largest cosmetics firms. "So she can peddle drugstore lipstick," Penelope said contemptuously. "No way is she gonna make this sale. Even if she's managed to slip between the sheets with more than half the House, she still won't get the votes. Ronkowski will eat her alive, eyeliner and all. Sorry—no story."

"No story? Laura Christen is gonna try to shoot the goddamn moon and become the first woman Speaker of the House in the history of these United States! And you want to be off sippin' Mai Tais with a bunch of bloody economists?"

"Those bloody economists will be going one-on-one with the President about the new trade bill, which *is* goddamn news, just in case you didn't know, Horace."

Marsten cocked his head to one side, considering it. "The trade bill *is* a hot issue," he admitted. "But I just heard it cooled off a little. Seems the guy the Russians sent to help push the bill along got himself arrested with an underage girl."

Penelope was annoyed with herself for not realizing that Jolly's Russian was the same one who'd come to plead with the President to endorse the trade bill. Not that it mattered. If the little idiot standing in front of her was aware of it, the story must have already made the wire. Old news. "My God, Horace, your horny Red notwithstanding, the trade bill is certainly more important than the Congressional Bimbo."

Marsten opened his mouth, then stopped himself. He had not stayed in his job for over a decade by telling prima donna columnists what he really thought of them. Not when they had the kind of following Penelope Krim had amassed at the tender age of thirty-five. Assuming a less hostile approach, he said, "Laura Christen is news, Penny. I got an advance copy of *People* with her very lovely face plastered over six pages."

"It must be their 'Sexiest Pol of the Year' issue," she snapped. He chuckled dutifully. "The headline reads: HONORABLE LADY!

and the photos have got her behaving like a combination of Abe Lincoln and Madame Curie. With maybe Kim Bassinger thrown in for good measure.''

''Time for a reality check, Horace. The man in the street couldn't care less about who wants to be Speaker of the House. That goes double for the newsman on the street. I can't believe you're taking it seriously.''

Horace Marsten gave her a brief wintry smile. Then he cooed, ''You're a pretty savvy customer, honey. You're carried in three hundred newspapers—''

''Three hundred and thirty-two. But who's counting, and what's that got to do with—''

''Just this, my dear,'' Marsten said, assuming his most avuncular tone. ''We have this sexy blonde congresswoman who's single-handedly attempting to drag the House kicking and screaming into the twenty-first century. Forgetting about your three hundred and thirty-two editors, do you really want your twenty million readers to wonder why you backed away from that story to talk to them about the romance of trade embargoes?''

Dr. Penelope Krim looked at the short, balding man with the ridiculous bow tie and knew that she would not be going to the Caribbean. She sighed. ''Shit . . .''

''It's the smart thing to do,'' he said. ''You want me to open those blinds for you before I leave?''

When she didn't reply, he winked, turned, and made his exit. She was sure she heard him chuckle as he shut her door.

''THE Rayburn House Building,'' Penelope barked at the taxi driver. After she adjusted her girth in the backseat, she began rooting through her oversized handbag for a Di-Gel. She'd blitzed a pastrami on rye while reading the *People* article. Fluff about how the Congresswoman spent her days in the nation's capital. Nothing about the nights, and precious little on Laura Christen's background and personal life.

''Turn up the heat,'' Penelope commanded the driver.

He waved his hand at the wintry sunlight. ''It's like spring outside, lady. In the fifties. And we're almost there.''

She shook her head. She couldn't even make a cabdriver see

things her way. She jerked her note pad from her bag and flipped through the scribbles she'd made on the story. She knew how it would end. The Speaker of the House was selected from the "old boys' club," the leadership of the majority party, which in this case was, as it had been for lo these many years, the Democratic Party. Not only was Christen a woman, she was an outsider, an "Independent."

Then there was the fact that you weren't supposed to campaign publicly for the job. You engaged in rather gentlemanly discussions with the party hierarchy, and the final decision was quietly resolved in the privacy of a party caucus.

"Geeze," the driver said suddenly, derailing her train of thought. "What's with this traffic, anyhow?"

Penelope was surprised to see the bumper-to-bumper line of cars creeping along Independence Avenue. Capitol Hill was usually a ghost town at this time of year, with most of the biggies in their home states, beaming over the November 7 elections and awaiting the arrival of the Christmas season with its family photo opportunities.

Everybody who was left in Washington, Penelope noted with annoyance, seemed to be headed toward the Rayburn Building. The crowd was thick with reporters, some of whom she hadn't seen out in the sunlight in years. All covering the absurd Christen spectacle. The old bastard Marsten had been right. It *was* turning into a bloody media event . . .

LINING the semicircular drive of the South Capitol Street entrance to the squat, gray marble Rayburn Building, one of the most expensive and least attractive structures in the city, were trucks and vans from the commercial and cable networks, aiming assorted satellite dishes skyward. Detroit iron and Japanese aluminum clogged the drive. Penelope slipped a ten-dollar bill through the plastic window that separated her from the driver and did not wait for the thanks that probably would not come.

She tromped up the walkway and passed between the Rayburn's entrance pillars only to face a makeshift sign that read: CONGRESS-WOMAN LAURA CHRISTEN PRESS CONFERENCE MOVED TO CAFETERIA

(B-124-8) RESCHEDULED TO BEGIN 2:30 PM. PRESS CREDENTIALS NEC-
ESSARY FOR ATTENDANCE.

The sign had carried two previous locations—Subcommittee
Hearing Room 217 and the larger Commerce Hearing Room 115.
It was another indication of the escalating interest in the Christen
press conference that it would now take place in the largest contig-
uous space in the building which, cleared of tables, would accommodate twelve hundred people. Penelope sighed. She had a half
hour to kill—and she devoutly wished she could find somebody
worth killing.

She walked back outside the building. NBC had set up its
cameras. A tall, earnest-looking middle-aged reporter in a black
trench coat was standing near the columns, speaking slowly and
with feeling into the red eye. ". . . the curious thing is that here we
have a woman of exceptional charisma, wealth, and power suddenly thrust into the limelight. Yet she has been doing her job in
the House for six terms—and doing it well. Perhaps it is true that
we pay far too much attention to the negative side of the news and
not enough to those dedicated persons who are making this our
world a better one to live in. . . ."

If there had not been a hot camera in the vicinity, Penelope
would have stuck a finger into her mouth in a don't-make-me-puke
gesture. Instead, she faced a throng of eager, chattering reporters
and begrudgingly decided that even if Laura Christen wasn't going
to be the next Speaker, she might conceivably make an interesting
flavor of the month.

She found a telephone booth just outside the door to the cafeteria
and claimed it as her own. Methodically, she used her charge card
to dial a series of numbers. As each was answered, she explained
that she wanted any scrap of hard news, gossip, or outright lie that
was available on Laura Christen.

While she was between calls a fat young man approached the
booth. From the corner of her eye Penelope saw the familiar
babyish face topped by wiry, pomaded black hair. He was wearing
a cocoa-brown cashmere coat with a mink collar.

"Could I cut in for a minute, love? Just for a quickie? Please."

"Bugger off," she said. "I'm busy."

"Well! If it isn't the bitch goddess of the Washington news corps. My, this *is* an A news event."

"It was until you showed up, fruitcake," she replied, punching in a new number.

His name was Jeremy Dunbar and he wrote a weekly gossip column for the *National Examiner*. In the past few years, the tabloid had been successfully sued several times because of Dunbar's unsubstantiated little libels. But its publisher wrote the costly defeats off to promotion and publicity, and the readers, in spite of considerable evidence to the contrary, kept their faith in the veracity of Jeremy's collections of vicious squibs.

"C'mon, love—I'll be just a sec," he said, extending a delicate, mauve-gloved hand for the receiver. Penelope slapped the hand away.

"Pretty please, Dr. Penny?" he said, reaching into his coat pocket and giving her a quick peek at a square envelope addressed to him at the *Examiner*. He giggled. "One call and I'll let you in on something juicy-juicy-juicy."

"What's that? Your latest libel suit?" Krim snapped.

"Oooooh, vicious lady! Better be nice or I just might tell the world about Dr. Penny and her hot-and-heavy with a *very* married old psychiatrist."

Penelope's eyes flashed. "If you do," she said evenly, "I won't bother suing you. I'll see to it that your fetid, backbiting body disappears forever from the face of the earth."

Something in her tone made the blood, what there was of it, drain from Dunbar's round face. He backed away, attempted a tough sneer, but only partially succeeded. "Keep reading the *Examiner,* sweetie-pie," he said. "I'll even spell your name correctly."

"Eat shit and die!" she suggested.

2

◆

"Nobody believes a rumor here in Washington until it's officially denied."

EDWARD CHEYFITZ

THE CAFETERIA WAS as hot and humid as a solarium by the time Congresswoman Christen and her daughter arrived. The windows were fogged with condensation, and several members of the restless assembly were waving their notebooks to circulate the stale air.

Catherine Christen Braden walked up to the hastily constructed podium and tapped a manicured fingernail against the microphone to test it. A few klieg lights came to life, adding to the room's discomfort, but Catherine, or as she would have it, Catsy, appeared remarkably cool in her orange wool Ungaro with a skirt short enough to bring a few of the TV guys out from behind their cameras. It *was* going to be a day of photo opportunity.

Some of those in attendance mistook her for the Congresswoman and scrambled for pens and cameras. Catsy looked like her mother. The twenty-two years that separated them spoke well for the care Laura had taken of herself, but not so well for the life that Catsy had thus far lived.

Catsy Braden was twenty-four but looked thirty-five and some days even forty; Laura was forty-six and looked forty and some days even thirty-five. As alike as their blonde hair, green eyes, prominent cheekbones, and elegant figures made them, their private lives were as different as those of Margaret Truman and Margaret Trudeau.

9

While adjusting the microphone upward for herself and her mother—with heels, they each stood nearly six feet tall—Catsy surveyed the crowd, pausing to lock eyes with several of the more interesting-looking men. One seemed very familiar—a tall, square-jawed specimen. He smiled at her and she remembered: John Kilmer, a newscaster at a local TV station, the only anchorman she'd ever met who had a sense of humor. He kept a hand puppet beside his bed—a very naughty hand puppet.

Kilmer wrapped his display handkerchief around his fist and waved at her. She grinned, then forced herself to look away. She spotted Laura chatting with the captain of the Capitol Hill police force. The captain was smiling, the way men usually smiled when her mother gave them her full attention. Well, Catsy thought, she could play that game too.

The remaining video lights flashed on as Catsy placed her note-book on the podium. She waited a beat for her eyes to grow accustomed to the glare. Actually, she loved it. Loved the heat, the attention. She basked in it.

She cleared her throat for attention, then introduced herself as Congresswoman Christen's press secretary. The words echoed through the suddenly silent room. She had a carefully cultivated, low and throaty voice. A man once told her that she could make "hello" sound like an invitation to spend the night, and she considered it a compliment. But it wasn't the effect she was seeking at the moment. She consulted her notes and then began, in her carefully articulated, efficient voice, to tell the occupants of the room everything they already knew about her mother's desire to become the next Speaker of the House.

PAYING only peripheral attention to Catsy Braden's rehash of current events, Penelope Krim focused her attention on Laura Christen. In her form-fitting, black silk gabardine Thierry Mugler suit, she looked revoltingly self-possessed and obnoxiously attractive. Captain Legrand, who was holding her in conversation, was nearing the drooling stage.

Then, suddenly, Jeremy Dunbar appeared at the Congress-woman's side. She turned to him. Words were whispered and Laura Christen turned to the attentive police captain and excused herself. As she and Dunbar edged away from Captain Legrand, Penelope began tracking them.

Catsy Braden's voice bounced around the room. "Sir—it would help if you'd identify yourself and your publication or broadcast group, or whatever, when you address questions."

Penelope pushed past a cameraman from Channel 4. Fifteen feet away, Laura Christen was frowning at Jeremy Dunbar, whose mouth was moving like a puppet's. Penelope was good at reading lips, but the best she could come up with was ". . . I might not have to use it." What the hell was "it"?

Penelope moved in close enough to hear Laura say, "You've been misinformed," in a harsh, flat voice.

Jeremy's hand emerged from his coat pocket. In it was a square envelope. He fumbled with its contents, a sheet of paper. He held it out to Laura.

The Congresswoman's face blanched. She reached for the paper, but Jeremy, with a sly smile, withdrew it and put it back in its envelope. "I'll call you to set up our chat . . . Laura . . ." he said, drawling her name in a mockery of intimacy.

Laura seemed about to reply, but Catsy Braden picked that moment to announce, "And now, for those who do not know her, I'd like to introduce my mother . . . Congresswoman Laura Christen."

Penelope moved back out of camera range while Laura Christen walked briskly away from the fat little gossip columnist to assume center-stage position on the podium.

There was a smattering of polite applause mixed with shouts from the Congresswoman's staff. Then it began to grow. Some of the television cameramen expressed themselves with whistles and catcalls which in another context—construction workers watching secretaries in tight skirts, say—could have been labeled sexist. Here, they merely added to the overall feeling of excitement.

Frowning, Penelope Krim looked away from the podium and tried to locate Jeremy Dunbar in the swirl of bodies. She spotted him edging closer to the door through which Laura Christen would undoubtedly exit. Not hesitating, Penelope stalked him.

"Thank you, thank you," Laura Christen said when the applause finally subsided. "I hope you gentlemen who were making the catcalls won't be too disappointed to learn that this is going to be a very dignified occasion." With that, she began slowly and gracefully to remove her suit jacket, exposing a soft white blouse that accentuated her full chest and thin waist.

Her eyebrows went up in mock surprise at the laughter that followed. "Well, it is extremely hot in this room," she said. "Feel free to take off your jackets if you like."

As Penelope edged past *The New York Times'* Jim Hafer, her eyes scanned his note pad. "Great looking! Exciting! Self-assured!" Hafer had just finished drawing a heart with the initials L.C. when he looked up and saw Penelope shaking her head disgustedly. He grinned at her and whispered, "I can't help it, Penny, I'm in love."

The object of his affection was warming to her subject. "Rather than keep us inside for too long on this glorious crisp winter's day, let me state simply that, yes, I plan on becoming the next Speaker of the House of Representatives."

More clapping and whistles. Penelope was appalled to see so many supposedly unbiased members of the Fourth Estate putting down their pens and notebooks to join in the applause.

Jeremy Dunbar stood only a few yards away from her, grinning oddly, his eyes focused on Laura Christen. Then Penelope was crowding in beside him, looming over him before he noticed her. "What've you got?" she whispered.

He smiled. "Judging by this reaction," he said, "nothing less than a very rich future."

"What's in that goddamn envelope?" she said aloud.

Faces turned angrily at them.

"You'll know soon enough." Dunbar sneered. "Or maybe you won't. It could go either way, sweetie."

He took a step back from Penelope and collided with a young woman who'd just entered the room. There was something about the graceful, almost unconscious way the woman regained her balance that piqued Penelope's interest.

The most obvious thing about the woman was her mass of brilliant red curls that seemed beyond taming by comb or brush. Not bottle red, but the real thing, with fair skin and emerald eyes to match. She was on the small side, compact-looking under a loose, black woolen sweater and forest-green corduroy trousers. She carried a parka in the crook of her arm.

Penelope knew most of the reporters on the Capitol beat, but this was someone new. She was young enough not to have been weaned from her tape recorder, but she didn't have one in evidence. No notebook, either.

Penelope had never been one to avert her eyes, and the redhead noticed her unwavering glare. She glared back. When that didn't work, the woman smiled sweetly and said, "It's rude as hell to stare, don't you think?" Then she strode past Penelope as though the columnist had ceased to exist, her attention focused on the star of the show, Laura Christen.

Penelope's mouth dropped open. *Well, screw her and the broom she rode in on.* Penelope gritted her teeth and scanned the room again for Jeremy.

There he was at the edge of the crowd, eyeing the Congresswoman, with his insipid smirk still in place. Penelope positioned herself between him and the door so he'd have to pass her on the way out.

TWENTY minutes and a dozen and a half questions later, the love affair between the media and Laura Christen had heated up. From the podium, Laura was saying, "The press packets at the door should contain the answers to most questions you still have. If you can think of any others, please call my office."

As some of the reporters started to move toward the door, Laura said, "There's something in the packet that requires a bit of explanation."

There was a sudden silence in the room as though the crowd could sense that Laura had led them up to a crucial moment. She held up a sheet of paper containing typescript. "Each packet contains a copy of this letter. In it I have informed my colleagues that Minority Leader Michael Roberts has pledged to me the support of the Republican Party. Further, more than twenty Democratic Party congresswomen have promised to be in my corner. Assuming we have counted correctly, and this impressive backing remains constant, I will have the votes I need to become the next Speaker of the House."

There was more silence as the crowd digested the fact that this lovely, well-spoken woman had just announced a coup. Then hands flew up and started waving, and voices shouted from everywhere in the room. Some reporters rushed for the exits to telephone their editors.

Penelope Krim did not notice the red-haired woman as she walked past her and out of the room; she was too busy gawking at Laura. Even Jeremy Dunbar and his envelope had been pushed to the back of her mind. She said, almost unconsciously, "It's a goddamned bluff."

Jim Hafer heard her. "If it is," he said, "it looks damn good on her."

The room was filled with questions. From an ultra-stylish *Vogue* editor: Was Laura joining the Republican Party? "No, I am still very much an Independent, though my leadership *would* give the Republicans control of the House." From Bob Todman of *The Washington Post:* Why did Mike Roberts decide to support her instead of running himself, as he had in the past? "You'll have to ask him that, Mr. Todman."

From *Time* magazine: "Do you have the President's support?"

"That's something you'll have to ask him," Laura replied with a confident smile.

There were more queries about Speaker Ronkowski, the seniority system, the women in Congress, her plans for improving the congressional process. Laura replied to each without hesitation, even if only to say that she had no comment.

Penelope listened attentively to it all, wondering if her original assessment of the woman could have been that wrong. Was there some substance under all those creamy curves? If so, why had Laura Christen been hiding it all these years, remaining Independent, traveling the country campaigning for a dead-horse issue like women's rights, doing everything to keep herself out of the political mainstream?

She didn't even play the social game. The columnist knew that, politician or no, the very rich often chose to maintain a low profile. And Laura Christen was very rich. But Penelope, who was invited to everything from carwash openings to private formal dinners for six, attended one or two functions each night, and she and Laura Christen seldom if ever crossed paths socially.

What did the woman do with her evenings? More important, with her nights? Penelope's quick calls to her sources had not revealed whom the Congresswoman had slept with, was sleeping with, would be sleeping with. Just about all of the sources, however, reported that Catsy Braden hit the sheets with anything in pants, as long as it was tall and brushed its teeth. *That* was a social philosophy Penelope could understand.

"I think we'll end on that note," Laura was saying as the columnist let go of her thoughts. "I want to wish you all Season's Greetings and a fruitful New Year."

As she moved almost regally from the podium, the bright TV lights went out like dying fireflies. Some of the members of the press were folding their notebooks and clicking off their tape recorders, but a persistent cadre continued to poke microphones in Laura's face, asking questions that ranged from inane to ludicrous. Did Laura have presidential aspirations? Did she sleep in a nightgown? What shampoo did she use?

Catsy Braden ran interference for her mother to the exit, allowing her to slip into the hall. Penelope hurried after them. From the corner of her eye she saw Jeremy Dunbar closing in on Laura. Then, suddenly, a man blocked his progress.

He was tall and very blond. His bland, not unhandsome face had the healthy glow of a deep tan. One of his large hands held Jeremy by the back of the neck while he bent down to speak to him confidentially.

Jeremy's eyes widened. He jerked away from the man's grasp. Then he turned and walked quickly toward the building's front door.

The man did not follow, merely stared after Jeremy with no expression.

Penelope had to make a quick decision—Laura and her entourage were getting into the elevator. Laura, she reasoned, would be available anytime. At the moment it was Jeremy who demanded her interest. . . .

As she went through the door almost abreast of the tall blond man she caught a whiff of cologne that smelled like industrial-strength Old Spice. It took several vigorous exhalations in the cold afternoon air to clear the odor from her nostrils.

The weather, which had been almost pleasant when they arrived, had shifted abruptly. The sky was hidden by heavy slate-gray clouds, and the wind was as damp as it was cold.

Jeremy was hurrying down the avenue, pausing every few steps to look over his shoulder. With an oath that would have withered a weed, Penelope gathered her large bag to her ample bosom and went after him.

The good thing about the chase was that Jeremy ran with an awkward, butt-wiggling waddle that did not allow for much speed. The bad thing was that any amount of exercise more strenuous than tapping the keys of a computer caused Penelope to wheeze and pant like a Saint Bernard after a hard day's romp in the Alps.

Jeremy turned right on Second Street, heading in the general direction of Folger Park, a small, square block of earth and benches. The cold weather had denuded the trees and bushes. Little puddles of melted ice rested on straw-colored lawns that in sultrier times boasted a healthy dark green color.

Penelope was only fifty yards or so behind the gossip columnist when he paused at a bench near the entrance to the park to catch his breath. He turned, saw her, and stumbled into the park.

Near its center, where several concrete paths converged, there was a parched concrete birdbath. Before Jeremy could gather up the energy to push himself beyond it, Penelope was on him. Wheezing like walruses, they looked at each other. When she had regained enough breath to speak, Penelope, her face an inch from his, demanded to know what was in the letter.

"Please," he whined, looking over her shoulder. "I have to go. I'm not feeling well."

He tried to pull away, but she grabbed the tail of his expensive cashmere coat and yanked him back.

"Time to talk, Jeremy," she said.

He opened his mouth. Then, quite unexpectedly, his eyes rolled back in his head. He leaped forward into her arms and began grinding his pelvis against her.

Astonished, she dropped her bag. Jeremy's head was against her chest, trying to burrow past her coat. His mouth was pushing against her left breast, making little biting motions. "Cut that out, you little shit!" she yelled, backing away.

Jeremy clung to her, bouncing against her. Through both their layers of clothes, she could feel his stiff penis battering against her hip. His face was turning scarlet. Flecks of foam appeared on his lips.

Suddenly he released her, stood completely still, and drew a sharp intake of breath. His right hand grabbed at his left arm and he grunted in pain. Then he fell forward onto the concrete walkway.

"Jesus Christ, Jeremy!" Penelope said, possibly aloud. She raised her head and looked about her. At the far end of the park a nursemaid was pushing a pram. Two little black girls were hip-hopping together, giggling. A homeless man lay on a nearby bench, snoring, covered with rain-soaked pages of the *Post*. No one was looking their way.

She heard a car door slam and spun around. The curb was lined with parked automobiles, a van, a panel truck. They all seemed to be empty.

She bent down to press her fingers against Jeremy's neck, the way she'd seen policemen check for a pulse on a hundred television shows. The flesh was still warm, but sans pulse.

If Penelope had been less of a newswoman, she might have panicked and run off to report the death. Instead, she took a deep breath and lifted Jeremy's body onto its side. Holding it with one hand, she used the other to fish the prized envelope from his inside jacket pocket. Then she lowered the body to its original position. As she did, she noticed an ugly red welt on the back of his neck. It resembled a mosquito bite—but there were no mosquitoes in Washington during the winter.

Let the coroner, or whoever, worry about the bite. The envelope, she observed, was addressed to Jeremy in care of his tabloid. She slipped it into her bag, stumbled to her feet, and forced herself to walk slowly and deliberately out of the park, without looking back.

At the corner she paused to allow a chocolate-brown panel truck to turn onto Independence Avenue. She'd planned on returning to the Rayburn to phone the police, but she had not yet decided if she would involve herself in Jeremy's death. A scream behind her made up her mind.

The two little girls had discovered Jeremy. Fine. She hailed a Yellow cab and gave the driver her syndicate's address on Maine Avenue. "Rain's gonna beat us there," the driver said. He might as well have been talking to himself.

PENELOPE fought her curiosity and won all the way back to her private office. There, she plopped onto her chair without bothering to remove her coat. As rain started pelting the window behind her, she placed the envelope on her desk and studied it for a few seconds. It had been postmarked in Los Angeles. She turned it over. It had a nice finish, might even be Crane. Using extreme care, she lifted the flap and withdrew a folded sheet. It read in neat handwritten block letters, DEAR JEREMY DUNBAR, IF YOU'RE LOOKING FOR A LEAD ITEM FOR YOUR COLUMN, WHY NOT ASK CONGRESSWOMAN CHRISTEN ABOUT HER BASTARD CHILD AND WHAT HAPPENED TO IT? It was signed, A FAN.

Penelope smiled. For the first time that day, she was genuinely pleased that she had missed her trip to the Caribbean.

3

♦

"Government is too big and important to
be left to the politicians."

CHESTER BOWLES

MARGARET STAFFORD'S ORIGINAL plan for the cold, damp D.C.
evening was to deliver a Welcome to the Building bottle of wine
to her handsome new next-door neighbor. Instead, she was sitting
in a parked car on dismal Delaware Avenue, watching rain blur the
windshield. But business was business. And anyway the neighbor
was much too good looking to be straight.

She flipped down the visor of her two-year-old Prelude and
glanced at her reflection with more curiosity than satisfaction. She
ran thin tapered fingers through her wild red curls and seemed
disappointed that they remained as untamed as ever. She wrinkled
her small, thin nose in frustration, disturbing the smattering of
freckles that dusted her chiseled features. With a sigh, she pushed
the visor back in place and stared through the car's rain-blurred
windshield. She scanned the street, which was as empty as one
might expect, considering the weather. Not even the presence of
the General Maitland Hotel, a dismal stained and chipped chunk of
granite and brick a quarter of a block away, seemed to be generat-
ing any activity.

The only other occupants of Delaware Avenue were three apparently empty parked vehicles—a black Buick Le Sabre, a nondescript Ford Probe, and a mud-colored truck belonging to
"Brookville," whatever that happened to be.

Margaret consulted the small quartz watch on her wrist. Five forty-seven. Thirteen minutes until her meeting. Given the opportunity, she would have suggested a livelier spot than the Maitland. An active staff had less time to spend observing the vagaries of the patrons. More important, she felt uncomfortable conducting business in unfamiliar surroundings. That was why she'd arrived early, leaving the neighbor untended.

Sighing, she wrapped her coat tightly around her slender, almost boyish figure, pulled down her rain hat until it almost completely hid her scarlet hair, set the car alarm system, and stepped into the rain.

She walked quickly down the street, trying to avoid the deeper puddles. A good portion of the downpour found easy access to her neck and ankles.

The alley behind the hotel was empty. A service entrance and a metal delivery door were both locked. The fire escape seemed rusty from disuse. In two filthy dumpsters, the rain was turning the garbage of the day into a watery soup.

She made a complete tour of the block, then returned to her car, pressed the electronic gizmo in her pocket twice, and unlocked the passenger door. A woman seated behind the wheel of a parked vehicle arouses suspicion. A woman sitting in the passenger seat is waiting for her husband.

At 5:58 a gunmetal-gray Lincoln splashed up the avenue and parked near the Maitland's front door. Its sole occupant was a man approximately six feet tall whose heavy build was enhanced by a lined trench coat that looked brand new. He made an ineffectual mini-umbrella of his large, beefy hand over his graying hair and ran into the hotel.

He was Margaret's partner, J. B. Murphy. She watched the street for two more minutes, then followed him in.

THE door to room 1421 opened on Murphy's ugly-handsome black-Irish face. Ever since she had first become aware of his existence—back when she was still a schoolgirl—he had reminded her of a less-wrinkled, spruced-up Andy Rooney. Fortunately, he didn't sound anything like Rooney. His rich baritone welcomed her with, "Meg, love, you're as welcome as blue skies to old man Noah."

Two other men were seated at a table near a television set with picture on and sound off. Like Murphy, they wore dark gray suits. She placed their ages as being close to Murphy's, too. Mid- to late-fifties. They'd been having a drink. A bottle of Dewar's was on the table, and beside it, the hotel's standard issue plastic bucket of ice.

Margaret allowed Murphy to assist her in removing her raincoat. She was wearing a russet turtleneck sweater and a short black skirt. The other men looked at her legs appreciatively and silently as she shrugged out of the rain garment. It didn't affect her one way or the other. Murphy threw her coat and hat carelessly onto the bed beside his Burberry, which was already dampening the tattered, earth-colored spread.

She looked around the room—pale orange walls, brown drapes, a faded light brown carpet. An ancient metal device along the wall made a gurgling sound and seemed to be producing heat. Two fire sprinklers disturbed the dingy ceiling. Definitely a "moderate" hotel. She wondered idly what the other two men had done with their rainwear.

"Meg, say hello to Mike Roberts and Charlie Stern," Murphy suggested. Then, working under the assumption that dignitaries never tired of hearing their titles bandied, he added, "Mike is, as you well know, Minority Leader of the House. Charlie is . . . hell, I'm not sure what your billing is these days, Charlie."

She studied Stern as the men stood. He was a tall, rawboned man with a thatch of iron-colored hair that bothered his brow. His leathery face broke into a grin. "I guess you might call me the current conscience of the Republican Party, Murph."

"Yeah?" Murphy raised an eyebrow and shrugged. "I thought that was Jesse Helms. Anyway, gentlemen: my partner, Meg Stafford."

"Actually, I prefer the name Margaret," she said with barely a trace of annoyance.

Mike Roberts, round and normally genial, with a perpetual five o'clock shadow, shook her hand and said, "A pleasure, Margaret."

Stern was too far away for a handshake and seemed disinclined to move into a position for one. He said, "The last time I saw you,

Margaret, you were behind the bars of a playpen in a rooming house in Cleveland Park.''

"You knew my parents?'' Margaret asked.

Stern's eyes moved to Murphy briefly, then back to her. "Oh, yes. Your father and Murphy and I were . . . warriors in a less complex time. Would you care for something to cut the chill? I'm afraid the selection is rather limited.''

She shook her head.

"To work, then,'' Murphy said, plopping himself on the bed and indicating that Margaret should take the remaining chair. He turned to the two other men. "Well, Mike, you said on the phone that you were in a time crunch. Here we are.''

The Minority Leader paused to stare at Margaret, absently scratching his dark beard stubble. Then he turned to Murphy. "How much were you able to pull together on short notice?''

"Given that I had just three hours and you requested I do the pulling together personally, not a hell of a lot.'' He leaned back and slipped two sheets of white paper from the folds of his trench coat and smoothed them on his leg. Then he removed a pair of half-glasses from his breast pocket. With them perched on his nose, he began to read. "Laura Christen, seventh-term congresswoman from the state of California. Independent. Member of the Comm—''

Roberts leaned forward impatiently and interrupted. "You can skip the lady's credits, Murph. What else?''

Murphy shrugged. "She was born on the twelfth of May, forty-six years ago, in Franktown, Colorado. Which I am informed is just south of Denver. Parents deceased. Raised by several foster families. Married one Robert Christen, now deceased. They resided in Aspen, had a child, a daughter, Catherine. She has something of a rep as a roundheels but is nevertheless her mom's press secretary.''

He looked up over his glasses, waited for affirmation, then returned to his notes. "The husband met his maker when a truck piled into his car. After a period of mourning, Laura Christen pulled up stakes and took the kid to Southern California, where she worked in public relations for one of the Hamilton Hotels, the Casa Bel Air. I prefer the plain old Bel Air, myself.'' He looked again at the two unsmiling men.

"Anyway," he continued, "things get a little fuzzy at this point. Something or someone evidently convinced the lady to put the screws to the company whose careless truck driver caused her husband's death. That resulted in an out-of-court settlement that she used to seed a small cosmetics firm in the San Fernando Valley. Some years later she sold her interest in the company for roughly twenty-five million, give or take a mil. And here she is, a fine, healthy figure of a woman, a popular politician, richer than Croesus, who expects to be the first lady Speaker the House has ever had."

"Is that all you have?" Mike Roberts asked.

"Jay-sus, Mike, you haven't hired us yet. The real dirty linen won't show for a day or two. That's how long it'll take one of our girls"—he gave Mcg a guilty sidelong glance—"one of our *assistants* to check our sources and root through the Congresswoman's press clippings."

"I was at the Rayburn for her news conference today," Margaret said. "She looked pretty good. Ronkowski is a sexist weasel who should be replaced. I hope she does it."

"Worse than a weasel," Mike Roberts said dryly, "he's a Democrat. Which is why my party is supporting Mrs. Christen."

Murphy sighed. "Why come to us now, Michael? It's a little late for a background check. You've already got into bed with the lady. Now you're asking to see her medical record?"

"Before we committed, I had a rudimentary background check made," Mike Roberts said. "I didn't really feel any more was needed. Mrs. Christen has been in public life for twelve years, and there hasn't been even a hint of anything dark and dank hiding in her closet."

"Then what's got you all hot and bothered?" Murphy asked, leaning back on his elbows on the bed.

Roberts paused, blinked, and said, "I received a letter in the mail a couple days ago. At my office. Here's a copy."

He handed Murphy a folded photocopy of a typewritten letter consisting of only two questions: "Are you sure that Laura Christen is the sort of person you and your party should be supporting? Do you know that her money springs from a tainted source?"

Murph handed the letter to Margaret. He asked the Minority

Leader, "Did you bring a copy 'cause you don't trust us, or did you misplace the original?"

Mike Roberts exchanged a look with Charles Stern and said, "It was inadvertently destroyed."

"What about the envelope?"

"Ditto," Roberts said. "My name and address were typed on the front, and the word 'Personal' was written by hand in green ink."

"Postmark?" Margaret asked as she returned the photocopy to Murphy.

"Marina Del Rey, California."

"That near L.A.?" Murphy wondered.

"Part of the sprawl," Charles Stern said.

"The message is sorta vague," Murphy said. "What money are we talking about? According to legend, some of Christen's loot came from settling the suit after her husband's death. Then she put that into the cosmetics company, which she later sold for more money. Who did the buying?"

Mike Roberts said, "Hamilton Resorts International. Ivor Hamilton had invested in the company early on, then increased his shares by picking up Mrs. Christen's."

"So? HRI's legit, isn't it?"

"No reason to think otherwise. Perhaps there's another partner that hasn't surfaced."

"Have you asked the Congresswoman about all this?" Margaret inquired.

"No," Mike Roberts replied. "I don't want to risk souring our relationship just because of some vague, unsigned bit of innuendo."

"On the other hand," Margaret said, "you're wondering if there might not be something in Mrs. Christen's past to embarrass you."

"Margaret," Mike Roberts said earnestly, "if you want to talk embarrassment, I would appear on the *Today Show* wearing just a loincloth and a boa if it would weaken the Democratic rule of the House."

"It's a pretty picture you paint, Mike," Murphy said. "But it doesn't tell us precisely what you want of us. Unless it's an investigation of the financial underpinning of''—he looked at his notes—''Lady Amber Cosmetics?''

''That, certainly,'' Stern said. ''We'd also like you to go over the Congresswoman's background completely. And we'd like to get as much of it done as possible before the President issues his own personal endorsement of Mrs. Christen. Without that, I'm not sure we can guarantee the backing of all the Republicans in the House. With it . . . well, you know how peevish the President can be when his will not be done.''

''When does he make his official statement?'' Murphy asked.

''The President is headed for the Caribbean to meet with some economists about the damned international trade bill. He returns Monday. That's when I'll need your report.''

''Four days? Cover forty-six years in just four days, and tiptoe around while we're doin' it? Why didn't you wait until tomorrow to bring us in, make it really tough?''

Roberts and Stern exchanged looks. Stern said, ''A couple of weeks ago, just after Mike and Congresswoman Christen agreed to agree, we put Stuart Wayland to work on a quick background check.''

Murphy cocked his head. ''Stuart's OK, for a one-man band.''

''Then, after that letter arrived, we called Stuart in again and hired him to fill in all the blanks.''

''What'd he find out?''

''We don't know,'' Roberts said, pouring another drink for himself. ''Stuart passed away this morning. He drove his rental car down the side of a canyon in Southern California. Caught fire. Horrible thing. He had the original of that letter with him. At least it wasn't among his effects.''

Murphy's face paled. He stood up. ''Well, I'm sorry as hell about poor Stuart. And I don't mind being in second position on your list. But poison pen letters, sudden death, *and* Southern California, it all sounds a bit rich for my diet. I don't think we can help you. Definitely not with a four-day deadline.''

''How long would it take?'' Stern asked.

''Five days,'' Margaret said.

Murphy scowled. ''Aww, honey. Our plate's full enough right now. And this has blood on it.''

She turned to Stern. "Is there any reason to think that Stuart Wayland's death was anything other than an accident?"

"Oh, hell no," he replied. "It was definitely an accident. The coroner out there says he had a heart attack, lost control of the vehicle, and went through a guardrail. He was probably dead even before the car touched down. Most assuredly an accident."

"OK," she told Stern. "It's a done deal."

Murphy moaned.

TWENTY minutes later the co-owners of the Murphy-Stafford Agency were alone in the hotel room. At Murphy's request the Dewar's had been left behind by the departing politicians. He took a swig from the bottle, then asked glumly, "Why for, Meg?"

"I've told you before: my name's Margaret."

"Your mother was Meg. You remind me of her."

"My mother was Meg. I'm Margaret."

"OK. Then why for—Margaret?"

"I've been your partner a while now, Murph. It's time I showed you what I can do with a case that counts."

"You don't have to show me anything, Meg. I know how good you are. I know who trained you. But you've got a pretty full caseload as it stands."

"Give it to the new kid, Pat Arthur."

"He's as green as Paddy's parsley."

"This is important to me, Murph," she said, standing. She threw on her coat. "I happen to think Laura Christen has the right stuff. But I'm almost as cynical as you are. If she's got any mud in her footlocker, I'll find it."

Murphy stood up, too. "You look just like *her,* Margaret, but you act just like *him.* Your dad was a hardheaded son of a bitch."

She smiled suddenly at the description of her father, which was totally accurate. Stubborn, opinionated, intractable. Her father, her best friend. "That's why I'm here," she told Murphy, "because that hardheaded son of a bitch knew his tomboy daughter wanted to follow in his footsteps."

"I've had no cause to regret that decision, darling."

"No," she said, the smile gone. "I do my best not to give you any."

She headed for the door, then turned back to him. "A question," she said. "It's storming outside. Why weren't your friends Roberts and Stern wearing raincoats?"

He smiled. "One of the things your dad and I learned during our graceless days fighting the secret war on foreign soil was that when you traveled with Charlie Stern, you traveled light. No hats. No coats. You never knew when you might have to make a very fast getaway."

OUTSIDE night had officially fallen, but the rain continued. Margaret ran to her Prelude, beeped open the door, and slipped behind the wheel feeling wet and on edge. She circled the block in the heavy rain, then parked behind the Probe. The Buick was gone. It was probably the car Roberts and Stern had come in. She saw Murphy exit the hotel hurriedly and drive away. She waited another five minutes just to make sure no one was following him. Then she started up the Prelude and headed for her apartment in Georgetown. Lately, she had begun to worry that the job was pushing her over the line into paranoia.

But she hadn't been paranoid enough. Shortly after her departure, the back door of the truck marked "Brookville" opened and a man in a camel's hair overcoat stepped out cautiously—the same suntanned blond who had whispered something to Jeremy Dunbar as they left the press conference earlier that day. He stretched, looked around for a moment, then moved through the rain as though he found it invigorating. He entered the Maitland, took the elevator to the fifteenth floor, then jogged down the stairwell to fourteen.

Using a pick, he entered room 1421.

He turned on the light and went immediately to the bed. Removing his rain-spattered black loafers but not his topcoat, he stood on the bed and reached up to unscrew a fire sprinkler that protruded from the ceiling. Inside the sprinkler was a tiny piece of electronic magic. He replaced the sprinkler, hopped from the bed, and slipped into his shoes.

Back in the "Brookville" truck, whistling to himself, the blond man fiddled with a tape recorder that was bolted to the vehicle's interior wall. The voice of Mike Roberts came through clearly.

Pleased with himself, the man clicked off the machine. Again ignoring the rain, he hopped out of the rear of the truck and walked around to slide behind the wheel.

He rolled down the window, breathed deeply of the moist, cold air. There just wasn't enough weather where he came from.

4

♦

"Greater love hath no man than this, that
he lay down his friends for his political
life."

JEREMY THORPE

LAURA CHRISTEN'S OFFICE was in the House building named for
Speaker Nicholas Longworth. Her seniority would have allowed
her space in the Rayburn Building, which was considered more
prestigious, but in her mind practicality always outweighed pres-
tige, and offices in the Longworth were larger.

Even so, Congresswoman Christen had to make do with three
rooms and a reception area, approximately 2,300 feet to accommodate herself and as many as twenty staffers. As her political adviser
and sometime escort Professor James Prosser had once noted, the
only people with more crowded conditions within the federal system were those occupying space provided by the Bureau of Pris-
ons.

At 6:23 in the evening, the Congresswoman was seated at her
desk, speaking by phone to Esther Cooper, the senior-most woman
in the House, who was explaining slowly and patiently why she
could not endorse Laura's nomination. "I've been a Democrat for
a hundred years, or so it seems," her dry voice with its slight New
Jersey accent was saying. "And I plan on being a Democrat for
another hundred."

"But you're the one who urged me to run," Laura said.

"My heart is with you," Esther Cooper told her, "but my vote
will of necessity be with Lew Ronkowski."

Laura thanked the elderly Congresswoman for her time and replaced the receiver. She turned to her computer screen and was scrolling through a list of possible converts to her cause when her daughter appeared at the door. Frowning. "There are two . . . policemen in the waiting room."

Laura checked her watch. "At this time of night? For me?"

"A Detective Gabriel and a Detective Skinner. Won't say what they want. Just that it's urgent they talk to you."

Laura sighed. "I know it's getting late, but could you stick around until they leave?"

Catsy hesitated, then answered, "Sure."

Laura had barely cleared her monitor screen before her daughter returned and seated the two plainclothes detectives. Skinner was a stocky man in his mid-twenties with a brown crew cut and a weight lifter's build. The only signs of animation on his square, ruddy face were piercing blue eyes that seemed to be exploring every inch of Laura. His inexpensive gray-and-black tweed sport coat was tight over his shoulders. His pants were black, as were the socks that didn't quite cover the expanse of ankle that showed when he crossed his legs.

Gabriel was a dapper man with a narrow, nut-brown face and matching eyes. He was dressed more expensively than Skinner in a charcoal three-piece suit with a small American flag pinned to its left lapel.

Skinner spoke with a New Jersey twang. He introduced himself and Gabriel and quickly got down to business. "Do you know a Mr. Jeremy Dunbar?" he asked Laura, his blue eyes continuing to move over her body.

"I know who he is, yes."

"He attended your press conference this afternoon?"

Laura nodded. "Yes. He was there."

"And you and he had some sort of conversation?"

"What's this all about?" Catsy demanded, annoyed.

Skinner shifted his piercing gaze to her and almost smiled. Then, without answering her question, he turned back to Laura. "Ms. Christen, could you tell us what you and Jeremy Dunbar talked about this afternoon?"

Laura leaned back in her chair. "I could, and I would, if you give me a reason why,'' she said. She thought she was remaining remarkably calm.

Skinner opened his mouth, but Gabriel put a restraining hand on his partner's arm. Skinner raised his head indignantly, as if sniffing smoke, then settled back against his chair.

"Mr. Dunbar died in Folger Park,'' Gabriel said to Laura. "Right after your conference ended this afternoon.'' There was a Jamaican lilt to his speech that suggested the man was being playful even when he wasn't. "A possible heart attack, although the coroner, Dr. Medray, is a bit uncertain on that point.''

"I'm not sure I understand,'' Laura said.

"Well, you see, Congresswoman Christen, we are living in an age of chemical creativity. Space age poisons—nuclear toxins. There are so many things that can cause heart failure. But Dr. Medray does his best to stay abreast of the latest developments. He's taking his time with Mr. Dunbar.''

"Are you saying it may have been murder?'' Catsy asked, once again inviting Skinner's blatant appraisal.

"The deceased was overweight, but young and with no history of heart disease,'' Gabriel said. "And the two little girls who found the body saw a woman running away.''

Laura leaned forward. "You think *I* might be that woman?''

"Not at all, Congresswoman. We know that you were returning to your office at the approximate time of death. In any case, the girls say the woman was built like an athlete—''

"A linebacker,'' Skinner interjected. "You don't exactly fit that description, ma'am.''

"Then I don't understand—''

"Captain Legrand of the Capitol Police was chatting with you at your press conference when Mr. Dunbar approached and whispered something to you. We were wondering what it might have been.''

"Why don't you ask the captain?''

Gabriel grinned. "We did, of course. He couldn't hear a word.'' He paused, waiting for Laura to speak. When she didn't, he said, "Forgive us, but we have been quite busy the past several hours. And there is still much to be done. We are not here to annoy you, but to discover if you have any information that might make our job a bit easier.''

"I assume you know that Mr. Dunbar worked for the *National Examiner*," Laura said.

Gabriel nodded. Skinner continued to stare at her. There was something in the man's determined, carnal expression that she found oddly exciting. She turned back to Gabriel. "He . . . wanted to interview me for his column. I told him to call my daughter, Mrs. Braden, who schedules such things.''

"Ah, then, regardless of the—how shall I say it?—the content of his publication, you considered giving him an interview?'' Gabriel leaned forward, brows raised in curiosity.

"That would have been up to Mrs. Braden," Laura told him, gesturing toward Catsy.

Catsy shook her head. "No way!"

"Did either of you see anyone else talking with Mr. Dunbar?"

Laura and Catsy moved their heads negatively. Gabriel was amused that the gestures seemed to be identical. Definitely mother and daughter. More like sisters.

He stood up. "Thank you for your time. Good luck in your campaign. I suppose you will be quite busy even during the holidays."

"I suppose," Laura said, standing and walking around her desk to see them out.

"We probably won't have to bother you again, Congresswoman," Gabriel said at the door to the reception room. "But allow me to leave my card in case something should occur to you that might aid our investigation."

Skinner did not follow his partner immediately. He paused at Laura's desk and took a small white rectangle from his pocket. "My home number," he said. "If I can do anything for you."

Then he was gone, followed by Catsy.

When she returned, Laura asked, "Do we know anyone with access to police records?"

Catsy smiled and pointed to the card on Laura's desk. "Young Blue Eyes," she said. "You've got his number."

"I'm being serious," Laura said. "I want to know about an envelope that should have been found on Jeremy Dunbar's body."

Catsy raised one suspicious eyebrow. "What sort of envelope?"

"Square, like a formal invitation. Addressed to him. He let me see it, then stuck it back into his pocket."

"What was in it?"

Laura was tempted to tell her everything—the accusation in the letter, the possibility that Jeremy Dunbar was killed because of it. But why worry Catsy until the police were sure Dunbar had been murdered and until she was sure who had done it? "Just another piece of unsubstantiated slander," she equivocated, "not unlike the malicious nonsense that fills newspapers like Jeremy Dunbar's. He was hoping to use it to force me to give him an interview."

"That hot, huh? C'mon, Mother. Let's hear it."

"Its contents are not worth discussing," Laura said firmly. "But I'd like to know what the police plan on doing with it."

"I'll see what I can find out," Catsy said. "But cops can be tight-lipped about evidence in a murder case."

Laura stared at Detective Skinner's card on her desk. She was half tempted to pick it up.

LATER that night the detective answered his phone with a gruff "Yeah?"

"Detective Skinner?"

"That's my name."

His caller stretched languidly on her bed. "Do you know who this is?"

He replied immediately, "I'd know your voice anywhere, Congresswoman."

She frowned, then smiled suddenly. "Of course you would. Well, I'd like to see you tonight."

"Business or personal?"

"What do you think?"

"I got this theory, Mrs. Christen—"

"Call me Laura."

"I got this theory, Laura. If I'm turned on by a woman, the feeling's gotta be mutual. And I am definitely turned on by you."

"Let's say your theory has some validity. Why don't we put it to the acid test?"

She gave him her address and placed the receiver back on its cradle. Yes, she was going to use him to find out about Jeremy Dunbar's envelope. But she was also going to provide quid pro quo. And she was certain she'd enjoy it.

She slid from the bed and began to prepare for his arrival. Before stepping into the shower, she paused to stare at herself in the bathroom mirror. "So, my horny, blue-eyed policeman, you would recognize my voice anywhere," she said aloud. "I hope you won't be too disappointed with the rest of me."

Showered, powdered, and dabbed with a hint of sensual 273 perfume here and there, she wrapped a sheer gown around her naked body and went into her living room. It was a comfortable space, soft furniture in muted colors, good prints, and one or two originals on the walls, a large, colorful Sarouk rug on top of the beige wall-to-wall carpet, a stone fireplace and above its mantel, a large gilt-edged antique mirror.

She turned down the thermostat and lighted the logs in the fireplace, then added sandalwood chips to the fire. She found an Oriental music tape that an army captain had donated to the apartment. He'd claimed that the combination of lute and other instruments produced a sound that worked on the brain to enhance orgasm. Brain, body, whatever, her orgasms were usually right on the money. But it never hurt to be sure.

As the room filled with the scent of sandalwood and the insinuating Oriental melodies, she removed a bottle of Gewürztraminer from the fridge and poured herself a glass. When the buzzer rang, she pressed the button that unlocked the lobby door. Then she turned off the lights and crossed the Sarouk to the door, which she unlocked. She retraced her steps and selected a position in front of the fireplace.

His knock sounded so quickly that she was certain he'd run up the stairs. She said, "Come in," and turned toward the fire, moving close to the mantel until her face was in shadow while her body would be clearly outlined under the sheer gown.

She could see the room reflected in the mirror as the door opened and Detective Skinner entered. He was wearing a leather jacket and tight Levi's. Perfect. He moved cautiously.

His blue eyes seemed to be glowing as they focused on her nearly nude body.

"Close the door," she told him. "Make sure it's locked."

He turned and fumbled with the button for the dead-bolt lock. "There's wine on the table with the tape deck," she said.

"I'm not thirsty," he croaked.

He started toward her but she said, "No. Wait. Are your shoes wet?"

"A little, I guess. It's been raining."

"Then take them off. The rug is very expensive."

She lifted a wineglass from the mantel and sipped at it, still observing him in the mirror.

He used the toe of one shoe to pry off the other. Then he started forward again.

She stopped him once more. "Socks."

Mildly annoyed, he pulled off his socks.

"The jacket looks wet, too," she said.

He suddenly understood what she was doing and smiled. "Yeah, I guess it is."

He removed the leather jacket slowly, in time with the odd music. "And this shirt's like a washrag," he said, pulling it over his head.

His body was almost hairless. Winter pale. Ivory muscles. "You must spend most of your life at the gym," she said.

"Just an hour a day," he said. "And this is all me. No steroids. A guy'd have to be an asshole to use stuff that softens your dick."

"Nicely put," she said.

He took a step onto the rug. "Those pants don't look very dry," she said.

"How could they be?" he asked. "I bet your gown's a little wet by now, too."

She put down the glass. "I believe you're right."

She shrugged and the gown slipped from her shoulders and down her body. She stepped out of it, then used one long, shapely leg to kick the gauzy material away from the fire.

She watched Skinner's reflection as he kept his blue eyes glued to her naked back and buttocks. Tired of the teasing game, he yanked down his trousers and Jockey briefs simultaneously and left them in a pile at the edge of the rug.

She raised her arms to the mantel as he pressed his body against her, hugging her. She pushed back on him, moaning at the size and hardness of him.

His lips were on her neck, his teeth nipping at her flesh, his right hand moving up her side to first cup her breast, then pinch the nipple more with passion than with play. His other hand moved down her stomach, fingers making a small circle.

She was more than ready. With a little cry of both pain and desire, she turned in his arms. Her mouth found his and accepted his tongue hungrily. She moved her hand between his legs. She touched him gently, almost as if to prove to herself that his erection was real. Then she squeezed him.

They fell to the rug, the fire warm on their naked flesh. Continuing the kiss, she moved under him, stroking him. He groaned and broke away, like a swimmer surfacing from a deep dive. His eyes opened, sleepily at first, then wide, staring at her. "Goddammit," he said, in wonder. "You're the daughter!"

She placed him inside of her and began to move under him. "You'd recognize . . . my voice . . . anywhere," she gasped.

"The goddamned daughter," he said, smiling.

"You're not . . . disappointed?"

"Hell no," he said between thrusts. "I still . . . have Mom . . . to look forward to."

She bucked beneath him. "I'm better . . . than she is . . . on her best day . . ." she barely got out.

LAURA was in her bed, reading, when Catsy phoned to tell her that no envelope had been found on Jeremy Dunbar's body.

"Maybe your source is holding back," Laura suggested.

Catsy chuckled. "I'd be surprised," she said.

Laura said nothing. She considered the import of the absent envelope. It had been in Jeremy Dunbar's possession minutes before his death. If it was now missing, it would lend credence to the murder theory. And to her fear about the motive for the murder.

She thanked Catsy for her help, keeping her voice carefully neutral.

"A pleasure," Catsy said. She hesitated a moment and added, "If you ever decide to start having sex again, have I got a guy for you!"

"What makes you think I've stopped?"

"I know you, Mother."

"Not well enough, apparently," Laura replied and hung up.

Catsy's amorality and total lack of discretion annoyed Laura. But it was her daughter's apparent abhorrence of a conventional lifestyle that was a source of genuine concern. And Laura blamed herself, attributing her daughter's inability to form a lasting relationship to some failure in her upbringing. Actually, she had been more attentive and loving than most mothers. But there is only so much a single parent can do, and, as any psychiatrist will attest, the way children behave is not always an indication of the way they were raised.

Still . . . she loved her daughter and wished that Catsy would find someone halfway decent and settle down before something really bad happened to her.

Relegating the specter of Catsy's future to some spot at the back of her consciousness, Laura began digging through a pile of magazines and newspapers on her night-table. When she found her personal address book, she flipped its pages, picked up the phone again, and dialed. After three rings, a recorded voice began its spiel. Laura waited patiently for it to finish, then identified herself, adding, "It is most important that I see you as soon as—"

A familiar voice cut in. "Laura—my beautiful Laura. After all these years, what can I do for you?"

5

●

"Politics makes estranged bedfellows."

GOODMAN ACE

JAKE ALBAN WASN'T sure he could handle the task before him. He paused at the polished glass entry to the Empire Features Building to observe the reflection of a tall, raw-boned man, vaguely uncomfortable in a coat and tie. He ignored it and went in, oblivious to the fact that he'd left two young women in the street wondering who he was and why the men in their lives looked so ordinary.

Jake ascended in the shiny brass elevator to the sixteenth floor too caught up in his thoughts to notice the brunette who was staring surreptitiously at his reflected image, at the strong jaw and clean-cut features that reminded her of some actor she couldn't quite recall, someone who used to be in Westerns. . . . And there was that intriguing little curved scar above his left eyebrow. Gathering her courage, she turned to stare directly at him, but to her surprise the move got no response. Those heart-melting gray eyes did not turn her way.

Jake's mind was on the job at hand. He was annoyed by his lack of confidence. He'd dodged Claymores, picked fights with drug lords, and stolen a kiss from a President's socialite daughter. So this situation shouldn't be that daunting. But he knew it would be. He assumed that was why he'd had the dream again the night before. It had been months since he'd been tormented and kept awake by the terrible images. His lovely wife, Danielle, seated across from him in the hot, ridiculously overdecorated Nicaraguan hotel dining room, smiling. The sudden stillness for no apparent reason. The doors bursting open. Curses in Spanish. Gunfire. The tinkle of glass overhead. The huge chandelier exploding. A thousand knives piercing his wife's flesh . . . her frightful, tormented scream . . . blood . . . Happy anniversary, Danielle. . . .

The elevator doors opened on the Empire editorial area and a prim, auburn-haired woman perched behind a teak module in the center of the waiting room. Jake provided her with the details of his appointment. She didn't seem familiar with his name—people rarely were anymore—but dutifully repeated it into her mouthpiece before suggesting he take a seat, her eyes never leaving his.

He sat at a coffee table, discovering that its surface was a monitor on which pages of syndicated news unspooled ceaselessly and soundlessly. His eyes were drawn to the amber letters on black surface. Terrorists did this . . . Protesters did that . . . the government pleaded for moderation.

He was, against his will, into the third graph of the latest developments on the "unfolding Russian diplomat scandal," when he heard his name being called. He looked up to see a thin, alert-looking young woman of average height standing a few feet away. "Mr. Alban," she identified him again, "Dr. Krim will see you now. My name is Louise Dubin. I'm her assistant."

She led him into a huge, bright area that bristled with activity. A hundred computer keyboards clicked an odd discordant symphony. "This way," Louise said, leading him past cubicles inhabited by workers whose only unifying characteristic seemed to be that they all looked like kids.

"I read your series on the Tongsun Park lobbying scandal," Louise informed him rather shyly. "It was brilliant work."

"That was quite a while ago," he said.

"Actually, we studied it in school."

"Ah," he said. He figured her for early twenties. He hadn't been much older than that when good old Tongsun Park and his sleazy lobbying scandal performed one definitely useful service—they made him a media superstar. If they hadn't, he wouldn't have been able to pick and choose his assignments, and he wouldn't have wound up in Nicaragua, and . . .

He derailed that train of thought. "Too bad you missed my coverage of Teapot Dome," he told the girl.

Louise paused and turned to look at him with a puzzled frown. Then her expressive face broke into a grin. "I'll be sure to check it out, next time I'm at the library," she replied.

PENELOPE Krim had her phone cradled between shoulder and neck. She continued to mumble into it while her eyes unashamedly appraised Jake's body. Apparently satisfied with his physique, she made a shooing motion with her left hand and Louise left the room, closing the door behind her.

Penelope covered the telephone speaker with a plump palm and mouthed the words to Jake: "Sit. I'll be just a minute."

He lowered himself into a chrome and leather cushioned chair and looked around the office. The blinds were drawn, and the only illumination came from the soft bulb of Penelope Krim's desk lamp. Jake thought that, pound for pound, she was probably the ugliest woman he had ever seen.

She winked at him and said into the receiver, "Have to run now, Kipper. There's a *beautiful* man waiting in my office. Let me know if anything's in the wind. Later. Ciao, darling."

She put down the receiver and leaned forward on her elbows, her impressive chest hovering precariously over the papers on her desk. "Care for a drink?" she asked.

"No, thanks."

"Can I get you . . . anything?"

Christ, she's flirting, he thought. *This godawful dragonlady— maybe my last ticket back into journalism—is coming on to me.*

"No. I'm fine," he said barely audibly.

"So you are. Well, what do you think of my proposition?"

"On the whole—it's good," Jake said.

"Empire will sign your weekly check, but you'll be working for me. Any problem with that?"

"Not at the moment," he said, daring a smile.

He was repaid in kind. "You were a *marvelous* reporter," she said. "You can be one again if it's what you want."

Did he want it? He hoped he did. It would mean that he was on his way back to a life that once was. But knowing what you had to do and convincing yourself that it was what you wanted were two different things. Since the time of the "incident" in Nicaragua that had taken his wife from him, he'd blown one opportunity after another, alienating editors who had bent over backward to accommodate his irritability, frequent nervous depressions, and unexplained absences. His newest and, he hoped, his final therapist, Armand Wexler, had made him understand that his clumsy attempts to burn his journalistic bridges had been his way of avoiding facing the situation that had brought about his sufferings. Other psychiatrists and psychologists had gently suggested that he find another line of work. But Wexler took the opposite tack: unless Jake faced a few of his collection of demons, he might never fully recover.

In any case, a journalist was what he had always wanted to be. So here he was. At the Last Chance Saloon. Facing an unexpected demon. He'd have something new for Wexler next week.

Penelope asked, "So, what made you decide to quit the newspaper game, anyway?"

He shrugged and replied with a bland non-answer. "Don't you ever get sick of deadlines and pressure?"

She hesitated, studying him harder now. "No. As a matter of fact I thrive on it," she snapped. "Maurice says you've been writing books."

Maurice was Maurice Speir, a Manhattan lawyer whom Jake used for an agent. "I've done a few biographies," he said.

"Oh? Anybody I know?"

"The books weren't very . . . significant." He had, in fact, ghosted several autobiographies of political figures, ranging from an ex-president to a current mayor under investigation for drug use. The money had been fine, but changing from a freewheeling investigative reporter to a tame, approved ghost writer had been hard.

"Maurice assures me that you're ready to do serious work again. I must say you look ready." She smiled at him and distorted the lower part of her mouth in an attempt at a seductive expression. To Jake it appeared as though her dentures were loose.

"My bags are packed," he said.

"I thought we might have a bite tonight, seal the deal."

He said, "When you phoned, you mentioned urgency. My plane for Colorado leaves at three-fifteen this afternoon."

Her face melted in disappointment. "How efficient of you."

"There was some material you wanted me to read."

"Yes. Louise has photocopied my complete file on the Congresswoman, such as it is. You're clear about what I need?"

"Research," he replied. "Legwork."

"Precisely," Penelope said. "Don't spend valuable time polishing your prose. *I'm* the writer on this team. As I promised, I'll credit you with the research. If we work well together on this"—again a leer—"I'll try to convince Horace to give you a shot on your own."

He nodded and stood up. She rose from her chair, too, and circled the desk. She moved across the carpet until she was standing less than a foot from him. "Aren't you the least bit curious, Jake?"

"About what?"

"About why I picked you for this job. I mean, there are probably a half dozen eager *young* reporters I could have used."

He looked down at the thickset woman who had just put a damp, heavy hand on his shoulder. "I assumed it was because of the Q and A I did with the Congresswoman eleven years ago."

"I did run across it in the files," Penelope said. "It was a fairly in-depth piece, considering the shallowness of the subject. Did she give you any trouble?"

Trouble? Jake tried to keep his face expressionless. From his first meeting with Laura Christen, he had been in trouble. She'd been too beautiful, too intelligent, too powerfully appealing for him ever to have written an unbiased article. On their second meeting, the "trouble" had intensified when he realized that the attraction was mutual. They were two healthy unmarried people who had had difficulty keeping their hands off one another and it had been inevitable that they make love.

Disturbed by the ethics of his position, Jake had delayed writing the article. Finally, facing an unavoidable deadline, he'd holed up in a motel for the week it took him to write it. When it was completed, much to his surprise he was satisfied by its objectivity. If anything, he had given too much space to the negative quotes from some of Laura's fellow congressmen.

His editor was pleased with the results, and Laura claimed to be.

They planned a celebratory weekend trip to Maine. But when he arrived at her Washington home, the maid informed him that the Congresswoman had flown to her California residence. The note she'd left read, "Dear Jake, I've decided our professions and goals are too incompatible for us to be happy together. Best wishes for a good life. I beg you not to try to contact me further." Signed Laura.

The next and last time he heard from her was shortly after his wife's murder. A brief, handwritten note: "Jake, Please accept my deepest sympathy . . ."

Penelope was saying, "The piece read as if she were being candid with you, trusted you. That could come in handy. I'd prefer you not approach her. But if all else fails, maybe we'll see if she'll open up to you, tell you the real nasties."

The idea of working for a columnist who would use trust to smear a subject revolted Jake. But since he had long assumed that the Congresswoman had gone to bed with him to influence his article, the idea of her opening up to him now for any reason seemed so beyond the realm of possibility that he decided not to bother discussing journalistic ethics with Penelope Krim.

She probably wouldn't have heard him. She was too busy explaining that the previous article was not the main reason she'd wanted Jake. She removed her plump fingers from his shoulder, then ran them playfully over his chest. She said, "When I first arrived here in D.C., I crashed a party that somebody was tossing for Jimmy Carter at the Jockey Club. You were there with the standard blonde bimbo, chatting with Carter like you were lifelong pals. Then you and the blonde left old Jimmy, and she whispered something to you and you both laughed and got the hell out of there. And I thought: this guy Alban is only a few years older than I and there he is, a Pulitzer winner with a byline in the *Post,* a bimbo on his arm, ducking a presidential party. I thought, how nice it would be to be Jake Alban."

The "bimbo" had later become his wife, Danielle. He stared at Penelope, trying to keep the revulsion from his face. "Anyway," she said, moving even closer, "that's what I thought then. Now I think, how nice it would be to spend the night with Jake Alban."

Jake looked into her small, glittering eyes and decided a little humor might help. He said, "I'm afraid it would be a bit dull. I'm asleep by ten."

Moving into her Sultry Seductress role, Penelope said, "I bet I could keep you *up* a little longer than that." She parted her lips, waiting for him to make the next move.

Aw hell, Jake thought. He hadn't even begun and it was all over, jigwise, to lift a line from one of his idols, S. J. Perelman. But he needed this chance so desperately. . . .

A reprieve came in the form of an opening door. Penelope took a quick step backward as Louise entered with a large manila envelope. She looked from her boss to Jake and back to Penelope and said, "You wanted these photocopies for Mr. Alban."

Jake smiled gratefully at Louise and stepped toward the open door. He turned to Penelope. "I told you I'd research Laura Christen's background, and I will. I do the job I'm paid for."

"I'm sure you do," she replied, smiling. "Work fast, Jake Alban, work fast and hurry back."

Somehow he managed to smile.

Louise walked with him to the reception area. "I'm sorry if I interrupted anything just now, Mr. Alban," she said mischievously.

Jake bent down and kissed her forehead. "May God bless you forever, my child," he said.

6

•

"Politics offers yesterday's answers to today's problems."

MARSHALL MCLUHAN

THE MURPHY-STAFFORD AGENCY was in the Paradine Building near Dupont Circle in what was known as Washington's "new" business district, the Nineteenth Street Corridor. When Murphy and Harry Stafford, Margaret's father, entered into their partnership, their office in the Paradine had been a small two-room affair on the nineteenth floor. That had grown to nearly a quarter of the seventh floor—two large offices for the partners, partitioned cubicles for the operatives, a small lunchroom, a mailroom, a combination conference room/client showcase and a library, which is where Murphy had spent the last hour, going over the biographies of the only members of Mike Roberts' staff who'd known about the Minority Leader's first meeting with Laura Christen.

None of them seemed like obvious suspects and he felt he'd probably wasted his time. He slid the background reports into their folders and replaced them in the large padded envelope in which they'd been delivered. He planned on having his secretary, Nina, put the envelope into one of the locking file cabinets, but she was not at her desk, so he carried the envelope into his private office.

There he found a young man in an ill-fitting light gray suit sitting in the visitor's chair. Murphy placed the padded envelope facedown on his desk and asked, "Trying the office on for size?"

"Oh, no. Nothing like that, sir. Nina wasn't out front, so I just walked in and waited. I hope that's all right."

45

"Depends on why you're here," Murphy said.

"To ask for more work," the young man said. His name was Patrick Arthur and he was, as of eighteen previous workdays, the Murphy-Stafford Agency's newest employee. Murphy glanced at his mop of brown hair, horsy white teeth, and easy smile, and wondered if the Kennedy look was back in vogue.

There was sudden movement at the door and his secretary, a short black woman named Nina, poked her head into the room. "Ah, you're back," she said.

"My mission was accomplished, sort of," Murphy told her. "I'm just chattin' with young Pat about this and that. Anything you need?"

"Nothing I can't handle," she said, moving away.

"There's too damn much efficiency in this office," Murphy said to Patrick. "So impress me with your ingenuity, lad. What's on the docket that you'd like to handle?"

"How's about my helping Miss Stafford?"

Murphy gave him a steadier look. "Do you know what she's workin' on?" he asked.

"No. But it's not listed on the office schedule, so it's probably high priority and maybe she could use another hand."

"I think she prefers to work alone," Murphy said. "Why don't you see what Mr. Digby's needs might be? He's still recuperatin' from his stay in the hospital."

Patrick stood up. "I'll do that. Thanks, Mr. Murphy."

"We're not that formal here, Pat," Murphy told him. "I'm 'Murph' and you can call Miss Stafford 'Meg.' "

Patrick smiled and seemed to canter from the room.

Murphy raised an eyebrow and looked at his desk top, where papers and notes were scattered and his daily calendar reflected an empty page for the current date. He studied his desk drawers. They were all closed. Then, more or less satisfied that Pat Arthur hadn't been poking about, he buzzed for Nina.

She responded to his buzzer wearing her round tortoiseshell glasses—the ones he didn't like. He said, "Is it a boyfriend who keeps luring you away from your desk?"

"Oh, Murph," Nina said. "You're turning into a real big-boss-man. I was away because those fools in Security called to say our

Christmas tree had been delivered. I went all the way down there and there were trees, sure enough, but none with our name on it. Then, when they couldn't find it, they started trying to tell me they hadn't even called up here.''

"The whole fabric of commerce is beginnin' to unravel in my declinin' years," Murphy said. "Well, would you please lock this," handing her the envelope with the biographies of Mike Roberts' staff members, "in the special cabinet?"

Nina turned to leave.

"And do you think you could anchor yourself to your desk long enough to do a little something for me?"

"You command and I obey, sir."

"Nina, I'd like you to find out what Congresswoman Laura Christen's schedule looks like for the next couple of days. Personal appearances, that sort of nonsense."

She raised an eyebrow. "Well, now, Murph. Is this business or pleasure?"

"You know very well, madam," he said, "that they are one and the same to me."

By 5 P.M. Nina had placed on his desk a sheet containing local radio and television appearances by the Congresswoman, luncheon and dinner engagements, and a charity affair that had something to do with the Ford Theater.

Murphy glanced at the events. The Congresswoman was going to appear on a special live interview during the course of that night's 11:30 newscast on Channel 8. Murphy thought he could handle that—observing the subject from the comfort of his own bedroom. Assuming he could stay awake long enough.

7

•

"I hate television. I hate it as much as peanuts. But I can't stop eating peanuts."
ORSON WELLES

THE YOUNG FEMALE guide with a fixed smile on her pale, angelic face and "Super 8" in white stitched to the pocket of her blue blazer led Catsy down a pale yellow corridor that wound, labyrinthian, through the backstage area of television station WSH. The place smelled of floor wax and ammonia. Catsy wondered what television people did that required such astringent cleaning preparations.

Her guide gave a little halt sign with her gloved hand and they paused before a closed, unmarked door. The young woman knocked once and leaned close to the door. "Jo— Mr. Kilmer, I have Miss Braden for you."

"Mrs. Braden," Catsy corrected.

John Kilmer, anchorman of WSH's nightly news show, threw open the door with a wide smile on his handsome, recently pan-caked face. A tissue paper bib protected his white shirt from the makeup. He winked at the young guide, thanked her, and closed the door on her. He stared at Catsy and said, "Damn if you don't look good enough to eat."

"Is that why you're wearing the bib?" she asked, looking about for a place to sit. There was one campaign chair, apparently Kilmer's, facing a brightly lighted makeup mirror. Another chair, beside a desk with a computer, contained a stack of books. A

couch, against one wall, was covered with newspapers and magazines.

Kilmer moved to the couch, lifted it, and dumped all of the
reading matter onto the floor. "I'm not used to visitors before
show time," he apologized.

Perching daintily on the edge of the couch, she said, "I've heard
that you're running women in and out of here every minute of the
day, show time or not."

Smiling, he spun the campaign chair around and used it. "I'm
cutting down, Catsy. Give me just three or four really profound
orgasms and I'm through for the day."

She frowned. "Four? We used to cover that in the first hour,"
she said mockingly, leaning back on the couch and at the same
time pulling her skirt back over her legs until the edge of her
stockings showed and just a fraction of garter belt.

"Oh, my," he said. "What lovely hardware. I bet you're even
wearing a merry widow."

"Made of black lace," she said. "And nothing else under the
dress but me."

"You remembered," he said. "Could I just have a quick peek
at the 'you' part?"

She shook her head. "We wouldn't want you too excited to
conduct a good interview."

"Is the Congresswoman here already?" he asked.

"Yes. Your producer took her off into the bowels of this cav-
ern," Catsy said. "I expect you to be very nice to her."

"I'm always nice to beautiful women," he said.

"Let me see what you're asking her," she said.

He leaned back and took a sheaf of papers from the makeup
counter. Catsy reached out to grab them, but he jerked them away.
"I'll show you mine if you show me yours," he said, grinning like
a naughty schoolboy.

She stared at him. Then she uncrossed her legs and slowly drew
her dress up over her thighs.

At the sight of her naked loins, he fell to his knees and tried to
embrace her, but she pushed him away and brushed her skirt down.
"You'll smear your makeup," she said. "Relax, Johnny." She

checked her watch. "In another forty minutes you can have a much more . . . in-depth look. Now it's my turn."

She took the sheets of yellow paper from him. On them, in large typewritten letters, was a set of nearly fifty questions. She skimmed them quickly, then said, "Don't use any of the ones about her personal life."

"Come on, Catsy. That's the stuff that viewers are dying to hear."

"That may be, but it's not why she's here and she won't answer them. It will make her look bad and the dead air will throw off your timing. So don't ask them."

"That's crazy," John Kilmer said. "The woman's a politician. She has to expect questions about her homelife."

Catsy thought for a moment. What would happen if her mother were trapped on a live interview show, fielding tough questions about her past? Maybe, Catsy thought, she would learn something about the people and events that she could never quite remember from her childhood—secrets, apparently, that her mother guarded so carefully that she kept them from her own flesh and blood.

Like why Catsy had been sent away to so many private boarding schools, though her mother doted on her when she returned during breaks. Like why she had never been introduced to any of the men her mother had been serious about.

There'd been a period during her teen years when she'd been convinced that her mother was a lesbian. But there had been signs to the contrary, the most notable being the diaphragm and contraceptive gels in her bathroom cabinet.

When she was very young, before she had reason to know better, she'd thought that her mother's old friend Tommy Hamilton had also been her lover. But Tommy, whom Catsy hated, in one of his more drunken moments had confided that her mother had been seriously involved with another man, unnamed. No matter how hard she'd pushed, neither Tommy nor her mother would say anything more about the mystery lover.

There was so much about the private Laura Christen that she wanted to know, but a television interview, even a local one, wasn't the best place to use as a confessional.

"Go ahead and ask her anything you want," she said. "But there's a very good reason why you shouldn't."

"And what's that?" he said.

She slid forward on the couch, reached out, and unzipped him. She pushed her hand inside and freed him. He immediately rose to full erection. It reminded her of the speeded-up blooming of a flower in one of those Walt Disney nature films.

She bent over and caressed him with her tongue and he sighed and closed his eyes. It was a few seconds before he realized that it was over. When he opened his eyes, she stood at the door, looking at him. "Good enough reason?" she whispered before leaving him alone and unzipped.

8

♦

"Anger as soon as fed is dead/ 'Tis starving
that makes it fat."

EMILY DICKINSON

PENELOPE KRIM WAS sprawled in the middle of her pink-satin-covered brass bed, propped up against its tufted headboard, staring at the huge Panasonic screen embedded in the opposite wall. She was wearing a woolen nightgown and over it a ratty white terry bathrobe. On her forehead were black eyeshades that looked like deflated Mickey Mouse ears.

She was watching the Christen interview on the Channel 8 Late News, alternately shouting at the screen and stuffing her mouth with handfuls of sticky caramel corn from a huge tin that was on a footstool beside the bed. The tin had been an early Christmas gift from her boss, Horace Marsten.

She had just heard John Kilmer ask Laura Christen why she felt women members of Congress were not being treated fairly. "Kilmer, you friggin' wuss!" she screamed. "Ask her the hard ones, like how many guys she had to lay to get elected."

Penelope suffered through Laura's smooth, thoughtful answer by devouring nearly four inches of caramel corn. She was now through the orange-flavored and was moving into the pink, whatever flavor that might be.

And what did the Congresswoman think about her rival, Speaker Lewis Ronkowski? "This is an interview? It's more like a god-damn testimonial to the bitch," Penelope shrieked.

She couldn't quite understand what was happening. Kilmer was known as a fairly tough talking head. Maybe not quite Mike Wallace, but close enough. And tonight it seemed as though Laura had written the script.

Suddenly Penelope sat up straight. Of course! He's screwing her. That had to be it. Kilmer the Killer and sweet little Laura C. She wiped her hands on the bedspread, then grabbed her telephone and dialed Jolly's number.

Her main purveyor of gossip picked up on the second ring. "Yeah?" he said cautiously.

"Jolly, this is Penelope Krim. Who is John Kilmer shtupping these days?"

"Kilmer? Who isn't he shtupping? The guy's liable to shtup a Venetian blind. I hear he's got this hand puppet that—"

Penelope wasn't interested in Venetian blinds or hand puppets. She said, "What about Laura Christen?"

"And Kilmer? This I never heard," Jolly said. "Hang on a minute."

In the background she could hear the electronic whirs and clicks of a computer. "Here we go," Jolly said. "Kilmer, John. A very long list. No Laura Christen, but her daughter made the team."

"Oh," Penelope said, glumly. That would explain the soft interview. There was absolutely no news value in an affair involving a well-known nympho and satyr.

"Like I put in the printout I sent you, Christen's probably screwing her adviser, James Prosser. But I got no hard—" She hung up on Jolly without saying goodbye. Who gave a shit about Prosser? Prosser was a dull university type. An intellectual. A widower. Even if Christen was screwing the guy blind every night, there was no real heat to that story.

On the large TV screen, a commercial had ended and Kilmer and Laura returned, this time with a telephone on the table between their chairs.

Kilmer picked up the phone and said, "Tell us who you are and where you're calling from, please."

"I'm Millie from Chevy Chase," came a female voice. "I was wondering if Congresswoman Christen found it hard to raise a daughter while working in politics all day long."

Laura smiled and said, "It's always trouble to raise a child,

Millie. But it's something that working mothers can do more easily if their employers are sensitive to their special needs. Fortunately, I was able to devote quite a bit of time to my daughter before she finally was on her own."

"On her own, huh?" Penelope snarled. "On her back would be more accurate."

"On her own already and you look so young," Millie said, milking her time with Laura Christen.

Penelope mimicked the caller's voice and grabbed another handful of pink caramel corn. It tasted like bubble gum.

The next caller identified himself as "Jim from D.C." His question, delivered in a mild Irish brogue, concerned the Congresswoman's personal finances. How had she become independently wealthy?

"A friend and I started a cosmetics company in my home state of California," Laura replied. "It was fairly successful. When I decided to enter politics, I sold my share of the stock, which made me independent, if not precisely wealthy."

"And how," continued Jim from D.C., "did you scrape the money together to start your company?"

Laura hesitated, and Penelope sat forward, squinting at the screen. The Congresswoman finally replied, "It's a very long story, I'm afraid. And not a terribly interesting one."

John Kilmer moved on to the next caller, but Penelope was suddenly smiling. "Maybe we should all judge for ourselves how interesting it is," she thought aloud.

She began searching the bed for something, poking into the covers. Apparently it was not there. With a grunt, she hopped out of bed, knocking over the tin of caramel corn. "Shit," she shouted when she stepped on the hard, sticky kernels, grinding them into the rug.

What she was looking for was her personal phone book. She found it on the chair next to her purse and strewn undergarments. She carried it back to bed with her, not bothering to scrape the corn from her feet when she slipped them under the covers.

She found the number of Jake Alban's hotel in Aspen and dialed it. She had something else to add to his assignment.

9

◆

Aspen, Colorado

◆

"If you've seen one redwood, you've seen
'em all."

RONALD REAGAN

MARGARET STAFFORD WAS in a crowded, noisy, no-frills tavern in
Cripple Creek, Colorado, a few miles away from the million-
dollar, two-bedroom-home community of Aspen. She was seated
at a scarred oak wood table, across from a diminutive man with a
crown of orange hair and yellow-tinted aviator sunglasses who was
telling the waitress, "Another Wild Dawg, precious! And a mocha
java for my ladyfriend." He gestured toward Margaret.

Feeling reasonably warm for the first time in two days, she
leaned back in her chair and observed the flamboyant little man
with a cynical, clinical eye. Because of the flame-colored strip
surrounding his tonsure, his milk-white face, and the pale yellow
parka wrapped around his thin frame, he looked like a human
matchstick. What he did not look like was The Wild Man of the
Washington Press Corps, the unofficial title that had propelled
DeWitt Taygard into the literary limelight. One book, *On the Bush
Bus,* and two collections of articles later, he had retired from
journalism to dabble in local politics in his hometown, the rough-
hewn, idiosyncratic community of Cripple Creek.

Margaret shifted her glance to the wall, where a large poster
depicted Taygard mugging outrageously while standing to the left

55

of Ronald Reagan, George Bush, and the current U.S. President back when the latter was merely a senator. The caption read: "Destined for greatness."

"Where was that taken?" she asked.

"Down California way at the Bohemian Grove just before they found out I wasn't Neil Bush and tossed me out on my bony keester." He chuckled a bit, then grinned at her. "So how the hell is my old pard, Murph?"

"Merry as Santa," she replied flatly. "He said you could fill me in on Robert and Laura Christen."

"To business, eh?" he asked, hoping she would suggest otherwise, but knowing she would not. "Well, I did a little digging for you, darling. It's not that easy, 'cause Aspen was a pretty different burg in the sixties. And I really didn't know the Christens to speak to, though his wife was sure a lovely thing to gaze upon. She looks even better now, but for some queer reason, I prefer redheads."

"Self-infatuation, maybe?" Margaret said, unconsciously tucking a tendril of her scarlet hair under her wool cap.

He stared at her, gave a little chuckle and said, "Touché, chérie. Goddamn touché." He withdrew a small spiral note pad from the pocket of his plaid Pendleton. "Let's see now. They showed up the summer of '69. She was heavy with child. Robert was a veterinarian. Was doing some kinda research project on the horses out at Hamilton Stables. Place is owned by the same family behind Hamilton Resorts International, if you can believe it. It's been closed down for years and it's definitely not for sale. They must be using it as some sort of tax boondoggle.

"Anyway, the old boy who's taking care of the property remembers the Christens pretty well, but he's not much of a talker. Carries a shotgun. You could give him a try, though."

"What's his name?"

"Clemson Granville. Been working there for eons," Taygard said. "I guess you knew that Tommy Hamilton was real tight with the Christens."

She nodded. She'd spent the previous day in Fort Collins, visiting the university where Robert Christen and Tommy had been roommates and the Presbyterian Church where the Christens had married with Tommy as best man.

"He is also just about the worst drunk I've ever met, even if he is running the show with Hamilton Resorts."

"Tell me about him," Margaret said.

"I don't think I will," Taygard said, frowning. "He got sick and puked on my boots once and I forgive no man that dishonor. I don't like him and I won't waste my time talking about him."

A waitress arrived at their table with a cup of coffee for Margaret and a tall glass filled with what seemed to be tan and brown sludge for Taygard. "About time, darling," he said to the waitress, who put the glass in front of him, gave a derisive snort, and left.

"What's in that?" Margaret asked.

"An Indian recipe for body warts, plus tequila and grappa and a jigger of crème de banana. A Wild Dawg. Wanna sip?"

"I'll pass," she said. "Let's cut to the car crash."

He looked puzzled for a few seconds, then he said, "Christen's car crash, you mean."

"Yes—that's exactly what I mean," she replied tartly.

Taygard slumped in his chair and looked at her through the yellow lenses. "Look, chérie—I just spent a bunch of hours driving around, phoning people and, in a word, busting my hump getting info that Murph said you needed. Now I'm not expecting anything priceless in return, like your fine pink body. But I sure as hell think a little civility is called for."

Margaret nodded. "You're right—and I'm sorry," she said. "Travel puts me on edge. Planes are always late. Rental cars aren't ready when you need them. And I hate cold weather. I'd like to wind this up fast and be on my way."

Taygard took a swig of his Wild Dawg and said, "Apology accepted. Only you ought to realize that it's not travel that rubs you raw, it's losing control. You strike me as a lady who likes to call all the shots."

Oh, God, Margaret thought. *Yesterday it was lost luggage, a car with a broken heater, and sleet. Today it was slick mountain roads, a stiff neck, and a sixties retread who thinks he's a psychologist.* She blinked at him and said, "That must be it. So tell me—what did you find out about the accident?"

He sighed, flipped a few more pages of his note pad. "Spring of '71," he said. "Bobby Christen was driving his VW on his way back home from Hamilton Stables. Out near Snowmass there's a road forms a junction with Highway 32. That's where he was kissed hard by a truck owned by the Maple Construction Company. Driver was a local boy named Buddy Radin.''

"You know him?" she asked.

"Yep. Sort of a simpleton, with pretensions of normalcy.''

"Did he have any dealings with the Christens before the accident?" Margaret asked.

"Who knows? It's a small town," Taygard replied. He leaned forward and said, "Jee-sus, you're not thinking this was anything but an accident, are you? If you're into that kind of paranoia, we might actually have a future together.''

"Assuming it was an accident, then, what are the specifics?''

"There was a broken booze bottle and the smell of spilled whiskey all over the wreck. So maybe Buddy was a mite pissed. But not so pissed he stuck around for the cops to find him. That boy took off like a greased gazelle.''

"How long before they found him?" Margaret asked.

"Didn't. Nobody ever saw him again. At the time, the cops figured he didn't stop running until he hit Mexico. You sure I can't get you something stronger than coffee?''

Margaret told him no. The place had grown noisy and hot and she was anxious to be gone. There was only a little more that Taygard had for her and she pushed him through it quickly.

In 1972 Laura Christen brought suit against the Maple Construction Company and settled out of court. It was the beginning of the end for Maple, which went into receivership two years later, ironically just before the big building boom of the mid-seventies.

Had Taygard talked with any of Radin's family? No, because there were no Radins left. The line ended with Buddy. He had not been able to locate anyone who'd worked for Maple Construction. The policeman who'd responded to the accident had moved on to God knows where. "And even the dame who wrote the whole thing up for the paper has vamoosed," Taygard ended his report.

"I'd like to see the newspaper clips," Margaret told him.

"Hell, I knew there was something I forgot to do. I suppose I could go to the library in town and copy it for you.''

"I'll do it myself," she said, rising to leave.

"I don't suppose it'd make much sense to suggest getting together later tonight?" Taygard asked.

"You're right."

"You are one feisty little woman," he said. "I love that."

"I knew you did," Margaret told him with a smile. "That's why I've been such a bitch. I've been flirting with you."

His guffaw followed her all the way to the door.

ON the drive into Aspen, she began to sense that she was being followed. There were several cars in her rearview mirror, but the one that made her frown was a dirty maroon Pontiac four-door. She'd noticed a similar car in Fort Collins. But the snow and sleet had smeared enough of the windshield to keep its driver's features blurred and vague. While she studied it, the car began to lose speed, drifting away behind her.

The next rise disclosed the little, relentlessly Victorian town of Aspen hunkering in its snowbanked mountain pocket. She forgot about the maroon car.

Five minutes later she was parked in front of the public library on Hoskins Avenue. Inside, she requested and received a leather-bound volume of *The Aspen Daily News,* dated January 1, 1971, to June 30, 1971. The article that described the Christen fatality was a perfunctory job of reporting by one Helen Belknap, the journalist who'd "vamoosed." Barely two paragraphs, it provided nothing that Margaret didn't know, except that Buddy's given name was Lester D. Radin and that he had been twenty-five years old at the time of the accident.

As she lowered the bound volume, she noticed a man at the next table reading a magazine. There were perhaps six people in the reading room, but he stood out. With alert gray eyes and an outdoor model's good looks, he did not belong in a library. She found him . . . interesting. But she had work to do.

She returned the bound collection to the desk and the librarian lifted it and said, "Heavy as lead. These volumes stay untouched on the shelf for years, and then today I barely put it back and you wanted it."

"Someone else been reading it?"

"That one and the 1968, '69 and '70. That gentleman right

over—'' She stopped because the table where she was pointing was now empty. "He was there a minute ago. Good-looking, gray-eyed devil. Darned if he didn't just leave that book right there on the table without bringing it back.''

Margaret went to the table, picked up a driving guide to the area, and returned it to the librarian.

FROM her room at the Hotel Jerome, Margaret phoned Clemson Granville, caretaker of Hamilton Stables. She told him she was a reporter preparing an article about the Hamilton family and the hotel dynasty. He replied that he wasn't sure what he could tell her, but that she could drive out to the Stables if she felt she had to. He gave her directions. "It's usually an easy drive," he said, "but the snow makes it a mite tricky."

Margaret thanked him and broke the connection. She tried phoning Murphy, but he was out of the office. She asked Nina to pass along to him the name of the man responsible for the crash that killed Laura Christen's husband, Lester "Buddy" Radin. "He left town for points unknown back in '71. Maybe Murph has some way of digging him up," she said, closing out the call. She paused to down a burger in the hotel coffee shop, then motored off to find Hamilton Stables.

She was a mile out of Aspen when she realized that the snow had frozen to a slippery glaze that covered the road. It was particularly treacherous in those areas where the asphalt sloped off into crevices hundreds of feet deep. Even with special tires, Margaret's car drifted unnervingly.

The snow began to fall again. Large fluffy flakes that made soft splats against the windshield. But it was still daylight and traffic was light. She would just have to settle for a slow and easy progress.

She poked along for about fifteen minutes. Then a driver behind her started blasting his horn. She steadied her rearview mirror. The impatient driver was in a maroon Pontiac. It moved closer until it was almost riding her back bumper.

Margaret was not easily intimidated. She slowed down even more. Her purse was on the seat near the passenger door. She drew it toward her.

The driver of the maroon car continued to honk.

Margaret stopped her car completely. Her hand was inside her purse, fingers touching cold comfort.

The Pontiac braked. Its horn blared. Then, with tires spinning on the slick macadam, it reversed. Its driver changed gears and it shot out into the oncoming lane, passing Margaret with a slap of wind and loose snow.

Its license plate was covered with hardened slush.

She returned her handgun to her purse and put her car back into motion. The road, both behind her and in front of her, seemed empty, but the snowfall helped to obscure the view. And the hills and dips in the countryside could easily hide a vehicle until it was upon you.

A glance at her instrument panel told her she'd been driving for nearly seven miles. The turnoff to Hamilton Stables should be approaching shortly.

She was creeping along, trying to stay on the road and searching for a sign, when suddenly a car appeared on the horizon—in her lane. The Pontiac. Moving directly at her at a tremendous speed.

She'd barely had time to form the word "asshole!" in her mind and to spin her wheel to the right when the car plummeted to within inches of her grillwork and made a miraculous swerve onto the other lane, disappearing into the distance.

But Margaret's rental was sliding now, bouncing along the shoulder of the road. There was maybe six feet of snowy land, then nothing but crevasse. A tree, possibly dry-rotted and of little use, stood twenty feet in front of her.

Margaret hit the gas pedal and the car's slide was transformed into a right oblique movement. It scraped against the tree with a grinding crunch, fishtailed, then nestled there.

She cut the engine and sat still, tense, making sure the car had settled to a complete stop. Then, shaken, she opened the door carefully and slid out, sinking up to her ankles in the snow, feeling the heavy wet flakes on her face.

She bent back into the car for her gun, which she shoved into the pocket of her parka. She locked up the car and began sloughing through the drifts along the road.

She'd progressed less than a quarter of a mile when a barely legible sign indicated the Hamilton Stables turnoff. She might have missed it completely from the car.

The snow had piled up along the private road. About a hundred yards from the highway, it masked a pothole that tripped her. She fell forward, her wrist trapped between her chest and the ground beneath the soft snow. Dizzy from surprise, she pushed herself upright. Miraculously, her wrist, hand, fingers seemed intact. But her parka and pants were coated with snow and she felt wet and half-frozen.

She started forward and experienced a sudden panic. The snowfall had grown heavier. She couldn't see more than a few feet in front of her. Was she moving away from the highway or back toward it? Or was she traveling cross-country? The place where she'd fallen had already begun to fill.

Her father had prepared her for self-sufficiency. She'd sailed through Outward Bound's grueling wilderness survival course. She could fish, hunt, start fires with twigs. She excelled in hand-to-hand combat and could subdue or calm most wild animals. But none of her training prepared her for freezing weather and snowstorms. She wanted to cry. Instead, she shouted "Dammit!" at the top of her lungs and trudged forward, wherever that would take her.

10

♦

Washington

♦

"A political leader must keep looking over
his shoulder all the time to see if the boys
are still there. If they aren't still there, he
is no longer a political leader."

BERNARD M. BARUCH

"WANT SOME COMPANY?" Catsy Braden asked as her mother took
her coat from the office closet.

"No, thanks. I've a hunch that Lew Ronkowski would prefer the
meeting to be one-on-one."

Catsy raised an eyebrow. "Oh? And who's going to be on
whom, exactly, Mother?"

"My daughter—queen of the double entendres. For your information, there is nothing, not even his promise of retirement from
politics, that would get me within friction distance of Pegleg
Lew."

"What do you suppose he wants?" Catsy wondered.

"I haven't the vaguest idea. The message he left was that I
should meet him at his formal office at four o'clock."

"We should get him to come here," Catsy said. "It looks
better."

"I don't have time for those games right now," Laura said,
slipping into her coat on her way out. The expression on Catsy's
face told her that her comment had sounded harsher than she'd

intended. She started to soften the rebuke, but Catsy gave her a curt nod and turned away, slipping out of the office.

On the walk to the Capitol Building, Laura's thoughts were once again about her daughter. When Catsy was a little girl, they'd been so close. When had that changed? Fourteen? Fifteen? Teenage rebellion, fueled by alcohol and sex. And drugs? Laura's attempts to talk out the problems had been met with sullen silence. Sensing that she'd lost control, she'd arranged for Catsy to see a high-priced psychologist, a Jungian in his fifties. Catsy spent the hours trying to seduce the man, who finally gave up on her.

During Catsy's college years, when they'd barely spoken for months at a time, a sort of truce was called until Catsy married Clare Braden, an arrogant twerp Laura had never liked. When Clare walked out on her, Catsy for some reason blamed Laura. The most recent truce had begun two years before, when Catsy joined her staff. Since then their relationship had been slowly improving. But there was a wide gap yet to be bridged. . . .

SPEAKER Ronkowski's young receptionist had been expecting Laura's arrival, but she was still a bit awed by her presence. "Good afternoon, Congresswoman," she said. "Please go right in." As soon as Laura had passed, the young woman picked up the copy of *People* magazine and looked at the picture spread once more. It was true what the aides had been saying: Laura Christen was even more beautiful in person.

The Speaker's secretary was fifty-something, with a matronly style of dress and a New England accent. She pressed her intercom button and said, "Congresswoman Christen is here, sir."

"Fine. Show her in, Lily."

Lily stood, smoothed her dark blue dress, and stepped over to a polished oak door that she opened for Laura. Past it was a remarkably overdone room that might have housed a *dauphin* during the reign of Louis XIV. From a distant ceiling not one, but an assortment of chandeliers dropped down to cast their glow over pale, almost sky-blue walls and an untrammeled carpet of royal red hue. Gilded molding matched the frames of ancient, faded seascapes and portraits that adorned the walls. Ronkowski was seated at an immense antique desk, directly in front of a marble fireplace topped by a gilt-edged mirror that was as tall as the elaborately draped windows that flanked its sides. In spite of herself, Laura couldn't help but think of ways that the room might be redecorated to undercut its almost absurd formality.

Ronkowski took his time getting to his feet to welcome her. He was a sturdy man in his late fifties, with a full head of gray-black hair that might have been trimmed with pinking shears. His pinstriped suit had a wilted look. His expanse of white shirt under his signatory bow tie was streaked with cigarette ash. His simian face was wearing what he thought to be his boyish smile. Actually, it made him look like a less intelligent Ollie North. "Come in, my dear," he said. "Let me get you a chair."

He moved from behind his desk and limped toward a plush, tufted visitor's chair which he moved closer to his desk.

His secretary asked Laura if she'd care for coffee, tea, or water. Laura politely refused them all. Then perhaps she could take Laura's coat for her. Laura replied that she didn't think she'd be staying that long.

The secretary exited and Laura used the offered chair. She watched Ronkowski limp to a polished wooden table, from which he lifted a silver pitcher. While he poured himself a glass of water, he asked, "Sure you wouldn't care for one?"

When she refused again, Ronkowski limped back to his desk. Laura knew that his bad knee, in spite of campaign rhetoric to the contrary, had had nothing to do with his service to his country during the Korean conflict. It'd been the result of a skiing accident in his youth. She also was aware that the limp got better or worse depending on the Speaker's mood.

"My dear Congresswoman Christen," he said, easing into the leather seat behind his desk, "I want to thank you."

"For what?"

"For opening my eyes to the inequity that exists in our august body. If there is one gathering in this great country that should be one hundred percent free of prejudice of any kind, it's our little club. And yet we have been acting as if our female membership had been sent there by second-class votes."

Laura stared at him, wondering what he'd say next.

"I know you're aware that quite a few of the fellows are happy the way things are. But I say, the heck with 'em. As we move through the complex and changing 1990s, I would like the history books to say one thing about yours truly: that he introduced procedures and practices to ensure that, male or female, all would be treated as equals in the United States Congress.''

He stopped, waiting for Laura's reaction, his ape's face pathetically eager. It was all she could do to keep from laughing. ''What will your first step be?'' she managed to say.

''Ah!'' He nodded. ''I'm setting up a committee to see how we can make this place less of a men's club. And then I fully intend to shove this right down the throats of those benighted s.o.b.'s who still think a woman's place is in the kitchen.''

''The home, I think that is,'' Laura said.

''Yes—the home. Anyway, Laura—if I may call you Laura—I would like you to head up this committee.''

Laura gave him a smile that was no more sincere than the one he was wearing. She said, ''I'm afraid I have to decline, Mr. Speaker. As you must know, I'm pursuing a different agenda.''

''Laura, Laura,'' he said, condescendingly. ''The peace pipe is on the table. Why not pick it up?''

''Smoking pollutes the air,'' she said sweetly.

He looked at her evenly, coldly. ''Lady, you don't have a hope of shoving this old boy off the throne. Even if every Republican in the Congress went along with the President—and you know they won't—you'd still need a lot of Democrats. And frankly, honey, there just aren't enough malcontents and troublemakers to push you through.''

She rapidly was losing her sense of humor. She started to stand, but he waved her down. ''Hold on just a minute, madam,'' he said, pushing himself to his feet. With a little hopping motion, he perched against his desk top, towering over her, trying to use his height as a form of intimidation. ''You're a good woman and a hard worker, the kind of politician we need. What you don't want to do is send your career into the dumper with an ill-advised move like this.''

She pushed her chair back, away from him, and stood. ''I don't think we've anything else to discuss.''

''Maybe one more thing,'' he said, causing her to pause. ''When you first moved to Los Angeles, what kind of business were you in?''

Laura stared at him. His forehead was wrinkled in mock concern, but his dark eyes were laughing. She said, "I was in the hotel business. In public relations. A long time ago."

"Yes—when we were all much younger," he said. "And probably willing to take more chances. Aside from the public relations stuff, wasn't there a little moonlighting going on?"

"Meaning what?"

He opened the top drawer of his desk and fished out a sheet of quality vellum. "I received this rather odd note a couple days ago." He handed it to her.

It read: "You might want to know that the woman who is challenging you is a disgrace to the Congress. When she first moved to the state she now represents, she made her living by selling drugs." Laura dropped the note on the Speaker's desk and looked at him, speechless.

"Now look here, honey—there's no reason for your fellow congressmen and congresswomen—or anyone else—to know about this . . . little fall from grace so long ago."

Laura shook her head in disgust and turned to go.

"Think it over. Think about that committee and all the good it could do." He chuckled.

Laura spun around, surprising the man so that he almost slipped off of his desk. "You're the one who needs to think," she hissed. "Think about what it will mean to *you* if that piece of paper is a lie and you banked *your* career on it!"

She turned on her heel and left through the door. Lew Ronkowski watched her go. The monkey smile returned to his face and he said in a voice much too soft for Laura to hear, "Don't try to bluff an old pro, baby. You're my meat and we both know it."

11

♦

"A party is perpetually corrupted by personality."

RALPH WALDO EMERSON

NINA LOOKED UP from her typing to find her boss gazing at the carpet near her desk. "What're you looking for, Murph? Roaches?"

"Our Christmas tree," he said. "Everybody on this floor is all set up already. This place looks like Scrooge's house."

She gave him a look of frustration. "I'll call Security again, see if it's come in yet."

"Before you do," he told her, "fill me in on this Ford's Theater bash tonight."

"You mean the Gilcrest do?"

He nodded and she explained that the wife of Senator John Gilcrest (Dem.–Ill.) was heading a committee to clean up the neighborhood around Ford's Theater, which had become dilapidated and overrun with drug pushers. Hence the party.

"I don't suppose we're providing security?" Murphy asked.

"Nope. Salinger Guards."

"Well, find out for sure if Laura Christen is going and if so, score me a ticket."

"You mean secure you an invitation?" She wasn't sure she'd heard him correctly. As long as she'd been working for him, he had not made such a request.

"Whatever it takes to get me past the front door," Murphy said. "And then see about our tree."

He went into his office and slumped onto his desk chair. He looked for a minute at the note Nina had given him earlier, underlined the name "Lester 'Buddy' Radin," then picked up the phone and punched its buttons.

The woman who answered had a voice like hail on a corrugated roof. She croaked, "Department of Motor Vehicles."

"Hello, my love," Murphy said.

"Oh, Gawd, Murph. How many you got this time?"

"Just one, but the guy's registration would have been in Denver, and you might have to go back a few years."

"How many years?" the woman asked guardedly.

"Twenty-one, twenty-two, something like that."

"That's a real grinder, Murph. Christmas is coming and our computers get real busy at Christmas."

"Think of how much brighter the season will be with a crisp new hundred in your stocking."

"This guy got a name?"

"A name and a nickname."

12

♦

"Life somehow finds a way of transcending politics."

NORMAN COUSINS

LAURA CHRISTEN HAD very little time.

She couldn't decide which clothes to pack. Finally, in desperation, she began throwing things into a bag. The problem was, she had no idea how long she'd be gone. She hoped it wouldn't look as if she were running away. Was she?

She suddenly remembered the Gilcrest party. It was the least of her problems, missing the party. Catsy would be furious, of course. And she'd be right. But with any luck, Laura would be back before Lew Ronkowski or anybody else knew she was missing.

It wasn't as if she were leaving the country. In any case, she had no choice. The new letter had made up her mind. She had to have some answers and she didn't feel she could trust telephones.

She clicked the locks on her luggage and carried it from the bedroom into the spotless hall that her maid had just cleaned.

She heard the Speaker's voice coming from her living room. She'd forgotten to turn off the TV. Speaker Ronkowski was grinning wolfishly at a bespectacled reporter who was holding a microphone rather combatively. "I greatly admire Congress*person* Christen," he was saying, making the word "admire" sound rather obscene. "And I don't really think our differences are all that great. But even if they were, to be bothering the American public with our, I must say, petty disagreements is a waste of all our time. She acted impetuously, as women sometimes do."

Laura snapped off the set angrily. That loathsome, blackmailing son of a bitch! Maybe she should just stay and let whatever happened happen. The thought of Lewis Ronkowski lying in state was not exactly repugnant. But one murder was more than enough. If murder it was.

She looked about the well-appointed room anxiously, then stepped quickly to a table where she scooped up a brown leather folder. She carried it back into her bedroom, where she paused, her mind churning.

The maid would be there on Monday, but she had her key. Catsy could take care of the excuses. *Catsy!*

She moved to a telephone, absently plucking off her earring before picking up the receiver. Catsy would be at the office. . . .

She had dialed three numbers before she changed her mind. She didn't really want to talk to Catsy. There would be too many questions for which she had no answers. Instead, she called her daughter's apartment and left a brief message on her answering machine.

She sat down at her makeup table and pulled her hair back from her face and secured it with a colored scarf. Then she put on a pair of very plain, very unfashionable square sunglasses. She smiled at her reflection. If she had been a movie star, the minimal disguise would have failed to do the trick. But even with the publicity that had been prompted by her press conference, she was not worried about recognition. It took awhile for the public to grow accustomed to a face.

She made one quick tour of the interior of her townhouse. Then, satisfied that she'd not forgotten some horribly crucial detail, she picked up her purse and her luggage and exited through the back door to the unattached garage where her car waited.

13

♦

Washington

♦

"I was never worried about any sex investigation in Washington. All the men on my
staff can type."

BELLA ABZUG

PENELOPE KRIM WAS trying to smooth out the portion of her body
that was bulging out of the bright red Valentino knock-off she'd
elected to wear to the Gilcrest affair. Apparently satisfied, she
turned to the black wig, and with some effort lifted it from its
plastic perch and placed it on her scalp. It looked like a pile of
black woodshavings sitting on top of her head. Did the women
really wear their hair like that in Lincoln's day? Her university
studies had made her fairly familiar with Lincoln the man and the
president, but she had no idea what the clothes looked like back
then. Or the women's hair. She had gone to Mr. Luis, her stylist,
and he had suggested a wig from his brother-in-law, Mr. Ramon.
So be it. She hated goddamn costume parties, anyway.

She was tucking a wisp of her own matted and oily hair under
the wig when the phone rang. She stuck her head out of the
bedroom and shouted down the iron stairwell, "Get that for me,
Sid, please?"

Sid, an outsized man in gray chauffeur's livery, moved to a
brand-new antique French phone, lifted it, and said, "Krim's."

A male voice said, "I'd like to speak with her. The name's Jake Alban."

"Just a sec."

Sid walked to the stairwell and shouted Jake's name.

Penelope paused mid-tuck and replied, "I'll pick it up here, Sid."

She flounced onto a settee, then paused for a beat while she got into what she thought of as her Desert Island mood. "Hello, Jake," she said, drawing out the words. "I've been waiting for your call."

The voice that replied wasn't Jake's. It said, "You want me to hang up this phone?"

"Yes, Sid, that'd be fine." She waited for the click, then asked, "Jake—are you there?"

"Yes, waiting patiently."

Across the room, Penelope's reflection told her that her wig had tipped to the right, rather like the leaning tower of Pisa. She tried to center it. "Exactly where are you, Jake?" she asked. "It sounds like a bowling alley."

He said, "I'm at a phone booth at LAX. I just flew in from Aspen. I was planning on staying there overnight, but that seemed pointless. Laura Christen lived there for just a few years with her husband. They had the one child, Catherine. But shortly after the husband was killed in a car accident, Christen headed to L.A. with the girl. I followed her example. If she did give birth to an illegitimate baby, this is probably the place it happened. Even your poison pen letter's postmark suggests that L.A. is the place."

Penelope had to agree with his conclusion. She went back into her kittenish mood. "Maybe you're just making up excuses so you can go swimming and tan that gorgeous, rugged body of yours."

He decided to ignore the implied insult and compliment. He said, "Her cosmetics company is here, too. If you want to know how she financed it, this is the place to find out. You realize that she got a nice chunk of dough from the company whose truck hit her husband?"

"That's in her bio," Penelope snapped. "I want to know the part she doesn't talk about. But you'll get that for me, won't you, Jakee-poo?"

His voice hesitated. "I'll do my best," he said. "There's something you should know."

"Yes?" She batted her eyelashes at herself in the mirror.

"There's a woman doing some sort of background check on Laura Christen."

Penelope frowned. It made her wig wobble. "What woman?"

"Her car rental slip says she's Margaret Stafford, from D.C. My guess would be a reporter."

"If she's by herself, then she's print media. Those TV divas can't walk across the street without a cameraman. I'll check her out."

"I need a favor," Jake mumbled.

"What did you say?"

"A favor," he pronounced more clearly. "Christen used to work at the Casa Bel Air Hotel. I'm going to need some cooperation from the management there. I was wondering if you could arrange it."

"Piece of cake," she said. "I love to throw my weight around."

He didn't reply. She thought she heard him cough. "Are you all right?" she asked.

"Fine," he said.

She relaxed. "Maybe I should fly out for a few days in the sun myself. We could spend some time together, find out a little bit more about one another."

"That'd be great," he said. "But give me a couple days to get the work done first."

"That's what I like to hear," she told him. "Work first, and then we play."

"Sounds like a plan," he croaked in reply.

14

♦

Aspen

♦

"Endure and preserve yourself for better things."

VIRGIL

THE LIGHT WAS beginning to fade when Margaret Stafford smelled the smoke. The snow had stopped falling a while ago. She'd lost any concept of time, but she imagined she'd been wandering around aimlessly for nearly an hour. She'd never been so cold.

There it was again! The smell of burning wood.

She saw a tendril of smoke above the tree line and headed for it.

As she trudged past two large, leafless trees, she sighed with relief at the sight of a flat, ranch-style building with its cheery lighted windows and a brick chimney from which billowed the smoke.

She stumbled to its doorstep. Shivering, she raised one heavy arm and aimed her gloved finger at the buzzer.

An elderly man answered. He wore corduroy pants with suspenders stretched against a thick wool plaid shirt. He had a shotgun in his hands, but it wasn't pointed at her, exactly. "Yes?" he asked suspiciously.

"I'm M—margaret Stafford, Mr. Granville," she said. "I c—called you from the H—hotel Jerome."

Clemson Granville's face softened. "Ah . . . the writer." He rested his gun beside the door. "I didn't hear your vehicle."

All she could think of was that the house was warm. Comfortable and warm. She basked for a moment in the heat spilling through the front door. Finally she said, "I had an accident less than a mile away—a car ran me off the road."

"Happens," he said, helping her inside. "You OK?"

"Just frozen," she said, gravitating toward the open fire. Granville called to a huge black dog who'd been hogging the spot directly in front of the fireplace.

"Better gimme that jacket," he said as the dog made way for Margaret, whining and growling unhappily.

Hesitantly, she surrendered the now-sopping parka with her handgun in its pocket. Granville draped it over the back of a chair and pushed the chair near the flames. "Warm yourself up some and I'll get you a cup of hot coffee with a shot of Kentucky in it."

He and the dog wandered off, leaving her alone by the fire. She moved quickly to her coat, found the pistol, and stuck it into her belt, covering it with her sweater. Then she returned to the fire, which smelled deliciously of smoky pine.

It was a large living room, she realized, with a ceiling much higher than she would have suspected from the exterior. The fireplace and mantel were rock constructions, but everything else seemed to be of wood. Pine-paneled walls were decorated with paintings of snowscapes containing elk and caribou and with sets of mounted skis that looked as if they were antiques. The floor was dark oak, covered by both cloth and animal hide rugs.

The old man returned, proffering a white mug of whiskey-doctored coffee. Margaret sipped at it, enjoying the feeling of the warm cup in her hands. The whiskey worked its way down her throat like hot honey.

She edged back toward the fire and sat down on the animal skin directly in front of the flames. The old man looked at her and said, "Sorry you had all this trouble for nothing. Like I said on the telephone, there's not much I can tell you about the Hamiltons that ain't been written about already."

Shivering, she said, "It's my job to talk to everybody I can."

Then, when she finally got her teeth to stop chattering, she took a deep breath and began the ordeal of Q & A.

Clemson Granville cooperated stiffly, but he didn't give her much that she didn't already know. The elder Hamiltons, a couple of ambitious British expatriates, had settled in Aspen because it reminded them of Switzerland, which they loved. Since Barnard Hamilton had worked for most of his young life around horses, they'd opened a stable that became so profitable they were able to purchase and refurbish a gone-to-seed ranch in Wyoming.

The resulting establishment, Owl Creek Ranch, held a huge appeal for city-dwelling tourists who wanted vacations with a touch of the Wild West. And in the postwar boom years, the Hamiltons' successful dude ranch paved the way for hotels in Beverly Hills and San Francisco.

By the mid-fifties, the Hamiltons' only child, a serious young man named Ivor, took over the reins of the company, renaming it Hamilton International Resorts in honor of new hotels in London and Paris. And Barnard and his wife relocated at the old homestead just outside of Aspen and took Clemson Granville, their loyal foreman, with them. His own wife had recently died and he was glad for the change of scenery.

"When did the stable close down?" Margaret asked.

"Eleven years ago. After the old folks passed on. They went one after the other. Pretty good way to go, for a husband and wife devoted to one another. It wasn't too much later when poor Ivor's heart gave out on him and Tommy became the big cheese."

Margaret asked, "Does Tommy ever come back here?"

"Nope," Granville said. "He lived here for a spell, after he graduated from State. Got a room in back that, on his orders, I haven't touched in twenty years, except to dust off. I doubt he'll ever come back. I suspect he'd have sold the place by now, if old Barnard hadn't put it in the will that I could live out my life here."

The whiskey had made Margaret a little drowsy. She shook off the feeling when Granville said he was going to see about her car. "You just sit here and relax," he said. "This is a real easy chore. The four-wheel does all the work. Shouldn't take more than an hour."

Margaret, warm and comfortable, watched him through a

frosted window as, jacketed, gloved, and booted he marched
through the snow to his truck. As soon as his four-wheel started
away, she went off in search of Tommy Hamilton's bedroom.

It was, as Clemson Granville had said, at the rear of the house.
Pennants on the wall. A flannel blanket in green with a large "CS"
in white at its center covered a queen-size bed. There was a small
sofa and matching stuffed chair, a floor lamp, a desk and chair, a
bookcase, and a stack of file cabinets. A huge round-screen color
TV with rabbit ears, an elaborate turntable-receiver outfit, a Web-
cor tape recorder, and a shortwave radio set.

The area was unheated. Even if Clemson Granville's return was
not imminent, the chill would have forced her to move quickly. On
the desk was a stack of spiral notebooks filled with handwritten
poetry—mawkish, overly sentimental stuff about unrequited love.

The wall behind the desk was covered with framed photographs.
Laura Christen was the subject of several candids. Laura in what
appeared to be an Angora sweater, pleated skirt and saddle oxfords, sitting on a blanket in the sun. Laura and a handsome young
man, dancing. Laura in cap and gown, receiving her diploma.

The handsome young man was the late Robert Christen. Margaret had seen his picture in the Colorado State yearbooks. She
recognized Tommy Hamilton's picture from the yearbooks, too. A
tall, attractive blond in tight denims and a polo shirt. There was
something posed about his stance, as if he'd practiced it in front of
a mirror before facing the camera.

The bottom desk drawer contained an amazing assortment of
perfume bottles, cheap costume jewelry, and the photo of a little
girl with blonde hair.

A noise in the hall froze Margaret in the act of opening a file
cabinet. Quickly she began to formulate a plausible excuse for her
being in the room. Then Clemson Granville's black dog poked a
curious nose around the doorjamb.

Margaret relaxed and grinned at the dog, which continued to
watch her suspiciously as she went through the top file cabinet. Her
search yielded mainly school textbooks and a collection of hotel
management home courses. In the bottom cabinet, however, behind an assortment of paperback mysteries, she found a rolled

notebook. Its cover carried a handwritten title, *On the Death of a Friend,* a short story by Thomas G. Hamilton.

Margaret closed the cabinet, turned out the lights, and left the room, the dog pat-patting behind her back to the living room. They were both settled before the fire when Clemson Granville returned.

"Car's driveable," he said. "The passenger side's mashed pretty good and the door don't want to open. But it'll get you back to your hotel. I'll follow you in."

"That's not necessary, Clemson."

He was frowning. Snowflakes in his eyebrows. "You know anybody in a dark Pontiac sedan?"

Margaret hesitated. "Why?"

"It passed while I was towing your car off the tree. Then passed the other way a minute later. I couldn't see the driver very well, but I got the idea he was pretty interested in your auto. I thought it might've been somebody you knew."

She shook her head. "I don't know many people in Aspen," she said. "But maybe I will take you up on that offer to follow me into town."

15

◆

"Don't be humble. You're not that great."

GOLDA MEIR

LAURA CHRISTEN'S CREAM-COLORED Seville whipped along New York Avenue in the general direction of the National Arboretum. The waning sun was trying to poke through a smudged sky. The car's tank was full, which meant she would not have to stop until she reached her destination. She leaned forward and slid the heater knob a notch higher, but the discomfort she was feeling was not totally the fault of the cold weather.

She had the sensation of running away from her work. In nearly twelve years, her membership in Congress had come before everything except her daughter. She had subjugated romance, friendship, sports, and home life. Now, at the most critical time imaginable, she was putting her political life on hold. Granted, it was not as if she were driving off the face of the globe. She'd arrive in Easton on Chesapeake Bay in just a few hours, even with the after-work traffic. Her plan was to be back in D.C. late that night, or at the latest, the following day.

But she would have to miss a gala she'd promised to attend. And she could afford no ill-will at all in her fight against Lew Ronkowski. The mere thought of the Speaker made her stomach tighten. He was everything that she had come to hate in Congress—a smug, self-serving upholder of the status quo. He did not seem to care that children were not being fed or educated in this country, or that women were still occupying a second-class status in nearly every aspect of life except homemaking, or that ever-increasing numbers of elderly citizens were being ignored by an unfeeling government. These were the citizens she'd become a congresswoman to serve. She hoped she was right in thinking she could serve them better as Speaker of the House.

She remembered the dinner she'd had with Esther Cooper after a long and frustrating meeting on the graying of America. Speaker Ronkowski's name had come up and Esther had expressed her disgust with his self-proclaimed chauvinism. "I've been in public service for nearly half my life," Esther had said, "and in all that time I don't think I've ever met another congressperson with so little regard for women as Lewis Ronkowski."

It was as they were sipping their after-dinner coffees that Laura suggested that Esther seek the position of Speaker. The elderly woman shook her head. "Bad timing," she said. "When I was young enough to take on a challenge like that, there wasn't a chance in the world a woman could be even nominated. We were lucky to get on the Education and Labor Committee. Now, I'm simply too old for that kind of fight. Lewis would not pull any of his punches." She stared at Laura. "But someone younger might just have a chance."

Laura said with a smile, "Might that someone younger have your support?"

Esther shook her head sadly. She had to remain loyal to her party. "But," she added, "that shouldn't deter a congresswoman who is popular and has a reputation for fairness and impartiality toward *all* citizens."

It had been at that moment that Laura had made up her mind to take the chance. There were drawbacks, of course. If she was defeated in her attempt, her effectiveness in Congress, not to mention her political future, might be in jeopardy. On the other hand, if she won . . .

She removed her sunglasses. The sky was darkening and it looked as if rain or sleet were on the way. She was approaching a toll bridge that would take her past Annapolis. Her dashboard digital clock informed her she was making good time.

If she won . . . She *would* win, she told herself. Hadn't she convinced Mike Roberts to back her move? Wasn't she worrying

Lew Ronkowski to the point where he was playing idiotic games like that supposed note about her dealing in drugs?

The confident smile froze on her face. A twenty-year-old memory suddenly slipped into place and she realized that the note might not have been an idiotic game at all, but a long-buried specter surfacing again. It was one more thing to discuss once she arrived at Easton.

16

♦

Los Angeles

♦

"This won't be the first time I arrested somebody and then built my case afterward."

JIM GARRISON

THE CASA BEL AIR was successfully hidden from the traffic along Bryson Road by a long row of impenetrable hedges slightly taller than Jake Alban's rented Jeep Cherokee. But he persisted until he found the hotel's unmarked entrance, then followed a winding road to its crowded parking lot.

There, a young man in a bright orange jumpsuit removed his canvas bag from the back of the Cherokee and presented it to a middle-aged porter dressed like a Spanish grandee in short tan jacket, belled trousers, and black sombrero.

Jumpsuit drove the car away and Grandee led Jake down a flagstone path to a towering powder-blue building of barely subdued opulence, surrounded by a water-filled moat from which another employee with a long pole was trying to fish a wedding bouquet without disturbing the swans and ducks floating by.

A sturdy drawbridge took them into a cool, high-ceilinged lobby where bright, efficient young men and women in blue blazers that matched the outside of the building satisfied the needs of arriving and departing guests.

A female clerk with perfectly coiffed cinnamon-colored hair

informed Jake that a wonderful suite had been reserved for him on the seventh level, with a splendid view of the city by night. "Julio will take care of your luggage," she said, indicating the Grandee. "Mr. Kerry Niles of Intercom, who manages public relations for the Casa Bel Air, has asked me to offer his apologies for not being here to greet you. He's out of town. He did say that Mr. Hamilton would be expecting you in his office at six."

Jake thanked her and followed Julio up to his suite. It turned out to be an impressive series of rooms in contemporary decor— kitchen, dining room, bedroom with balcony that extended across a living room with floor-to-ceiling windows.

Jake paused on the balcony to look down on Sunset Boulevard just as the sun was setting in the west and the streetlights blinked on. Cars like cockroaches clotted the streets. The Strip was aglow with neon Christmas trees and holly. Towering vanity billboards saluted rock stars and authors and motion pictures that would be as faded as their pasteboard images a month later. Hovering over all this was an ominous, obviously unhealthy, yellow-tinged smog that didn't quite complement the darkening purple sky.

Julio joined him and handed him the door key. Jake took out his wallet, but Julio said, "Please, sir, no. Señor Niles takes care of everything."

Kerry Niles definitely did not stint. A large basket of fruit had been deposited on a table in the dining room, along with several bottles of California wines and one fifth each of Bell's 12 and Stoli. Niles' business card had been stapled to a press kit an inch thick, filled with photos of Tommy Hamilton, the various Hamilton Hotels, and a biography that seemed to Jake to be rather thick for a guy still in his forties whose main achievement had been being born into the Hamilton family.

Jake poured a shot of Bell's and took it and the bio to the couch in the living room. As he leafed through the information, most of which he already knew, his mind drifted. In the days when he had been a confident young reporter, he had always believed his hunches. Tommy Hamilton had, according to all reports, been a close friend to Laura and her husband. Jake's hunch was that if Laura Christen really had given birth to an illegitimate child, Tommy was the Pick of the Week as the father.

He only had to wait until six to find out.

17

◆

Airborne

◆

"I'd much rather be having fun in the bedroom than doing all this talking in the living room."

ELIZABETH RAY

"NORA SAT AT the end of the pier; her long, tanned legs, as if carved from rarest teak by loving hands, dangled inches above the Atlantic's rippling waters. There was a halo, an ethereal nimbus, surrounding her flowing, golden tresses. Troy, his heart fairly bursting, looked at her longingly. He had never seen anything quite so beautiful as this woman-goddess that Fate had cruelly placed within his grasp then made untouchable."

"Oh, Jeeze, Louise!" Margaret Stafford muttered, mainly to herself, as the jumbo jet she was on soared through the evening sky. "Woman-goddess! Cruel fate! Give me a break."

The first class flight attendant asked, "Champagne?"

Margaret looked up from Tommy Hamilton's manuscript and said, "Oh? Champagne? Why not?"

Her glass filled, she shifted in the comfortable bed she'd made from two wide-body seats and returned to one of the worst pieces of chauvinistic trash-tripe she'd ever come across. Tommy Hamilton's yarn was set on the Mississippi Gulf Coast, where its youthful protagonist, Troy, had invited his married friends, Barry and

Nora, to spend the summer at an oceanfront mansion owned by his aged grandparents.

Margaret had worked her way through nearly two-thirds of the novella-length story, past episodes involving the grandfather's incipient senility, Nora and Troy colliding during a volleyball game on the beach and sensing *"the electricity of the moment,"* Troy getting drunk watching Barry and Nora close-dancing at a Yacht Club party.

The story progressed with Troy and Barry taking the motorboat out onto the choppy Atlantic for a day of water-skiing, leaving Nora back on the beach, tanning *"her lovely goddess body."*

"Troy steered the craft into the wind, to give Barry an easier ride, letting the novice skier take the waves head-on. The breeze felt good on Troy's face, clearing the effects of the champagne from his brain. Staring at the soft, billowing clouds, his mind wandered to Nora's body. Her breasts—round and firm and proud and, in his imaginings at least, aching for his touch."

"Oh, brother . . ." Margaret said, wincing and feeling her toes curl in embarrassment for the then-young author.

With Troy's fevered brain continuing to be tantalized by the woman-goddess Nora, the mood of the piece shifted abruptly. Barry's ski connected with a bit of flotsam and he was thrown off-balance. Troy, suffering the effects of too much champagne and too much fantasizing, reduced speed. The slack in the line added to Barry's trouble and he hit the water, losing both skis. Troy punched up the speed suddenly and Barry was jerked forward. In his panic, he continued clutching the handle of the taut towline, even when it dragged him toward an anchored sail craft.

"Barry disappeared beneath the sailboat's stern. Then the boat gave a violent shake. The towline popped free." Troy cut his boat's engine and dived into the water. Within seconds, he found his friend *"wedged between the rudder skeg and the companionway hatch."* He freed the body and got it into the speedboat, but *"he knew that his friend was beyond mortal care."*

She rested the notebook on her knees. She wondered just how autobiographical the story was. Had Tommy Hamilton been in some way involved in Robert Christen's death? And, if so, did it affect her specific assignment?

She picked up the notebook again, flipping pages past the trans-
porting of Barry's body back to shore, where Nora fell apart at the
sight of her dead husband. Troy could not bring himself to tell her
of his complicity in the accident.

Margaret flipped ahead past the descriptions of the death trip
back to their East Coast home, past passages of Troy's guilt and
self-loathing, past the condolences of friends at the funeral, past
the burial, to where Nora finds herself alone in the graveyard with
Troy. He is so distraught that in her sadness she begins to comfort
him. Finally, she tells him that she's going away.

" *'I'm leaving in the morning,' she said. 'It's best for us both.
We would be constantly reminding one another of how much we
both loved Barry. It's time we moved on from that.'*

*"He nodded and they stood, arms encircling one another, say-
ing goodbye until the sun set and the dusk melded into night. Then
she was gone. Forever.*

*"Somehow, he found his way to The Sea Chanty, a beer and
burger sawdust shack that the three of them frequented. He sat at
their table and looked out at the crowded room and sipped his stein
of beer.*

*"A young couple he knew slightly asked if they might share his
table. The husband was carrying their young child in a back
pouch, a lovely little girl with blonde curly hair and a sweet smile
that melted Troy's battered heart.*

*"Looking at the beauty, he realized suddenly that life hadn't
ended for him. There was a reason to go on. His beloved Nora was
lost to him forever. But he would find another love, another golden
girl. And this new one would be undisturbed by an adult's con-
cerns, unmarked by life's cruel touch, eager for his guidance, his
wisdom, his love.*

*"He smiled at the little girl resting comfortably in her father's
pouch and wondered if she might be the one."*

Margaret looked up from the completed manuscript to find the
flight attendant beside her seat. "More champagne?"

"Maybe just a touch," Margaret replied. The chilling ending to
Tommy Hamilton's little epic had sobered her.

18

♦

Los Angeles

♦

"Now is the time for all good men to come to the aid of the party."

ANONYMOUS

THE CASA BEL AIR'S office staff evidently ran from the place when the quitting bell rang. The clean, modern space on the second floor of the main building was empty when Jake Alban arrived at 5:45, fifteen minutes early for his meeting with Tommy Hamilton.

He walked quietly through the dimly lit pale blue waiting room into a shadowy larger space containing six vacant secretarial desks and two closed doors. The opaque glass panel on the unmarked door at the far left corner was aglow. Tommy Hamilton's private office.

Shadows on the glass panel indicated he was not alone. A voice, possibly Hamilton's, was saying something about "thug tactics."

Another voice, not quite so deep, replied, "Just listen to who's lecturing *us* on morality."

"You can get the hell out of here," the first voice snapped furiously. "My days of *cooperation* with scum like you are over."

Jake edged closer to the door as a feminine voice purred, "It's your decision of course, Tommy. But if news about your little girlfriends came out, just think what it would do to your family trade." She laughed.

"Screw you—and the bastard you work for."

"Now, Tommy," the woman cooed, "I bet you wouldn't be so mean if I introduced you to a cute little girl in one of my classes. She's fifteen, but she has the body of a twelve-year-old."

"Get out!"

Jake picked out a desk to hide behind, but there was no need. He heard a door opening inside Tommy Hamilton's office. A rear exit. The door slammed shut.

The office was quiet for a few seconds. Then Jake heard the distinct sounds of a man weeping. He moved very quietly back the way he'd come.

TEN minutes later, an apparently recovered Tommy Hamilton greeted Jake in the empty outer office. He was a large man in his mid-forties, with a long, slightly puffy face that sun and alcohol had turned the approximate deep red color of a side of beef. His hair had been tinted blond and combed back in a leonine sweep that ended just past the starched white collar of his tuxedo shirt. His thick chest was covered by an obviously expensive rough silk tux jacket that fitted as if it were made for him, which it was.

"Excuse the monkey suit, Jake," he said, then explained that he was wearing it because John D. Slaten, the Vice President of the United States, was being honored at a $1,000-a-plate dinner in the hotel's Corrida Room. "Should be quite a crowd. Poke your nose in the cocktail party as my guest. It's always fun when Washington and Hollywood meet for a little mutual stroking and back-scratching."

As he was ushered into Hamilton's private office, Jake decided that the man's soft brown eyes seemed too sensitive and kind to go with the rest of his face. "Well, fire when ready," Hamilton suggested. "Or would you like a drink—hard or soft?"

"No drink," Jake said flatly, gawking at the thing that was behind his host's desk. It was a remarkable piece of furniture. A chair—wood painted with silver leaf. It resembled a sitting skeleton, its garish shiny skull atop sparkling curved ribs. Shiny silver armbones joined with bent fleshless legs. The only part not based on a parody of the human anatomy was the seat, a curved silver slab.

"That's amazing . . ." Jake said.

"I suppose it is," Tommy Hamilton replied with a smile. "I've had it so long I've grown used to it. It was inspired by the Day of the Dead ceremonies in Mexico. It's really quite comfortable. Try it."

"I'll take your word for it," Jake said, sitting down on a contemporary chrome and leather chair facing the desk. His host sat, too, a formally attired businessman perched on a silver skeleton.

"A distracting element in your office," Hamilton said affably, "keeps your business opponents off-balance. Actually, it was a gift from one of my ex-wives."

Jake removed a notebook from his pocket and began his "interview." He took his time talking about the expanding Hamilton empire, but finally he said casually, "I understand that Congresswoman Laura Christen once worked here."

Tommy Hamilton nodded. "We're old friends, the Congresswoman and I. From college. She needed a job and I called my father, who was running the show at the time."

"What did she do here, exactly?" Jake asked, knowing the answer from his long-ago interview with Laura Christen. He'd reviewed it during his cross-country plane trip.

"Worked her way up to become our director of public relations. In those days, publicity was handled in-house. Now we use Intercom," Hamilton said, and Jake was surprised to see his lip curl on the word.

"What kind of job is Intercom doing?" Jake asked.

Tommy Hamilton hesitated, then replied, "Oh, a *fine* job. . . . But according to my father they couldn't compare with Laura."

Laura hadn't mentioned Tommy Hamilton's name during their interview. But there was something . . . he couldn't quite bring it to mind. Something Laura had mentioned, off the record, about a romance that had soured. It hadn't been in his notes.

"Do you remember any specific examples of her expertise?" Jake asked.

"Like I said, my father was the head man then. I was living abroad." He paused, his brown eyes hardening. "Is this article of yours about Hamilton Resorts or Laura Christen?"

Jake wished he'd known more about Laura when they'd last met. If he'd asked her the right questions then, it might have made his job now much more simple. He said, "Mrs. Christen is news these days, and she did work for HRI. Was her friendship with your father the reason Hamilton Resorts invested so heavily in Lady Amber Cosmetics?"

Hamilton blanched. Recovering, he smiled and said, "All of that took place long before I took over. All I know is that it turned out to be a damned fine investment." The silvered bones of the skeleton glittered malevolently as he shifted on the chair. "I'm sorry, but I have to attend the Vice President's cocktail party shortly. If you have any more questions, give a call. I'll answer 'em if I can."

The big man walked Jake to the elevators. "I meant it about the cocktail party," he said. "The Corrida Room, on the mezzanine. Tell 'em Tommy sent you."

WHEN Jake entered his suite, he found a young woman in the living room watching a cartoon show on the TV. She was short but full-bodied, with hair and lips made up to resemble the late Marilyn Monroe. She was wearing a blue leather miniskirt and a bright yellow spandex tanktop that didn't quite cover her breasts.

"One of us seems to be in the wrong room," he said.

"Oh, no," she said, leaping to her feet. She ran into the kitchen, opened the refrigerator, and removed a container of ice in which a bottle of champagne had been wedged. "I didn't want the ice to melt too quickly," she explained. "We're all compliments of Mr. Kerry Niles."

"Mr. Niles is too generous," Jake said wryly.

She grinned and began fiddling with the bottle, trying to remove the cork. "He thought maybe we could have a little vino, then have some dinner, and then—whatever."

She studied him for a reaction. *She is rather sweet,* he thought, *seems pleasant, obviously available.* He wondered why he wasn't interested. "I'll be sure to thank Mr. Niles, but I'm a little busy right now. Work to do."

"I could wait. This is a wonderful, big TV. I could just wait here and when you're ready for a little company, all you have to do is whistle. I got that from a movie!"

"You're a hundred movies rolled into one," he said. "But right now I just need a little time by myself."

A bit of the wattage went out of her smile. She nodded. "I came on too strong, didn't I?"

"Not at all," Jake told her. "If I wanted to be with a beautiful woman tonight, it would definitely be you."

"Ah," she said, brightening a little. "I bet I could get you in the mood."

"No doubt about it," he said. "But I really have work to do. No kidding."

"Well, it was nice meeting you."

"Take the champagne if you want it," Jake said.

"You really are working, then," she said, plucking the bottle from its ice cube nest. He nodded. "This is nice. My boyfriend and I both love to lie in bed, have a few drinks, and watch old movies. Tonight we do it in style." She held up the bottle and made her exit.

Jake stepped over to the bar and poured a short scotch, carried it to the balcony where he stretched out on a chaise lounge. It was winter everywhere else in the world, but here it was still in the high sixties. He closed his eyes. A pleasant night breeze fluttered by. He felt strangely peaceful. And then the delicate tinkling of wind chimes flashed the familiar montage of horror before his eyes. Shouts. Gunfire. The huge chandelier exploding. Glass shards darting down like sharpened diamonds. The gleaming white table-cloth, suddenly scarlet. His wife's half-severed hand still grasping a wineglass. Glistening daggers slicing through Danielle's perfect oval face, cutting apart exquisite pale flesh. And, as she opened her bleeding mouth to scream, the remains of the chandelier crashing upon her, covering her like a crystal shroud. . . .

He sat up suddenly, spilling the scotch. His hand was shaking. Slowly, reality began to crowd out memory. And with it came self-doubt. What was he doing wasting his time in Los Angeles? Why was he working for a woman like Penelope Krim? What was he trying to do with his life? What was he searching for? How would he know it when he found it?

19

♦

Maryland

♦

"Deliver me from your cold phlegmatic
preachers, politicians, friends, lovers and
husbands."

ABIGAIL ADAMS

THE GRAYNESS OF both water and sky began to darken as Laura
Christen drove over Chesapeake Bay Bridge. Night was not so
much falling as slamming down with a wintry vengeance. The last
view she had of the Bay was of ice forming where the slate-colored
water lapped the deserted beach.

She remembered when she'd first seen the Bay two decades
before, from a private plane that eventually landed at Baltimore-
Washington International. From there she'd been driven by limousine to a yacht resting in a slip at a nearby marina. An international
financier named Theo Koriallis had been aboard, waiting to take
her on a cruise down the Bay to his "East Coast home."

She'd met him two months before, at a cocktail party at the Casa
Bel Air in Los Angeles. She'd been a rather introverted, newly
widowed young mother, and this incredibly romantic man who
was like the hero from an Ayn Rand novel was ignoring all of his
friends and associates to dote on her every word and gesture. He
was beyond handsome, a tall, wiry, dark-complexioned man in his
forties. Smoldering dark eyes staring into hers. Irresistible, dynamic presence focused on her alone.

He had insisted on driving her home in a car the Italian name of which she would never remember. He had not tried to kiss her at the door. Nor had he after their date the following week.

On the third week, a stunning brunette woman had approached him in a restaurant and whispered something in his ear. She had then looked at Laura and given her a friendly salute. Later, in the restroom, the brunette had sidled up to her and asked her what she thought of Theo's equipment. "Have you ever experienced anything so wonderful before?" Then, amused by Laura's stammer and blush, she had flitted away. That night, convinced that he would at least kiss her, she waited for his lead. But again, she was left at her door, confused and, for the first time, sexually frustrated.

Nearly a month went by without a word from him. But just as she had assumed she would never hear from him again, he phoned from New York. Would she like to join him for a long weekend? She would, but she was a working girl.

He had already spoken with her boss, Ivor Hamilton, who was an old friend. He would send his private plane for her.

By the following Thursday afternoon, she was on his yacht in Chesapeake Bay. They had barely left the marina when he took her face in both hands and kissed her with a passion and intensity that she had never before experienced.

It was as if an electric current had passed through them. All that power and strength. And passion. She was not aware of the ocean beneath them or of the roar of the ship's engines.

She could not recall how they arrived at the stateroom, only her clothes being impatiently removed from her body. Then, silk sheet beneath her. His hands touching her, hurting her, soothing her, toying with her. Then his mouth. Then his lean, muscled body pressing against hers. When he entered her she felt her heart stop, then start again.

Remembering, Laura smiled bitterly. Happiness always had a price tag and that one had been higher than she'd wanted to pay.

She left the highway at the turnoff to Easton. The road took her past quaint little towns that would have looked closed for the winter except for the smoke coming from chimneys, and the occasional lighted window.

Passing through Easton, she had to swerve to avoid a group of men in hunting gear who had just exited a pub with their dogs and were crossing the road to their vehicles. A bit north of the town she turned onto a secondary road that led past vast fields that were all but hidden in the moonless night. Her only clear view was of the ground illuminated by her car's headlights. It was like driving through black velvet.

She turned on her brights in time to spot a sign nailed to a tree. It read EUREKA, the name of Theo's estate. It marked the entry to a private country trail next to property surrounded by a high barbed-wire fence. To Laura's dismay the trail was still unpaved and strewn with large boulders to discourage trespassers. Testing the Seville's shocks to their limits, she forged ahead, discovering too late that the trail was beginning to narrow.

Apprehensive but persistent, she continued on, but it was becoming apparent that she would soon have to leave the car and continue on foot. Before that happened, however, the trail ended and a smooth, evenly cindered road began.

She followed it and the high wire fence another five miles and arrived at an iron gate. Suddenly the area was brightened by a row of lights. An amplified voice said, "Please identify yourself."

She lowered her window and shouted, "My name is Laura Christen. Mr. Koriallis is expecting me."

Within seconds the gate swung inward and she drove through it. As she passed the gatehouse, she saw a man's face in its window, grinning at her.

The two-story stone house was a mile from the gate. On the front steps was a black man wearing a red parka and a red hunter's cap, his breath freezing on the air. "Good evening, Mrs. Christen," he said as she stepped from the car. "My name is Albert. I'll take care of your luggage. You just go on inside the house."

The place, she remembered, was like a contemporary version of an English castle, but there was a different atmosphere in it now. Thick stone walls were still brightened by paintings by Picasso and Miró and even a Warhol lithograph of Theo himself, but in the dimness of the room, even they seemed drab and shadowy. The slab floor was covered by the rich Oriental rugs she'd recalled, but they were streaked with mud. The massive hearth had housed a roaring, crackling fire, even in summer, but it was now cold and dreary.

Albert followed her inside, placed her small suitcase on the carpet, and closed the solid oak front door. It took all of his strength to do it. He said, "I'll show you to your room, madam. And then I'll get Cook to prepare your dinner."

"Won't I be dining with Mr. Koriallis?"

"He left Eureka a few hours ago," Albert said without expression. "I'm not sure where he went or when he will return."

Laura was annoyed. She'd come with the understanding that they would talk that night. Otherwise she could have stayed in Washington and attended the Gilcrest party. "Is there anyone here who might know when he will return?" she asked.

"We have a small staff here, but I will ask. First allow me to show you your room."

"Are the guest rooms still in the west wing?" she asked.

He nodded. "Then Madam has been here before?"

"Madam has."

"Before my time then," he said. "I would have remembered."

She wished she could forget.

20

♦

Washington

♦

"Give me the hand that is honest and hearty,/Free as the breeze and unshackled by party."

JAMES MONTGOMERY

J. B. MURPHY, resplendent in a dinner jacket that was tugging a bit at his midsection, turned over his gray Lincoln to a parking attendant who seemed to disapprove of his choice of transportation. As attendant and car zoomed off down Tenth Street, Murphy cast a jaundiced eye at the unusual activity on the block. Across the street, Ford's Theater was lighted in all its refurbished glory, proudly proclaiming the appearance of *Our American Cousin*. Murphy turned to observe the guests entering a building across the street and to the left of the theater, where Senator Peter Gilcrest (Dem.–Ill.) and his wife, Marcy, had invited a small crowd of two hundred or so of their nearest and dearest friends to a gala designed to kick off Marcy's latest project—the sprucing up of the neighborhood surrounding Ford's.

That section of downtown Washington did need a bit of sprucing. In spite of the historical lure of the museum that had been established inside the playhouse where John Wilkes Booth had sent a bullet into the brain of Abraham Lincoln, there was considerable flotsam, both animate and inanimate, cluttering up the landscape. But to Murphy it wasn't nearly as off-putting as the sight of

Washington society, in crinolines and stovepipe hats, swarming into what the invitation described as a "Come as You Are, April 14, 1865, Party," with instructions reading: "Costume or black tie."

Murphy had nearly balked when his secretary, Nina, had informed him of the costume aspect of the party. "Just wear your tux," she'd replied sweetly. "It shouldn't be more than a few years off."

The gala was being held next door to the Peterson House, where the mortally wounded President had been carted and where he'd passed away. Evidently that restored building had been unavailable, or possibly deemed too tiny, for the blowout. So, when a blast of winter wind pierced the piqué bib of his dinner shirt, Murphy found himself double-timing up to the house next to the house where Lincoln died.

He watched approvingly as the appropriately costumed security guards moved the crowd easily and cordially into the party, smoothly leading those without invitation to a section of the building where their credentials might be checked. An attractive young woman in a yellow ball gown accepted his invitation, glanced at it, and said, "Thank you for joining us, Mr. Murphy. Your host and hostess are in the main room."

Murphy moved on, following a short, round Abe Lincoln and his tall, bejeweled Mary Todd into a crowded, noisy, very active room filled with costumed revelers. Someone, an antic interior decorator or a theatrical set designer, had transformed the space into a large, turn-of-the-century ballroom, complete with chandelier and orchestra and parquet dance area. The bewigged band was playing its historical heart out on an up-tempo version of the "Blue Tail Fly," but the guests were more interested in the bars front and back and a room just off the main area where several tables were heaped with hors d'oeuvres running the gamut from Alaskan crab to Swedish meatballs.

Aside from the band, the only other attraction that was being totally ignored was the display of the architect's dimensional rendering of how the new, improved neighborhood would look, with a little luck and $14 million in taxpayer dollars.

Murphy turned his back on the display, too, wandering through the room, picking up snatches of conversations charged with political rhetoric, sexual innuendo, and combinations of both. It was the sort of atmosphere that had kept him away from such social gatherings for the past thirteen years.

He was staring at a melting ice sculpture of the Lincoln Memorial and wondering why he'd come when someone shoved a drink under his nose. Charles Stern said, "Your wish is my command, sahib." The tall, self-proclaimed "conscience of the Republican Party" was dressed more or less the same as he'd been for their meeting at the Maitland Hotel, which made him the only man in the room wearing neither costume nor tux.

"I admire your outfit, Charlie," Murphy said enviously, accepting the drink.

"I decided to come as a descendant of John C. Breckinridge," Stern said.

"And who might that be?"

"He lost to Lincoln in the election of 1860."

Murphy chuckled and sniffed at the drink he'd been handed.

"It's bourbon and branch," Stern told him, pronouncing the whiskey "booor-bon." "The gentleman's drink."

"Bourbon, huh? I don't recall your being a son of the South, Charlie." The truth was, Murphy couldn't recall any of Stern's pre-service biography.

"We are born," Stern said, "we age, we die. Specifics don't matter much to anybody but the historians, and we know what liars those bastards are. How are you progressing on that certain matter?"

Murphy sampled the drink. He hadn't tasted bourbon in years. It was sweet. He said, "We're moving right along."

"There's some other business I might throw your way. Something very, very nasty. Should be just your cup of poison," Stern said, "considering the personnel."

"Am I supposed to guess?" Murphy asked.

Stern shook his head. "It's still a bit . . . premature for any discussion." He brought his glass to his lips and lifted his eyes to survey the crowd.

"Just between us girls, Charlie, what exactly *is* your connection to the Republican Party?"

"Hell, Murph, you know I'm a bipartisan sort of guy. I was just keeping Mike company."

"Then who *does* issue your paycheck? The FBI, the CIA, the National Guard?"

Stern gave him a wintry smile. "I suppose I'm sort of an independent . . ." He paused, distracted by someone or something in the room. "I hope you don't mind if we take this up later, eh, Murph," he said, already angling away through the crowd.

As always, Charlie Stern moved fast once he decided to move. Murphy watched him maneuver toward a man wearing a silk shirt and tights. Black curly wig and a moustache. The detective wondered who the guy was pretending to be. Then he got it. With all the Lincolns in the room, there had to be at least one John Wilkes Booth.

And this one's chiseled profile looked oddly familiar.

Stern and "Booth" were engaged in conversation now, and Murphy was wending his way toward them when he was halted by a formidable woman in a low-cut, bright red gown who planted herself in his path. The wig atop her head tilted precariously to the right like a lightning-struck oak. "And just what are you doing here, Murphy?" Penelope Krim demanded.

Murphy gave her a dazzling smile. "Slummin', my dear. But don't you look nice and . . . Lincolnesque."

Penelope Krim raised an eyebrow. "I've never seen you at one of these shindigs before. Ergo, you must be working. For whom?"

Murphy tried to keep sight of Stern and "Booth" over Penelope's shoulder, but that proved impossible. He said, "My analyst tells me I should become more sociable. Get out more."

"Can the paddy bullshit. You're here and you're working." She paused, her eyes widened, then narrowed. "Your partner's name is Stafford, isn't it?"

"Meg?"

"Margaret!" she exclaimed. "Margaret Stafford—I knew that goddamned name seemed familiar. I think you'd better fill me in on what you and *Meg* are up to."

He had no idea what the reference to Margaret was all about, but he certainly was not going to discuss her, or anything else, with Penelope Krim. He'd made that mistake once before. She'd hired the agency for what was supposed to be a simple stakeout on the home of a freshman senator. The result had been that Penelope had gotten a scoop and in the course of the full-out political scandal that had ensued, Murphy had spent hours appearing before a variety of investigative committees, hours for which he had not been paid.

He gave the big woman a wink and said confidentially, "Our hot case of the moment involves John C. Breckinridge."

"Who?"

"Breckinridge. You know. The presidential hopeful."

"But we've just had an election," she said, frowning because the name *was* vaguely familiar.

"That's why he hired us," Murphy said, winking. "To find out why he didn't do better." This last was said with his voice raised to cover the distance he was putting between them. He waved to her.

Three Capitol Hill secretaries on the prowl separated them and he turned to pursue Stern and the man in tights. But they were no longer in the room.

In frustration, he edged toward the bar, where he traded in his bourbon on a scotch and soda. The band had moved on to "The Love Theme From Phantom of the Opera," which Murphy doubted was a relic of Lincoln's day. A couple at the food table caught his eye. The man, a tall, model-handsome fellow wearing a Union officer's uniform, was of little interest to him. It was the woman—tall, blonde, beautiful in her soft cocoa gown—who drew him closer.

He thought she was Laura Christen, and it was not until he was standing beside her that he realized his mistake. It was not the Congresswoman but her daughter, Catherine Braden. She was telling the officer an off-color joke, inching closer with each word until she had invaded his space so completely that he was having trouble lifting a skewered shrimp to his mouth.

She ended, triumphantly, "Then the garter snapped and the woman yelled, 'Here goes nothing!' "

The Union officer chuckled politely and Catsy Braden added in a serious tone, "It actually doesn't sound all that outrageous. And it might even be fun to try. . . ."

She looked up at the young man hopefully. He smiled and Murphy was pleased to see that blushes hadn't quite disappeared from the earth. He was about to introduce himself to Catsy Braden when a thin, timid-looking man joined the couple. He was wearing a dark, ill-fitting waistcoat and a string tie—his only acknowledgment of the party's theme.

Catsy introduced him to the Union officer as Professor Jim Prosser, a member of her mother's staff.

"Have you seen Laura?" he asked Catsy curtly.

Frowning, she turned her attention from the officer to Prosser. "Not yet, but she said she'll be here."

"I called her to see if she needed a ride," Prosser said, "but all I got was her machine."

"How long ago?"

"At least an hour."

"She *said* she'd be here." Catsy turned quickly and peered around the room. "I can't believe she'd do this to me."

"We should talk," Prosser told her. He asked the young man if he could have a minute or two alone with Catsy. Her eyes flashed with annoyance, but she managed a smile, touched the officer's arm, and told him she'd be right back.

Murphy, noting the look of relief on the young man's face, followed Catsy and the Professor from the main room, down a hall to the rear of the building.

Prosser opened a few doors to rooms filled with furniture that had been removed from the party area. Finally, he found an empty chamber that could have been a maid's room.

The Professor closed the door behind them, but not completely. Murphy edged it open a few inches with the toe of his shoe. He could hear their conversation clearly, even though the band had begun again in the main room.

"I think we took a big step over the line, Catsy," Prosser was saying.

"Relax, Jim. It's going to be fine. We just have to make sure that everybody knows the script."

"We should have told Laura about the letter when it arrived."

"It was a judgment call," Catsy said waspishly. "And it was perfectly correct. You know Mother. The first thing she would have done was to hand the whole thing over to the FBI. And you know how good they are about keeping secrets. It's much better this way. We've turned a guaranteed disaster into a probable victory.''

''It could still be a disaster. You say she told you Jeremy Dunbar had a letter.''

''But not what was in it,'' Catsy said. ''In any case, the letter's missing. Relax, Jim. Everything's fine. Go with the flow. Get drunk. Get laid. That's my game plan.''

''Where do you suppose Laura is?'' Prosser asked.

''God only knows. The Senator and Marcy will be mad as hornets if she's a no-show. But that's their problem. If she arrives late, wonderful. If not, we send an apology and a check to help the renovation.''

Murphy heard them approaching the door. He backtracked quickly and seemed to be just entering the hall from the party when they appeared.

Catsy was in the lead, evidently anxious to, as she put it so charmingly, get drunk and get laid. Murphy stared at her until their eyes met. He gave her his most beguiling Irish smile. She looked straight through him as if he didn't exist. He stepped aside to let Catsy and Jim Prosser pass and then, with a sigh, rejoined the party.

THE room was elbow to elbow with desperate fun-seekers. A drunken couple was trying to dirty-dance to ''Oh, Susannah!'' The Lincoln ice sculpture was making a puddle on the carpet. Two junior senators were squirting people's ears with water pistols. A young, pretty woman tripped on the carpet and spilled the contents of her drink onto Murphy's tux, giggled, and moved on without a word of apology. Penelope Krim stood beside a food table clutching several tiny hamburgers, masticating in tempo with the music while her beady eyes unblinkingly scanned faces. Was she looking for him?

Murphy downed his scotch and decided not to wait for Laura Christen to put in an appearance. He'd had enough of the Washington social swim to last him another thirteen years.

21

◆

Los Angeles

◆

"If I have to lay an egg for my country, I'll
do it."

BOB HOPE

THREE HOURS AFTER her arrival in Los Angeles, Margaret Stafford
was sitting at a tiny table in the Amigo Lounge of the Casa Bel Air
which had been closed for the night for a private party for John D.
Slaten, the Vice President of the United States. She was watching
every Republican in the film industry and more than a few Democrats maneuvering for a moment's recognition by the guest of
honor, a rather gray man with a nervous smile.

"Makes one wonder who the real superstars are, doesn't it," her
amused escort said. Wagner Mills was a middle-aged man who
might have been born wearing a cummerbund. With his neatly
trimmed moustache and brittle manner of speech, he resembled a
member of the British aristocracy. Actually, he was an amusingly
affected native Californian, a former restaurateur whose extremely
popular establishments had made him famous and allowed him to
retire to a life of indolence and ease, except when asked by friends
to perform little favors. He was doing one now, having arranged,
on very short notice from his Korean War buddy J. B. Murphy, an
invitation that would get him and Margaret past the Secret Service
men at the door.

Finding herself in the midst of Bob Mackie sequins, Vicky Tiel chiffons, and Valentino black satins, Margaret looked down at her short hunter-green skirt and oversized tunic sweater and mumbled, "I feel like the whole world's gone formal and I'm a pair of Day-Glo tennis shoes."

Wagner patted her hand. "There, there. It's not totally formal. The mayor's in his nice shiny blue suit and, ah yes, there's a true nonconformist." He pointed to an actor, arguably the most popular performer in films, whose oft-photographed biceps were covered by a deep purple suit, a light purple shirt, and a green bow tie.

"He looks like the Joker on steroids," Margaret said. She scanned the room. Over the years, the line between show business and politics had grown exceedingly fine. She thought that tonight they were erasing that line. "What's the deal, here?" she asked Wagner. "I mean, it's sort of a kick to see the V.P. sipping a soda, but these people aren't here just to gawk."

"Movies and television can make you very rich and beloved," Wagner said. "But politics can give you power. They believe that it might rub off on them. The magic might touch them. It touched Reagan, and he never came within two zeros of carrying a hundred-million-dollar film."

She shrugged. If movie stars wanted to be politicians or politicians wanted to be movie stars, it made no difference to her. Right now the only thing on her mind was meeting Tommy Hamilton. Her plan was to meet him socially, chat a bit, and then hit him with a few well-chosen questions about Laura Christen, based on his autobiographical novella. She had no idea what the results might be, but some information might shake loose.

She frowned at the sight of a man entering the room. She pointed him out to Wagner. "The bruiser with the gray eyes?" he asked.

He was the man from the library in Aspen, the one she suspected of having tried to run her car off the road. "I'd like to know who he is," she said.

"So would I," Wagner replied. He left their table and strolled casually to the entrance to the room. He smiled at the Secret Service man and bent down and whispered something into the ear of the woman who was seated at a table, checking invitations. The woman smiled, nodded, and made some reply.

Wagner returned to the table and informed her that the man's name was Jake Alban. "He's a newsman working with the columnist Penelope Krim. They're doing something on Hamilton Resorts and Tommy put him on the list. Do you want to meet him?"

To his surprise, she replied with a definite "No." She pointed to another section of the room, and added, "But I would like to meet *her.*"

Wagner turned to see an extremely well-preserved statuesque blonde of forty-something years, her black cocktail dress cut low to display her apparently still-youthful breasts. She and her breasts appeared prominently in the advertisements for her company. Lady Amber Hall McNeil, the titular head of Lady Amber Cosmetics.

"She's definitely her own best advertisement," Margaret said. "Who's the fud with her?"

Chuckling at her choice of words, Wagner explained that the cadaverous, balding fellow was Amber's chemist-husband, George McNeil. He added, "Murph said you wanted information on the company's financial structure."

"Specifically, the sources of the original investment capital," she replied, watching Amber Hall meet and mingle with the other guests.

"So far I've discovered that Hamilton Resorts is a majority stockholder. Seems Tommy's father ponied up a large hunk of the initial investment."

"Tell me what you know about *her,*" she said, indicating the blonde woman.

Wagner replied that Amber had been a cosmetologist at the very hotel in which they sat. She met her husband when he was behind the counter of a nearby pharmacy. It was he who'd come up with the formula for the wrinkle cream that launched the company.

Beauty and the brain, Margaret thought, then became annoyed with herself for assuming that Amber was any less intelligent than her husband. She watched the woman gesturing to a friend, smiling, poised but also a bit apprehensive.

"George is responsible for most of the beauty miracles that Lady Amber has gifted us with," Wagner noted, "including the amazing Maintain. Sales are over three million units a year."

Margaret rolled her eyes. "My God, guys don't really use that stuff, do they? An over-the-counter medicine for impotence? Oh, please!''

"It never did much for me, I admit," Wagner said. "But I don't suppose it hurt, either. In any case it definitely helped to improve Lady Amber's financial picture. How nice for Tommy to have all of HRI's properties paying off so well. And speak of the devil—''

A thick-chested man with a mane of yellow hair that made his sun-reddened face seem almost purple entered the room. The years had not been kind to Tommy Hamilton, Margaret thought, recalling the photos she'd seen of him in his college days. He pressed the flesh of a half dozen hands before making his way to the guest of honor who greeted him like, if not a brother, than at least a major contributor to the party.

Margaret got to her feet. "Introduce me," she told Wagner.

But as they approached, Hamilton began to usher the Vice President from the room. It was the end of the cocktail hour. Margaret and Wagner followed the crowd to a large private dining room on the mezzanine that had been set aside for the dinner.

They were seated at a table in a far corner of the room with a Las Vegas comedian and his wife, a judge, the wife and daughter of an independent producer who had been unable to make the dinner at the last minute, and a Secret Service man wearing an audio headset who scanned the room like a hawk guarding its nest.

Margaret saw that Tommy Hamilton and the McNeils were at a table next to the dais. She said to Wagner, "I don't suppose it was possible to seat us at Tommy Hamilton's table?''

He shook his head and whispered, "Not for a Democrat who celebrates Gay Pride Week.''

"Well, the bottom line is that I need to spend some time with both him and Amber Hall McNeil.''

"She'll be the more difficult," he said. "We can't use the old *Vogue*-comes-calling approach, because she absolutely refuses any sort of media involvement. I'll work on it.''

An employee of the hotel, dressed in gray slacks and blue blazer, moved through the tables to deliver an envelope to Tommy Hamilton. Margaret watched the hotel owner read the message and saw his face pale beneath the sunburn. He found a smile from somewhere in recent memory and turned to the others at the table, muttered a brief apology, and made his exit.

"If I'm not back for dinner," Margaret said to Wagner as she rose, "tell them just to go ahead without me."

As she left the dining room, she saw that Tommy Hamilton was standing before the elevators, waiting for a car to appear. She decided to wait with him.

Even in his rather overwrought condition, he paused to eye her appraisingly. "Enjoying yourself?" he asked.

"I always do," she replied.

The elevator doors opened and he allowed her to enter first. She pressed the button beside "Floor 8." His destination was the second floor. He inquired if she was traveling alone. Yes, she was. Then perhaps she might like to meet him later for a drink at the Amigo Lounge? How much later? she asked, not wanting to appear too eager. He looked at his watch. Ten o'clock? Ten o'clock would be fine.

Grinning, he stepped from the elevator onto the second floor.

As the doors closed, Margaret quickly pressed the third-floor button. When the elevator opened, she stepped into a brightly lit hall. She headed for the exit sign and took the concrete stairwell down a flight.

That exit door opened on a small room with a tile floor and two doors. One was unmarked. It was also locked. The other, labeled RESTROOMS, proved more accessible. A faint night-light led her past the plumbing down a narrow hall to another room filled with filing cabinets.

Beyond the files was the main office space with its empty desks. It was in darkness except for the light from an entryway to her left and another from the open door to a private office to her right.

Cautiously, she stepped into the room. There were odd noises coming from the office, as if someone were choking. Then someone said, *"What the hell?"*

She moved toward the center of the dark room until she could peer into the private office. What she saw sent a chill up her spine. On the other side of his desk, Tommy Hamilton seemed to be embracing a silver skeleton, gasping and groaning, thrusting his body against it. His face was the color of blood.

A man joined him and tried to pry him from the skeleton. Then Hamilton straightened, uttered a guttural cry, and fell forward over his desk. His apparent assailant leaned over him. It was Penelope Krim's legman, Jake Alban.

22

♦

"In this world nothing is certain but death
and taxes."

BENJAMIN FRANKLIN

JAKE ALBAN HAD stayed at the cocktail party for the Vice President
until Tommy Hamilton arrived. Then, assuming that the hotel's
offices would be empty, he climbed the firestairs to the second
floor. He tried the door that probably led to Hamilton's private
office and found it locked. When he discovered that the other door
led to filing cabinets, he smiled. They were precisely the reason for
his evening visit.

He'd brought a pocket flashlight that had long been part of his
travel equipment and used it to study the labels on the file drawers,
narrowing his search to those marked PERSONNEL. He limited his
scope even further by focusing on a drawer that purported to
contain files for personnel whose name began with "CA" to
"CZ."

He flipped quickly through the folders but could find none
marked "Christen, Laura." He began pulling files at random,
checking to see the dates involved. Maybe the very old files were
being kept elsewhere. But no, the file for "Lee N. Cady" went
back to 1968.

He thumbed through the drawer slowly. Perhaps the Christen
records had been misfiled. But it was not in that particular drawer.
He opened the one atop it and was starting to leaf through those
folders when he heard the elevator doors open.

He clicked off his penlight and moved to the entry to the office

area in time to see a tall, almost pretty-looking blond man with a
very dark tan stroll casually into the room. Humming a tune that
Jake could not identify, he walked past the empty desks toward
Tommy Hamilton's private office.

He tried the door, found it locked. He withdrew a ring of keys
from his pocket and opened the door. He closed it behind him. Jake
heard the lock click. He waited for the lights to go on in the office,
but they did not.

After five minutes had passed, Tommy Hamilton arrived and
walked quickly to his office. Moving closer, Jake saw him unlock
the door and go inside. The light went on and Hamilton uttered a
startled cry. Then he snarled angrily, "What the hell do you think
you're doing? Playing games?"

The visitor's reply was too soft for Jake to hear. He edged closer
to the door. He caught the word "Koriallis."

Tommy replied harshly, "That's stupid. Koriallis doesn't give
a shit about Laura. Never did."

Koriallis. Jake knew the name, of course. The infamous
wheeler-dealer Theo Koriallis had once been an associate of the
late Howard Hughes before launching his own considerable financial empire. But Jake had no idea what the relationship might be
between Koriallis and Laura Christen. Had she known him back
when Jake had written his article? He was beginning to realize how
very superficial that "in-depth" article had been. How little he had
known about her. How little she had let him know. By encouraging
their brief romance, she had effectively steered him away from
anything vaguely close to her personal life. Now he had a chance
to set the record straight.

"Koriallis is opposed to what we're doing," Tommy's soft-
spoken visitor replied. "Just like you."

"Maybe if we got together," Tommy snapped, "we could get
rid of you."

"It doesn't work that way, Tommy. It's us who do the ridding.
I've been instructed to inform you that unless you cooperate with
us, we might even see that you get put away. Doing naughty things
with little girls will stick you in there with the hard-timers."

There was the crash of metal against wood and Tommy Hamilton snarled, "Get the hell out of here, you scumbag. And tell the

bastard you work for I won't be threatened by him or his flunkies. Two can play the exposé game.''

The office door opened and Jake ducked into the kneehole of a desk. Peering over the modesty panel, he saw the tan blond make his exit, slipping a leather cigar case into his pocket. "Good night, Tommy," he said as coolly as if they'd parted the best of friends.

Jake heard the elevator doors open and close. For a few seconds there was silence. Then a strangled cry came from the private office.

Jake rose from under the desk. He hesitated, but a second even more desperate cry drew him to the office.

Tommy Hamilton was losing control of his body. With tiny, jerky steps, he threw himself on top of his bizarre silver chair and began pushing his pelvis against its shiny surface. "What the hell!" Jake exclaimed.

Jake rushed to him and tried to pull him away from the chair. But Tommy Hamilton refused to be pulled. His strength was incredible. Jake could see the neck tendons and the veins on his forehead puffing out as he strained. Flecks of foam were forming on his lips as he kept repeating "Got to . . . got to . . . got to . . ."

Then suddenly he straightened to his full height, clutched at his right arm, and sighed. His eyes snapped shut. His rigid body relaxed and toppled over onto the desk. Jake reached down to find a pulse in Tommy's neck, but there was nothing.

He was with a dead man. He fantasized a cordon of Los Angeles police arriving by stairs and elevator to beat him senseless before he could explain his presence. Perhaps there was something in the desk or elsewhere in the office that might aid his investigation of Laura Christen, but at the moment he just wanted to be a million miles away from Tommy Hamilton's too mortal flesh.

He backed out of the office, turned, and ran to the file room. The door at the far end was just closing. He ran faster, pushed it open. Someone was on the fire stairs. A woman, running away. He didn't pause to reflect on why she was there. He just followed her down the stairs. By the time he arrived at the lobby level, she was gone. But he thought they would be crossing paths again. He had seen those bright-red curls twice before.

23

♦

Washington

♦

"Honey, I've never taken up with a congressman in my life. I'm such a snob, I've never gone below the Senate."

BARBARA HOWAR

THE RINGING PHONE awakened Catsy Braden to the fact that it was morning and there was a strange man in her bed. Not strange, exactly. Unique might be more accurate. Insatiable would be right on the money.

She tried to reach out a slightly achy arm and discovered that her hand was tied to the bedpost with a man's belt. "Oh, God," she moaned, recalling just a little bit more of the night. She reached across her breasts with her free arm and awkwardly drew the receiver to her ear. "Yes?" she mumbled, unable to keep the sleepiness from her voice.

"It's nine-thirty and this is your wake-up call," announced the sarcastic voice in her ear.

"What?" Sitting up now, the hunk next to her stirring. . . .

"This is Dr. Penelope Krim," the voice continued. "I want an interview with your mother. Today."

"Uh . . . today. I'm not sure that's possible." Looking wildly around the room for an indication of what day it was.

"Get it in gear, honey. Rise and bloody shine already. Read my column about a very odd death on the West Coast. It cost the paper an arm and a leg to get it into the final edition. Tell the Congress-woman I had a lot of information I didn't put in the column. I'm sure she'll agree to talk with me.''

''Uh . . . Dr. Krim . . . how did you get this number?''

''Oh, please,'' Penelope Krim said, as if the question were too naive for discussion. ''I'll expect your call within the hour. *My* number's in the book.''

Catsy put the phone back on the cradle and moaned, ''Shit. Oh, shit . . .'' She began untying the belt.

The hunk beside her stirred. ''Hey—what's for breakfast?''

''I'm all out of Spam.''

''Huh?''

''Refresh my memory,'' she said, shaking blood back into her now free hand. ''What is it you do?''

He yawned. ''Anything your heart desires.''

It was one of those rare moments when she was not in the mood for sex. ''You're some kind of lobbyist?''

''I work for Ralph Nader,'' he said.

''Oh, Christ!'' It was not going to be her day.

While he bathed, singing off-key all the while, she sat on a couch, sipping coffee and trying to stay warm in a flannel robe, listening moodily to a secretary at the office reading Penelope Krim's column. It concerned Hamilton Resorts International CEO Thomas Hamilton's sudden death, apparently by heart attack. Hamilton had succumbed only minutes after leaving his table at a dinner for the Vice President of the United States that was being held in his hotel. The column noted that the discovery of his body during the Vice President's discussion of new funding for the arts had put something of a ''damper'' on the evening.

A tag line noted that Hamilton had been ''an old family friend'' of Congresswoman Laura Christen.

Catsy hung up and started to dial her mother's home. The Nader's Raider entered the room dressed and carrying his coat and tie. He said, ''Have you seen my belt?''

''On the floor near the bed!'' she snapped.

Seven. Eight. Nine rings. Her mother was not at home.

Her guest returned, adjusting his belt. ''Could I call my office, tell 'em I'll be late?''

"No," she replied, annoyed by his continuing presence.

Undaunted, he asked, "When can I see you again?"

"Never again in public."

"What?"

"Scribble your number on that pad," she said. "I'll call you."

As she looked at the pad, her eyes landed on her answering machine with its blinking red light. She rewound the tape.

Hurt and puzzled, he handed her the pad with his phone number. "I thought we had a good time," he said.

"It was fine," she said. "Better than fine. But an old friend just died and I'm busy now. So please go."

"Right," he said, miffed now. "Right," he repeated. Then, for want of some more clever course of action, he made his exit.

She barely noticed he'd gone. Her mother's taped voice was saying, "Sorry to leave you in the lurch, darling, but there's something I have to clear up. Needless to say, it's serious. I'll be gone just a day, two at the most. Help Holly juggle my schedule. I'll phone again later."

A day or two? Could her mother be in Los Angeles, where Tommy had just died? Would she have gone with the Vice President's party? Certainly not without telling her.

She stood up, drew the robe tighter around her, and marched into the damp bathroom. Using just thumb and finger, she gingerly lifted the Nader's Raider's wet towel from the floor and dropped it into the dirty clothes hamper. One thing was sure. That Krim bitch was going to live long enough to lose forty pounds before Catsy would be returning her call.

24

◆

Maryland

◆

"Knowledge of human nature is the beginning and end of political education."

HENRY ADAMS

LAURA CHRISTEN AWOKE from a dreamless sleep that morning to
find herself in a beautifully appointed bedroom with peach-colored
walls and off-white furniture and fresh logs aflame in a small
fireplace. Above the fireplace mantel two tall windows looked out
on a blue sky and snow melting from leafless trees.

The bed was round and soft and she could feel the warmth and
comfort of flannel against her skin. She burrowed deeper under the
down comforter. She turned her head and saw a single pink rose
in a stem vase on a bedside table. She wondered where one found
a rose in that part of Maryland in the winter. It had not been there
when she'd finally gone to sleep at midnight, giving up on the
possibility of Theo Koriallis' return.

The pink rose—she remembered waking in one of Eureka's
other guest rooms long ago. Theo lay beside her, wearing only a
deep green towel, his body burnished by the summer sun. He held
out a pink rose.

She took it, pricking her finger on a thorn. He reclaimed the rose
and sailed it across the room angrily. He held her injured hand
tenderly and kissed her wounded finger.

Then he was kissing her wrists, her arms. Her finger was forgotten by them both as they began to make love. Slowly at first. Then . . .

The memory became shockingly real. Laura sat up in the bed. She saw that she was alone, the discovery bringing more relief than disappointment. She slipped from the bed, quickly threw a rough woolen robe over her naked body, and walked to windows that looked out over fields that were barren except for the sections left to feed the winter birds. In the distance, outside the Koriallis compound, she could see a group of men in red caps, sitting in duck blinds with their dogs.

She moved closer to the windows, feeling the cold emanating from the glass panes. Below her, two men in checked parkas and hats strolled listlessly around the house, shotguns draped across their arms. She assumed they were not duck hunters.

She turned from the windows. It was time to call Catsy. But she could find no phone in the room. A jack, but no phone.

Annoyed, she walked quickly to the heavy oak door that led to the rest of the house. It would not open. She shook it furiously. There was the sound of a key in the lock, and the door swung open. Albert stood there in a purple flannel shirt and thick-ribbed black corduroy trousers with red suspenders. "Can I help you, ma'am?"

"Why was the door locked?"

The man was unperturbed. Apparently it was a permanent condition. "For your protection, ma'am," he replied as if it should have been obvious.

"Protection from whom?"

"Mr. Koriallis' enemies."

"I'd like to speak with Mr. Koriallis."

"I'm sorry, but he's away."

"He still hasn't returned?" she asked in frustration.

"Oh, he's in the compound," Albert told her. "He's out checking a break in the fence in the northeast corner. Perhaps you'd like breakfast while you wait for him to return."

"Yes," she said, suddenly hungry. "Breakfast would be fine."

He nodded and stepped into the room. He walked to an antique armoire and opened it, exposing a sound system and a large television screen. "We have a satellite dish that works pretty well. I find it makes the time pass quicker. I'll get your breakfast now."

He left the room, carefully shutting the door behind him. And locking it. *Damn,* she thought, *I forgot to ask about a phone.* It was so absurd, being kept in a room. After so long, Theo Koriallis was boxing her in again, making her dependent on him.

In the past she had been both afraid of and angry at his possessiveness. Now she was merely angry. She picked up the TV remote-control device and pressed the channel selector until she saw the familiar dour countenance of Robert Novak. Then she went into the pink-tile bathroom and took a long, hot shower.

She was dressing, slipping a nubby wool sweater over her head, when the grating voice of Lew Ronkowski suddenly boomed from the television. He was in front of the Capitol Building, his bow tie wiggling over his Adam's apple, chatting with CNN's Bob Franken. "I'm not sure where you get your facts," the Speaker of the House was saying, "but I can tell you they're out of date. From everything I've been told, Congresswoman Christen may have changed her mind about opposing me. You know that's a woman's prerogative. I'm sure if she was carrying out her plans she'd be here talking to you, too."

"We tried to contact the Congresswoman," Bob Franken said, "but we were informed that she was unavailable."

"My point exactly," Ronkowski cooed. He turned to the camera. "If you're watching, Laura, won't you *please* let us know what you're up to? Your people seem a little confused."

Laura lifted the remote device and clicked off the set on the Speaker's obscene monkey grin. She slumped hopelessly on the stuffed chair and cursed Ronkowski for being such a pig. She cursed Theo Koriallis for keeping her a prisoner. She cursed Ted Turner, too, for bringing her the bad news.

25

◆

Los Angeles

◆

"Accuracy in a newspaper is what virtue
is to a lady. But a newspaper can always
print a retraction."

ADLAI STEVENSON

AT 7:15 IN the morning, Margaret was lying on the carpet of her
hotel room, feet tucked under the bedboard, doing sit-ups, when
Murphy phoned her from his office in Washington. He read a few
highlights from Penelope Krim's column about Tommy Hamilton's death. He wondered somewhat sarcastically whether Margaret had made it to the dinner for the Vice President, or had they
blown the $2,000 at Spago's instead?

Flexing the muscles in her legs, she matter-of-factly told him
about leaving the dinner to follow Hamilton.

"You saw the bugger have his heart attack?" he asked, as-
tounded.

"It wasn't your usual heart attack, Murph. He seemed to be
having sexual relations with a chair that resembled a squatting
skeleton."

"Jay-sus, what is it," Murphy asked, "something they put in
the granola out there?"

She straightened an arm toward the ceiling, then dropped fore-
arm and hand behind her head, letting it swing there lifelessly. "I
think it's the smog," she said. "Anyway, the papers have got it

120

wrong. He wasn't alone when he died. There was a guy named Jake Alban with him. He works for Penelope Krim. He might have said or done something to push Hamilton over the top. Maybe you should phone the Krim woman and see if he's really on her payroll."

"Phone Penny?" Murphy gasped. "I'd rather drink near beer." He paused, then said, "I don't have to. She asked about *you* last night, so we can assume that your Alban's reporting back to her.

"In any case, darling, remember that in two days the President is gonna want to know if it's okay for him to personally endorse Laura Christen. That's our interest in all this mess." He paused, then continued, "I am reminded, however, that Stuart Wayland, the operative on this job before us, also succumbed to a heart attack. Stuart was a young man, as young as Thomas Hamilton."

"And they both were connected at least tangentially to Congresswoman Christen," she said.

"I knew we shouldn't have gotten mixed up in this," he said. "How much longer are you gonna be out there among the palm trees and sudden death?"

"As soon as Wagner can line up a meeting with Amber McNeil, I'll be catching the next flight back to D.C. It may be cold and damp, but at least the men there don't behave like priapic lunatics before they die."

"They don't?" he said with an exaggerated moan. "I was hoping I had something to look forward to."

AN hour later she was having breakfast in an outdoor café on Sunset Boulevard, trying to ignore the tacky Christmas decorations adorning the lampposts. Wagner Mills, in slacks and a peach-colored sweater, sitting opposite her, had observed her consume a waffle with butter and syrup, two sausage patties, two eggs, four pieces of toast, and two cups of coffee. "Do you always eat like this?" he wondered.

"Ever since I was a kid," she told him, "I've porked out in a big way when I travel." The memory of those youthful trips, following her father from one far-flung locale to the other, took hold of her suddenly. She shook her head to throw it off.

"Everything all right?" Wagner asked.

"Just chasing the ghosts of Christmases past."

He unfolded the paper he'd been carrying and placed it beside the plate she was currently emptying. It was a week old. He turned to the second page, where a small headline read, COUPLE CLAIMS RIGHT TO REFUSE SERVICE. Accompanying the item was a grainy photo of a man and a woman standing in front of a building. Its caption stated simply, "Club managers Gordon and Darla Lavery."

Margaret looked up at Wagner questioningly.

He explained that the Laverys were being sued by a woman who'd been denied entrance to their nightclub.

"Is this information key?" she asked.

"Rather," he said, smiling. "Gordon Lavery used to be Laura C's boss at the Casa Bel Air. Even better, when he was canned, she took his place."

Margaret grinned and looked at the photo again. The man was tall, rather gaunt, with dark circles under his eyes. He wore a small moustache. "I bet he loves our Laura to pieces."

"His answering service says he'll be at his club tonight," Wagner said.

"What kind of place is it?" she asked.

"The lady is suing the Laverys because she was told she was too fat and too ugly to be allowed inside. It's *that* kind of place—relentlessly arrogant staff, dreadful music, badly mixed drinks, currently very popular with the oat bran and cocaine crowd."

"Sounds like my idea of heaven," she said glumly.

"Also, I have an idea about how to get you and Amber McNeil together," he said, his eyes sparkling at the sight of her leaning forward with interest. "Lady Amber has a spa just outside of D.C., near Chevy Chase. Suppose we tell Amber's p.r. rep you were sent here from Washington to take a look at their operation."

"There must be more to your plan," Margaret said. "So far I can almost feel the door slamming in my face."

"What self-respecting company could afford to slam their door on a representative of the White House here to find out about their services on behalf of the First Family?"

Margaret was amused by the audacity of the plan. "They wouldn't really buy that, would they?"

"Welcome to Hollywood," he said, "where nothing is beyond belief."

26

◆

THE CASA BEL AIR's idea of mourning its CEO, Jake Alban discovered as he made his way past the lobby, was to replace the silver
Christmas wreath on the front door with a black one. There was no
sense rubbing the guests' noses in death.

Earlier, Jake had placed a call to Lady Amber Cosmetics to set
up an interview with its president, Amber Hall McNeil. He'd been
informed by Mrs. McNeil's assistant that all requests from the
press would have to be channeled through the company's public
relations firm, Intercom, Inc. That was why Jake was approaching
the desk and the same clerk with the cinnamon-colored hair who'd
welcomed him the day before.

Of course she remembered him, she said. Mr. Niles? Of course
she would give him Mr. Niles' number. And would he care to use
a phone in the office?

Unfortunately, all of the clerk's cordiality was negated by Kerry
Niles' secretary, who curtly informed him that her boss was out of
the office. Was he in the city? Yes. At least she thought so. Would
the caller care to leave his name? The caller would.

IT occurred to Jake that Niles had probably pulled funeral duty and
was busying himself somewhere with arrangements for the plant-
ing of Tommy Hamilton's body in the cold hard ground. Rather

than waste the morning waiting for the p.r. man's call, he drove to the new, contemporary Los Angeles Public Library, where he worked his way through an assortment of newspaper and magazine articles about Lady Amber Cosmetics.

In his early days as a reporter, he'd hated research. He'd been much more interested in exploring the present than in delving into days gone by. Now he rather enjoyed the time spent in the stacks and files.

His interview with Laura Christen and the material from Penelope Krim had provided very little information about the Congresswoman's ex-partner, Amber Hall McNeil. And there wasn't much available from other sources.

Just a few short notices about her marriage to George McNeil the year following the debut of Lady Amber Cosmetics. The small wedding had taken place in the courtyard of the Casa Bel Air, with its owner, Ivor Hamilton, giving the bride away. One of the brief articles mentioned in passing that Amber's earlier marriage had been to UCLA sports figure Wesley Hall, an entertainment industry lawyer with the firm of Morley, Dane and Bernstein.

When Jake left the library, the first thing he did was phone the law firm and learn from a receptionist that Hall was there no longer. The information operator located his name in the Burbank phone directory.

The voice that responded to the Burbank number was aggressively masculine. After a few perfunctory questions, he replied, "Amber? Sure, Amber and I used to be married. So?"

Jake explained that he'd like to talk to him about his ex-wife. "What sort of stuff you looking for, bud?" Wesley Hall asked. "The hearts and flowers or the down and dirty?"

Jake replied that he'd be glad to listen to whatever Hall wanted to tell him. "Come on out, then. I was just watching *Wheel of Fortune,* anyway."

HIS directions led Jake to a sloppily painted green and white Burbank neighborhood bar named Hall's Hall of Fame. Inside was a shrine to Wesley Hall's sporting life—trophies, pennants, a basketball hoop screwed to the wall, pictures of a handsome, square-

jawed young fellow shaking hands with Mayor Sam Yorty and
Governor Ronald Reagan.

A considerably aged version of the young man in the photo was
seated at the bar, dressed in polo shirt, shorts, and unlaced, sock-
less sneakers. He was sipping a beer and gaping at a flickering TV.
"You better get up on the roof again, El," he told the room's only
other occupant, a dour, bald-headed bartender. "The goddamn
pigeons are back."

"Aww, Wes. I *hate* getting up on that friggin' roof. The tar
sticks to my shoes."

"Well, I'm sure as hell not gonna—" Wesley Hall saw Jake's
reflection in the mirror. He spun around on his stool, smiling. His
once-strong jaw had developed dewlaps. He was soft all over, but
even with the Pillsbury Doughboy waist, there was still a sugges-
tion of brute strength.

"You must be Jake," he said, hopping from the stool and
extending his hand. Jake was expecting a bone-crushing shake and
tightened his grip first. The former athlete grinned at him, impressed. "Hey, you must've played ball somewhere."

Jake shook his head. "Lugging a portable typewriter around."

"Yeah? Well, I'm Wes and that's Eldon there in the apron.
Want a beer? We got Watney's on draft."

"A Watney's sounds fine."

Wesley Hall waited until Eldon had filled a glass for Jake, then
led the newsman to one of the six or seven empty tables. "What
kind of story are you doing on the lovely Amber?"

"A profile."

"Warts and all. Jesus, I hope it's warts and all."

"Sure," Jake said.

"When I met her she was just another blonde with knockers out
to here trying to get into movies," Wes began. He continued on for
some time, thinking he was getting all the bitterness out of his
system, but just filling up with more. He ended his tirade with, "So
I got all that actress bullshit out of her head, gave her a condo in
Brentwood and a great little kid. And class, don't forget the class.
She was like some *hick* when we met. I do all that for her and she
dumps me flat, for no goddamn reason."

"She must have had some reason," Jake said. "Maybe the McNeil guy?"

"That dipstick? Hell, no. She didn't meet him until we were through. Actually, it was this dumb thing. This little slut at my office. It wasn't my fault, was *not* my fault. Hell, I'm only human . . . anyway, Amber found out and just went nuts. Claimed I'd been screwing around on her our whole married life—a piece of absolute fiction—and kicked me out.

"Hey, Eldon, another Wat-ney for the boss, huh?"

"When was the last time you saw her?" Jake asked.

"You mean except for the goddamn billboards and ads? It's like a bad dream: your ex-wife's picture all over the country in her underwear." His rueful smile was like a nervous habit. "I haven't seen her in the flesh in years. Not since our kid went off to college. Haven't seen either of 'em. So who cares?"

"How well did you know Laura Christen?"

Wes' face darkened. "I met her a few times," he said. "One of those do-gooders, always getting into other people's business. I met her maybe twice when she and Amber were roommates with the dope dealer. For some reason—maybe she was hot for me herself—Miss Laura Christen kept putting it into Amber's head that she was better off without me."

"Did I understand you to say that Amber and Laura Christen were rooming with a dope dealer?"

Wes grinned. "Sure. Sweet, pure little Amber moves out on me, takes *my* kid with her, and moves in with some drug peddler who eventually gets sent up the river. Really great for the kid, right? It wouldn't surprise me to find that Amber and Laura were getting a piece of the action, too, though the cops evidently thought otherwise."

Jake couldn't quite see Laura Christen carting drugs around in her handbag, but there was so much about her that was a mystery. He said, "I don't suppose you remember the roommate's name."

"Darla Sullivan," Wes said brightly. "Good-looking head. She married the guy who she was in business with, Gordon Lavery. That's her name now, Darla Lavery. They didn't spend much time in prison. The slick ones never do. I should know. I used to practice the law."

"It sounds like you've been keeping track of 'em," Jake said.

"Naw. I was just reading about 'em last week in the *L.A. Times,*" Wesley Hall said. "Hey, Eldon, you still got last week's papers stacked up somewhere?"

27

♦

Maryland

♦

"I'm the most liberated woman in the
world. Any woman can be liberated if she
wants to be. First she has to convince her
husband."

MARTHA MITCHELL

THE LAST LINK to Laura Christen's late husband, to her youth, was
gone.

The news of Tommy Hamilton's death had been like a slap to
her face, driving all other thoughts, including the upcoming battle
with Ronkowski, from her mind. She'd concentrated on the television monitor, waiting to find out more. But there wasn't much
more to be said. Heir to hotel chain succumbs. Vice President
among those mourning the death of the popular businessman, a
friend to the powerful and famous.

A well-groomed news reader began toting up Tommy's awards
for service to state and country. His coldly impersonal reportage
threatened to rob Tommy's passing of any impact. The medium
seemed to be conquering death by reducing it to sixty-second bites.

She turned off the set and tried mourning Tommy without its
distraction. She thought of the days at State, the three of them—she
and Bobby and Tommy—inseparable. She thought of the weeks
after her husband's death, when it was difficult to know who was
taking it harder, she or Tommy.

He arrived at her apartment one Sunday afternoon, on the tail end of a marathon drunk, sick, unkempt, bottomed out. She helped him into the kitchen, where she fed him scrambled eggs and coffee, the first food he'd eaten in three days.

That night they sat in her tiny living room, watching the baby Catsy sleep fitfully while Laura tried to convince him to let the past go and think about the future. In doing so, she managed to convince herself.

She told Tommy that she was going to take Catsy to a large city—Chicago, New York, Los Angeles, she didn't much care, as long as it was a place where she could get work. A BA with a political science major might not be of much practical use, but she'd find something.

He picked up the phone, made a long distance call to his father. Two days later she received a large envelope containing personnel forms, an airline ticket to Los Angeles, and a letter from Ivor Hamilton offering her the job of assistant to the public relations manager of Hamilton Resorts International at a then-respectable $350 a week.

Tommy had driven them to the airport. He'd toyed with the idea of moving to L.A. himself—his father was anxious for him to start working for the company. But Laura, who understood his feelings for her and who could not offer him anything but friendship in return, had not encouraged him. Eventually he decided a year or two in Paris might be a better idea. He would work on the novel he'd always talked about.

She lost track of him during the next year. It was a hectic one for her. A new job in a new city. Her boss, an odd, moody fellow named Gordon Lavery, had arranged for her to share a comfortable home with his girlfriend, Darla Sullivan, and a woman in the hotel's beauty salon, Amber Hall, a divorcée with a son Catsy's age.

It seemed like the perfect situation. The house on Doheny was a large two-story with three bedrooms. Laura and Amber quickly became friends and shared the expense of a nurse for their children. Darla, who remained rather aloof from them and who had no interest whatsoever in their babies, was rarely at home.

At the office, the job was exciting, working with the press and tourist agencies, planning seasonal campaigns, arranging lunches and dinners and celebrations. Lavery was the one drawback. He would be charming and thoughtful one day, unreasonable and demanding the next.

Her personal life was nonexistent. She went to hotel affairs and on rare occasion to parties with Amber and Darla. But there was too much to learn about raising a child and operating in the business world for her to have any time for serious romance.

At the beginning of her second summer in Los Angeles, a bearded Tommy appeared suddenly at her desk with a bouquet of yellow daisies that he swore he'd picked from in front of the Beverly Hills City Hall. Over lunch he told her about his vaguely debauched life in Paris, and she told him about her rather chaste one in Hollywood. She felt much more comfortable with him than she ever had before. His emotional dependence on her seemed to have evaporated.

That night she forced him to sit through a lecture by an anthropologist named Margot Needham, a frequent guest at the hotel whom she had befriended. Later, they had coffee with Margot, an avowed feminist who foresaw a bright future for Laura in whatever endeavor she chose to pursue. Tommy had remained uncharacteristically quiet in the woman's presence, and on their way back to Laura's home his silence persisted.

At her door, he told her that he agreed with Margot Needham. Laura could do anything she put her mind to. He, on the other hand, had very limited aspirations. He was flying back to Paris the next day. It was the only place he could be happy.

She'd asked him why and he'd replied that what was looked upon as scandalous and even criminal in the United States was considered only mildly unconventional in Paris. He would not be more specific.

She was not to see him again until his father died nine years later. They had written, of course. His letters, she understood with her increasing awareness of sexual politics, were blatantly chauvinistic, with him referring to his partners as "girls," never "women." But they were also amusing and chatty. Hers were filled with news of the hotel and the city, but were, as he often complained, very impersonal.

She had written nothing of the dreadful scandal that had resulted in the arrest of Gordon Lavery and Darla Sullivan for dealing in drugs, though the news did reach him by some other means. Probably through Ivor, who had managed to keep Hamilton Resorts out of the mess, a remarkable feat considering that Lavery was using the facilities of the hotel to make his deliveries.

A few years later, when she and Amber celebrated the start of their cosmetics company, Tommy had wired them a case of French champagne with a note that they should toast Gordon Lavery for having made Lady Amber possible by introducing them. It would have been more amusing had not Lavery sent them several threatening letters from prison suggesting a similar debt with the demand for a considerably more substantial acknowledgment. Shortly after she showed Theo the letters, they stopped coming.

By the time Tommy returned to take the place of his late father, he had changed. His drinking had begun to show in his face, which, though still handsome, had a florid puffiness to it. In college he had been partial to denim pants and shirts with alligator logos. His expatriate years had turned him into something of a dandy, with an Italian-French wardrobe that matched his flamboyant lifestyle.

He rapidly became a part of the social whirl of Southern California, escorting actresses and socialites alike, without entering into relationships with any of them. Laura was well into her political career, spending more time in Washington than in Los Angeles, but they would have dinner several times during the year, and there was a three-month period in the early eighties, when her Malibu home was being renovated, that she and Catsy had occupied a wing of his Palisades estate.

Though they were never again as close as they had been when Bobby was alive, they had still remained friends. She had never told him why she had sold her Lady Amber stock back to HRI or given a reason for the coldness that had developed between her and his father. To do so would have been to admit her knowledge that he was not really the CEO of Hamilton Resorts, but a front man for—

A heavy knock at the door broke her train of thought.

"Yes? Come in."

The lock clicked and Albert entered. "Mr. Koriallis has returned, but he's in conference," he announced. "He has asked me to prepare a dinner that will be served on the plane."

"What plane?"

"Mr. Koriallis assumed you would be flying to Los Angeles for the funeral of Mr. Hamilton. Is his a correct assumption?"

Laura admitted that it was.

"He will be accompanying you. Mr. Hamilton was an associate."

"I know," she said with some bitterness.

This time, when Albert left, he did not lock the door. He didn't even close it. Somehow Laura did not feel liberated.

28

◆

Washington

◆

"Speech was made to open man to man,
and not to hide him."

DAVID LLOYD

J. B. MURPHY was removing his topcoat as he pushed through the
agency's glass doors. His secretary, Nina, looked up from her desk
and said, "Your protégé, Mr. Patrick Arthur, has been buzzing
around, wondering why you were still on your lunch hour at four
P.M. I was wondering that myself."

"I've been buying Christmas presents for the good little girls
and boys at the Murphy-Stafford Agency who mind their own
business," he said. Actually, he'd spent the afternoon in Georgetown, in the guise of a representative of D.C. Power and Light,
chatting with Laura Christen's housemaid and neighbors. Those
conversations, coupled with her failure to appear at the party the
night before, convinced him that the Congresswoman had flown
the coop for reasons unknown. The news depressed him enough to
take his mind off Christmas, a season he loved.

He barreled into his office, threw his topcoat onto the hook on
the back of his door, and went to his desk, flopping onto his leather
chair. He was reaching for the intercom to summon Pat Arthur to
his lair when the phone rang.

"Mr. Stern on one," Nina informed him.

Charles Stern said, without preamble, "That matter we discussed at that lousy party last night has become more pressing. You remember Larry Newfield, of course.''

Murphy's depression took an even deeper nosedive. He now understood why the man at the party in the John Wilkes Booth outfit had seemed familiar. Newfield had been part of Murphy's team in the late sixties; they had lived and worked together for nearly three years. Murphy should have recognized that familiar tilt of the head and other body language immediately, even under a black wig. ''How could I forget good old Larry?'' he said to Stern. ''Don't tell me he's your problem?''

''I don't know. That's where you come in.''

Murphy hesitated, then asked, ''What's the situation?''

''I've opened the lid on a loose-cannon operation that makes Ollie North's wheeling-and-dealing look like a DAR tea party. Dirty tricks. Drugs. Blackmail. Brain-twisting. The works.''

''And where does Larry fit in?''

''He's part of it,'' Charles Stern said. ''He's the counterman.'' Translated, it meant that Newfield was acting as front man for the organization. ''But he says he's unhappy and he's willing to provide us with the operational blueprints—names, places, who did what to whom. The full directory.''

''What's he asking in return?'' Murphy asked.

''Immunity. Some cash. How far can I trust him?''

''You're asking the wrong guy,'' Murphy said. ''Years ago I booted him out of my unit after a prisoner he was 'interrogating' died, with his chest caved in. Larry's excuse was that the prisoner was choking and he went a little overboard on the Heimlich. We weren't even supposed to be in the area, so there was no way I could bring charges against him. But I sure as hell didn't want him around. He's smart. Got a mind full of razor blades. But he's the meanest, coldest son of a bitch I ever dealt with. Maybe he's changed, but I'm happy he's your problem and not mine.''

''He's *our* problem,'' Stern shot back. ''There seems to be a link between Laura Christen and Newfield and his gang.''

Murphy scowled and asked Stern to explain. But Stern wouldn't. ''Not on the phone. Never know who's on the party line,'' he said. ''My wife talked me into attending a chamber music thing at the Corcoran at eight. You and I could get together before it starts. Just outside the Hudson River School exhibit. Around seven-thirty." He didn't wait for Murphy's reply.

The detective stared at his telephone receiver for a beat, then replaced it on its cradle. He wandered out to Nina's desk and asked her for the "doodad that chases the bugs away."

She rooted into a desk drawer and removed a small object that resembled a paging beeper. The logo on it said that its name was The Pocket Sentry. He carried it back into his office, studying it warily. He disliked gadgetry. For years he'd had a framed *New Yorker* cartoon on his desk in which a detective explains to a prospective client, "I'm an old-fashioned private eye, Miss Jones. If this little mystery of yours has anything to do with computers, forget it."

Still, Murphy realized he could not afford to bury his head in the sand of antitechnology. He telescoped The Pocket Sentry's antenna and began pacing his office, using the device like a divining rod and feeling like a paranoid jackass.

Then The Sentry began to vibrate near his visitor's chair. He ran his hand under the seat and removed a little metal object. He placed it on his desk top and returned to the hunt in earnest.

An hour later there were three identical metal objects on the desk and a slightly different fourth object that he had removed from the speaker of his telephone. He went to the doorway and told Nina, "Have that woman who sold us The Sentry come in as soon as she can. Get her to check all the phones and all the offices. Even the latrines."

Nina took The Sentry and put it away. "Are we working for the government again? Seems every time we do, we have to sweep the office."

"Doesn't it just," Murphy said grimly.

He went to a neighboring office belonging to a periodontist to phone Charles Stern with the news that their earlier conversation had been compromised. But he was told that Mr. Stern had already left for the day.

When he returned to the agency, the newest employee, Pat Arthur, was standing at Nina's desk, waiting for him. His JFK hair was hanging over a forehead wrinkled with youthful concern. Murphy waved him into the office.

"What can I do for you, Pat?"

"Digby says he doesn't need me anymore. I'm tired of sitting in my cubicle studying crime stats."

Murphy picked up one of the little metal objects from his desk. He handed it to Pat. "Know what this is?"

"Something for a computer?"

"It's a bug. It transmits stuff over a signal. The signal is picked up by a receiver that's not more than fifteen hundred feet away, usually connected to a small, noise-activated tape recorder. The recorder is probably picking up every word we're saying right this moment."

Pat studied the bug as if he were amazed by it.

"I want you to try to find the receiver."

"But, how . . . ?"

Murphy sat down behind his desk. "You go up, down, or all around, son. The choice is yours."

"I'll try the office above ours first," Pat said.

"No. Start with the agency. Chances are it's right here somewhere."

"But that would mean somebody who worked here—" Pat looked flustered.

"Hey, Patrick, I pay a living wage," Murphy grumbled, "but I sure don't match bribery rates. Get Nina to give you the handy-dandy whatever, The Pocket Sentry, and show you how it works. Maybe you can pick up some more of these fellas." Murphy scooped up the remaining bugs and deposited them in his desk drawer.

He watched Pat Arthur leave his office, then leaned back in his chair and closed his eyes. Bugs in the office. Laura Christen missing. Larry Newfield muddying up the water. And Meg out in Los Angeles. He began to whistle a tune that only another Irishman might recognize as "Dougherty's Party."

By 7:45, Charles Stern was a no-show at the Corcoran Gallery of Art, and Murphy, who had arrived early, had run out of patience with the Hudson River School. He strolled through the large, complex building until he found the auditorium where the chamber music ensemble was setting up.

Stern was not among the music-lovers filing into the room. However, his Southern-born wife, Suzanna, was. The handsome middle-aged woman was headed toward her seat with a shorter, plumper lady. Murphy intercepted them.

"Well, of all people to run into at a recital," she said, offering her cheek to be kissed. "I didn't know the violin was your instrument, Murph. Forgive me. Liz Weller, J. B. Murphy—an old friend."

Murphy barely nodded to the plump woman. "Isn't Charlie coming, Suzanna?" he asked.

"Oh, you know Charlie," she said. "He got one of his last-minute calls and that was that for the recital. Fortunately, Liz was game for it. Please sit with us."

"Actually, Suze, I was kinda looking for Charlie."

"Oh?" She gave him a long, serious look.

"No problem," Murphy said, finding a grin that he'd hidden away for just such an occasion. "Just the usual nonsense. Enjoy the show, Suzanna. Nice meeting you, Liz."

At the exit, he turned. Suzanna Stern was staring at him, frowning. She'd lived with Charlie long enough to read the signs. Murphy cursed himself for having spooked her. But he was a little spooked himself.

29

♦

Airborne

♦

" 'Tis said that some have died for love."
WILLIAM WORDSWORTH

IT WAS TO be a two-plane trip, Albert explained as he and Laura traveled by Range Rover to a small landing strip on which rested a small high-wing single-engine craft that resembled a Cessna Turbo Stationair, but had been modified with nearly half a million dollars' worth of electronics gear.

A sallow-complexioned man, wearing a dark suit under his parka, helped Albert transfer an assortment of full pots and bags of groceries from the Rover to the aircraft. Wondering if Theo Koriallis was going to arrive in time for takeoff, Laura climbed aboard and discovered a cabin that was compact and cozy, with seats for six.

The sallow man, whose name was Georgio, and Albert eventually took their seats away from hers. As the plane's props began to spin, she shouted to Albert, "I thought Mr. Koriallis was joining us."

"He is," Albert said with a rare smile. "He's our pilot."

WITHIN minutes they touched down at Baltimore-Washington International, not far from a sleek gray private jet with the Eureka logo emblazoned in red on its side. While Koriallis guided the smaller plane into a hangar, Laura accompanied Albert and

139

Georgio as they carried the various covered pots across the icy field and into the jet.

The interior of the Eureka craft was all rounded surfaces, soft leathers, and deep pile carpets. The seats reminded her of comfortable office chairs, placed far enough apart to allow for a 360-degree turn. A color TV monitor had been built into the rear bulkhead. Beside it was a thermostat set for 72 degrees.

As Albert and Georgio headed aft to the galley, Laura called out, "Is Mr. Koriallis flying this one, too?"

"No," a voice answered behind her. "Mr. Koriallis is not fool enough to spend five hours looking at an instrument panel when he could be looking at you."

She turned to face a man who had aged greatly since she'd last seen him. Five years ago, he could have been in his late forties. Now he looked every day of his sixty-three years. His hair was completely white. His dark face was lined and very tired. She said, "If you're trying to make up for keeping me locked in a room for twenty-four hours, without a telephone, it's going to take more than a broad compliment."

He was dressed in a dark suit of soft material, probably cashmere. He was smiling and the smile looked genuine. He opened his arms but she stayed seated. "My beautiful Laura," he said, stepping closer, taking her hand. She let him kiss it.

"It's a little late for charm," she said. "What happened to our meeting last night?"

He took a seat opposite her and said, "Shortly after your phone call, it became necessary for me to drive to Washington. Our cars may have passed on the road. Then I was forced to stay longer than I had anticipated. I'm sorry. You have my full attention now."

She was about to speak when the pilot's voice echoed through the cabin, notifying them that takeoff was imminent and requesting that everyone remain seated with belts attached. Then the craft began to vibrate and hum.

The jet moved out onto the runway. Through the side windows Laura could see the brightly lighted airport.

Then they were speeding forward and gliding into the night sky. Laura waited for the familiar feeling of apprehension to subside and said, "Basically, I had one question to ask you and I wanted to see you when you answered. Are you responsible for the death of a newspaper columnist named Jeremy Dunbar?''

He raised one eyebrow. ''Why would I do such a thing? I don't even know the man you speak of.''

''He was threatening to print an item about an illegitimate child that I have never claimed.''

His glance was unwavering. ''How do you know this?'' he asked.

''He told me. He showed me his 'source,' a poison pen letter.''

''And so you assumed that I would dirty my hands on this slime?'' She knew how rarely he allowed his emotions to show. The anger that distorted his face made her think she had misjudged him. He was, of course, a master at deceit. ''I'm surprised you don't accuse me of having Tommy killed, also.''

''It had not occurred to me. Did you?''

''Why in God's name would I?''

She shook her head. ''I don't know. I only know that whenever something unpleasant and inexplicable takes place in my life, you're usually at the bottom of it.''

''You wrong me this time, Laura, I swear to you.'' He unsnapped his seat belt. ''Tommy suffered a heart attack.''

''They say the same thing about Jeremy Dunbar. All I know is that two people who knew about our . . . our baby . . . are dead.''

He scowled. ''I have had nothing to do with any murders.''

''There was a time when I was so naive I believed everything you told me. About us. About my career. All lies.''

''I was afraid of losing you.'' The dark eyes looked moist. Past his shoulder, the moon seemed to be peeking in one of the round windows.

''I believed you when you said that you understood why I didn't want you as a partner in Lady Amber. But that understanding didn't stop you from secretly becoming our partner.''

''So you sold your stock,'' he said. ''A good thing, as it turns out.''

''Why is that?''

He seemed uncomfortable. ''The company is . . . troubled.''

''And Amber and George?''

He shrugged. "I know nothing more than rumors and I don't wish to repeat rumors."

"Don't play with me, Theo. You know everything about—"

"No longer," he interrupted her. "I am no longer in a position to know everything."

"But you own—"

"I own nothing," he said. "In the game of the deal, someone wins and someone loses. And I have lost. The new powers have rendered me helpless. But I am still on the board of Hamilton Resorts, a 'gray eminence' is the phrase, I believe. I talk, but they do not have to listen and rarely do. If I were not on the board, I would not be in the sky right now, going to the funeral of a man for whom I had little respect. Forgive me, I know Tommy was a close friend of yours, but he was a fool and a wastrel—and worse. If he had been making the decisions for his company, it would now be in bankruptcy." He smiled suddenly. "Then again, if it were, I would no longer need the services of bodyguards like Albert and Georgio."

"Is that what they are?"

"Among other things. But it is their main function. I am at some risk. And, my dear Laura"—he leaned forward, placing his hand on her arm—"so are you, I fear."

"Me?"

"It is why I left Albert at the house, to look after you. It is also the reason I drove to Washington, to try to change their minds. But their minds do not change."

"Who are *they?*"

"It would do you no good to know."

"This is maddening," she said heatedly. "You hint at some terrible secret but you won't say more. Is this your idea of helping me?"

He hesitated, then said, "The only thing I can do is warn you to retire from public life, find a quiet place to stay for a while."

"It's absurd to think I would ever do that. Certainly not now."

"There is no way they will let you become a public figure."

"Why? What harm can that be to them, whoever 'they' are? Did 'they' kill Jeremy Dunbar?"

"I have no knowledge of that. I am merely a retired financier, recently widowed, trying to enjoy the sunset of my life on Chesapeake Bay. I—'' He paused as Georgio entered the cabin carrying a round tabletop on a metal rod. Using his toe, he edged back a flap in the rug between her and Theo and exposed a round hole into which the rod fitted snugly. Theo waited for Georgio to test the table's sturdiness and exit before repeating, "If you hope to save your life, you will have to retire, at least for a while."

The idea angered her. "If you think I'd take your advice without more information, then you don't know how much I've changed."

He held up his hand. "Enough," he said quietly. "We need not be cruel to one another. I've told you what I think you should know. What you do with the information is your own affair."

Georgio returned with a tablecloth and silverware which he placed in front of Laura and Theo. Within minutes they were dining on fresh clams, sweet and still frosty from the bay, followed by stewed duck with turnips, which was Albert's specialty.

Their conversation during dinner was mainly about the food. When the plates had been cleared away, Theo insisted they watch a videotaped movie to pass the time. Laura was not surprised that it was a bootlegged copy of a film currently in the theaters. Two-thirds of the way through it, she turned to find Theo sleeping peacefully in his chair.

She turned off the movie and tried sleeping herself. As tired as she was, sleep did not come easy. When it did, her troubled dreams were filled with faces—Tommy with tears in his eyes, Catsy, Theo, even Lew Ronkowski. All of them kept giving her the same advice: "Retire."

30

◆

Los Angeles

◆

"Nostalgia's not what it used to be."
ANONYMOUS

MARGARET SAT WITH Wagner Mills in his classic beige Jaguar XKE, staring across the wide street at a large barn of a building that had once housed a savings and loan but no longer even remotely resembled a place of higher finance. Its exterior was painted a stark white. Blue checked curtains hung in windows once protected by burglar bars back when no one realized that the real burglars were sitting on the S&L's executive board. A mock Astroturf front yard was surrounded by a three-foot white picket fence. The subdued white neon sign over the door spelled out BEAVERVILLE.

L.A. is not a late-night city, but 8:15 was still a bit too early to witness Beaverville in full bloom. A scattering of young, post-punk fun-seekers was starting to line up beside the picket fence. They were dressed like school kids from the fifties—the men in baggy khaki pants, striped T-shirts, baseball caps, the women in fuzzy sweaters, short dresses, floppy white socks, saddle Oxfords.

A gawky young man with a bored expression stood beside the door, garbed in a bright red windbreaker and khaki pants. His hair dusted his forehead in an imitation of the late, never-to-be-forgotten, James Dean. He was guardian of Beaverville's gates.

"It's sort of amusing," Wagner said.

"You don't think it's just the tiniest bit sexist?"

144

He frowned. "What's sexist about Bea— Oh, I see. No, you miss the point. The reference is to Beaver Cleaver."

"Who?" She seemed genuinely confused.

"The Beav'. *Leave It to Beaver.*"

"Oh," she said. "A television show."

"Family life in the fifties. That's what they're mocking over there. Not the female anatomy."

"I wasn't even alive in the fifties. And I spent most of my childhood out of the country. Will we have a problem getting in without costumes?"

"It depends on whether you conform to that thug in the windbreaker's idea of attractiveness," Wagner said. "I, myself, wouldn't be caught dead inside. I'll wait here for you."

She stepped from the Jaguar, clutching a leather drawstring purse. She said, "It would save time if you could pick up the Lady Amber corporate ownership papers from your lawyer buddy. I'll catch a cab back to the hotel."

"You don't catch cabs in L.A., Margaret. You must phone for cabs."

"Then I'll phone for one," she persisted.

Wagner did not look happy.

"You and Murph are giving me an inferiority complex," she said.

He tried a tiny smile of encouragement, then turned on the ignition. "There's a little bistro on Melrose called Ragout," he said. "Your cabdriver will know it. I'll meet you there in an hour."

She watched him drive away. The damnable thing was that he and Murph were right. She was not exactly a seasoned hand and there was obviously something sinister at work. But she had confidence in herself. Most of the time.

She brushed past the people on line, staring unblinkingly at the James Dean clone who pushed himself from the side of the building and blocked the entrance. He appraised her legs, her short skirt, her tight-fitting sweater, then graced her with a smile that was half sneer and winked. "Lookin' good, Red. Have yourself a ball, baby." He opened the door for her. She entered, feeling the angry eyes of the people on line boring into the back of her neck.

The interior of Beaverville was mainly flat black paint and key

lights and an assortment of vaguely Warholian lithographs of the
Cleavers and their friends and neighbors. They were just faces to
Margaret. Right past the entrance was a series of illuminated
counters at which patrons might purchase candies or cookies or
children's items like rubber baseball bats and water pistols.

Next was a long, milk-white bar behind which a juvenile delin-
quent type wielded bottles of vodka and rum while preparing
drinks with such nonalcoholic names as Beaverville Milkshake or
Beaverville Iced Tea. Margaret asked him where she might find
Gordon Lavery. "In the back, if he's here," the j.d. said. "The
office is to the left of the apple pie."

The apple pie. Sure. Margaret passed the area called the Family
Room, where a scattering of customers sat at tables drinking and
talking while two big television screens, perched against a back
wall past an empty stage area, displayed clips from the now leg-
endary black and white sitcom. Speakers pounded out some hard-
rock ditty that seemed totally out of synch with the videos.

A pin light at the far corner of the room illuminated a sculpture
of a four-foot apple pie on a tin plate. A triangle was cut out of the
pie, and in among the plaster apple pieces were portions of baby
dolls, an arm here, a leg there.

Margaret turned left at the pie and found herself in a dark
hallway leading to a door labeled PRIVATE. DO NOT ENTER.

She disobeyed the sign and entered an office that was ultramod-
ern on the cheap. Naugahyde sofa and chairs. Assorted knock-
downs of Italian originals, including an imitation Olivetti desk.
Seated at it was a woman in her early fifties with frizzy black hair,
scribbling in an order book. She was wearing a beaded black dress,
cut too low for her sagging breasts. She paused, looked at Margaret, and said, "You must be illiterate or you'd have read the sign
on the door."

"I'd like to speak with Gordon Lavery."

"Oh?" The woman tore a section from her order book—a white
page and a yellow page separated by a sheet of carbon. She threw
the carbon away and placed the pages on stacks of other similarly
colored stacked sheets. "And why were you looking for him?"

"Is he in the club?"

The woman stood up and circled the desk. "I asked why you

wanted to see him," she said. "For your information, I'm *Mrs.* Gordon Lavery."

"I'm here about Laura Christen," Margaret said. She'd decided to follow that up with a moderately serviceable lie about an article she was writing on Christen. But Mrs. Lavery's reaction made that unnecessary.

"So the bitch has come to her senses, eh?"

Margaret tried to maintain a steady voice while she bluffed, "Didn't you think she would?"

"Gordon did," she said. "But back when we were roomies, Laura rarely did what you thought she would." She indicated an empty chair and went back to hers. Margaret found her face interesting. It was no longer pretty, if it ever had been, but there was a vibrancy in the dark eyes, the pointed chin and nose. Mrs. Lavery looked like a particularly alert fox.

"Drink?" she asked.

Margaret shook her head. She said, "You and Laura were roommates?"

"Oh, yes." Mrs. Lavery picked up a spoon and stirred a cup of coffee that rested on the desk top. Then she licked the spoon and placed it on the desk very carefully. "We shared an old three-bedroom house on Doheny. Me, Laura, and that cow Amber Hall. Three little maids were we. So you work for Laura?"

"Yes, I do."

"In Washington?"

Margaret nodded.

"And she sent you all the way here? She could have just Fed-Exed the money."

What money? Margaret wondered. Then she knew the answer: blackmail money. "She's not convinced she should pay it. That's why she sent me."

The woman scowled. "Not convinced? How much convincing does she need? We gave her a sample of what we can do. Next time we'll do more than write a letter. She should realize we're only asking for what's rightfully ours."

"Yours?" Margaret's mind was revving, but her face remained impassive, mildly curious.

"I should have been a partner in Lady Amber. I was their

goddamn roommate. I even introduced her to Daddy Bigbucks, without whom nothing would have happened. Just because I was *away* when the deal went down—''

''Away?''

The woman's eyes narrowed. ''Didn't she tell you anything?''

''Only that I was to come out here and pay you and Gordon Lavery what you'd asked,'' Margaret said, ''assuming you can convince me that you won't be asking for any more.''

''Fifty thousand will do us fine,'' Mrs. Lavery said, smiling suddenly. Margaret stared at her as the smile froze on her face and her eyes dulled. ''I was away at T.I.,'' she said. ''That's this little facility they've got down at San Pedro. Terminal Island. Gordon and I did ten long years. Just for spreading a little happiness among the idle rich. We never sold to kids or people who couldn't afford the stuff. Victimless crime. Those bitches Laura and Amber saved their asses by cooperating with the d.a.'s office, but they helped us deliver the merchandise. I've got proof of that.''

''Was that what you meant by 'the source of her money'?'' Margaret asked, quoting the letter that had been received by Minority Leader Mike Roberts.

Lavery's wife looked confused. ''Source of her money? The source of her money was the goddamned cosmetics company!''

''But your letter—''

''Our letter didn't get into the drug thing,'' Mrs. Lavery said quickly. ''Where'd you get that idea? The note we sent the columnist was about the kid. I don't remember the exact words, but it didn't have anything about money or drugs. Gordon thought we should start with the kid, because that was more personal and showed we were playing hardball without running the risk of getting her booted out of office.''

Letter about a kid? Margaret suddenly realized that the Laverys had not sent the letter to Mike Roberts. Their letter was one she knew nothing about. Fortunately the talkaholic Mrs. Lavery didn't seem to notice her confusion. ''The minute the cops came down on us,'' she rattled on, ''sweet, honorable little Laura took Gordon's job. Before the desk chair was cold. We served the time and she and Amber dragged in the dollars. That's why Laura owes us money.''

"Why'd you wait so long to try to collect it?"

"You may find it hard to believe, but we haven't spent our whole lives brooding about her. We've been busy. But we saw her on a news show. And we remembered a debt was owed."

"What about Amber's debt?"

Mrs. Lavery blinked and licked her lips. "Amber . . . isn't as vulnerable as Laura is. And it wasn't Amber who had the little bastard."

Little bastard? Margaret calmly asked, "How'd you find out about the child?"

"Find out? It was me who—" Mrs. Lavery stopped talking even before Margaret heard the door slam behind them. A tall man strolled in. His gray hair was combed back neatly with just the hint of a pompadour. He looked a bit less decadent than his picture. In fact, he reminded Margaret of the film actor Alan Alda, with a slightly vulpine profile that belied the innocence of his pale eyes. He was wearing a black silk coat, an open-neck green shirt patterned with blue teardrops, and cream-colored, pleated pants that broke neatly over his alligator shoes. "I've been trying to find out the deal with Tom—" he began, then spotted Margaret.

He ran his eyes over her body and began to smile. "Well, well, who is this, now?"

"Laura sent her," his wife said. "She's got the money."

Lavery stared at her.

"Not on me," Margaret said. "You don't expect me to walk in here lugging $50,000 in cash?"

"Frankly, I didn't expect you to walk in here at all," he said. "Go back to Laura and tell her it was all a misunderstanding. We don't want her money. We don't want anything of hers. And we have no intention of causing any trouble for her whatsoever."

"Jesus, Gordy," his wife complained, "hitting Laura up for the money was *your* idea."

He grinned a sheepish smile. "It was a gag," he said to Margaret. "Nothing for her or Mr. Koriallis to get upset about. Tell her that. Just a little joke."

Koriallis? The name was a familiar one to Margaret. Theo Koriallis. Some sort of shadowy business type.

"Nighty-night, sweetie—time to go," Lavery said.

Margaret hesitated. She could change her story. She'd tell them she was a reporter doing a hatchet job on—

"Out, now!" Lavery ordered. "And tell your people that we have nothing more to do with Laura. We don't recall ever having met her."

The shrill chirp of the office phone made Margaret jump. Lavery glared at her while his hand went to the phone. He nodded to his wife, who walked to Margaret, took her by the arm, and pushed her toward the door.

BEAVERVILLE was beginning to fill up with night people, most of them in costume. Near Margaret, at the bar, with her back turned, sat a strange-looking woman in a polka-dot topcoat, though it was hot in the club. She also sported purple-framed cat's-eye glasses and an enormous beehive hairdo—the first Margaret had seen except in photos. Margaret blinked. *Now that's what I'd call Big Hair.*

The woman was looking intently into the mirror behind the bar. Margaret looked at the mirror too, and discovered that the beehive was staring at *her*. The woman turned and began talking with a muscular young fellow on the next stool who was wearing a UCLA varsity sweater and white slacks.

It was only after Margaret had pushed her way through the crowd and out onto the now-teeming sidewalk that she realized she'd forgotten to phone for a cab.

A block away, Hollywood Boulevard pulsed with traffic. She walked toward the noise and the cars, assuming that there would have to be some cabbies who believed in cruising for fares.

But after five minutes of watching the dizzying parade of speeding cars, she began to lose faith. She was about to look for a phone when a hand pushed the center of her back, propelling her off the sidewalk directly into the path of the oncoming traffic.

Disoriented, caught in the glare of headlights, the noise of boomboxes, car horns, and screeching tires filling her ears, Margaret struggled to return to the safety of the sidewalk. An electric-blue Ford lowrider swerved at the last second and grazed her hip with its gleaming bumper. She fell to the street and looked on in helpless horror as a black sedan bore down on her. She tried to roll away.

Then she felt hands under her shoulders, yanking her out of the car's path, onto the sidewalk. She sat up, breathing hard, and turned to face her rescuer. It was Jake Alban.

She twisted out of his grip, got up unsteadily, leaned against a broken newspaper display machine, and adjusted her dress. Her side hurt, one shoe was badly damaged, and her dress was torn, but otherwise she seemed intact. No one had paid the slightest attention to the incident. The crowds along Hollywood Boulevard were used to far more exciting events: dope busts, real-life shoot-outs, and hookers.

"Why didn't you finish the job?" Margaret asked.

"Beg pardon?"

"You pushed me out there and then you pulled me back, didn't you? Why?"

"You were pushed by a woman in a polka-dot topcoat and a beehive hairdo."

"The Big Hair beehive," Margaret said.

"I was parked across from the club," Jake said, "and saw you leave. Then I saw her going after you. I followed you both on foot because I was curious. She ran back in the direction of the club."

"You just *happened* to be parked by the club?" Margaret asked incredulously.

"That's right. I was trying to get a fix on the place before going in to chat with the owners."

She rubbed her hip. He offered his hand but she waved it away.

"What made you think *I* pushed you?" He closed his eyes for an instant. "Never mind. I get it. How much did you see at the Casa Bel Air?"

Margaret looked at him without expression.

"I saw you running away from Tommy Hamilton's office last night," he said.

"Really? And I saw him die with you bending over him."

"What about the other guy, the beach-boy type with the suntan?"

"Oh, please," she said, shoving away from the newspaper box

and hobbling toward the curb. "And I suppose you didn't try to run me down in Aspen."

He shook his head. "All I did in Aspen was look in your car to find out who you were."

Margaret took a deep breath. "You're pathetic," she told him, wincing from the pain.

"I'll give you a lift to wherever you're going," he said. "Maybe we can even figure out a way to stop stepping on each other's toes."

"I don't think so," she said. "Even if you're not some sort of hit man, you're working for one of the sleaziest humans on the face of the globe. I don't think we have much to say to one another."

He followed her down Hollywood Boulevard. "Let me drive you to an emergency ward. Get an X-ray."

"That's not necessary." Forcing herself not to limp now. "I'm fine. I'll get a cab."

"Cabs don't cruise in L.A.," he said, watching her waving her arm in the general direction of the traffic. "It's against their union or something."

But at that moment a cab pulled in to the curb. Margaret turned and flashed Jake a triumphant smile. Then she got in and slammed the door behind her.

Through the rear window, she saw him standing there staring after her, too damned handsome to be believed. She gave the cabbie the name of the restaurant where she was scheduled to meet Wagner Mills. Then she settled back against the seat and smiled. All in all, it had been a very interesting if painful night.

31

◆

Washington

◆

"I was so naive as a kid I used to sneak
behind the barn and do nothing."

JOHNNY CARSON

BECAUSE OF HER mother's disappearance, Catsy's day had been one
of those truly horrible experiences. When not canceling appointments, meetings, and lectures, all the while issuing the most abject
of apologies, she'd had to dodge the ever more insistent Penelope
Krim, who had actually camped out in the Christen reception room
for nearly three hours in the afternoon. Catsy had been forced to
enter and exit through the fire door.

When anchorman John Kilmer called at 5 P.M., she almost wept
with relief. They had an early dinner at a tiny Greek restaurant near
the station. Then, instead of the quick tryst he had been hoping for
in his dressing room, she suggested he come to her apartment after
his newscast.

He was in favor of immediate gratification, but she reminded
him of the oil massage and other delights that would make the wait
worth his while. Then she kissed him, using her tongue to touch
that unguarded spot in the corner of his lips that made him moan
and pull her closer.

She arrived at her apartment shortly before ten o'clock, to find
an assortment of messages on her machine, most of them from

men, several from Penelope Krim, whose calls were becoming increasingly more strident, filled with threats and accusations.

Still no word from her mother. This sort of silence was so unusual that Catsy began to imagine she was being punished for something. She hoped that wasn't the case, but even if Laura was annoyed at her for some reason, Catsy knew she had devised a plan that would change her mother's mind and earn her eternal gratitude. It was just a matter of time.

The only caller who piqued her interest was Detective Skinner of the D.C. Police. He of the marble-white limbs and amazing endurance. She thought of responding, but remembered that John Kilmer would be arriving within the hour. She'd save Skinner for another night.

Yawning, she went into the kitchen and removed a bottle of her favorite Gewürztraminer from the fridge. She half-filled a crystal goblet and took it with her to the bedroom, where she turned on the TV. John Kilmer was looking at her with an earnest expression, discussing the state of the world, which seemed to be deplorable as usual.

She lay down on the bed and closed her eyes just for a second. Kilmer was saying something about the Saudis. . . . Then she was awake. She had no idea how long she'd been asleep, but the newscast had been replaced by a dreadful comic from one of the local clubs and someone was pressing her door buzzer.

Feeling slightly woozy, she turned off the TV and stepped into the hall. The buzzing continued. "Hold on, John," she said, wondering how he'd gotten inside the building. "We've got the whole night to—" She was going to say more, but when she opened the door she discovered her caller was not John Kilmer. It was Penelope Krim.

"Gotcha!" Penelope said.

Catsy took a deep breath and regained her composure. "What can I do for you, Dr. Krim?"

"Make it Penny, dear," Penelope said cheerily, looking past her into the living room. "Expecting somebody else, huh?"

"It's very late, Dr. Krim." She started to shut the door but Penelope stuck her foot in the way.

"Just between us gals," Penelope said, pushing her bulk inside the apartment, "would you tell me where the hell your mother is?"

"I . . . at her home, I assume," Catsy lied. She was wondering what the consequences would be if she had this grotesque woman arrested for trespassing. Or breaking and entering. Anything.

"Assume again. She's not there," Penelope snarled. "The police are very interested."

"The police?"

"Yes," Penelope said. "The least I could do was to report that my dear friend Laura Christen seemed to be missing."

"You did *what?* Who the hell gave you the right—"

"Maybe I did act precipitously," Penelope said, her voice dripping with . . . concern. "But I know you'll forgive me when I remind you that another of my good friends, Jeremy Dunbar, died so suddenly just after Laura's press conference. And then when I discovered that your mother was missing—"

"Missing? What makes you think she's missing?"

"My people and I have been watching her home and her office." Penelope edged farther into the apartment, looking past Catsy, eyes exploring every nook and cranny. "She hasn't been at either location. So I put it to you—if she's not working or resting, just where the hell is she?"

"It's not exactly your business where she is."

"It most certainly is, my dear," Penelope said, giving Catsy her full attention. "Lew Ronkowski is walking around like a rooster with the gout, crowing about how he has, and I quote, 'kicked the butt of that rich bitch bimbo who doesn't believe in this country's two-party system.' Is your mommy nursing her kicked butt or is she just running away from life in general? Or is she somehow involved in poor Jeremy's death? Did you know that the police think he may have been poisoned?"

"No, I didn't."

"They haven't been able to identify the toxin," Penelope said. "But they will. And then there's the death of your dear family friend, Thomas Hamilton."

"All I know about that is what I've read in your column," Catsy said.

"That's not good enough."

"Your column's not good enough, Penny?" John Kilmer asked from the door. "I've heard other people say the same thing lately."

Penelope turned and looked at him. "Ah, the Mr. Integrity of the nightly news."

"Well, Catsy, you didn't tell me this was going to be a media party," he said.

"Dr. Krim was just leaving," Catsy said.

"Dr. Krim is not leaving until she finds out where Laura Christen can be reached," Penelope said.

"Swell," John Kilmer said, shutting the door. He dropped the sports bag he was carrying and moved beside Penelope, putting his arm around her broad back. Unnoticed by her, he winked broadly at Catsy and proclaimed, "I bet there's enough love oil for all of us."

Penelope shrugged free of his embrace. Kilmer removed his coat, draping it on a chair. He walked over to Catsy and suddenly took her in his arms and whispered, "Play along." Then he kissed her, a long passionate wet kiss.

Catsy was amused and aroused. Immediately understanding his plan, she broke the kiss and said, "Make yourself at home, Penny. There's white wine in the fridge. Pour yourself a glass. Get loose."

Penelope Krim eyed them suspiciously, skeptical of this sudden shift in the atmosphere. Then she unbuttoned her coat and said truculently, "Maybe I will."

She pointed a pudgy finger at John Kilmer's sports bag. "A change of underwear?"

"No," he said. "That's Little Johnny."

He unzipped the bag and removed a hand puppet, made for him by one of his exes. It was a foot-high naked man with a face that was an easily recognizable caricature of Kilmer's. It was also physiologically complete, with an exaggerated penis that was almost as long as the little fellow's legs. Kilmer slipped his hand into the puppet, his little finger manipulating the hyperbolic member, moving it up and down. "He seems to be under your spell, Penny," Kilmer said.

"Tell him to come back when he's bigger," Penelope said.

"It's not size that counts," Catsy said. "It's the rhythm."

Penelope snorted and went off in search of wine. She found it in the kitchenette, filled a glass, and took it back into the living room, where John's puppet hand was busy turning down the lights. Catsy was near the fireplace, putting a match to the neatly stacked logs. "This should be a very interesting evening," Catsy said. "Do take off that frumpy coat, Penny."

"It's a goddamned Kamali," Penelope snapped, removing the coat and draping it over the couch. She then sat beside it, staring unblinking as John's little hand puppet picked up Catsy's glass for his master to drain. "I'll get some more," Catsy said. But John stopped her. "No. Penny won't mind filling my glass. Would you, Penny?"

Penelope grunted to her feet, determined to play along with whatever game was in progress. She snatched the glass from the leering puppet and took it into the kitchen. When she returned, she saw that John and Catsy were stretched out on the couch, fully dressed, pressed against one another and kissing feverishly. The lewd puppet seemed to be crawling up Catsy's backside.

Irritated, Penelope yanked her coat from under their feet and carried it with her to a chair facing the couch. John moaned and ground his body into Catsy's. Penelope, fascinated, began to lean forward toward them.

John wormed his way under Catsy until she was on top of him. They had barely begun a gyration when John raised his head and saw Penelope staring at them, gaping. "I'd *love* some of that wine, Penny," he said.

Penelope pushed herself off of the chair and slowly waddled toward them with the wine. Catsy turned to watch her; the pupils of her eyes seemed tiny; her mouth was slack and moist. She was frowning, as if in pain, and her tongue flickered on her lips.

Penelope paused and held out the wineglass.

John's hand with the puppet had disappeared under Catsy's skirt. The other was lost in her blouse. "Come, put the glass to my lips, Penny," he whispered.

Penelope, who was no shrinking violet, began to feel acutely uncomfortable. As much as she enjoyed a good lay, she was not certain she wanted to be a party to whatever was happening here. But she bent down and with a trembling hand pressed the wine-glass to John's lips.

As she did, Catsy's hand grabbed her leg. It made her jump and wine spilled onto John's chin and neck.

"Hey," he said. "Don't waste it."

Catsy's hand crept up Penelope's leg until the journalist could stand it no longer and took two backward steps. Catsy looked up at her and said, "C'mon, Penny. Into the bedroom where the three of us can get . . . comfortable. Tomorrow we can shout at each other again, but tonight we'll play."

Penelope liked to think of herself as a sophisticated woman of the world, but in truth she had not been one to expand her sexual boundaries. She had grown up in a home where lovemaking was tolerated as a method of procreation and nothing more. She had been a late bloomer, a moody, overweight, angry child who matured into an antisocial, basically friendless young woman. She made it all the way to graduate school with her virginity intact. She lost it there to a similarly hostile, lonely young man she met at a history seminar.

The breaking of her hymen and the resulting blood so frightened her timid, bespectacled young lover that he was never able to speak to her again. But he had served his purpose. Penelope's sex life was launched, and from that moment on, she began to pursue a certain type of man—one whom she could dominate by strength of will, since beauty was not one of the weapons in her arsenal.

She had slept with many men, but had had ongoing affairs with very few, the most recent being a married psychiatrist, a quiet, deeply passionate man whose failing health had brought about an end to their relationship. She had never slept with a woman. Which is why Catsy's invitation disturbed her as much as it intrigued her.

John and Catsy struggled off the couch, staggering toward the bedroom. "C'mon, Penny," John called. "The more the merrier."

She hesitated, then followed them into a large room with a long mirrored wall. The bed was magnificent—a plump four-poster king that Catsy had had made, covered by a soft peach-colored down comforter and several small lacy pillows.

John put his hand puppet on a pillow and began unbuttoning his shirt. Catsy stepped out of her skirt and hopped onto the bed. Penelope still wasn't sure how much of this she wanted. Catsy slithered toward her over the comforter. "Take off some of those drab old rags, Penny."

John slipped onto the bed beside Catsy and said, "Where's the good stuff?"

"I'll go get it," Catsy said, and bounded from the bed.

"Drugs?" Penelope asked warily.

"Just a little heroin with a cocaine chaser," Catsy said, opening a drawer beside the bed.

"I . . . I don't use drugs," Penelope said.

Catsy handed John a little teakwood box, then moved around the bed to Penelope. She reached out a hand and stroked Penelope's face with the tips of her fingers. "But it makes you feel so *good,*" Catsy purred. "You have to try it."

Penelope's face twitched. The sex business she might be able to handle, might even enjoy, but a drug scene was beyond her. "No," she said. "You people are killing yourselves."

"But what a lovely way to go," John said. "Come on, Penny. Get naked and loosen up."

"No! This is crazy!" Penelope shouted, backing out of the room. Catsy, a look of profound disappointment on her face, started to follow.

Penelope grabbed up her coat, then made a dash for the front door. She rushed out of the apartment, feeling frustrated, foolish, and furious.

WHEN the door closed, Catsy breathed a sigh of relief and slipped the lock. Then she went back to the bedroom. John grinned up at her from the bed. He was naked, propped up against the headboard with the wooden box on his stomach and the puppet on his right hand. "Little Johnny is disappointed," he said. "His girlfriend ran away."

Catsy laughed delightedly. "I can handle you both," she said, grabbing the puppet and pulling it from Kilmer's hand. She took the puppet's penis in her mouth and bit down hard.

"Owwwww," John Kilmer groaned. "Don't even joke about something like that."

Catsy's throaty laugh echoed in the room as she tossed the puppet aside and removed her black lace panties and bra. She groaned. "For one horrible moment, I was afraid we were going to have to sleep with the cow."

"And you would have, wouldn't you?" he asked.

Catsy shook her head. "She would have been all yours."

"I don't know if I could have gotten it up," he said, looking thoughtful. She hopped onto the bed and moved in on him, taking his face in both hands. Her tongue entered his mouth as she pressed against him.

When she pulled away, she looked down at his erection. "Ha! That's how difficult it is for you to get it up."

She took the wooden box from him, opened it, and plucked from it a dark bottle. She moved over to him on her knees and straddled his waist, then uncorked the bottle and poured its contents into the palm of her hand. She handed him the bottle and the cork and he placed it onto the bedside table.

She began rubbing the oil onto his chest, kneading his flesh. Its musky perfume filled her head. "Some heroin," he said sarcastically, laughing.

"The prospect of a threesome wasn't chasing her away. I had to try *something,*" she said.

"She'll probably spread the story all over town."

She paused, considering it. "There's only one way to handle people who are out to do you harm," she told him. "You let them hang themselves. If Penny even hints about my drug usage, I'll take her to court and pick her clean. I haven't used any kind of drug in years, and any test would prove that."

Kilmer stared at her for a minute, surprised at her sudden seriousness. "In any case," he said, "heroin dulls sex. On the other hand, this love oil"—he picked up the bottle and looked at its label, "this Lady Amber Love Potion # 9 is supposed to be 'Cupid tested' to strengthen a man's mighty sword."

"Let's not take Cupid's word for it," she said.

32

◆

Los Angeles

◆

"I would rather be attacked than unnoticed."

SAMUEL JOHNSON

RAGOUT WAS A tiny French restaurant on the newly fashionable Melrose Avenue in Hollywood that just missed being trendy. Margaret sipped her after-dinner coffee and watched Wagner as he opened his briefcase and extracted from it a folder his lawyer had finagled, containing a financial report on Lady Amber Cosmetics.

"With these privately held companies," he said, "it's not easy to get precise figures, but I am assured these are close to the mark." He positioned his Ben Franklin glasses on his nose and stared through them at his notes. "HRI ponied up approximately $1.7 million in return for 51 percent of the voting shares in Lady Amber. Laura's $1.1 million bought her 31 percent, and the McNeils, who were then unmarried, split the remaining 18 percent."

"And Christen's money came from her settlement with Maple Construction Co.?" Margaret asked.

Wagner shuffled through his papers. "She collected $1.3 million," he said. "My lawyer says she sold out too cheaply. Considering that her young husband, a new father, was the main breadwinner and had the potential for a long and lucrative career

161

in veterinary medicine, she should have gotten double that amount."

"So she had a lousy lawyer," Margaret said.

"Actually, a very good one. The late Jacques Bloomfield, a Hollywood legend. Worked for Howard Hughes for a while, financial pooh-bahs of that ilk."

"Theo Koriallis?" Margaret asked.

Wagner was impressed. "Yes, indeed," he said. "In fact, he was supposedly the guy who arranged for Koriallis to buy and sell and rebuy the Federated Broadcasting Company without using a pennyworth of collateral."

So, Margaret thought, *that was probably how Laura had become Jacques Bloomfield's client.* "I wonder why he didn't get her more money," she said. "She might have become the majority stockholder in Lady Amber." She brightened. "Maybe that was the whole point. To make it necessary for her to find another investor, Hamilton Resorts. Could Hamilton have been a Bloomfield client?"

Wagner made a note on a sheet of paper. "One more little thing to look into," he said. "This is so much more fun than retirement."

A waiter appeared at their table with a tray containing two pale amber liqueurs. "Compliments of the owner, Monsieur Maurice," the waiter said, indicating a small man with a thin moustache standing at the rear of the restaurant. Wagner raised his glass to him in a salute and the little man winked and nodded his head.

As the waiter moved on to another table, Margaret lifted her tiny glass and sniffed at the liqueur. "Smells sort of orangy."

"Cointreau. My favorite," Wagner said. "Try just a taste."

Margaret let a bit of the fragrant liqueur roll onto her tongue. She liked it. She continued to sip it as Wagner reported that, in order to open the company's first spa, in the Mexican border town of Rumarosa, and to introduce a new line of cosmetics for men, Laura Christen managed to find a bank with a woman loan officer who agreed to provide a $5 million loan. A short while later, Laura had tried to purchase the Hamilton Resorts shares of the company, but Ivor Hamilton had refused to sell at any price.

"He was right, of course," Wagner said. "There are now seven spas in operation in the U.S., besides the one in Mexico. And the Lord Ambrose men's line is topping Aramis and Halston, thanks to Maintain. Even in 1976, when Laura Christen sold off her stock, the company was rock solid.''

Margaret frowned. "In '76? She didn't run for Congress until 1980. But she sold her stock in '76. Why?"

"I imagine you'd have to ask her."

Margaret shrugged. "Did Hamilton International buy all of her shares?"

"All 31 percent," Wagner said, closing his folder and slipping it back into his leather case. "Does that do it for the night?"

"Do you suppose," Margaret asked, "that I might have another shot of that Cointreau?"

In between sips she asked Wagner to look up the newspaper accounts of the Laverys' drug arrest. "Darla Lavery claims that Laura and Amber were part of the operation. I'd like you to check on that, too."

Wagner opened his case and removed the folder again. He made a notation. "Is that all, Margaret?" he asked. "I can get by on five hours' sleep, but it makes my moustache droop."

As they were leaving the restaurant a tall blond man with a deep California tan was headed for the door at the same time. He bumped into Wagner, begged the former restaurateur's pardon, and continued on. Margaret thought that he looked familiar.

A few minutes later, as Wagner piloted his Jaguar down Sunset toward Margaret's hotel, chatting about the cheesiness of the half-hearted holiday decorations, he began scratching his left wrist. "Dammit," he said. "I think I've been stung by a bee."

"Bees don't sting at night," Margaret said. "They're asleep."

He held his wrist out to her. She saw a small, angry bump on his wrist, illuminated by the streetlights. "What do you suppose that is, then, if not a bee sting?" he asked.

"Spider bite."

"That's *better?*" he asked with some alarm.

"Remember, Wagner," she said, "that which does not kill us, makes us strong."

"I'll . . . bear that in . . .''

Suddenly he turned left off Sunset, rolling down a hilly deserted sidestreet.

"Where are you going?" Margaret asked. "My hotel's two blocks in the other direction."

Wagner twisted the steering wheel and parked the car head-in to the sidewalk in an unlighted section of the block. He was breathing heavily.

Margaret looked at him in alarm. His face was turning crimson. "Wagner, what the heck is—"

He pushed himself up in his seat and leaped at her, grabbing her, pulling her to him.

Margaret drew back against the door, her hip screaming in protest. "Wagner, for Christ's sake—" She managed to get the door open and staggered out into the street. In the car, Wagner was making grunting noises and thrusting himself against the steering wheel.

"My God, Wagner!" Margaret exclaimed. He looked at her and said, "Sorry," then, with shaking hands, he put the car in gear and roared off down the street.

Margaret stared after him, wondering if all Southern Californians were crazy, or just the ones she happened to meet.

33

♦

"Keep the home fires burning."

IVOR NOVELLO

IT WAS SHORTLY after 2 A.M. when the Laverys exited the rear door of Beaverville and walked to the silver Porsche parked under a tin roof off the alley. The personalized license plate on the car read BEAVI.

Jake Alban had been behind the club watching the Porsche for nearly an hour. The engine of his Cherokee was humming as the silver car passed. He eased into its wake, staying slightly to the right, in its blind spot.

The Laverys led him up Laurel Canyon for about a mile, then suddenly doglegged onto an unmarked cutoff. The Porsche stopped almost at once in front of a stairwell leading to a small house that had been built on a plateau about twenty feet higher than the road. Jake backed out of the cutoff and parked the Cherokee on Laurel, headed downhill for a fast getaway.

By the time he returned to the house, the Laverys had gone inside and were in the midst of a loud argument. Jake eased up the stairwell. As he neared the front door the voices grew louder. ". . . said nothing about that," Darla Lavery was complaining defensively.

"So you just let her in and started yapping about Laura. What happened to your goddamn brain?" Gordon Lavery snapped. Jake heard what sounded like the clank of a bottle against a glass. He moved to the side of the house. The plateau on which the house rested had been carved out of the side of a mountain. There was

165

a path of about ten feet between the building and the mountain. Jake crept along it until he was at a window, looking into an untidy living room filled with assorted mismatched pieces of furniture and litter—newspapers, unopened bills and junk mail, bits and pieces of plastic, rumpled bags, dirty glasses and ashtrays filled with cigarette stubs.

Gordon Lavery was at a wet bar at the rear of the room, fixing a drink. A phone resting on the edge of the bar rang. Lavery eyed it warily, then lifted the receiver. "Yes?" he asked cautiously.

Darla entered the room, looking at her husband anxiously. "Who?" she mouthed silently. Lavery ignored her. He was obviously too upset by the call. "He's coming to L.A.? Shit, I should have figured that when I heard about the Hamilton guy's death." He looked at his watch. "We'd better get rolling. Thanks for the warning." He replaced the phone and repeated, "Shit."

"What's the matter?" Darla asked him.

"We're going to the desert for a couple days till this 'situation' takes care of itself."

"What about the club?"

"Throw some clothes into a bag," he snarled, lifting the phone again. "I'll wake Dougie up and tell him he's got to take care of things for a few days."

"Dougie's a jerkoff," Darla said.

"Would you rather close the place down?"

"No. But why do we have to go? I mean, do you really think they'll try to—"

"Try thinking yourself. Maybe that gossip guy, Dunbar, really died of natural causes. And maybe Tom Hamilton did, too. But if there is a hit list, I can guarantee that we're on it. They may even blame us for starting all this shit."

"What do you think Theo would do if he knew about the receipts?" she wondered.

"If you keep telling the world all our secrets," her husband replied, "it won't be Koriallis you have to worry about. Now go pack the goddamn bags."

She shrugged and left the room. Lavery wiped his perspiring hands on his pant legs, picked up the phone again, dialed, and told Dougie he'd be acting manager of Beaverville until further notice.

Dougie wanted to know if that meant he'd be getting more money and Lavery told him they would discuss it when he returned. Jake thought that Darla must have been right about Dougie being a jerkoff, because he apparently believed Lavery would play straight with him.

In ten minutes Darla had filled two pieces of luggage and one bulging hanging bag. Jake watched as they closed the windows and shut their house behind them, then tried to load the luggage into the Porsche's small trunk. "You're going to have to keep the hanging bag on your lap," Lavery told his wife.

"All the way to the desert? You're nuts."

"Then we'll just leave it right here," he said, dropping it on the road.

"I hate this shitty little car," she said, picking up the bag. "It's the kind of car guys buy when they're going through the male menopause."

"Get in or I'll dump your ass right here," Gordon Lavery informed her.

Darla muttered something, then got into the car with the bag draped over her knees. He squeezed behind the wheel and they were off.

Jake waited at the side of their house for about fifteen minutes. Then, satisfied that they wouldn't be coming back for some forgotten item, he circled the house until he found a window that had not been bolted shut. He worked it up a couple of feet and rolled over the sill into the living room.

Besides the living room, there was a dining room, a tiny kitchen with a stove that looked as if it had never been used, two bedrooms, one of which was being used as an office-den, a bathroom with an elaborate sunken tub, and, at the rear of the house, a laundry room with a half-bath. Behind the house was a tiny yard that barely supported a redwood hot tub.

Using his penlight for illumination, Jake worked his way slowly through the house, pausing longest in the den with its file cabinets. They were filled mainly with business papers pertaining to Beaver-ville and a place called The Oval, the Laverys' previous enterprise—a gay bathhouse that they'd opened shortly before the AIDS devastation.

It was well after three when he spotted the heating vent in the laundry room and went back to check the rest of the house to make sure there were no vents anywhere else. That confirmed, he returned to the laundry and removed the faux vent's cover. Inside was a metal box. In the box were the Laverys' marriage certificate, a small diamond ring, and a cardboard folder containing a stack of yellow slips of paper—carbon copies that seemed to be merchandise receipts, all dated 1972, the year the Laverys peddled their drugs.

He started toward the front of the house with the folder. He was going to exit through the main door, as if he owned the place. But curiosity stopped him. He put the folder on top of the dining room table and, holding the penlight with one hand, riffled through the yellow sheets. Each was dated, and included scribbled notations. First, a description of the merchandise: "1 Mari," "3 Mesc," "1 doz. LSD." This was followed by a set of initials and a destination: "JG in Rm 224," "ML at Lido Club," "VG in Hacienda Room." Finally there was a single name, which Jake assumed referred to the person making the sale or the delivery. Among the "Judis" and "Kims" and "Pattis" he discovered several "Lauras" and "Ambers."

Jake was still leafing through the receipts, congratulating himself on his find, when he heard footsteps on the front stairs. He clicked off the penlight and jammed the yellow receipts into his pocket. A back-door retreat seemed the best move. But when he approached the rear, he heard someone coming in that way, too. He had barely ducked into the half-bath off the laundry room when the back door crashed open and a man in black slacks and a black sweater entered carrying a large tin filled with something liquid.

Jake backed farther into the half-bath. The man began to spill the contents of his container onto the tile. Jake recognized the pungent fumes of gasoline. And he realized that the man was heading his way.

He checked his surroundings for a possible weapon. Nothing. Except the toilet.

The man entered the half-bath, dumping the fuel. He never saw

Jake swing the heavy porcelain tank lid at the back of his head. There was a dull thud and the man reeled backward and collapsed silently. His gasoline can clanged against the tile floor.

Without knowing why, Jake carefully eased the tank lid back into its proper position, then moved to the rear door.

"Is that you, Carl?" a woman's voice called inside the house. Jake didn't answer. He went through the door and out into the fresh air, gulping quickly. Crouching low, he headed toward the front of the building.

A man was blocking the stairs leading to the road. He was powerfully built and wore a dark double-breasted suit that made him look even more formidable. His black hair was cut in a crew style so extreme the top of his head glowed white. While Jake tried to think of some way of getting past him, the female voice called, "Something's happened to Carl!"

The crew-cut man hopped up the stairs and disappeared into the house. Jake descended the stairs as quickly and quietly as he could. He squeezed past a black Mercedes sedan parked near the bottom step. He could not see through its smoked windows, but he prayed the car was empty.

As he jogged away down the road he turned and saw that the car's plates read IC4.

He slid behind the wheel of his car, the sweat flowing from him. His hands were shaking badly, but he managed to get the key into place. The engine turned over easily and he was on his way. He'd barely reached the bottom of Laurel Canyon Road when he noticed a glow coming from the direction of the Lavery home. By the time he had stopped at a pay phone to call in the fire, the whole hillside seemed to be ablaze.

34

♦

"Power is the ultimate aphrodisiac."
                                        HENRY KISSINGER

MARGARET STAFFORD WAS in her hotel bedroom, nude, studying her injured hip in her floor-to-ceiling wardrobe mirror, when there was a knock on the door. She stared a moment longer at the enormous bruise, which was made up of a variety of hues, none of which complemented her complexion. Then she wrinkled up her nose and grabbed a white terrycloth robe that the hotel had provided.

She limped across the bedroom and peeked through the peephole. Her brows knit in anger.

She unlocked the door and stood back as Wagner Mills entered with a box of long-stemmed roses in his arms, a newspaper, and a sheepish look on his face. "I appreciate your seeing me," he told her hoarsely, looking down at the floor.

"You've got three minutes," she told him. "Then you're out of here."

"When I . . . regained control of myself last night, I dragged my doctor out of a comfortable bed and forced him to take a sample of my blood."

"Wagner, I don't—"

"Please. Let me get this out, Margaret. I am not a . . . a pervert. I've never . . . behaved that way before. I was drugged." He held out his wrist. There was still a slightly pink lump where he'd been "bitten" the night before. "It was the most powerful aphrodisiac I have ever encountered. And I have encountered a few. Believe me, Margaret, even with Rush casting its romantic glow, I have never before been aroused like that.''

Margaret stared at him for a beat, then said, ''I'd like a copy of your doctor's report.''

''As soon as it's available,'' he said, placing the flowers on her rumpled bed. ''I wasn't sure how you'd feel about flowers, but I didn't want to come empty-handed.''

''The flowers are fine.''

''You might want to look at this morning's *Times,*'' he said. ''It says Tommy's funeral service will take place at eleven at the Wee Kirk O' the Heather church at Forest Lawn. In case you'd like to observe Amber McNeil once again.''

''Thanks for the information,'' she said.

Wagner made a helpless gesture with his hands and then said, ''I'm sorry, Margaret, but I swear to you I was a victim of some astonishing chemical.'' He made another helpless gesture and left her.

She went to the door, locked it from the inside, then hobbled, muttering to herself, back to the phone and used it to make a long distance call.

Murphy was curious about her progress, but that wasn't why she'd called him. She wanted to think over the Laverys' accusations about Laura's involvement with drug dealing before spreading the word. So she asked Murphy how well he knew the widow of the detective Mike Roberts had used before hiring them, the one who'd died of a heart attack in Los Angeles.

''Stuart Wayland's wife?'' Murph asked. ''I suppose I know her to say hello to.''

''Well, say hello to her—and see if she'll tell you something about the state of Wayland's body when they found him out here.''

''State?'' he asked, surprised. ''It was supposed to have been burned to a crisp.''

''See if she'll let you look at the coroner's report.''

''What am I looking for?'' Murphy asked.

Without the flicker of a smile, she said, ''I'd like to know if he died with a hard-on.''

35

♦

"You can't go home again."

THOMAS WOLFE

As THEO's MERCEDES limousine sped down the Pacific Coast Highway toward Laura's California home, he tried once again to convince her of the danger she was in. "If you will not believe me," he told her, "then at least humor me. Be very careful while you are here."

"I'm two days behind in my work and I'm fighting a very difficult battle in the House. My plan is to attend Tommy's funeral, then fly immediately to Washington. I don't suppose you're heading back today?"

He shook his head. "There will be many discussions about the future of Hamilton Resorts and other matters I care rather passionately about. My influence may have waned within the company, but I will at least have my say."

When they arrived at her beachfront home, he insisted that Albert remain behind with the sedan to drive her to the cemetery. She agreed. She did not feel as if she were in any real danger, but Albert was an undemanding and perhaps even reassuring presence.

The handyman-gardener who cared for the house while she was in Washington was surprised by her unannounced arrival and suspicious of the big man seated in the car parked near the front door.

"That's Albert," she told the old man. "I bet if you get him a beer, it'll be like taking a thorn out of his paw. He'll be your friend forever."

She went directly to the sunken living room that looked out on clear blue skies and frothy waves breaking against a clean white beach. Ah, California. She turned her back to it, picked up a cordless phone, and dialed her office in Washington.

When the receptionist finally located Catsy, her daughter's voice began with a cool, "Nice hearing from you," but quickly degenerated into a mildly frantic, "Where the devil have you been?" followed by a grocery list of problems ranging from appointments missed to Penelope Krim's going to the police to report her missing.

Laura tried to explain her inability to telephone before, but Catsy responded with, "When I was attending that awful school in Connecticut and forgot to phone one week, you tried to guilt-trip me with a 'You couldn't find ten minutes to give your mother a call.' I'm saying the same thing to you now. You must have known I'd be climbing the walls."

Laura wondered what her daughter would think if she explained she was locked in a bedroom without a phone. Instead she said, "I knew that you could handle whatever came up."

There was a moment's silence on the other end of the line. Then Catsy replied, "Okay, as your press secretary, I accept the compliment. As your daughter, I think it's a little glib."

"I simply couldn't phone until now. I've been on a plane for the last five hours, and I just this minute walked into the Malibu house."

"Malibu? But, my God, tonight's the NOW dinner."

"I'll try to make it on time. But if I'm a little late, explain to them that I had to attend the funeral of one of my closest friends. You won't be lying."

Catsy said, "Of course. Tommy. I was sorry to hear about him." But there was no sincerity in the words. At approximately the same time that their mother-daughter relationship had been at its most strained, Catsy began to exhibit hostility toward Laura's friends, Tommy included.

Before hanging up, Catsy said, "Oh, and by the way, Ronkowski is claiming that some of your more chauvinistic Republican pals in the house have privately agreed to back him. If true, Jim says you're now lacking the votes needed to win."

It was a wrist slap posing as an exit line.

36

♦

*"I'm a candidate for no office but heaven
and I have no Republican opposition."*

SAM ERVIN

THE FREEWAYS WERE less congested than usual and Jake Alban, dressed in the only suit he owned, made the trip to Forest Lawn in Glendale faster than he had expected. It gave him an opportunity to find a parking spot near the Wee Kirk O' the Heather where within the hour the bereaved would be arriving.

According to a brochure he picked up in the memorial park's Memento Shop, the little picture-postcard chapel was a rough approximation of the Scottish church where Annie Laurie once said her prayers. Inside its comforting walls, Gable had served as a pallbearer for Jean Harlow, with Jeanette MacDonald and Nelson Eddy singing at the service. Ronald Reagan had married Jane Wyman there. It was a place of history. And another milestone was taking place that day.

Jake stood near the chapel's open doors watching the assistants of the funeral director make the final arrangements, while, in the parking area, the paparazzi began to gather.

In the next few minutes, the pre-funeral activity increased. The TV crews arrived, behaving even more intrusively and with a rudeness far greater than the still photographers who were merely shouting for the rich and famous to please look their way.

The celebrities, for the most part, were not playing the game. No poses today. No philosophical musings on mortality. No discussions of the vital issues of the day. Not even for the lady from

Entertainment Tonight who kept asking, "What's your favorite memory of the deceased?" The celebrities politely declined to comment, moved on, shook the hands of a few distant relations of the deceased, and filed into the chapel, where the unmistakable strains of an organ could now be heard.

The members of the business community, less recognizable to the swarming, snapshooting mob, made their way into the chapel relatively unhindered. Jake placed a few faces with names from the financial pages. He perked up considerably at the arrival of Theo Koriallis. The financier was with a tall, sallow man who might have been his son or nephew or bodyguard.

Jake wondered how he might approach Koriallis. The conversations he'd heard between the tanned blond and Tommy Hamilton, and at the Laverys', indicated that Koriallis was very much a part of the situation involving Laura Christen.

Suddenly the paparazzi began swarming around a newcomer and the TV crews barged into the fray. Jake saw a flash of blonde hair and then the woman he'd just been thinking of strode into full view. Laura Christen was ignoring the media's entreaties, gracefully but firmly. She was wearing a demure black Chanel dress with just one string of pearls, her eyes hidden by sunglasses more functional than fancy. She moved in his direction, then stopped, facing him.

"Jake?"

"Hi, Laura. Been a long time."

Suddenly she seemed to be looking over his shoulder. He turned and saw Theo Koriallis glancing their way before entering the chapel.

"It's about to start," she said. "I'd better go in."

"Could we talk later?" he asked, not sure which of many motives prompted the question.

She hesitated. "Yes . . . I'd like that. Later."

Then she was walking toward the chapel, nodding to the other mourners.

The paparazzi began to re-form around a popular television star and her husband. Past them, Jake watched a Mercedes limousine defy all roadblocks to enter a special path reserved for members of the family. Its license plate read: "IC1."

He pushed through the crowd toward the limo. The driver, a nondescript young man in a dark suit and mirrored sunglasses, slid from behind the wheel and opened one of the rear doors. A large, overweight cleric in black staggered out of the car, his face bulging dark red from the effort. Behind him, a trim middle-aged man in a conservative gray suit emerged with the grace of a professional athlete. Under a short, serious executive hairstyle, his face consisted of planes and ridges. He reminded Jake of Kirk Douglas minus the dimple in his chin. Jake didn't know the man, but he did recognize his fellow passenger. The overweight man was Dr. Frederic Corvin, the official chaplain of the House of Representatives and the host of a TV talk show broadcast each night from Washington over public television.

Jake stepped into his path. "Hello, Dr. Corvin. Jake Alban. Good to see you again." The only times Jake had seen the man had been on TV, but the cleric shook his hand with all the warmth of an old friend.

Jake turned to the other man and Dr. Corvin said, "Of course you know Lawrence Newfield?"

"I don't believe so," Jake said. Newfield's hand was like an iron vise. His eyes stared at Jake, unblinking.

"Larry's the president of Intercom," Dr. Corvin said. Something caught his eye and he jerked his head so quickly that his red-veined cheeks almost flapped. "Ah, there's Reverend Muller over there waving to me frantically. Nice seeing you, Mr. Alvin."

Jake watched Corvin waddle through the crowd, pressing the flesh. Newfield recaptured his attention by saying, "You did some fine work in 'Nam. You came the closest of any reporter to telling it like it was."

Newfield's voice was distinctive, broadcast quality with a little more determination behind it. Jake said, "Thanks. I gather you were over there?"

"On and off," Newfield said, leading him toward the chapel.

"And you started Intercom during the off-period?"

Newfield smiled. "I didn't start it. I just sort of worked my way up in it. I understand from our guy out here, Kerry Niles, you're doing a story about HRI. I'm afraid this is a rather downbeat ending."

"I'll work around it," Jake said.

Newfield gave him an appraising look. "I bet you will. If you need anything, just tell Kerry."

As Newfield started away, Jake asked, "Is Kerry here? We've never met."

Newfield studied the crowd for a minute. "Don't see him. But he should be around somewhere. He handled most of the arrangements."

Newfield gave him a manly wink and sailed easily through the crowd. The cameras were grinding and clicking at a handsome, voluptuous strawberry blonde and a thin, bookish-looking man— Amber Hall McNeil and her husband, George.

Jake followed the McNeils into the chapel. Dr. Corvin was beginning his sermon with a Shakespearean quote about the refusal to fear death. Jake barely heard it as he searched for Laura Christen. She was seated in the first pew beside an elderly woman who was weeping softly.

Newfield was several rows back, next to the owner of a fast-food chain and his large family. Theo Koriallis was on the opposite side of the chapel. The McNeils had found a seat not far from where he was standing. Just to their left was a familiar mop of red hair. Margaret Stafford! Somehow she'd passed Jake without his seeing her. So much for the observant newsman.

The Reverend Corvin continued to wax Biblical. " 'God created man to be immortal, and made him to be an image of his own eternity. Nevertheless through envy of the devil came death into the world.' That reminds me of something my friend Fr. Andrew Greeley once told me about Satan . . .' "

Jake slipped outside to find that the TV crews had departed and most of the photographers had gone on to other chores—developing, cropping, peddling their wares. He found a stone bench a short distance away from the chapel. It was shaded by a tree. He sat down and watched the remaining photographers sweat in their rumpled windbreakers. He watched the driver of the hearse try to move the vehicle around Newfield's limo. He listened to the organ music, then the choir singing something that sounded like the old Marty Robbins tune "El Paso."

He looked across the patio and saw a large black man in a dark suit seated on a bench similar to his. The black man's sunglasses were pointed directly at him.

TWENTY-FIVE minutes later the chapel's doors opened and Tommy Hamilton's mortal remains were transported through them by Theo Koriallis and seven other pallbearers. They placed the cherrywood coffin onto a sliding shelf at the rear of the hearse. An attendant pressed a button inside the vehicle and the tray and the coffin were drawn into its interior.

Laura and a few other friends of the dearly departed commenced their sad pilgrimage over the manicured lawn to Tommy's final resting place. The large black man with sunglasses stood up from his bench and followed them. Most of the mourners went back to their cars to escape onto the freeways and head for home.

When Lawrence Newfield appeared and started for his limo, Jake moved to intercept him. But Margaret Stafford was there before him and Jake kept his distance, settling for an unobstructed view of their byplay. He heard her call Newfield by name.

"Have we met before, Miss—"

"Margaret Stafford. I've seen pictures of you with my father, Harry Stafford."

Newfield seemed genuinely surprised. "Harry's daughter? I'll be damned. Your dad and I went back a long ways. Didn't I hear that you and Murph were—"

"Yes," she interrupted, spotting Jake. She turned away from Newfield and lowered her voice, but he could hear her say to him, "Could you spare me a few minutes?"

Newfield glanced at his watch. "I've got a meeting to go to in Beverly Hills. Drive with me and my guy can bring you back for your car."

Jake watched them get into the limo and drive away, then walked slowly in the direction of the burial party.

The coffin was resting on the last shelf of a mausoleum that had the Hamilton name carved on a stone tablet at its top. In addition to the eight pallbearers, there were twelve other people in attendance, including the large black man, who was standing apart from the others.

Jake kept his distance, too, waiting for Dr. Corvin to administer his finishing touches.

That accomplished, the remaining mourners began to disperse. Koriallis' sallow companion winked at the black man as they passed him on their way to the parking area. Laura paused a moment to say something to the McNeils, then started back to the chapel.

When she saw Jake she smiled. She was much more beautiful than he remembered.

He approached her awkwardly, uncertain as to how intimate their meeting should be. A friendly hug? A kiss on the cheek? On the lips?

But the black man was moving between them, facing him. Laura said, "It's all right, Albert. He's an old friend." She extended a gloved hand and Jake held it briefly. "I didn't realize you knew Tommy," she said.

"I'd just met him," Jake said, glancing at Albert, then back to Laura. "I'm working on an article about Hamilton Resorts."

She continued walking toward the chapel and Jake stayed in step with her. Albert brought up the rear. Laura said, "Are you living out here now?"

"Nope. Just visiting. Staying at the Casa Bel Air. How long will you be in town?"

"I'm going back to Washington now."

He nodded, feeling his heart sink. "Too bad. I was hoping we might have dinner."

"I'd like that," she said, "but—duty calls."

They were passing the chapel now, walking slowly toward the parking lot. Jake felt as if there were only seconds left for him to say something, do something, or she would go out of his life again, this time forever. He said, "I'll be in Washington myself within a day or two. We could have that dinner then."

She stopped, turned to him, and put her hand on his arm. "Promise me you'll call when you get in town."

"I'll need a number."

"Call the office. Leave your number and I'll get back to you." She shook his hand, then kissed him briefly on the cheek.

Then the muscular Albert was opening the back door of a black sedan and she was getting inside. Albert pointed his sunglasses at Jake a final time, mumbled something, then squeezed beneath the steering wheel and slammed his door.

Jake watched the sedan vanish and wondered if he were really going to see her again or if he'd just been treated to a refined variation of the old "Don't-call-me" brush-off.

37

♦

"They're not going to get married or anything. They're only nine."

LILLIAN CARTER ON GRANDDAUGHTER
AMY'S FIRST BOYFRIEND

AS THEIR LIMOUSINE glided down the Golden State Freeway in the direction of the Burbank Airport, Lawrence Newfield turned to the redheaded woman beside him and said, "Well, Margaret, are you here only to pump me for information about my clients? Or is there something else on your mind?"

"Your clients will do," Margaret replied. She tried to remember if she'd ever met him, thought not, though she'd met a number of her father's friends.

"Well, business talk is a small price to pay for your company," Newfield told her, leaning forward to open the limo's polished wooden bar. "Let me make a quick guess: You're a scotch drinker."

"Not before noon."

He poured her a drink. "In Washington it's almost three."

He dropped in a few ice cubes and handed her a drink, fixed one for himself. When he leaned back against the seat again, he was somehow closer to her, his arm pressing against hers. She tried not to be too obvious about moving away from him. He'd been her father's friend, after all.

He clinked his glass against hers. "To making new acquaintances at funerals," he said.

She barely wet her lips with the scotch. "What sort of services does Intercom do for its clients, Mr. Newfield?" she asked.

"Please call me Larry. Your father did. What we do depends on the client. Every one of them has a different, special need." His gesturing hand idly brushed her arm. "We're salesmen, matchmakers, psychiatrists, business consultants, publicists."

"Since you work for Hamilton Resorts, does that mean you work for Lady Amber Cosmetics, too?" she asked, moving to the far corner of the seat.

"What exactly are you and Murph after?" he asked. "I hope it's nothing that would make trouble for HRI or Lady Amber."

"I can't tell you precisely what our job is," she said. "But making trouble is not our goal."

He shrugged. "To answer your question, Intercom was hired by Hamilton Resorts International, and since Lady Amber is under that umbrella, we work for that company, too."

"What was Tommy like?"

"A nice enough fella. Maybe a little, ah, disinterested, to be running a major corporation. But smart enough to find a few old pros to help keep things rolling along."

"And what happens now that the last Hamilton is gone?"

"When you can't find a real Hamilton, you get a substitute, I guess. That's what I expect to discover at my meeting."

"Who will make that decision?" she asked.

"The board."

"And who's on the board?"

"Ah, Margaret, how like your father you are. Straight ahead."

He was pushing the father button, and she was usually a sucker for it, but not at the moment. "As Dad might have said, 'Who's on the board?' "

"Suppose I asked you which client sent you out here?"

"I couldn't tell you."

"Then you see my situation."

"So let's go back to Lady Amber."

He sampled his scotch before replying. "A very solid firm. The product is moving well. The spas are constantly expanding."

"Have there been any problems?" she asked.

"My, but you do demand a lot of your new friends," he said.

He shifted his legs until one knee pressed hers. He smiled. "Why don't we have a little lunch, Margaret?"

"You've got a meeting."

He pressed a button on a panel under the side window that apparently opened an intercom to the front of the limo. He asked, "I've got to be at the Beverly Building by 1:15. Can we squeeze in a quick lunch somewhere we won't have to leave the car?"

The driver nodded and Newfield turned off the intercom and refocused his attention on Margaret.

"We were talking about problems at Lady Amber," she said.

"Well . . . there's been nothing catastrophic. At the Mexico spa there was a minor drug problem. Some of the massage room guys were peddling a little coke. They were booted out and that was that. At the Atlanta spa a good ole boy beat his wife rather badly. Domestic violence. Nothing to do with Lady Amber, of course. Thanks to Intercom the media were none the wiser."

"I'd like to meet Amber McNeil and have a chat with her," Margaret said. "Could you arrange it?"

"I'd need to give her a damn good reason. There's a company policy against interviews."

"Since there's a Lady Amber Spa in Washington," she said, "couldn't we say I'm out here representing the First Family and would like to speak with Amber about their doing a little toning up at the spa?"

He nodded. "We could," he said. "But it's a pretty wild tale, and I might be jeopardizing my relationship with Amber. Why should I do that, Margaret?" His eyes locked onto hers.

"I don't know, Larry," she said. "Because of your friendship with my father? Because you act impulsively every now and then? Because you're trying to impress me?"

He laughed. "I am trying to impress you, but I believe in quid pro quo. I'll do it . . . for a kiss."

She was momentarily speechless. By the time she'd thought of a comeback that wouldn't be too insulting, he had picked up the car phone and dialed a set of numbers. The connection made, he identified himself and asked to speak to Mrs. McNeil. "Oh," he said, "won't be back until then, huh? Well, I'm with a Miss Stafford from the White House who wishes to meet with Mrs.

McNeil later today to discuss the facilities at the Rollingwood spa
. . . Yes, I realize that Mrs. McNeil wouldn't handle this sort of
thing ordinarily, but, as I said, Miss Stafford is representing the
White House . . . Yes, *that* White House . . . Yes, precisely . . .
Thank you!''

He slammed down the receiver. ''The people out here have so
much smog on the brain you have to hit them over the head with
a lie. But you'll get your meeting at three P.M.''

''Thank you,'' she said. The business with the kiss bothered her.
He was probably joking, but if not, she really didn't want any kind
of a scene.

''You've barely touched your drink,'' he said.

She took another sip of scotch and felt its warmth spreading
through her body.

The limo turned into a parking lot beside what appeared to be
an abandoned streetcar. On its side was painted, MAME'S RED CAR
DINER. Newfield eyed the establishment with skepticism as his
chauffeur asked if they wanted the steak sandwich or the fish
sandwich. Everything else, especially the chili, was chancy. Grinning, Margaret ordered fish. Newfield, steak.

While they waited for their lunch, he removed a bottle of Chardonnay from the cooler. He noticed Margaret staring at him.
''What?'' he asked, as he worked the cork out of the wine bottle.

''I'm wondering why I haven't heard more about you and Intercom.''

He gave her his widest smile. ''There are two sides to public
relations. You must know how to get publicity and how to avoid
it. I avoid it because there is no client on earth that wants to hire
a p.r. man who is better publicized than they are.''

''So that's why I haven't read about you in the press,'' she said.
''Why haven't I heard Murph talk about you?''

''That's another story,'' he said. He cocked his head as if in
thought, then continued. ''Murph's never had a very high opinion
of me, I'm afraid. He's a tough man to turn.''

''That he is.''

He found two goblets and began to fill them. ''Could I ask what
your relationship is to Murph?''

''Relationship? We're business partners.''

"Nothing else?"

"No. Nothing else. He's old enough to be my father."

"So am I," Newfield said.

"Yes," she said, feeling somewhat relieved, as if that settled it about the kiss.

He sighed. "Do I look like a dirty old man to you, Margaret?"

She didn't know what to say.

"Best two out of three," he prompted. "Dirty? Old? Man?"

There was a knock at the window. The chauffeur had their food—two soggy French bread sandwiches on cardboard plates. "Isn't this haute cuisine?" Newfield asked. Then he suggested the chauffeur grab a bite for himself in the diner.

They ate without speaking for a few minutes, observing one another warily and listening to soothing music on the limo's CD player. Then Newfield opened a black leather briefcase that had been beside him on the floor of the limo. He withdrew a dark brown bottle the size of a half-pint of whiskey. He uncapped it, inhaled its contents, and sighed with contentment.

Margaret watched him curiously.

"Care to join me?" He held out the bottle.

"What is it?"

"Something not yet on the market. It's still being product-tested. It's supposed to make food taste better."

"What's in it?"

He smiled. "That's something they don't tell us. All I know is that the FDA gave it the nod."

She accepted the bottle and sniffed at it tentatively. It smelled of sandalwood, not unlike his cologne.

"Now try a bite of your sandwich," he said.

She lifted the sandwich to her mouth, nibbled a piece. She could taste the yeast in the bread, the peppers and marinade that permeated the fish filet, the butter in which it had been broiled. She could taste the Mame's Red Car Special Sauce with its tangy tomato-bouillon-brown mustard base. It was the most magnificent sandwich she'd ever eaten.

Ravenous now, she put the bottle on a burled wood ledge and devoured the fish and French bread. When she finally paused to look over at Newfield, he was finishing his steak sandwich with the same voraciousness.

"Offhand," she announced, "I'd say the product is an unquali- fied success. It could bring back TV dinners."

He dabbed at his lips with his napkin and placed it and their empty plates on the tin tray. He put the tray on the limo's floor and moved toward her.

She put up her hand and he stopped. "Don't forget our deal," he said.

The strange thing was that suddenly she wasn't all that op- posed to a little kiss. But no, he was a contemporary of her *fa- ther*.

He was watching her, amused. "I think you'll be sorry if we don't."

"Sorry?"

"An opportunity wasted."

"I'll take that chance," she said and straightened in the car seat. "You don't want to be late for your meeting."

Whatever else Lawrence Newfield might have been, he was a man in control of his emotions. Sitting back against the cushion, he took a deep breath, exhaled, and pressed a button on the arm- rest of the car. He said, "I hope that this no doesn't mean never."

"Well, Mr. Newfield—"

"Larry."

"Okay. Well, Larry, maybe if you were the last man on the face of the earth. And I were in my forties—"

He laughed. "You're tough, Margaret. But I like tough. I may take a run at you again sometime."

The chauffeur exited the diner and got into the limo, started the engine, and they were off. Newfield picked up the little brown bottle and put it back into his briefcase. "Not quite the miracle it was cracked up to be," he said.

"You can count on me for a testimonial."

"We'll see."

The Beverly Hills traffic made him a bit late for his meeting. He was out the door even before the limousine had come to a complete stop in front of the building. "We'll meet again, Margaret," he called back to her. "You can count on that." And he was gone. All that remained was the faint scent of sandalwood. Whether it was the odd new product or Larry Newfield's cologne she couldn't tell.

38

♦

Washington

♦

"Politician—any man with influence
enough to get his old mother a job as
charwoman in the City Hall."

H. L. MENCKEN

WOODWARD & LOTHROP'S, or "Woody's" as it is usually called by
residents of the Nation's Capital, is a department store chain with
links scattered throughout the metropolitan area. Its largest and
oldest branch takes up a complete city block in downtown D.C. At
approximately 4:30 P.M., J. B. Murphy was in the bakery department of the original Woody's accepting a box containing a lemon
meringue pie when Mike Roberts bore down on him through a
crowd of mainly female shoppers.

The Senate Minority Leader's face showed more than a five
o'clock shadow. His brow was knitted and he did not seem in a
pleasant mood. His first words were a hissed, "What's so damned
important we have to meet in public?"

"This isn't public, Mike," Murphy replied. "It's Woody's.
Pick up some brownies for the kids. I've just bought a pie to go
with the steak dinner I'm having tonight with my niece's family.
They think I'm a lonely old coot."

"I'm too tired for whimsy, Murph. What's on your mind?"

"Charlie Stern," Murphy said, looking longingly at a rack of
fresh oatmeal cookies. "I can't find him. His secretary says he's

not at his office. His wife says he's not at home. Nobody else seems to know where Charlie is. I was hoping you might.''

"He drops in and out," Roberts grumbled. "You know how he operates. What do you want with him, anyway?''

As he guided the Minority Leader past windows filled with everything from gingerbread men to elaborate cakes in the shape of the Washington Monument, Murphy explained about Stern's no-show at the Corcoran Gallery. He concluded with his concern that some ill could have befallen their friend.

"Charlie's a survivor," Mike Roberts said. "And he doesn't exactly keep office hours. But I admit I haven't heard from him in two days, which is a little odd. I'll make some calls. Meanwhile, how about Lady X?''

"Well, I'm trying to convince Stuart Wayland's widow to let us look at her husband's body.''

Roberts frowned. "Why, for God's sake?''

"It's Meg's idea. She thinks he might have been slipped some sort of mickey that induced his heart attack.''

"And this has something to do with . . . our situation?''

" 'fraid so,'' Murphy told him. "Making me all the more anxious about Charlie.''

"This is incredible.'' The Minority Leader looked stricken.

"Mike, this may be Woody's, where people are more interested in buying than spying. But I'd still try to keep it calm and polite.''

Mike Roberts nodded and twisted his face into a grimace of a smile. "Do I tell my boss that we should start bailing?''

"We've nothing to suggest that Lady X has anything to hide, just that some of her friends may be sorta *de trop*. I'd love to know where she spent the last two days, however.''

"She was at Tommy Hamilton's funeral on the West Coast this morning,'' Mike Roberts said, "looking as beautiful as ever, even on the small screen.''

"They didn't have any coverage on her yesterday,'' Murphy replied. "She sorta dropped out for a brief time. Maybe she was with Charlie.''

"Is that a joke?'' Roberts snapped.

"Not a good one,'' Murphy admitted. "You know Lawrence Newfield?''

"Not personally. He's the top man at Intercom."

"Charlie said Larry might be helping him with something. Any idea what?"

Roberts made a gesture of helplessness. "Newfield's been lobbying lately."

"For or against Lady X?"

"No involvement there that I know of," Roberts said. "He's been working hard to block the international trade bill."

"Who's he representing?"

"My God, Murph, don't you even read the papers? He's repping unions and manufacturers who want to levy an anti-Japan, anti-China, anti–unified Germany, anti-Russia, anti-every-goddamn-foreign-country-in-the-world tariff that could conceivably carry us back to colonial times. The problem with the spread of capitalism is that it makes this nation's manufacturers so very, very nervous."

"And friend Larry is waving the Buy American flag?"

"And practicing what he's been preaching," Roberts said. "I hear Intercom is dumping all of its executive Mercedes for Ford Probes."

Murphy scratched his jaw, gave in, and pantomimed an order for a salesgirl to box four eclairs. "The Larry I knew wouldn't change his lifestyle just for a principle."

"How well did you know him?" Roberts asked.

"How well? I once tried to shoot the son of a bitch in the head. But that was a long time ago, when the world was young and we were all pretty innocent. Today I'd aim for a more vulnerable spot."

39

◆

Los Angeles

◆

"We agree completely on everything, including the fact that we do not see eye to eye."

HENRY KISSINGER AND GOLDA MEIR

IT WAS ONE of the most eye-catching billboards Jake Alban had ever seen. Driving along Victory Boulevard in the San Fernando Valley—not the most colorful of land masses—he'd spotted it in the distance. Protruding from a shimmering black background were two gigantic, perfect bright pink lips in bas-relief. They were full and slightly parted, and he could almost hear them whisper "Lady Amber Cosmetics," which was the caption written in a comic strip balloon floating above them.

The billboard rose from the flat roof of a white and pink three-story building that contained offices and the reception area of Lady Amber, Inc. The building, like the others occupying the city block area of company property, appeared to date back to the WWII days, when stucco and wood trim were all the rage.

Spreading out from each side of the main building was a twelve-foot-high chain fence that encompassed the whole property. Jake circled the block to make sure. Then, satisfied that there were no rear entrances, he parked his rental car near the front building.

Except for its main door, the only other entry to the area was a drive-through gate, twenty yards away, guarded by a sentry wearing a uniform that was military with a touch of the millinery—an Army-like peak cap, severely starched short sleeve shirt, and short trousers, knee socks, and brown shoes. Shirt and trousers were khaki, the cap cover, the socks, and a holster at his side were the same shocking pink of the buildings and billboard lips.

Jake decided he would not be able to bluff his way past the gate. He'd have to try his luck at the front door.

It opened easily enough, offering a cool, breatheable respite from the tepid, smog-laden Valley air. Jake stepped into a small pink and white room. In front of him were two pebble-grain windows and a closed door. To the right was a reception nook with three pink chairs and a round coffee table on which rested an assortment of magazines and a stunted pink Christmas tree with white ornaments. There was the scent of magnolias in the air, though none in evidence.

Margaret Stafford was seated on one of the chairs, an open magazine on her lap.

One of the pebble-grain windows was lowered suddenly and a thin young woman asked, "Yes?"

Jake put on his most sincere smile and stepped forward. He almost whispered, "Thank you. I see my associate is already here." The receptionist raised her window and he turned and walked across the room to take a chair next to Margaret.

"Did I hear you say you were with me?" Margaret hissed.

"So you're a detective, huh," he said, ignoring her question. "Isn't that a rather tough job for a woman?"

"And you're working for Penelope Krim. Isn't that a tough job for a . . . man?"

The window dropped down. "Miss Stafford? What precisely is your title at the White House?"

"I assist the social secretary," Margaret replied without a moment's pause.

The receptionist asked, "And your associate?"

Margaret turned to Jake, frowning. "He's not—"

"I'm with White House Security," he cut in. "My name is Andrews. James Andrews."

"Thank you. Mrs. McNeil will see you in a moment."

The window lowered again. "White House?" Jake asked, rolling his eyes.

"You're not coming in there with me," Margaret said between clenched teeth.

"Oh, no, Miss Assistant Social Secretary?"

"If you screw this up for me, I'll kill you," she said, and it sounded to Jake as if she meant it.

A door across from them opened and a tall brunette wearing an orange silk dress and a bit too much makeup arrived to escort them to Amber Hall McNeil. Following her, Jake patted the breast pocket of his coat and was reassured to hear the rustle of paper. It was a surprise he had for later.

Amber's large, airy office was painted a soft off-white. It's wall-to-wall carpet was the signature pink. Still wearing the same black dress with white accents from the funeral, she was seated at a white desk with a side pedestal containing a pink computer. The walls were covered with reproductions of Lady Amber print ad campaigns under glass. The famous "Pink Fling" photo featuring the Lady Amber model dressed in bra and panties strolling nonchalantly through the Los Angeles Raiders' locker room. The "In the Pink," shot with the model, attired in an even briefer bra and bikini pants, walking her dog through the stock market during a frantic rally. The "Amber Is the Name, Pink Is the Color" page in which the model, nude, with crucial areas nearly covered, posed for an assortment of hunks pretending to be artists, but with their canvases noticeably blank.

In all of the illustrations, as in all of the Lady Amber ads, the model was the very same woman who was welcoming them to her office. Amber McNeil was incontestably Lady Amber. "Please sit down," she said with the hint of a Southern drawl, indicating a white sofa, "and tell me exactly what I can do for you."

Jake could have withdrawn the objects from his coat then, but he decided to wait and see what was on Margaret's agenda. He looked at her, wondering how she was prepared to answer Amber's question. She replied, straight-faced, "We want to make sure that your spa in D.C. at Rollingwood would be a proper place for a member of the First Family to . . . shape up a little."

"Well," Amber McNeil replied, "I may be a bit prejudiced, but

I happen to think that our facilities are the best this country offers.''

"Could you show us a little of your operation here?" Margaret asked.

Amber hesitated. "It's not terribly glamorous. And it won't give you much of an idea about what the spas are like."

"But it would let us know something about Lady Amber's efficiency," Margaret countered.

"I suppose we could take a short tour," Amber told them, rising from her chair.

She led them back through the main building, past the large office spaces filled with dozens of retail order processors seated at computer terminals, wearing telephone headsets, fingers clicking away at keyboards. Past a smaller cadre of wholesale order takers.

From there they went to a small bungalow where marketing decisions were made and from that to an identical bungalow where a handful of young men and women worked at drawing boards redesigning existing product containers and designing bottles and boxes for future products. Her employees seemed both surprised and intimidated by Amber's informal stroll-by.

At the rear of the lot was a two-story stucco building devoted to the spas. As Amber took them past reservations areas and design centers and a department labeled TERRITORY ACQUISITIONS, she gave them a brief history of the spas and their phenomenal growth, with special emphasis on the Rollingwood spa.

Watching the names of guests scroll by on the reservation screens, Margaret asked, "Can you guarantee privacy?"

Amber's sweet, rosebud face seemed to radiate health and sincerity. "We can and have used code names when necessary. Total privacy at the spa itself is possible, but that means that the program would be limited somewhat. There is a small, private gym that is available at Rollingwood, but it isn't quite as well equipped as our main gyms. The best way to achieve complete privacy would be for us to send a trainer to the White—to the client's place of residence on a regular schedule.''

"That's a possibility," Margaret said.

The tour moved swiftly through four huge, clean, automated

warehouses packed to the rafters with cosmetics. Then Amber directed them back to the main office.

"What's that building over there?" Margaret asked, pointing to the only structure that did not conform to the stucco bungalow architecture. It was a rectangular bunker with glazed windows slightly beyond the warehouses, partially hidden by shrubs.

"That's our New Products Lab."

"It sounds interesting," Jake said.

Amber raised her hands in a gesture of helplessness. "It's my husband's special place," she said. "Off-limits to just about everyone, including me. Over here are the company workout areas. You might find them interesting."

These were two connected bungalows that had been transformed into gyms. In the first, a combination exercise room and day care center, very young children were being taught simple gymnastics. In the other, several adults were being put through their paces by a sinewy blonde in spandex. "Put that butt in motion, Frank," she called out to a plump, perspiring fellow in his middle years. "You can bend more than that, Alice," she chided a pale thirtyish woman.

"This is Luna's domain," Amber informed them. "She's worked out schedules for every employee, and she also trains most of the young people who staff the spas."

Luna evidently knew her business, Jake thought, staring at her glistening body. There was something about her that seemed dimly familiar to him, but he couldn't imagine what. Nor could he imagine why Luna was looking their way with such obvious annoyance.

Apparently oblivious to this sole sign of employee pique, Amber whisked them through the company cafeteria, around an Olympic swimming pool that had been closed for repairs, past a laundry for workclothes and lab smocks, and finally into the cosmetician labs where experts passed along the secrets of the makeup game to hopeful young women and men eager for a career in Lady Amber's many salons.

On the return trip to the main building, as they walked past a car park area, Margaret slowed her pace until Jake and Amber were several yards ahead of her.

Jake noticed her absence a fraction of a second before Amber did. When they turned, Margaret was standing beside a car, adjusting her shoe. She joined them smiling innocently.

Back in Amber's office, Margaret continued to improvise her fanciful story about that certain White House occupant. "We must be very careful of our selection, you understand. In securing the services of Lady Amber, it's much the same as the First Family endorsing your company. And before we did that, we'd have to know a bit more about you."

"I understand your concern," Amber said, somber businesswoman now. Jake was amused to spy her eyes flicking to the "Pink Is the Color" ad where she appeared nude.

"We are aware of problems you've had," Margaret said.

"Problems?" Amber asked, eyebrows raised.

"Drugs at the Mexican spa," Margaret explained. Jake listened, fascinated, fingering the objects in his coat pocket.

"That was a while ago," Amber said. "It was taken care of immediately and it certainly did not reflect on the company in any way. We have more than a thousand employees nationwide and you can't expect us to be responsible for their individual failings away from the workplace."

"What about the potential difficulty?" Margaret asked.

"I'm not sure what you mean?"

"The tragic death of Tommy Hamilton," Margaret said innocently. "How will this impact on Lady Amber?"

"Tommy was an old friend, but I doubt his death will have any major effect on us."

"Wasn't he a majority stockholder?" Margaret asked.

There was a hard edge to Amber now. Before their eyes she was turning from figurehead to businesswoman. "He was never involved in the day-to-day operation of this company."

"Maybe his successor will be more hands-on."

Amber frowned, as if she hadn't considered the possibility. "We'll just have to see," she said.

"Is there anything about Lady Amber, past, present, or future, that might prove embarrassing to the White House should we proceed?"

"Definitely not."

Jake thought the time had come to break the ice. He hated to use pressure tactics, but sometimes they were all that were left. He said, "I understand you and Congresswoman Laura Christen used to be roommates."

"Yes," Amber said. "The Congresswoman was one of the co-developers of Lady Amber."

Jake took from his pocket several of the yellow receipts he'd lifted from the Lavery house before it was torched. "Do these mean anything to you, Mrs. McNeil?" he asked.

Margaret eyed him suspiciously.

Amber's china-blue eyes were guileless. "What are these?" she asked, then began to study them more carefully. "I really don't understand—"

"I got them from Darla Lavery," Jake said flatly, definitely not enjoying himself now. "I think you knew her as Darla Sullivan when you and she and Congresswoman Christen shared a house."

"Oh, my God!" Amber muttered almost to herself.

Margaret's glittering green eyes moved from her to Jake.

"Here's an entry," he said, reading from one of the receipts. " 'July 21, 1972. Fifty grams of c to P.K. in Room 407. Laura.' "

"We had no idea what we were doing," Amber said. "Gordon Lavery asked us to drop off packages for him. We had no idea what was in them."

"Were you and Laura Christen paid to deliver the packages?" he asked.

"Paid?" she asked, still dazed by the receipts. "Of course not. And when we found out what was going on, we went to Ivor Hamilton at once. He notified the police. It was all so long ago. . . ."

"What I'd like to do," Jake said, "is discuss this privately. I'm sure Miss Stafford would excuse us."

But Amber McNeil wasn't listening. "I don't understand the purpose of all . . . of course, this isn't about me at all. It's about Laura. You're doing some sort of dirty-trick number on her."

"No. Not at all," Jake said.

"Laura Christen is the finest woman I've ever known. That's all I have to say about it. Now get out of here." She reached over, balled the receipts in her hand, and threw them in Jake's face. "And take your trash with you."

Jake swallowed the bile that was gathering at the back of his throat. Amber turned to Margaret. "And you. Are you really from the White House? Is the President of the United States actually involved in a plan to destroy the reputation of Laura Christen? Have we reached a point where anytime a woman raises her voice politically, she immediately becomes the target of every sleazy—"

"Mrs. McNeil," Margaret said. "I don't know anything about what this man is saying. You must believe—"

"Get out, both of you."

Jake stood. "Mrs. McNeil, please forgive me. I handled this badly. It's not my intention to smear anybody. Not you, not Laura Christen. I just need some information—"

"Get out now!" Amber McNeil screamed, and pushed a button on her desk.

ON the sidewalk in front of the main building, Jake said to Margaret, "That went pretty well, don't you think?"

"I think you're either a sleazebag or an idiot and probably both," she said evenly. "But I'd like a look at those receipts."

"Are you suggesting an exchange of information?"

"My problem with that," she said, "is the loathsome bitch you work for. I won't betray my client confidences."

He nodded. "Whatever you tell me will be off the record. I don't feel compelled to pass along everything I find. I'm not trying to crucify your client."

"Who do you think my client is?" she said.

"Laura Christen."

Margaret shrugged noncommittally. "Let's see the papers."

The midday heat had still not subsided and the smog level had gone up. Jake suggested they continue their conversation in his air-conditioned car.

It took the car nearly five minutes to cool. By then Margaret had seen enough of the receipts. "Where'd you get 'em?" she asked.

Jake told her how his meeting with Amber's ex-husband had led to his being in the Lavery home when the arsonists arrived. He mentioned the woman's voice and described the stocky man in the double-breasted suit who'd been waiting beside the Mercedes. "I think he works for Lawrence Newfield's company, Intercom."

"Why?" Margaret asked, suddenly alert.

"Because he was driving a Mercedes with a personalized plate that read IC4. Your pal Newfield's Mercedes had plates reading IC1."

"How do you think Newfield fits in?"

"I don't know. He's based in Washington. Maybe he's not aware of what's going on out here. His man on the West Coast is a guy named Kerry Niles, who never seems to be around. I've been trying to find him ever since I got here."

Margaret digested the bits of information, then asked, "What do you want out of all this, a good story?"

He didn't reply at once. Then he said, "I was a writer once. A journalist. Then I had some bad luck. Now I've got another chance to get back to what I do best."

"So you're looking for a good story."

"Not even that. I'm just doing research."

"I see," she said. "You dig up the dirt and Penelope Krim dishes it out."

He didn't respond, because her statement was too accurate.

"What's she expect you to find out about Laura Christen?"

Should I tell her? Jake wondered. *Would it hurt Laura or help her? And which do I want to do?*

"It has to do with a gossip columnist who died of a heart attack in D.C. Jeremy Dunbar. Shortly before his death he was sent a poison pen letter about Laura Christen having an illegitimate child."

"How do you know?"

"Somehow Penelope got hold of it," Jake said. "And that's the story I'm trying to prove. Or disprove."

"Have you found any proof?"

He shook his head.

"And you say this Dunbar died of a heart attack?"

He nodded. "Unless the D.C. Metro Police have decided otherwise. Penelope says the coroner is still withholding his official report." When Margaret remained silent at this news, he continued, "Judging from what I heard at the Lavery house, Darla and her husband probably sent the note to Dunbar."

She nodded impatiently, as if that information wasn't new.

"Your turn," Jake said. "Have you heard anything about Tommy Hamilton having a thing about very young girls?"

"No. Why?"

Jake described the conversations he'd overheard. "Could the man and woman in Tommy Hamilton's office have been the Laverys?" she asked.

He shook his head. "They didn't sound anything like them."

She shrugged. "Well, thanks for the information," she said and opened the car door.

"Hold on! What about our deal?" he shouted.

"Considering what you just put me through with Amber McNeil, I figure we're even," she told him. "In any case this is my day for backing down on deals. Especially with people who peddle gossip."

He watched her run to her automobile, start it up, and drive away. He made no attempt to follow her. He had no heart for it. She'd nailed him with the "gossip" crack. That's exactly what he was peddling. He didn't like what he was doing. During the years he'd been writing his insipid as-told-to's, a change seemed to have taken place in the profession of journalism. He wasn't so sure he wanted to be a part of it anymore.

40

◆

Washington

◆

"It is the function of vice to keep virtue
within reasonable bounds."

SAMUEL BUTLER

THE SUN HAD not quite set when Catsy Braden entered her apartment building. She scooped up her mail, mainly bills, and was
unlocking the lobby door when she heard the outer door whoosh
open behind her. She turned to find Detective Skinner staring at
her. "Well," she said, "is that a gun in your pocket, Detective, or
are you just glad to see me?"

Skinner looked uncomfortable. He said, formally, "Good evening, Mrs. Braden." Then he stepped aside to make room for his
partner, Detective Gabriel. The small, dapper black man looked
briefly from Skinner to Catsy and nodded.

"Mrs. Braden," he said, "we have been trying to reach you and
the Congresswoman by phone."

Catsy had told the receptionist at the office to tell Gabriel she
was out. "We've been working so hard," she said. "And then
Mother felt she had to go to the funeral in Los Angeles."

"In Los Angeles," Detective Gabriel repeated, giving the words
his odd lilt. "Yes, we know she is there, but not precisely where
in that city. We have phoned her home, her California offices.
They have no knowledge of her whereabouts."

"I spoke to her earlier today. She'll be in Washington shortly," Catsy said.

"We thought that with her being unavailable, you might be of some assistance," Gabriel said.

"I hope you haven't been waiting outside for too long," Catsy said, though in fact she didn't care if they'd been out there since breakfast.

"An hour or so," he said. "But our days have been so long since the murder of Jeremy Dunbar, the wait was recuperative. Might we come in, please?"

Should she refuse? She did not think they could follow her in without a warrant. But why not cooperate? "Sure," she said. "Come on in."

Once inside the apartment, neither man would take off his coat or accept a drink. Skinner was so tense that she began toying with him, striking poses similar to the ones she had struck, nude, for him the last time he was there.

Gabriel sat on the edge of his chair, knees together. He asked, "Mrs. Braden, am I correct in thinking that you knew the deceased Mr. Dunbar?"

"I may have met him once or twice. I certainly knew who he was," Catsy said. "He was rather infamous."

"Oh?" Gabriel's ears almost perked up.

"He was careless, always being sued for inaccuracies."

Gabriel stared at her, his dark eyes searching for something. He said, "You seem tired, Mrs. Braden."

"I am. My days are long."

"Mine, too. I wonder if I might use your facility," he said.

"Of course," she said. She stood and showed him the door leading to the bathroom and the bedroom. When he had shut it behind him, she turned to Skinner. Before she could speak, he shook his head and mouthed the word "Later."

When Gabriel returned, he did not sit down. Skinner and Catsy both stood up, too. Gabriel asked, "Could you tell us when we might converse with the Congresswoman?"

"She'll be at work tomorrow," Catsy said. "I'm sure she'll make time to see you. Could I tell her what it would be about?"

"The late Mr. Dunbar, of course," Gabriel said. "Perhaps you yourself could give us some idea of the extent of his relationship with Congresswoman Christen?''

"Relationship? They had no relationship. She talked with him briefly at her press conference. That's about it.''

"Ah,'' Gabriel exclaimed, as if satisfied. "Fine. We would still wish to speak with the Congresswoman. Shall we say tomorrow at three?''

"If she's in town,'' Catsy said. "I'll phone you tomorrow to confirm.''

Detective Gabriel shrugged his thin shoulders and shifted his overcoat so that it hugged his back and collar perfectly. He thanked Catsy for her cooperation.

Skinner waited until his superior had stepped into the hall. He turned and tapped his wristwatch. Then he opened and closed his fingers into a fist twice, nodded, and said, "Be seeing you, Mrs. Braden.''

He was back in ten minutes. Catsy was not overly affectionate. Just a peck on the cheek. He was disappointed. "Can I get you a drink?'' she asked wearily.

"Not if you're not having one,'' he said. He sat on the couch and indicated that she should join him. She was careful not to sit too close. She didn't want to start anything. She had to get back to the office.

"What was that all about?'' she asked.

"You've got to watch out around the Cockroach,'' he said. When she looked bewildered, he explained. "Gabriel. You know how cockroaches are, you can't get rid of 'em. They're too sneaky. That's Gabriel, all right.''

"What's he want?''

"We, uh, talked to some people over where Dunbar worked,'' Skinner said. "This secretary says he got a letter of some kind about your mother. He didn't tell her what it was about, just that he was gonna show it to Congresswoman Christen at her press conference and see what effect it would have.''

Catsy remembered her mother's concern about a letter. "Have you found it?'' she asked.

"What? Oh, the letter, you mean. No. The secretary says he took it with him. But it wasn't on his body. That suddenly makes it very important. So the Cockroach wants to ask your mother about it. Tomorrow at three. I'd make sure she keeps the appointment. The Cockroach looks sort of meek and laid-back, but he does not screw around.''

''You guys waited out front for over an hour just to get an appointment to see my mother?''

''No,'' Skinner said, staring at her. ''We stayed outside because we didn't have a search warrant. We were waiting for you to invite us in.''

''I still don't understand,'' Catsy said.

''We got a report that you had drugs in your apartment,'' Skinner said, enjoying her look of surprise. ''Now, we don't give a good goddamn if you stick anything up your nose, but if we find some dope up here, then that would cut through a lot of bullshit. We could hold it over your head and get you and your mother to stop waltzing us around about Dunbar. That's the way the Cockroach works. I told you he was a sneaky son of a bitch. He didn't have to go to the toilet. He was searching your bathroom and bedroom.''

Catsy was thinking about Penelope Krim, not kindly. ''Poor little Cockroach,'' she said. ''All that waiting in vain.''

''I could have told him,'' Skinner said. ''I know what gets you high, and it ain't drugs. But what would make me so smart? So I had to sit out in the goddamn car, listening to his goddamn singsong. So am I gonna get laid now, or what?''

''I just came home to take a shower. I have to go back out.''

''Date?'' he asked, too casually.

''No,'' she replied truthfully. ''Working dinner. I thought the shower might wake me up.''

''I want to get laid. You want a shower. Let's kill two birds.''

Catsy figured she owed him at least that much.

41

◆

> "Women sometimes forgive those who force an opportunity, never those who miss it."
>
> TALLEYRAND

AS MARGARET APPROACHED her hotel's front desk, the clerk, a weary-looking man whose complexion was not complemented by the gray pinstripe blazer he was forced to wear, notified her that a gentleman was waiting for her in the Fundebar Lounge. That the name was a tacky play on the German word *wunderbar* was evident as soon as Margaret entered the lounge with its heavy carved furniture, Black Forest murals, and Prussian ambience.

She thought for one terrible moment that Larry Newfield had tracked her down, but it was Wagner Mills who was seated at the bar, discussing imported beer with the bartender, a solid, ancient-looking man with a Franz Joseph moustache, soup bowl haircut, and a Heidelberg scar, possibly genuine, rising a half inch from his upper lip.

Wagner, the Fundebar's sole customer, was dressed in a tan camel's hair sport coat, cocoa slacks, and a piqué shirt buttoned to the neck. A large brown envelope rested on the bar beside his half-filled pilsner glass.

"Ah, Margaret," Wagner welcomed her, stepping away from the bar. "Can I get Hermann, here, to pour you a Dortmunder?"

"Sure," she said. "Driving in this heat can build a thirst. Been waiting long?"

"Not long. I could have just left this for you"—he handed her the envelope—"but I wanted to discuss the lab report." He lifted their two glasses of beer from the bar and carried them to a table in the corner of the room.

She opened the envelope and discovered a stack of photocopies—newspaper articles concerning the arrest of Gordon Lavery and his wife, Darla Sullivan. She shuffled past them to a computer printout from Thurston Labs. Margaret looked it over. "What does this tell me?" she asked.

"The analysis of my blood chemistry disclosed small amounts of methyltestosterone and strychnine, which my doctor tells me are used to reverse the effects of impotence. They are available in a number of brand-name remedies like Maintain."

"What's this second analysis?" she asked, indicating an additional printout.

"Because of the bump on my wrist, I assumed that the drug was administered there. It would have had to be injected through my French cuff. So I had them run a test on the shirt cuff, too. They discovered a section containing a third element and one that was probably absorbed in my bloodstream. Yohimbine. It acts in conjunction with the other two to form a considerably more potent stimulant. If my sleeve hadn't soaked up so much of the dose, it could have resulted in a stroke."

"Or a heart attack," Margaret added.

"Or that."

"What about this?" She read a headline on one of the photocopied pages. "This 'Two Arrested in Drug Raid'? Hot stuff?"

"Indeed. But no mention of anyone we know except the Laverys. No political person. No cosmetics chairwoman."

"Not even as witnesses?"

He shook his head.

Margaret stood up, draining her glass of beer. "Thanks, Wagner. I'm sorry about all this mess."

"So am I, dear. I think we should both walk very carefully for a while."

"Yes," she agreed. "I've come to that same conclusion myself. Unfortunately I've got one more very risky errand to run."

"Shall I assist?"

She shook her head. "This is the sort of thing I was trained to do alone."

42

◆

Washington

◆

"The public weal requires that men should betray, and lie, and massacre."

MONTAIGNE

AT THE EARLY dinner at his niece's home Murphy had consumed too much wine, probably too much filet mignon, and definitely too much pastry. Driving back to his home in the overheated car, sleet blurring the windshield, feeling bloated and chilled and depressed, he decided to stop off at the agency to perform a task he could no longer avoid.

As he walked down the shadowy hall away from his office he was amazed how spongy the carpet felt when you couldn't get a good look at it. He turned a corner and was surprised to see a rectangle of light against a far wall.

He walked toward it and found Pat Arthur in his cubicle, surrounded by telephone books, staring at the phone, ashen.

"Well, Patrick," Murphy said, causing the youth to jump, "burnin' a little midnight oil?"

Pat stared at him guiltily. "I . . . I just did something stupid, I think," Pat said. Murph looked at him questioningly and the young man continued. "It's that guy you were looking for, Lester Radin."

"What makes you think I've been looking for a Lester Radin?"

208

"A woman from the DMV who phoned. She located a New Mexico driver's license in the name of Lester Radin."

"She phoned you?"

"No, sir. She phoned you, but Nina wasn't around and the phone was ringing when I walked by, so I answered it. Anyway, Nina helped me run the name through a bunch of city directories, but I didn't come up with the match until about twenty minutes ago."

"Good work. Did you give the number a try?"

"Yes," Pat Arthur said. "Just now. This guy answered and said he was with the Las Cruces police, that Lester Radin had committed suicide only a couple of hours ago. He wanted to know who I was. And that's when I did the dumb thing . . . I just hung up."

"It was the right thing to do."

"Really?"

"You don't want to get yourself involved in a suicide you know nothing about," Murphy said, relaying the information through his mind. "When did you say that call came in from the DMV?"

"This morning," Pat said. "I spent most of the day nailing down the town."

"The address should have been on the license."

"Yeah, but it was out of date. It had him in Albuquerque, and he'd moved from there years ago."

Murphy stared at the floor for a beat, then asked, "You gonna be here much longer?"

"If you need me," Pat said eagerly.

"Naw. Let's both call it a night."

"Go ahead," Pat Arthur told him. "I'll close up here. Nina showed me the security system combination."

Glumly, Murph retreated down the dark hall to his office and dialed Nina's home number. She didn't sound happy to hear from him. "What do you need, Murph?"

"Something the matter, Nina?"

"The building's TV cable has frozen or blown away or something and I'm missing the last third of *Citizen Kane*."

"No problem," he said. " 'Rosebud' is the guy's wife. Now let's move on to something a little more serious. You know that I have nothing but the highest regard for your feelings about things.

What does your keen insight tell you about Pat Arthur? Is he for real?''

She was silent for a minute. Then she said very carefully, "He's almost too rah-rah . . . you know?''

"Yeah, I know. But did he bug my office?''

"I wouldn't go that far. But I don't feel comfortable around him.''

"Then why did you give him the security lock combination?''

"Why did I do *what?*''

"You didn't?''

Her indignation turned to anger. "Mr. Murphy, you know very well I wouldn't do something like that without asking you.''

"Sorry to bother you, Nina. My best to Citizen Kane and his missus," he said, replacing the receiver.

He sat at his desk for a while, staring at the wall. Then with a groan, he slowly got to his feet and dragged himself into the reception area. He picked up his damp topcoat from the couch where he'd tossed it upon entering and shuffled out into the cold, wet night.

He dialed Margaret's hotel in Los Angeles from a restaurant-bar on M Street. While waiting to get through to her he saw the wife of a senator he knew heading in the direction of the ladies' room. She didn't make it. A young waiter with olive skin and curly hair met her in the alcove. The senator's wife, a bit tipsy, grabbed his arm, pulled him to her, and kissed him. Murphy moved farther into the phone area and prayed they wouldn't see him. He sighed unhappily. It was getting so that there was hardly anybody in Washington you could look in the eye without blinking.

The couple disappeared through a doorway to the right just as Margaret lifted her receiver. Her first question was to ask if he was drunk. "Merely disenchanted," he replied. "We've got a quisling in our midst, Meg." He told her about Pat Arthur's overeagerness, the listening devices, Pat's explanation for knowing the combination to the office security system, and Nina's denial.

"You have two choices," Margaret told him. "You can fire him or keep him on to find out who's behind him."

"Aw, Jesus, but I hate this sort of thing."

"How seriously have we been compromised?"

"Enough to have cost somebody his life."

"Who?" Margaret demanded.

"Lester Radin, the guy you tell me did in la Christen's husband in that car accident. My friend at the DMV called in his approximate location this morning. Now it appears the poor sod has gone and got rid of himself, just hours ago. I am not happy about the timing." He paused. "I wonder what Radin might have told us that was that important?"

"Maybe he wasn't responsible for the crash," she said. "Maybe it was Christen's car that went out of control."

"Then why did Radin run?" Murph asked.

"Because he was paid to."

"By whom?"

"Let's save that for later," she said. "Right now I want to lay a few things on you that are a bit more pressing." When they'd talked earlier, she hadn't told him about the drugs or the child born out of wedlock or the probably connected death of the Washington gossip columnist. She spun that yarn now, adding the details of the confrontation with Amber McNeil. She ended with the Wagner Mills lab report.

For once in his life, J. B. Murphy was speechless. Finally, he croaked, "Jay-sus, but I need a drink. Murder, sex, drugs, blackmail. And in the middle of it all, a fine-looking congresswoman. Maybe it's time for me to retire from this goat's nest."

He paused while the senator's wife and her waiter surfaced again, adjusting their clothes. "So soon?" Murphy muttered.

"What?" Margaret's voice asked in his ear.

"Sorry. Just part of the passing parade on this end." He rubbed the back of his neck, but it didn't help the stiffness settling in. He said, "With all this stuff flying, I'm inclined to tell Mike Roberts to cut the lady loose."

"Not just yet," Margaret said. "The way I see it, all she did was get herself a little too much publicity with her announcement about replacing the Speaker of the House. That lured the Laverys out from under their rock. They tried to put the bite on her, and when she refused, they started spreading rumors about her."

"But how did they know where to address those rumors?" he

asked. "Mike Roberts got his letter before there was any public announcement that he was getting behind her."

"I haven't figured that out yet," Margaret said.

"Then there's the bottom line," Murphy said. "Do the Laverys' claims have substance?"

"So far we only know about two of them," she said. "Mike Roberts' letter mentioned tainted money. If it has any validity, it's probably a reference to the money she took out of Lady Amber. But when she took the money, she disassociated herself from the company. A long time ago. I don't get it."

"What about the letter that Penny Krim seems so vitally interested in?" Murphy inquired.

"It may have some basis," she said. "But, assuming that the Laverys are the ones telling this tale, the baby would have been born sometime around 1972 or 1973. That's a long time to keep a child a secret."

"What do I tell Mike?" Murphy asked.

"Stall him. I'm going back to Lady Amber for a look around."

He opened his mouth but censored himself. She took his silence as concern. "Don't worry, Murph." Her voice was arch. "I take care of myself."

"Sure you do, Meg. You eat well and you have a good suspicious nature and you're sound of mind and body. But your impatience gets the better of you some—"

"I'll watch that," she cut in, proving his point. Then she called his name in a softer voice.

"Yeah, kid?"

"Tell me about Larry Newfield?"

Murphy felt a sudden chill. "What do you want to know?"

"I met him this morning, at the funeral. I was wondering what you thought of him."

"What was he doing at the funeral?" he asked without a trace of his usual playfulness.

"His company, Intercom, handles publicity for Hamilton Resorts," she said. "For Lady Amber, too."

"That's certainly interesting," Murphy said. "One of my last conversations with Charlie Stern was about Larry. He's apparently on the inside of something rather dicey."

"I'm not interested in what Charlie Stern has to say about him. What do *you* say? Were he and Dad good friends?"

"Your father got along with everybody," he told her. "I suppose he tolerated Larry well enough. But friends? I wouldn't say that, exactly. And he surely wasn't foolish enough to offer Larry his back."

She was silent for a moment. Then she said, "That's the general impression I got. Only I don't think he was interested in my back."

"You'll do well to go with your instincts, Meg," he told her. "You've got what it takes. It's in your genes."

He replaced the phone feeling ancient and depressed. A spy in the office. Larry Newfield going after Meg in L.A. Too many heart attacks to be believed. And Laura Christen was looking very tainted. It had not been a good day.

He didn't know it, but there was worse to come.

43

◆

Los Angeles

◆

"A pessimist is a man who thinks all
women are bad. An optimist is one who
hopes they are."

CHAUNCEY DEPEW

JAKE HAD SPENT nearly an hour trying to reach Penelope Krim in
Washington to pick her brain for information about Theo Koriallis.
But Penelope seemed to be among the missing. Not at the syndicate. Not at her home. Her assistant, Louise, said she'd been acting
mysteriously all morning, even humming to herself.

Not caring enough to speculate on the reason for Penelope's
behavior, he otherwise occupied his thoughts by sorting through
Darla Lavery's drug receipts, counting the number of times
"Laura" made deliveries. None of the packages were sent to a
"T.K.," which did not mean that Koriallis was on the side of the
angels, only that his relationship with Laura probably had nothing
to do with the Laverys' drug trade. Jake wanted to believe Amber
McNeil's story that she and Laura were innocent of the contents of
the packages. But there were nearly fifty slips carrying their
names. He wondered what had become of the other messengers.
Had they, too, achieved a degree of fame and were now paying
Darla and her husband for their silence?

Another, more important question: What should he do with the
receipts? They would obviously send Penelope into paroxysms of

delight. But he didn't want to hand them over to her. Still, that was the job he was paid to do, and the censoring of information was precisely what he hated most about his "as-told-to" autobiographies.

Annoyed by this moral dilemma and bored with the confinement of his hotel room, he put the receipts back into a folder and tossed it onto his bed. He threw cold water from the bathroom tap on his face, then headed for the hotel's garage to pick up his car.

HE'D expected the Lady Amber offices to be nearly deserted, but the nightshift was just arriving. He cruised past the bustling auto gate and drove down a side street, parking at the rear of the fenced area. He left the car and began slowly and carefully to examine every foot of fence. There had to be a way onto the grounds other than past the guards.

He circled the area twice and had convinced himself that Lady Amber's security was simply too tight when he spotted a familiar figure inside the compound. Looking through the chain links of the fence, he felt a mixture of frustration and admiration as Margaret Stafford exited the laundry area. Garbed in a white smock and carrying a clipboard, she strode purposefully toward the ultrasecret New Products Lab as if she owned the place.

44

♦

"With almost all doctors, population experts, and drug manufacturers male, is it really a surprise that oral contraceptives were designed for women to take and men to promote?"

ELLEN FRANKFORT

MARGARET STAFFORD HAD arrived at Lady Amber at twilight. The guard at the gate had barely glanced at the employee pass she'd lifted from the dash of a parked car while on Amber's tour.

She'd wedged her rental into an empty space among the other employee cars, then gone directly to the laundry, where she tried on several soiled white smocks until she found one that fit.

There was a clipboard hanging on a hook by the laundry door that she took along as a prop. By then, night had officially fallen. The glow of a dimly lighted window drew her to the rear of the tantalizingly secret New Products Building.

A cement path took her within three feet of the light. It was filtered through a glazed window that was open a few inches from the sill, too narrow for anything or anybody to be seen. She thought the glow might be coming from a night-light in the empty lab.

Except that it suddenly went out.

She looked down at the white smock, which was nearly glowing in the moonlight. What had been protective coloring was now exactly what she didn't need. In the semiprivacy of a shadowy tree, she removed the smock, folding it carefully and placing it on the ground, covered by the clipboard.

Considerably less conspicuous, she approached the now-darkened window. She listened. Did she hear breathing? She couldn't be sure. Slowly, she circled the building.

As she rounded the rear corner, she heard a woman scream. She stopped and listened. Night sounds. Distant traffic. Branches scraping. Faraway laughter carried on the still air. And a thumping inside the lab.

She moved closer. *Thump-thump-thump.* Something pounding against the back wall. Then another short scream, and a prolonged moan. Margaret grinned in the darkness. Someone was getting laid in the lab.

It would be only a short time before the deed was done. Safely in shadow, she sat down with her back to the building and waited.

In a matter of minutes she heard loud gasps and the thumping stopped. She got to her feet and pressed an ear against the exterior wall. Conversation inside, but she couldn't understand a word of it.

The light was turned on. Margaret went in search of the lab coat. She took it and the clipboard to a dark, concealed spot under the branches of an oak tree just to the right of the lab. From there she could keep an eye on both the front and rear doors. She doubted that the lovers would be leaving by a window.

Another few minutes went by and the rear door opened. A woman was outlined clearly as she stepped into the night. Luna, Lady Amber Inc.'s physical culturist. Her sinewy body was wrapped in a white cotton warm-up outfit.

A man joined her at the door. George McNeil, Amber's husband, grinning sheepishly. He closed the door behind them and locked it.

They left, passing within feet of Margaret's hiding place.

When they were no longer in her line of sight, she put on the lab coat and, carrying the clipboard, approached the lab's front door. Using a pliable plastic strip, the kind that was being whipped around the wrist of every kid in America, she slipped the lock.

She stepped into a dimly lighted room and paused, senses acute, hearing only the sound of her own heartbeat. The space contained file drawers and cabinets and a desk that was bare except for an ivory phone.

Two doors led from the room. One took her into a small half-bathroom with a toilet and basin, the other to a large lab that smelled of chlorine and something equally pungent but unidentifiable. She removed a small flash from her pocket and used it to get a sense of her surroundings. In the subdued spotlight of its red bulb, a long counter stood like an island in the center of the room. At the far end of the counter were four gas burners and, hovering over them, an assortment of beakers and bottles. Nearer to her was a deep metal sink surrounded by a laminate countertop covered with jars and more bottles.

Against the back wall was a convertible black leather couch that had been hastily remade, a bit of bed linen poking from between one of its folds. Next to the couch was a wooden chair with a small bottle resting on its seat, uncorked.

Margaret walked past the couch and the back door to a bare wall broken only by a framed advertisement. In it, Amber Hall McNeil, clad in bra and panties, shared the stage with a symphony orchestra whose tuxedoed and bearded conductor was pointing his baton at her with a broad smile on his face. She was standing in the solo spot, placing a lipstick to her lips. The caption read: ''You and Lady Amber, Such Lovely Music.''

Margaret poked the frame. It was secured to the wall, top and bottom, but it slid to the right, exposing the ugly steel face of a safe. Margaret frowned at it. She was hopeless at safecracking.

She slid the frame back into place and was reaching for the uncorked bottle when she heard the key at the back door. There was no time to do anything but drop down beside the counter in the center of the room.

George McNeil entered, flicked on the light, and walked to the chair near the couch. Margaret held her breath while he picked up the bottle, corked it, and carried it to the counter.

Doubled over, Margaret was putting too much pressure on her damaged hip and was afraid her leg would collapse. And, in another second, McNeil would see her. She decided to take the offensive and stood up.

McNeil made an ''Ah'' sound and stumbled backward. Margaret simply looked at him, saying nothing. It was a few seconds before he could get himself under control enough to demand indignantly, "Who the hell are you? And what are you doing in here?"

Margaret didn't reply.

Taken in by the white smock, McNeil got tough. "What department are you in, young woman?"

"How long have you been sleeping around on your wife?"

He paled and teetered slightly. "What the devil are you talking about?"

"I saw you," she said. "And heard you. Luna's a screamer, isn't she?"

"It's none of your damned business."

"Maybe it is," Margaret said, unzipping the lab coat and draping it on the couch. "Maybe I've been hired to find out what you've been up to here in the lab at night."

He paled even more and a tic developed under the pouch of his right eye. "Hired by whom?"

"I'm not at liberty to say."

"Oh, God, you're another of Kerry's people, aren't you?"

She stared at him blankly.

"Well, you misinterpreted what you saw," he said. "Ask Luna. Luna will tell you. I was testing the new sample."

She laughed. "Is that what you call it?"

"Really," he said, holding out the bottle. "It was a test. Honestly."

Margaret took it from him, held it to the light. The liquid in the bottle seemed clear. "What is it?" she asked.

"Don't you know?"

"Kerry doesn't tell me everything."

"It's something new. A variation on our Love Potion No. 9," George McNeil said with a straight face.

"Oh, please."

"Really," he said, defending his invention. "It actually . . . aids . . . romance."

"It works like a charm," she said with a wink, "judging by what I could hear through the wall."

His cheeks turned red. He reached out a hand for the bottle, but Margaret placed it on the counter instead. "What's in the safe?" she asked casually. "More love juice?"

He turned his head toward the framed advertisement, then back to Margaret.

She moved across the room and pushed the frame back. "Open it up for me."

"You're not working for Kerry, are you?"

"What's the difference? I caught you and Luna in the sack. That should give me a little leverage."

He sat down on the couch and shook his head from side to side morosely. "I can't imagine who would care whom I sleep with."

"Not even your wife?"

"Amber? She lost all respect for me when this whole mess began."

"What whole mess?"

He looked up at her. "Who are you?"

"I'm not here to cause you any more grief," she said. "I may even help. Tell me what's in the safe."

"I can't. They don't trust me with the combination."

"Who's *they?*"

He ran a hand across his forehead and made no reply.

Margaret frowned. "Sooner or later the police are going to ask you questions tougher than these."

He gave her a stricken look, got up unsteadily, and crossed the room. Standing before the sink, he twisted the tap, wet his hands and patted his eyelids with damp fingers.

"Who are you?" he asked again. "My God, you're probably with *them,* after all. This is some sort of additional torment. Just tell me what the hell you want."

"Who owns Lady Amber?" she asked.

His face twisted into a rueful smile. "Amber and I. We are . . . the parties responsible. On paper at least."

"According to all records, the only other participant involved in Lady Amber is Hamilton Resorts International."

"That's correct," he said bitterly.

Margaret picked up the bottle and uncorked it. "Then the crucial question seems to be, who owns HRI?"

He shook his head. "I . . . I don't know the specific names, only that they are . . . despicable people."

"Who's Kerry?" Margaret asked.

"Kerry Niles. He works for them. He's . . . a bully, a vicious, awful hoodlum."

She sniffed the bottle's contents. The odor of sandalwood filled her head and caused her chest to tingle. She held out the bottle. "What's in this . . . love potion?" she demanded.

"A combination of things that produces a mild aphrodisiac effect. Lowers inhibitions. Heightens the sexual urge. It won't turn hatred to love, but if a person were to be interested in another party, that interest could be vastly enhanced."

"What's it do to your appetite?"

He gave her a wan smile. "That's what I thought I was working on—something that would enhance the taste of healthy food. But that proved to be of only secondary interest to *them.*"

Margaret felt anger rising inside her. "What's the main ingredient?" she asked between tightened lips.

"I . . . I'm not sure that I should be—"

She smashed the bottle against the metal sink, shattering the glass and splashing away its contents.

"Look, Georgie," she said, trying her damnedest to sound tough, "I'm fed up with you and your damn experiments that mess around with human emotions. *What's the ingredient?*"

Margaret's intensity fully unnerved McNeil. He stared from her to the broken glass. "It's a form of the drug Mazindol."

"What kind of drug is it?"

"An anorexiant."

"A diet pill?" she asked, doubtfully.

"Sort of. But it also has the effect of stimulating nerve receptors."

"And what's in that safe you can't open?" she asked. "An industrial-strength version of this? Or maybe a lethal version of its brother drug, Maintain?"

"I don't even know," he said in despair. "They have their own chemists and lab technicians. They come in, demand or take whatever they need from my notes and files, and do what they wish. I'm not even allowed to observe them. They own the goddamn place, don't you understand? I'm here at their whim."

She didn't bother to ask him again who *they* were. She knew as soon as she sniffed the Mazindol cocktail. As she headed for the

door, George McNeil said, "Don't make any more trouble—
please."

She offered him no such assurance, merely stepped through the
rear door and closed it behind her. She took a deep breath and let
it out. Trespassing. Breaking and entering. Industrial espionage. If
George McNeil had called in his security guards, they would have
begun with those charges and gone on from there. But she'd
mau-maued him and won.

Humming to herself and feeling rather smug, she started down
the cement walk toward the parking area. A figure stepped from
the shadows.

It was Luna, and she had a Walther 9 millimeter automatic in her
hand.

"Hello, Margaret," she said. "Time for the pros to take over."

LUNA marched her away from the parked cars, toward the un-
developed wooded area at the back of the compound. The night air
suddenly felt heavy and gritty against Margaret's face and arms.

Occasionally Luna would give a direction, but otherwise she
was silent until they approached the high wire fence that marked
the rear of the area. Then she told Margaret to turn around. Luna
held the gun steadily in her right hand, as if she were used to its
being there. She said, "Now I want you to climb up that fence,
Margaret."

"How do you know my name?"

"Margaret Stafford. You live at 1223 Rock Creek Park Road in
Washington. You were born in Quantico, Virginia on March 3,
1968, while your father was off somewhere near the DMZ in South
Vietnam. You're a private investigator licensed in the District of
Columbia. You've a one-inch scar on your upper right thigh and
you're a registered Democrat. We know quite a lot about you,
Margaret." Luna smiled slyly. "March 3. An Aries," she said.
"Tough, assertive. But no match for Gemini!" She gestured with
the gun. "Now go ahead. Climb, Margaret."

Only in L.A., Margaret thought, would you find an assassin who
was interested in your astrology sign. She looked at the wire fence
and wondered if it was electric. No, that was a bit too dramatic for

just a cosmetics company in the San Fernando Valley. Except, of course, that Lady Amber was considerably more than that. . . .

Luna jammed the barrel of the gun into her right kidney. Margaret gasped, then put one cautious hand on the wire fence. There was no instant, deadly jolt, so she relaxed slightly. "What now?" she asked. "I get to the top and you shoot me as a prowler?"

"You *are* a prowler, Margaret," Luna said. "But there's always the chance I might miss. You might get lucky—like you did the other night on Hollywood Boulevard."

"You pushed me?"

"That was me," Luna said proudly. "Now climb!"

Margaret hesitated, then put one reluctant toe into the chain link about three feet from the ground and stepped up. It was an easy climb to the top, where four strands of barbed wire had been stretched. She didn't think Luna would let her get that far.

"Did you try to run me off the road in Aspen?" she asked, looking over her shoulder at Luna and trying to gain time.

Luna merely stared at her. No reaction. Nothing else on her mind. "In a way," Luna finally said. "I was not there—but I was. Gemini."

Deadly and demented. A bad combination. Margaret realized that she had to pretend to obey Luna's orders. She would take one more giant step, as far up as she could, pause, then push off backward and hope. Her father hadn't raised her to submit to fate.

She pulled herself up and dug her fingers and toes into the links. Behind her, she heard Luna say, "Goodbye, Margaret."

Suddenly a car roared down the street that ran parallel with the fence. When it was abreast of them it made an abrupt turn and braked, pinning them in its headlights.

Already tensed and ready, Margaret launched herself with all her strength. In her short, awkward backward flight she connected solidly and heard Luna's grunt of rage as they fell to the ground, Margaret on top.

The car lights spotlighted the scene.

Margaret twisted around, rolled clear of her opponent's flailing arms, and got to her feet. Luna, momentarily stunned, was on her knees, scrambling for the Walther that she'd dropped.

Margaret kicked it away. With a snarl, Luna hopped upright,

using only the force of her legs. It was quite a stunt—Margaret was impressed. Then the car lights went out. Luna didn't even glance in their direction. Nostrils flaring, she slowly circled Margaret, who imagined she could see the woman's formidable muscles bunching, then relaxing, under the loose workout suit. She waited as Luna approached on the balls of her feet, bouncing slightly. Luna's right hand shot out, fingers pointed toward Margaret's eyes. Margaret shifted her weight sideways but Luna unexpectedly pivoted on one foot and slammed the other against Margaret's injured hip.

Margaret yelped and fell back against the fence. Luna pranced back and forth a few feet away, certain now of victory. Margaret held out her hand, palm up, apparently a bid for mercy.

"Aries," Luna said contemptuously, then turned her back briefly and stooped down for the gun.

Margaret saw her chance and again threw herself onto Luna. The two women grappled in the dirt and dried leaves, reverting to a fighting style that soon was devoid of the usual martial arts techniques. They fought silently until fatigue, pain, and the hot, smoggy night air began to wear them down.

Panting, Margaret was the first to break their embrace, crawling away to assess the damage as Luna lay motionless but alert, watching.

Dirt-filled scratches covered Margaret's naked shoulders and arms, and her slacks and blouse were in shreds. But nothing seemed to be broken. The pain in her hip was excruciating. She was too exhausted to run.

Luna was gradually regaining her strength. There was a wide gash on her forehead and the blood was partially blinding her. Her clothes had fared better than Margaret's, but she was favoring her right foot.

Margaret knew that Luna was stronger, and in better physical condition, but she hadn't been trained in close combat by professional soldiers. That had been another of her legacies, like the half ownership of the agency.

She took a deep, cleansing breath, fluttered her eyelids, blanked her mind to pain, and attacked. Luna immediately assumed a defensive, half-standing crouch, right fist back and clenched, left arm positioned slightly forward, favoring her injured foot. Margaret stopped, waited for her to take a short, awkward step backward, then feinted sideways and threw herself against Luna's knees, sending her onto her back. Margaret pressed the advantage, pinning her arms. Then she pushed Luna's head back and reached for her throat, not attempting to choke her but carefully feeling for the right spot. She pressed it hard until Luna lay still. Then she removed her fingers quickly. She wanted to neutralize her enemy, not kill her.

Margaret waited for a minute to catch her breath and to check that Luna wasn't in fact dead or possibly faking unconsciousness, then stood up. She remembered the car that had saved her life. It was still there, facing the fence, lights out. Inside, someone sat watching her. Then the engine started and it backed into the street and sped off.

Margaret knelt beside Luna, who was breathing laboriously, and searched her. No wallet, no keys, not even Kleenex. Margaret suddenly became aware of the time. A guard would be making his rounds soon, and she wanted to put considerable distance between herself and the unconscious body of Lady Amber's High Priestess of Physical Fitness.

She backtracked to the laundry rooms, where she began to make herself presentable enough to get past the guard at the gate.

45

♦

"After all, even a politician is human."
SEN. MIKE MANSFIELD,
ON THE CHAPPAQUIDDICK TRAGEDY

PARKED DOWN THE street from Lady Amber, Jake watched the cars trickle through the front gate past the guards. When Margaret's exited, he started his engine. He waited for her to drive past, then pulled out into the street and followed.

Their procession lasted three blocks, when he began honking his horn. She pulled over to the curb and he stopped behind her.

She turned to look at him as he approached her car on foot. It was impossible for him to read the expression on her face. When he was standing beside her, she said, "I want to thank you for distracting that woman—"

"It looked like you were in trouble—" he began.

"—but I don't know why the hell you didn't do something more constructive than just sitting there, enjoying the show."

"So what did you want me to do, notify the security cops?" he said angrily.

"You could have tried to climb over the fence to help me," she said. Then she shook her head. "No. I guess you really didn't understand what was happening. All you saw was a Lady Amber employee holding a gun on me, then the fight."

"Actually," Jake said, a little embarrassed, "I remembered where I'd seen her before. She was the woman in the beehive who pushed you into the traffic on Hollywood Boulevard."

Margaret's anger returned. "So you *knew* she was capable of killing me!"

"That's why I shined the light on you both. It's all I could think of doing at the time."

"I'm sorry. You did save my life. Again. I should be more grateful, but—"

"But you hate to owe me anything—right?"

"Something like that," she said wearily. "Instead of spending your valuable time following me around, why don't I just give you my itinerary. . . . I'm on my way back to my hotel. I'll be checking out right away and heading for the airport to catch the United flight to Washington. If you want to keep hounding me, go ahead. I'm too damned tired and sore to care. But you'd better be prepared to catch that 9:35 flight. Maybe we can sit together if you'll let me sleep."

"What did you find back there?" Jake asked, indicating the Lady Amber compound.

"I just picked up some free lipstick and eye liner."

Jake walked back to his Cherokee. He followed her as far as the Hollywood Freeway, then, from lack of interest, let her disappear.

FORTY-FIVE minutes later he walked into his hotel room to find his red phone light glowing. The message center informed him that "a Mrs. Christen called. She's in room 907 of the hotel."

Jake didn't wait to hear any more. He broke the connection and then dialed the three numbers, praying that she was still in her room.

She was. She'd decided to take a later flight. She wondered if he was still interested in dinner.

He didn't want to say yes too eagerly. Was her large friend with the sunglasses going to join them?

No, Albert had gone away. Would Jake mind dining in her room instead of going out? She was trying to avoid the press.

He reminded her that he *was* the press, but said her room would be fine.

In half an hour, then? And would she allow him to select the menu?

He informed her anything would be fine except lima beans and sweetbreads.

46

◆

Washington

◆

"I do not believe that the men who served
in uniform in Vietnam have ever been
given the credit they deserve."

GENERAL WILLIAM WESTMORELAND

J. B. MURPHY had just fallen asleep when the telephone rang. It was
Margaret at Los Angeles International Airport. "I'm flying in
tonight," she informed him.

"Good." He yawned, looking at his watch. Already well past
midnight. "Spend too much time on the West Coast and you start
looking and thinking like an orange. Come on home where it's
bitter cold and wet, the way Christmas should be."

"I've got several things we should talk over," she said. "Tomorrow, first thing, at the office."

"I'll be there."

It seemed to him that he'd barely replaced the receiver and put
his head back on the pillow when the phone rang again. But in fact,
forty-five minutes had passed.

It was a woman's voice, hard and hoarse. "Is this Murphy?"

"Yeah," he said, "Sleepy Murphy."

"I'm Lil," she said. "I waitress at The Dublin Inn. In Bethesda,
Dublin Street and Wisconsin. Maybe you know it?"

"I don't think so," Murphy said wearily. "Is this a solicitation
call?"

"Huh? No. Fella named Charles Stern was just here and he asked me to phone you. He wants for you to meet him at the Sleepwell Motel at 1334 Crabapple Street."

"Hold on," Murphy said, reaching out to put on his bed lamp. Then he rooted around on the end table for a pen. He scribbled the address on the sports page of the *Post* that he found on the carpet near the bed.

He read back the address to her.

"That's right," she said. "It's near the Ford Rec Center in Rollingwood. Just over the state line. He said he'd be there, in cabin number thirteen. He also said I should tell you that it's Gomer Pyle time. It doesn't make much sense to me, but he tipped me a fiver, so I figure he's entitled to be a little weird."

"Thanks, Lil," Murphy said, hanging up the receiver and swinging his protesting body out of the bed. He paused, bunched his toes on the carpet's cool nap, and felt the damp chill attack his bare ankles. He shook his head a few times to clear some of the cobwebs. Then he was up and getting dressed.

"Gomer Pyle time" was a phrase that he and Stern and Harry Stafford had come up with way back in the mid-sixties, when then-president Lyndon Johnson had dispatched them to snoop around Saigon after a bomb wiped out the U.S. embassy there. The reference had been to the popular "Gomer Pyle, U.S.M.C." television series. In the parlance of Murphy and his small band, "Gomer Pyle time" was when you found yourself in a situation where you were so helpless you needed a buddy to lead you home.

Murphy was dressed, in his car, and whizzing past the National Zoological Park within fifteen minutes. The thought flitted through his mind that Larry Newfield had been along on that particular tour of duty. He would have known about Gomer Pyle time, too.

47

◆

Los Angeles

◆

"It takes a wise man to handle a lie; a fool
had better remain honest."

NORMAN DOUGLAS

LAURA CHRISTEN TOOK special care in selecting the dinner in her
hotel suite. It began with Artichokes Santa Anita, the hearts of the
'chokes covered with foie gras and the meat from crab legs; followed by Poodle Dog Trout, fish filets broiled in butter and corn-
meal, named after a Gold Rush restaurant that created the recipe.
This was accompanied by a splendid California Chardonnay that
was especially recommended by the sommelier.

Through it all, she had kept the conversation light and impersonal. But she knew that eventually they would have to address the
events of a decade before. Actually, she wanted to clear the air.

They had just put an end to the banana fritters and were sipping
their coffee when they were interrupted by the phone.

She excused herself and took the call in the bedroom. It was
Catsy, telling her that the National Organization for Women dinner
meeting had gone as smoothly as possible with Esther Cooper as
a last-minute substitute. "Unfortunately, Congresswoman Cooper,
being a Democrat, didn't feel right about trashing Lew Ronkowski
the way you would have," Catsy said. "And any questions about
the upcoming fight in the House were smoothly sidestepped by
her. She's a real pro."

Catsy then began listing an assortment of new crises requiring Laura's personal attention. Laura interrupted her. "I'll definitely be there by two tomorrow afternoon and we'll go over everything then. Right now I want to get back to my dinner guest."

"What guest?" Catsy was intrigued.

"A very nice man I used to know," Laura told her. "He once wrote a very flattering article about me."

"Oh, God, not a reporter. You're *not* sleeping with a reporter. What's his name?"

Annoyed, Laura hung up. She looked at herself in the mirror, decided her lipstick was OK, and returned to Jake Alban.

He was sitting on the couch in the living room. He'd brought their after-dinner brandies with him. "Problems?" he asked.

"Nothing I can solve tonight," she said, sitting next to him on the sofa. "I'm sorry we were interrupted. Where were we?"

"You were telling me about your plans to change the Congress," Jake said. "And I was wondering what happened to us ten years ago."

She stared at him for a beat, then took a sip of her brandy. "It's not easy to explain."

"Let me help," he said. "Was it another man?"

"Yes," she said. "But not what you think. Any affection between us had died a long time before I met you. But there was something else—"

"And this something else came between us?"

"You have to understand the kind of man he is." She paused, trying to get it straight in her mind. "Ten years ago during one of our interview sessions, he phoned. Do you remember?"

Jake looked thoughtful. Then his face told her that he'd made the connection. "Of course! You asked me if I'd mind giving you a few minutes alone. When you asked me back in, you'd been crying. I wondered what was the matter—"

"And you remember what I said?"

"You said that you had a friend who—"

"That wasn't the first thing I said."

He looked at her blankly.

"I asked you if what I was about to tell you was off the record and you said that it was. Then I made a vague confession about a 'friend' who had caused me a great deal of pain in the past. You never questioned me about him again. Weren't you the least bit curious?''

''Very curious,'' he said, picking up his brandy. ''But as a reporter, I didn't want to discover anything that would tempt me to put the information on the record. And as a man falling in love, I obviously didn't want to remind you of an old, painful romance.''

She desperately wished that were the truth. ''I've never even told my daughter about him,'' she said. ''But it's time that you know. I want so much to trust you.''

''Tell me what you can.''

''I met him shortly after I moved to Los Angeles. One of my new roommates introduced us at a party in this hotel. He was totally unlike anyone I'd ever known. Much older than my late husband. More worldly. Soft-spoken, but there was a dynamic aura about him and an element of danger—a dark side. You could see it in the way people treated him at the party. With more than deference. Even Ivor Hamilton. It was as though he held power over them.''

''Power is the word,'' Jake said. ''And you fell for him.''

She considered that for a moment. ''Yes—you could say I fell for him.''

''But you didn't live happily ever after.''

''No. I got pregnant. And he picked that time to tell me he was married. He said he loved me, but that divorce was out of the question.''

Jake frowned and looked down at his glass.

''The baby made no difference?''

''Oh, he wanted the baby,'' she said. ''His plan was for me to have the child, then he and his wife would adopt it. Naturally, I refused.''

Dammit, she thought, *I'm making myself cry again.* She willed the tears to stop, then tried to think of a quick way of getting back to the point—the thing that had ended her romance with Jake. But he wasn't quite ready to make that jump. ''So what happened to the baby?''

She waited a breath, then replied, ''He died in the hospital.''

''I'm sorry.''

"It was a long time ago," she said. *Maybe this is the best way. Let him ask his questions.*

"Did . . . you continue seeing him after the baby died?"

"No. He'd lied to me," she told him. "About his marriage and about something else. He helped us start Lady Amber. I thought it was because he cared for me. But he saw to it that he controlled the company and therefore kept control of me."

"How did he control the company?"

"He was secretly involved in numerous corporations, including Hamilton International. He pushed poor Ivor into providing the money we needed and demanding, in return, a majority ownership of the stock. As soon as I discovered that he was our controlling silent partner, I made a clean break with Lady Amber by selling all my shares. I assumed that had severed my last connection to my 'friend.' "

"But when we met, you were still connected."

"He's an extremely powerful man, Jake," she said, glad to be getting to the point, finally. "And a very possessive one. We had stopped seeing one another, but he continued to show he had not completely lost his hold over me. Back then he still was capable of manipulating me."

"I don't understand. How?"

"By playing on my doubts and fears. The day his phone call interrupted our interview, he told me that I was being very foolish to risk going out with a reporter. I suppose we must have been seen together." She smiled. "He said that you were toying with me, that you had a reputation for seducing—that was the word he used—seducing women into telling you secrets that you later used against them."

"You believed that?"

"Not at first," she said. "But when I told you off the record about the man who had hurt me, while it was the truth, it was also a test that he suggested."

"But I passed the test," Jake said. "I didn't mention it."

"He sent me a photocopy of the manuscript you submitted. It included a passage about my being in pain over a lost love."

"There was nothing like that in my article."

"My 'friend' said he pulled strings to get it edited before publication."

"That's total bullshit," Jake said. "He conned you."

"Not total bullshit. He was a major shareholder in the company that owned your former syndicate. It could have happened the way he described it."

"I did not betray your confidence," Jake almost shouted.

She studied his face and said, "The reason my 'friend' is so successful at his little games is that he can read people. He knew I had doubts about being in public life and having an affair with a reporter. So he played on that. Over the years I've come to understand him better. And myself as well. His hold on me these days is tenuous at best. In many ways I think I'm now stronger than he."

"You should have told me what was going on."

"But don't you see? That was the beauty of it. You were a reporter—I wasn't sure I trusted you."

"I'm still a reporter and you're still in public office. Do you trust me now?"

"I want to. I think I do."

"Then tell me your friend's name," he said. "On the record."

She hesitated only a second. "Theo—"

"Koriallis," he completed. "I know. This was *my* test."

He looked hard at her and then smiled. The tension that had been building in the room floated away. *My God,* she thought, *maybe it isn't too late for us after all.*

48

◆

Washington

◆

"Half a truth is better than no politics."
G. K. CHESTERTON

HAVING WATCHED her mother's political adviser, Professor Jim
Prosser, devour nonstop three large slices of cajun sausage pizza
and now nervously chew the inside of his mouth, Catsy Braden
wondered if the man was on the verge of some sort of breakdown.
They were the only occupants of her mother's office. It was nearly
midnight. They had been putting out brush fires all day and working out schedules during much of the night.

The pizzas had been delivered twenty minutes before. She'd had
only one slice. When Prosser's hand went out for even more, she
said, "Jim, will you for God's sake relax."

He drew back his hand as if she'd slapped it. "What was it Laura
told you, exactly?"

"For the fourth time," Catsy went on, "she said she would be
returning tomorrow, sometime in the afternoon. She's got a meeting at three."

"Who with?" Prosser asked, going for the pizza again.

"Two policemen—about the Dunbar thing."

Prosser's face was impassive. "They think she did it?"

"Of course not!"

He shrugged as if it didn't matter to him either way. Catsy
realized that she shouldn't have told him that her mother was

having dinner with another man in Los Angeles. But she had never quite absorbed the fact that though her mother, to her knowledge, did not consider Prosser to be her lover, Prosser might have seen things differently.

In any case, something was up on the West Coast. Her mother had sounded like a teenager on the phone.

Prosser finished his current pizza slice and began prying a chunk of sausage from yet another. Catsy asked him, "Are you sleeping with my mother?"

He looked up at her through his thick glasses and replied calmly, "That's nothing we should be discussing."

"It's no big deal, Jim," Catsy said. "Humans make love. I was just wondering if you and Mother—"

"If there's a reason you think you should know, she's the one you should ask." He stood up. "If you don't want any more pizza, I think I'll take it back to my office."

Alone at her desk, with the lingering smell of cheese and sausage still in the air, she was suddenly annoyed with herself for chasing the Professor away. She liked him. She was depending on him to keep a secret they shared.

Getting into her coat, she continued to brood about her mother's love life. After such a long fallow period, when Laura did decide to let herself go, it was with a guy who didn't meet with Catsy's approval—a goddamned reporter. What was wrong with a governor or senator or just an ordinary run-of-the-mill multimillionaire? Catsy would have to find out this new stud's name and have a background check done on him. She didn't want anything or anyone to suddenly screw up the plans she had for her mother's political career. Or for her own.

49

•

"The end move in politics is always to pick up a gun."

BUCKMINSTER FULLER

IT WAS NEARLY 1:30 in the morning when Murphy's gray Lincoln parked in front of The Dublin Inn on the corner of Dublin and Wisconsin. The sleet had stopped, but the temperature had dropped a few crucial degrees. Puffing plumes of frost, he did a little jog from his car into the building.

The neighborhood bar and grill had called it a night. Chairs were piled atop most of the tables. The Christmas tree lights that had been strung over the bar, possibly years ago, were dark. Two elderly waitresses were chatting with a bartender. One of the women had "Lil" stitched in white on her orange uniform.

"Yep," she informed Murphy. "There's only one Lil here, and it's me who called you."

He had a question to ask her. He could have asked it by phone, but he wanted to get a look at her, to make sure she was really a waitress (no doubt of it now). "Could you be good enough, Lil, to describe the fella who told you to call me?"

She didn't try to hold him up for money, which was a good sign. She just said, simply, "He was tall, a rugged-looking guy."

"Hair color?"

"I dunno. Gray, sorta."

"How'd he talk?"

"With his mouth," she said and gave him a loud braying laugh.

"I mean, what kind of voice?" Murphy asked patiently.

237

"Strong. Sure of himself. He was something."

So far so good.

Murphy took a five-dollar bill from his wallet and gave it to her. "Thanks, Lil," he said.

He was turning to leave when she added, "And he sure does dress nice. I haven't seen a topcoat that fine since Cary Grant stopped making movies."

He thanked her again and asked where he might find a pay phone. She directed him to a dim hallway. The phone was beside the door to the men's room. Using his scarf to keep the biting disinfectant smell from his nostrils, he dialed the airport and left a brief message.

Then he walked through the main room, informed the bartender that his lavatories smelled like roses, and, whistling an off-key version of "Jingle Bells," he left The Dublin Inn. As long as Murphy had known him, Charlie Stern had never worn a topcoat. Not even in weather this bad.

He looked up and down the deserted, ice-covered street, crossed the sidewalk, unlocked the door to his car, and got in.

He pushed the key into its slot and turned it to the right. The engine started with a hesitant grunt followed by a roar. Then someone called his name from the backseat.

Murphy adjusted his rearview mirror. It was a man he'd never seen before. A tall, blond man with a tan he certainly didn't get in Washington in November.

The man said, "Mr. Newfield thought you'd go straight to Crabapple Street, but I thought you might come here first."

"Well, you won," Murphy said. "What now?"

The man leaned forward. He had a gun in his gloved hand. Colder than the night was the touch of metal against the back of Murphy's neck. "Now we drive."

Ah well, Murphy thought to himself, *it's one way of finding out what happened to poor old Charlie.*

50

♦

Los Angeles

♦

"Practical politics consists in ignoring the truth."

HENRY ADAMS

JAKE TRIED TO remember the precise steps that led to their first kiss, but there were those few moments, just after they'd stepped onto Laura's balcony, with a cool night breeze carrying sweet scents of the gardens below, that seemed lost to time. He recalled turning and finding her suddenly beside him. Were words spoken by either of them at the time? He couldn't recall.

What he did recall was the exquisite sensation of the kiss. Lips meeting, then becoming more demanding. Her mouth opening slightly. Their bodies pressing together. A moan. His or hers?

She pulled away suddenly and his heart sank. But she only wanted to lead him inside the suite. Past the sofa and into the bedroom, bathed in moonlight. The cover on the bed was turned down and there was a foil-wrapped candy on the pillow.

She plucked it up, peeled the wrapper. She broke the chocolate circle in two. She placed one section into his mouth and kept the other for herself. It tasted bittersweet. He brought her hand to his lips and began to lick the chocolate smudges from her thumb and fingers.

Then they were on the bed, hugging, fondling, kissing. The frenzied removal of clothes. He had a vivid memory of the way she maneuvered her blouse over her head, cross-armed, as quickly as a magician making a paper bouquet disappear. But no magician's trick was ever as dazzling as the magic of her naked body in moonlight. If anything it was even more desirable now than it had been ten years before.

A shiver went through him as she touched the small scar over his eye with her finger. Turning the wound around. Replacing pain with pleasure, memory with desire. And when they made love, when her body arched under his and she muttered "ohyes-ohyes-ohyes," when he had lost himself in a rush of pleasure, he realized for the first time that living for the present was definitely the way to go.

HE awoke to find her staring at him in the semidarkness. "You cried out in your sleep."

He didn't reply. He'd been having the dream.

"It sounded like a woman's name," Laura told him. "That's not very flattering."

"Danielle was the name. My wife's," he said, his mouth dry. "I was having a nightmare."

She was silent for a moment. Then she said, "Would it help if you told me about it?"

He wasn't sure if it would. But he wanted to be as honest with her as he could. And so he told her.

He explained that he had been assigned to cover the war in Nicaragua. His wife, a freelance photographer, had insisted, after a long argument, on joining him. They'd been in Managua for two weeks and had filed an assortment of stories and photos when Danielle had informed him that it was their anniversary. In celebration, they'd reserved a table in the restaurant of one of the more modern hotels. It was called the Crystal Room, a large space just off the lobby with pale, blue-flocked walls, electric-blue carpet, and a gigantic chandelier that supposedly had been made especially for the hotel on the Italian island of Murano.

He told her about the gunfire; he told her about the chandelier exploding; he told her about the senseless and bloody death of his wife, Danielle.

"For a while I seemed to have been untouched by the whole

thing," he told Laura. "Then the nightmares started. I began overreacting to loud noises—'exaggerated startle response' was how a shrink put it. I couldn't work. Everything and everyone irritated me."

"What did the shrink say about that?" Laura asked.

"That I was a walking, breathing textbook example of post-traumatic stress disorder. It had been my job as a journalist that had placed me and Danielle in jeopardy. Therefore it was my fear of reexperiencing the trauma that was forcing me to seek a less dangerous occupation. His advice was that I should go with the flow."

"Did that help?"

"For a while. That's when I started writing 'autobiographies' for politicians. They kept me in food and drink, but I wasn't wildly happy. And then one night, about a year ago, I was walking home from the neighborhood deli and this kid, couldn't have been out of his teens, stuck a gun in my neck and took my wallet and watch and twenty-five bucks' worth of cheese and cold cuts. And left me a basket case."

"You look pretty solid now," she told him.

"It's taken time." He didn't bother to mention his new psychiatrist, Dr. Wexler, who thought he should "work through" the problem of returning to journalism. Instead he said, "The thing that stays with me is the feeling of guilt. I know that if I hadn't been a reporter, Danielle wouldn't have died."

She shook her head and pulled him against her. She said very slowly, "It was her decision that she go. Not yours. That's another thing that's wrong with chauvinism. It makes some men feel responsible for things over which they really have no control."

"I could have told her she couldn't come."

"And she could have been hit by a car while you were away. You would have blamed yourself for that, too. It's time to give it a rest, Jake."

"Yes, it is," he agreed and held her close.

At midnight he bent over the bed to kiss her cheek and say, "Your plane leaves very early. You'd better try to sleep. I'll just stagger back to my cold, lonely room."

She smiled lazily.

He asked, "When can I see you again? This weekend in Washington?"

She was suddenly solemn, a worry frown creasing her forehead. "Give me a little time to . . . clear up a few problems first."

"Anything I can do to help?"

"You might call tomorrow. Just to say hello."

He promised that he would. Then he kissed her again. He knew that he should tell her why he was in Los Angeles. He could end by saying that he was phoning Penelope Krim in the morning and quitting. But could he make good on that promise? Penelope was vindictive enough to spread the word about his "unreliability." He might never get another chance to work as a journalist. And where would that leave him? Back writing puff books. Hardly the occupation of choice for the consort of a beautiful and charismatic political figure.

He tried to maintain a mask of confidence as he left her. But the gnawing conflict of career and affection was still on his mind when he let himself into his hotel suite. As a result, he overlooked the pile of scribbled notes beside the phone in the alcove and the half-empty glasses on the wet bar.

It was the light in the bedroom that alerted him. That and the rattle of paper.

He picked up a heavy glass candlestick from the marble mantel and moved toward the bedroom cautiously. He peeked around the corner, expecting the worst, but what he saw was beyond even that.

In the center of his bed was a mound of flesh wrapped in a silk see-through nightie. It was encircled by four plump pillows, sipping at a pale green drink, and scribbling notes on a legal pad.

Penelope looked up at him and smirked. "Well, lover boy, it's after two. Bars all closed?"

"Hello, Dr. Krim," Jake said evenly, placing the candlestick on the dresser. "What a surprise."

She capped her pen and put it and the legal pad on the floor near her pink satin pumps. Then she patted the bed beside her. "Come tell Penny how you've been getting along."

Jake didn't move.

She said, "Since Laura Christen was out here, I thought I might as well come out myself. I don't suppose you've seen our Laura?"

"She was at Tommy Hamilton's funeral."

"So I saw on the news. Come! Sit!"

But the lapdog did not obey.

"Don't be so standoffish, Jake. We've been working. Now we play."

"Like you said, it's late."

"Late? Don't give me late, lover. It's close to dawn in Washington, but do I look sleepy? I took a catnap earlier. I don't want to waste our time together by sleeping." She dimmed the lamp and raised a plump hand to a pendulous breast. She then began to fondle it while licking her lips and staring at him.

Oh, please, he thought. *This can't be happening to me. Heaven and hell in one night.*

"C'mon," Penelope said throatily, "show the boss lady you're glad to see her."

Think fast, he commanded himself. And the answer came to him. "I'm . . . I'm afraid to come any closer," he whispered.

"Don't be," she said. "We're free, white, and twenty-one." She giggled.

"You don't understand," he said. "I'm afraid I won't be able to stop myself from making love to you."

"That's the general idea, you goose," she said, shimmying down into the bed, her nightie rising up over acres of cellulite. "That's what boys and girls do when they're all alone in hotel bedrooms."

"I guess I'd better be honest with you, Penny," he said. "I'm going to be contagious for at least another week."

"Contagious?" Her lip curled on the word. "What the hell have you got?"

He sighed. "Nothing fatal," he said. "Just old-fashioned herpes."

Penelope bounced from the bed, rubbing frantically at her body. "Jesus!" she screeched and ran into the bathroom, slamming the door behind her. A second later she opened the door, peeked out, and demanded, "Have you used the toilet since the maid swabbed it?"

"I don't think so," he replied, keeping a straight face.

She slammed the door again.

Penelope emerged a few minutes later, fully dressed and fuming. Jake was lying on the bed. He successfully maintained a guilty, pained look on his face while she called the desk, ordering a separate room.

"This is the last time I hire anybody without a goddamn health certificate," she spat at him as she threw her clothes into her bag.

"I can't tell you how awful I feel," he said. "It's like Robert Browning said, 'Never the time and the place and the loved one all together.' "

"Screw the poetry. You better have some solid research for me in the morning. I'll expect you in the dining room at nine and not a goddamn minute later. And don't sit too close to me."

She did her best to slam the door to the suite behind her, but it was on a pneumatic arm.

Jake rolled over on the bed and started to laugh. Then he was struck by a very sobering thought.

He got up and made a quick search of the room. The Lavery drug receipts were gone.

51

♦

"Politics is not the art of the possible. It consists in choosing between the disastrous and the unpalatable."

JOHN KENNETH GALBRAITH

LAURA EMERGED FROM her shower and stared at her glistening body in the bathroom mirror. She grinned. Yes, she definitely had the glow of someone in love. She grabbed a thick hotel towel and began to dry herself. Then she wrapped a fresh towel around her damp hair, threw on a terry robe, and strolled dreamily into the bedroom.

Theo Koriallis was standing there.

Fear fluttered briefly through her and was replaced immediately by anger. She opened her mouth, but he only shook his head and placed a finger to his lips. He moved to her bedside lamp and lifted it to reveal an electronic listening device attached to its base.

Confused, she allowed him to lead her by the arm back into the bathroom, where he turned on all the water spigots. He shut the door and said, "I think you've provided them with enough drama for tonight."

"Theo, just what the devil are you doing here?"

"You must leave this hotel immediately," he said, ignoring her question.

She studied his solemn face. He seemed to have aged another decade since she last saw him. "What's happening?" she demanded. "Why is my room bugged?"

"The only thing you must know is that the situation has worsened. You must leave this hotel, this city. Come with me to Eureka. I can protect you there.''

"Protect me from whom?"

"From people who feel you are a threat to their plans."

She frowned. "But how could I be a threat to people I don't even know?"

He sighed and explained in an exasperated tone, "Laura, your recent activity in Washington has brought you into the public eye. Because of this, everything about you will be scrutinized by the press—your lifestyle, your philosophy, your past."

"But I have nothing to hide," she said.

"Perhaps not. But when the spotlight is turned on you, it will also shine unblinkingly on others who are far from innocent."

She was watching him closely now; her head had cleared and she could focus her thoughts. She looked at him skeptically. "How?" she asked. "I want specifics, Theo."

"You have no time. Believe me. They'll be coming for you any minute. Let me help you."

"I'll take my chances here," she said. "Eureka is nice enough to visit, but I wouldn't want to live there."

"Understand me, Laura. I was at the meeting. The decision has been made to kill you."

"You're telling me that I'm going to be murdered because I'm getting too much publicity?"

"You came to see me about the death of a gossip columnist. I will tell you now that he was assassinated. As was a detective from Washington named Stuart Wayland. And Thomas Hamilton. I myself am on their list. All because of you."

"Don't try to guilt-trip me, you bastard. I've matured past that phase."

"This has nothing to do with you and me and what we may have been. It's about people wanting to keep secrets."

"I'm not exposing anybody's secrets."

"But you are. It's their activity at Lady Amber that they're trying to keep hidden. And your new bedmate is very curious about Lady Amber."

She could feel the blood rushing to her face. *That's it, of course. His goddamned jealousy.* "Get out of here, Theo," she rasped.

"My bedmate, as you so charmingly put it, is none of your affair. I never realized how low you were. Placing listening devices in my bedroom and blaming them on some mysterious bogeyman. How suave. How continental."

"I repeat—your *bedmate* is interested in Lady Amber."

She hesitated. "Why should he be?"

"Because"—and he could not keep the vindictiveness out of his voice—"your beloved, upright Jake Alban is working for a smutty columnist named Penelope Krim. Out to smear you and anyone else they can."

Laura's knees suddenly felt weak. She leaned back against the shower door.

"He's with Krim at this very moment. They are sharing a suite in the hotel."

She shook her head. "No. You're lying. Like you lied to me before about him."

He removed two small white cards from his coat pocket. The first was the Casa Bel Air Guest Information Card that Jake had signed when he checked in. The second was the one Penelope Krim had signed just that afternoon. The room numbers were the same.

Laura dropped the cards onto the bathroom floor. "Boy, I can pick them, can't I, Theo? With you, I had the excuse of being young and naive. These days I have no excuse at all."

"Don't worry about your petty infatuation," Theo snapped. "Worry about staying alive."

"Who ordered my death?"

"Why look for names? Look instead for ways of escape. I am powerless in this matter. All I can do is warn you. Leave here now. If not to Eureka with me, then to some other retreat. Announce your retirement from politics and you may be allowed to live. Otherwise you have no hope."

"I'm leaving, all right," she said, bristling. "But I'm not going to any goddamned retreat. I'm going to Washington, where I intend to carry on my business as usual. If I am asked, I will refer any questions about Lady Amber or murders to you, since you do seem to know so much about them."

"Laura, please—"

"No! I went to you for information and you fed me fantasies. Now, for some perverse reason, probably having to do with the fact that I slept with another man, you're elaborating on them. Well, I won't have it. All right, I made a mistake with Jake Alban. It's one I'll rectify. Just as I once rectified the mistake I made with you."

He stared at her a moment, his face stricken. He knew that there was nothing he could say, nothing he could do that would convince her of the danger she was in. He had made a serious mistake bringing Alban into the discussion. Instead of working for him, it had made her suspect his own motives. It was like a business deal that had gone irrevocably sour. There was no way to start over. He said, "Goodbye, Laura," and left her.

Laura took a deep breath, then moved quickly into the bedroom. She began throwing her clothes into her bag. She'd seen a friend buried, slept with a cheat, and, finally, she'd nearly allowed herself to be manipulated again by Theo Koriallis. She'd had her fill of Los Angeles.

52

◆

Washington

◆

"Self-preservation is the first principle of
our nature."

ALEXANDER HAMILTON

MARGARET WAS AMONG the first sleepy passengers to get off the red
eye express when it landed in Washington. She half-ran along the
nearly empty corridors of the terminal, for the first time barely
noticing her injured hip. Suddenly a loudspeaker called her name,
requesting her to pick up a courtesy phone.

She spotted one in an alcove.

Murphy had left a message for her. She listened to it carefully,
her mind suddenly alert, and asked that it be repeated. Then she
hung up and continued on through the terminal, but more cautiously now.

Nothing seemed out of the ordinary. She caught up with a
handful of other disheveled-looking riders from the red eye at the
baggage area and watched the luggage wobble slowly along a
clanking treadmill. Hers was as usual the very last to arrive. As she
jerked it angrily off the treadmill, she thought she saw a familiar
face in the sparse crowd.

Mistrusting her senses after so little sleep, she blinked and
looked again. She did know the face, but it was attached to the
wrong body. The last time she had seen that thin, almost pointed
nose, those high, Slavic-looking cheekbones, icy blue-green eyes,

and drooping, oversized lower lip was on the homicidal Luna, Lady Amber Priestess of Physical Fitness. Now the features belonged to a tall, blond, deeply suntanned young man standing near the exit.

Margaret realized that even if Luna hadn't referred to herself as a Gemini, it was now obvious that she was a twin, the other half of which stood at the exit door, trying not to be too obvious about scanning the crowd. For Margaret. As she cautiously approached the exit, she observed the man out of the corner of her eye. Could he have been the same tall blond who had brushed past her in the L.A. restaurant and pricked poor Wagner's wrist, infecting him with some bizarre drug—from the Lady Amber lab?

She walked past the official checking luggage tags. When she passed the blond man, he seemed to be vitally interested in something at the far end of the hall. But then he spun about and followed her out of the terminal into the pre-dawn chill.

Parked illegally in the yellow zone was a mud-covered truck marked "Brookville." Margaret remembered seeing it near the Maitland Hotel the night she and Murphy had met with Mike Roberts and Charles Stern. Mr. Gemini had been onto them right from the start.

An annoying mechanical voice repeated over and over that cars left in the yellow zone would be towed "at the owner's expense." Margaret left the voice behind her as she sprinted across the roadway, still holding her lightweight bag, her breath visible in frosty puffs. She was shivering under her leather, fur-lined jacket.

She chanced a look back. The blond paused by his truck, then continued after her.

She yanked open a door to the stairwell of the parking structure.

The blond was closing the gap. He arrived on the structure's second level in time to see the door closing. Cautiously, he entered the building. Before him stood endless rows of cars. Margaret was nowhere to be seen. He walked toward the closest car, unsure of his next move. Then he saw Margaret's flight bag, almost at his feet, unzipped.

"Behind you," Margaret said.

He spun around. She was leaning against a nearby wall, gun in hand.

"Down on the ground," she ordered.

He looked down at the grimy, oil-smeared cement and gave her an imploring look. She snapped her fingers and he reluctantly lowered himself.

"Now give me one push-up and hold it."

When he had done that, she approached him from his left side, holding her gun behind his head, aimed at his neck. She reached under his arm, across his chest, and withdrew a pistol from his shoulder holster. It was small, remarkably lightweight. The name Nova was stamped onto its blue barrel. She liked it.

He said, "I've a permit for that."

"Good," she said, slipping the gun into her pocket. "Let's have a look." She moved her hand back under his coat. She felt him tense and said, "I don't mind killing you," so softly that he believed her. Her fingers found something too bulky to be a wallet. It seemed to be a black leather cigar case. Wrinkling her nose, she slipped it back into his pocket and moved on to his wallet. He did have a permit. And a number of identification and credit cards indicating that his name was Kerry Niles and that, surprise, surprise, he was an employee of Intercom, Inc.

"I can't hold this much longer," he gasped.

"Then drop," she said, "but stretch your arms out in front. And keep your face down."

"On the goddamn cement? It's *cold* and it's *filthy.*"

She kicked him gently in the leg. "Then do it carefully."

She bent over his body and rested his wallet beside his head. Then she patted his topcoat pocket until she located the keys to his truck. He stirred. "Wait a—"

She poked the barrel of her gun into his neck. "You boys with your car toys," she said.

"What are you going—"

"Turn your head and watch," she ordered. He saw her toss his keys through an open window, heard them clang against something metal at ground level.

"Facedown again, Blondie," she said.

She zipped her bag and backed slowly away with it to where she had parked her Prelude. She tossed the bag onto the backseat.

As she was getting into the car, Niles started to move, so she pointed the gun at him and commanded him to lie still.

Niles, face pressed into the concrete, heard the engine turn over and then the car pulling away. As he started to get up, he saw that a trio of travelers was standing a few feet away, gaping at him. One of them stepped over and asked in a heavy German accent if he needed any help. Niles ignored him as he leaped to his feet, ran to a window, and caught a final glimpse of Margaret's little sedan as it headed for an airport exit.

MARGARET did not continue on to D.C. Instead she quickly circled the airport and returned to a spot a few hundred yards from where Niles, covered with oil stains and filth, was on his knees among a collection of garbage cans, rooting about for the keys to his truck.

53

◆

Los Angeles

◆

"A lie can get you in a peck of trouble, but
so can telling the truth."

HUEY LONG

BLISSFULLY UNAWARE OF how much trouble he was in, Jake Alban
lay on the couch in his hotel sitting room, watching the Late News.
Actually, he was listening to the news with his eyes closed and his
mind on Laura Christen.

Then suddenly he was sitting up, staring at an attractive Oriental
anchorwoman—would he ever live to see an Oriental anchor-
man?—who was nattering on about a Los Angeles couple, unnamed until relatives could be found and notified, who were
speeding to their home from Palm Desert when their car evidently
spun out of control. Both were killed instantly when the car, a 1985
Porsche Roadster, smashed into the median, overturned, and
caught fire. "But here's the surprising part," the anchorwoman
said, her bland face suggesting that nothing would surprise her,
really. "The lovely home they were racing back to had just burned
to the ground. Talk about your bad luck . . ."

It had to be the Laverys. That added two more to the Laura
Christen hit list.

Jake picked up the phone and dialed her suite. After the tenth
ring, he gave up.

There was no reason for alarm. She had unhooked the phone. She had fallen asleep with earplugs. He had misdialed the number. The hotel switchboard had inexplicably blown a fuse.

He tried to think of one more impossible reason why Laura had not answered. Then he did what he'd been wanting to do since he left her an hour before. He threw on his clothes and went back to her room.

Her door was open. He rushed into her suite. It was empty. No clothes in the closet. No luggage.

Frantic now, he raced to the elevator.

A clerk at the front desk informed him that Congresswoman Christen had checked out only minutes before.

He ran through the lobby and out the front door. The timbers of the moat rattled as he raced over them to the parking area, where Laura was stepping into a limo.

He ran toward her, calling her name.

She turned and stared straight through him.

"Laura, wait—"

"Why don't you and Penelope go peddle your papers, little boy," she said, slamming the limo door in his face.

The chauffeur stared at Jake with a mixture of embarrassment and apprehension. Jake's hand went out to the car door but both he and the chauffeur could hear the snap of the lock, activated from the car's interior.

The chauffeur took that as his signal to return to the car. Jake withdrew his fingers from the limo's door handle a second before the vehicle leaped forward.

He watched in frustration as it passed a line of cars parked along the drive parallel to the man-made moat. One of them eased into the drive, as if lured on by the scent of the limo's exhaust. It was a Mercedes with a plate that read "IC4."

Jake rushed back to his room for his car keys. He would go after them, stop Laura's limo, warn her, convince her of how he felt about her.

He burst into his suite. All the lights were on, and the television had been turned to MTV, not loud enough to disturb his neighbors, but loud enough to muffle sounds in the room.

His first thought was that Penelope was back. Then two men stepped from the bedroom. One was Albert, minus his shades. The other was the sallow man who had accompanied Koriallis to the funeral.

54

♦

Washington

♦

"Doubt is not a pleasant mental state, but
certainty is a ridiculous one."

VOLTAIRE

YAWNING, MARGARET sat in her car watching Kerry Niles looking
for the keys to his truck. It was too bad they had landed among the
garbage cans; she'd hoped they would fall someplace in plain
sight.

She wondered what kind of mess Murph was in. His message
had been brief: "Welcome home, Meg! I may be in for a long,
difficult night with our pal Larry. I don't know where the party is
being held, but try to find out and then join us. Love, Murph."

Our pal Larry! What an odd duck Murph was. She wondered
how he managed to send her a message if he was in fact in trouble.
Could Murph be the bait in a trap set for her? She would proceed
very carefully.

But if he was in serious trouble, had she time for caution?

She sat up straight. Niles had found his keys and was running
toward the truck, which miraculously had not been towed.

She waited until he had aimed the vehicle toward the east, away
from the airport, then followed at a discreet distance. She assumed
Niles would be traveling the Access Road to the Dulles Connector
and then via I-66 into the heart of Washington. It was the fastest
way into town and he seemed to be in a hurry. She felt she could

afford to allow him a nice long lead for at least the next twenty-five miles. Then, as they neared the city, she'd have to close the gap a little.

The car heater was working perfectly. She felt good. She was back in a city she understood, among people who behaved, if not exactly rationally, at least with some definable purpose in mind.

Of course she may have misconstrued the whole thing. Perhaps Kerry Niles wouldn't lead her to Newfield and Murph. She chewed on that thought for a while, then said aloud, "Nawww."

She was in control of the situation.

55

♦

Los Angeles

♦

"Power corrupts, but lack of power corrupts absolutely."

ADLAI STEVENSON

ALBERT AND HIS friend escorted Jake from his suite down flights
of stairs to the second floor and the business offices of the Casa Bel
Air. The last time Jake had been there, he'd seen Tommy Hamilton
die. He wondered what this visit would bring.

He had tried talking to the men, but they didn't seem to care for
conversation.

At the door to the office once occupied by the unfortunate
Tommy Hamilton, the sallow-faced man knocked twice. A male
voice told them to come in.

Theo Koriallis was seated on the chrome skeleton chair. Behind
him, the safe was open. Jake assumed that its contents were the
folders and ledgers now resting on the desk.

Koriallis stared at him, then said, "I know who you are, Alban.
A liar, a male prostitute, a seller of secrets. A man looking for
trouble. How marvelous to be you."

"This is just what I need," Jake replied, "a well-known international crook and third-rate, overaged Don Juan giving me lessons
in ethics."

Albert stepped forward scowling, but Koriallis smiled and held
up a hand in a restraining gesture. He leaned back against the

skeleton. "Mr. Alban," he said, "if by some rare stroke of luck you should still be alive by sunup, I want you out of this hotel, out of this city, and most definitely out of Laura Christen's life. Find some other story to amuse yourself and the swine you work for."

"You never give up, do you?" Jake countered. "How many times does Laura have to break clear of you?"

"You're a foolish scribbler who understands nothing. I have no illusions about Laura and myself. All I want is for her to be safe from the harm people like you can bring her."

"Me harm her? I want to help her."

"Then stay away from her," Koriallis said. He waved his hand. "That's all I have to say to you. Please go."

"Are you the new top man at Hamilton Industries?"

"Goodbye, Mr. Alban," Koriallis said, picking up a folder and emptying its contents onto the desk.

Jake felt Albert's steel-clamp fingers grab his arm, moving him toward the door. He twisted his head and yelled, "Who's calling the shots at Intercom, you or Lawrence Newfield?"

"Wait," Koriallis said quietly and the fingers on Jake's arm relaxed. "What exactly do you think you know about Intercom?"

"I know that its activities are very diverse. I know that its employees set fire to houses, maybe even kill people. I know that one of them is following Laura's limousine right now."

"What?" Koriallis leaned forward, forgetting the papers on his desk.

"When she left the hotel a Mercedes with an Intercom license plate was following her limo."

Koriallis frowned. "Dammit. I warned her." He stared at Jake. "I told her what she had to do, but she's a very willful woman. She's flying back to Washington. I don't know if they will try to stop her here or when she arrives. I only know they will try to stop her."

"Who's 'they'?"

"The mercenaries who work for Newfield. He has decided that she is a danger, throwing too much light on his activities at Lady Amber."

"Maybe I can help her," Jake said.

Koriallis paused. "Not very much."

"More than if I stay here talking with you."

Koriallis stood up. He searched for a slip of paper on the desk, found it. He said, "Laura's plane for Washington leaves in less than an hour. Here is the information. She made the reservations under her maiden name, Laura Foster. If they have not already intercepted her limousine and if you hurry, you may be able to find her. There will be a reservation for you by the time you arrive. Be especially watchful when you reach Washington. Newfield's power emanates from that city."

Jake was confused and suspicious of Koriallis. But he saw no alternative course of action. He grabbed the slip of paper and rushed from the room.

"See that he leaves here without incident," Koriallis told his two associates.

"Should we follow him, sir?" Albert asked.

"No," Koriallis said. "We may not have removed all of the listening devices from this room. If that is the case, I will be needing you here. There are only so many bodies you can guard at one time. Remember whose is number one."

56

◆

Washington

◆

"If God had wanted us to think with our
wombs, why did He give us a brain?"

CLARE BOOTHE LUCE

MARGARET WAS EXPECTING Kerry Niles' truck to follow Route 66
into D.C., but instead it turned north on Highway 495 along the
Capital Beltway. Circling Bethesda, it continued on until the Connecticut off-ramp.

Wishing there were more traffic to mask her car, Margaret took
the turnoff, too, following it along the East-West Highway until
Beach Drive when Niles made a right turn.

Margaret's car and the brown truck had been the only two
vehicles on the road at that early hour. There was no way she could
follow without Niles spotting her, so she continued on along the
highway toward Silver Spring. At the next exit, however, she made
an abrupt exit, then doubled back toward Beach Drive.

The truck was nowhere to be seen.

Cursing, she cruised slowly down Beach until she passed some-
thing that brought a smile to her face. It was a large walled area.
Thick, carved wooden letters sunk into the wall read: BROOKE-
VILLE—A LADY AMBER SPA.

Beside a closed iron gate there were two other signs. One said:
PRIVATE—GUESTS ONLY. The other: NO SOLICITATIONS! NO TRES-
PASSING!

Just past the gate was a brightly lit booth in which two guards sat, warm and cozy in the frosty pre-dawn morning.

Margaret drove around the four-mile circumference of the spa. Then she started around it again, parking her car along a perpendicular, residential side street. Her reason for choosing that particular street was the proximity of an oak tree growing close to the wall, its branches picked clean by the frost.

Sighing, she opened her flight bag and removed a pair of black pants, a dark sweater, and black gym shoes. With some difficulty, she shimmied out of her jacket, her blouse, her skirt and, shivering in the cold that was finally overtaking the car's preheated air, she worked her way into the dark clothes.

She reached a hand into her bag to find her pistol. Instead, she came up with Kerry Niles' little 9mm Nova. She checked its magazine. Eight rounds. She snapped the magazine back into place and tucked the pistol behind her belt.

Stepping from the car, she felt a familiar painful twinge in her hip. It reminded her precisely how much grief she owed Newfield and his friends.

57
♦

Los Angeles

♦

"Knowledge is power, if you know it
about the right person."

ETHEL WATTS MUMFORD

LAURA'S LIMOUSINE WORKED its way toward the Santa Monica
Freeway, where it joined the light flow of traffic south to LAX.
The phone in the limo began to chirp. She saw the chauffeur lift
his receiver, then heard his voice over an intercom. "Mr. Koriallis,
Congresswoman. He says it's very important."

She nodded and lifted the receiver. "I don't want to hear any
more, Theo. Not about you, or Jake Alban, or Lady Amber. I
thought I made that clear."

His reply was lost as she replaced the receiver. She pressed the
button on the intercom and asked, "Is there a way to disconnect
these phones?"

"Yes, ma'am. I'll take care of it."

She leaned back against the cushions and looked out at the dull,
artificially lighted landscape rushing past—billboards, marquees,
flat, clapboard houses selling for only $300,000 because they were
too near the Freeway. Southern California. Her home. Oddly
enough, when she was in Washington, she missed it.

AT the United terminal she tipped the chauffeur and, over his
protests, took her luggage to the departure counter herself to check

it. With her ticket she was handed a small envelope with the name "Laura Foster" written by hand.

It was a phone message that had come in for her. She opened it and removed a memo sheet from which the name Theo Koriallis leaped. *My God,* she thought, *he even knows the name I'm traveling under. Well, it won't do him any good.*

She crumpled the note, unread, and deposited it in a waste receptacle, moving on to the metal detectors.

She found a moderately comfortable chair near her departure gate and stretched out on it. She had barely shut her eyes when she felt someone shaking her and looked up to see an airline official standing before her anxiously. "Ma'am," he said, "your flight is boarding."

ON the plane, she asked the flight attendant if the seat next to hers was going to be vacant. "I'd like to get a little sleep," she explained.

"Let me check, Miss Foster."

In a minute the hostess was back. "The seat has been assigned, but we're taking off in five minutes and it looks as though he may be a no-show."

"Afraid not," Jake Alban said, waving his boarding pass.

Laura glanced at him, then turned to the attendant. "Are there any other vacant seats?"

"I'll go check," she said.

Jake sat down next to Laura. She turned away, facing the bulkhead window.

"Please listen to me."

"There's nothing I want to hear."

"How about the fact that I'm in love with you?"

"Is that supposed to make me feel privileged?" she asked tartly. "I'm loved by a man who sleeps with Penelope Krim?"

"What? Come on, now. Sleep with her? I mean, Penny is beautiful, and kind, and generous. But she's just not my type."

She turned to face him. "This isn't funny."

"Who said it was? I'm serious."

"Penelope Krim is as beautiful, kind, and generous as . . . as an angry rhino," Laura said. "Which she vaguely resembles."

"I guess it's all in the eye of the beholder," Jake said. "But let's assume you're right, Laura. If she were a disgusting, selfish, arrogant insult to the female sex, why would I want to sleep with her? Why would I even want to work for her?"

"But you do work for her."

"Not as of"—he looked at his watch—"an hour ago."

The flight attendant was standing beside them. "There's an empty seat in the first row, Miss Foster."

"That's too close to the cockpit," Jake said.

Laura stared at him, then turned to the attendant. "It is a little close," she said. "Thanks, but this seat is fine."

The hostess shrugged and moved on to satisfy the whims of some other first-class passenger. "If you have something to tell me, I'm prepared to listen," Laura said to Jake. "But I want the whole story from the top, not the edited copy."

"Yes," he said. "You deserve at least that. But first I want to show someone to you."

He pointed to a man seated across the aisle slightly forward of them, studying a magazine. He was thick-chested, wearing an expensive gray suit. His dark hair had been cut in a severe crew style, so that his white scalp showed through. His eyebrows were thick and black. "Look familiar?"

She shook her head. "Not at all."

"He works for Intercom. He and his friends set fire to Gordon Lavery's home."

"Gordon Lavery's home? I don't understand."

So he told her what had happened during the last few days, and about the bad trouble they both were in.

"But," she protested, "I don't know anything about Intercom except what I've read in the papers, and I'm not sure I've ever heard of Lawrence Newfield."

"Well," Jake told her, "he has definitely heard of you."

58

◆

Washington

◆

"He who asks questions cannot avoid the answers."

CAMEROONIAN PROVERB

MARGARET, IN BLACK from head to feet and with her pistol tucked into her belt, paused on the top of the wall surrounding Brookeville, braced by the overhanging branch of an oak tree. Shivering, she stared out across several acres of cold earth and wintry woodland, purposely landscaped to resemble the non-landscaped.

It was the area where the spa's enthusiastic fitness teams led the overfed and underdeveloped of the capital and its environs on revitalizing jogs and walks in the wee small hours. Margaret saw no movement of any kind, human or animal. The odds were that there would be no guard dogs that might nip the paying customers by mistake, but one never knew.

She ran a gloved hand along the wall and felt no alarm wires. *Well, here goes nothing,* she told herself as she dropped to the earth inside the grounds. Her destination was a complex of red brick buildings that appeared to be living quarters.

She circled the buildings, peeking into windows, observing the early morning kitchen crew at work preparing breakfast and, farther on, a yawning woman at a desk in the lobby, jotting down notes while consulting a computer screen. An assortment of young men and women in brown uniforms were dusting the halls and the large dining room.

Margaret had followed Niles in the hope that he would lead her to Murph and Newfield. But the building was immense. Too many rooms to try each one. And too many people wandering about. And the maddening thing was that she wasn't absolutely certain that Murphy was there.

That concern disappeared when she spotted his gunmetal-gray Lincoln, parked among several dozen other vehicles in an open-air port topped by a tin roof.

The Lincoln was unlocked. No one was about. She entered the car, hoping to find some clue as to what to do next. What she found was a large smear of dried blood on the driver's headrest.

59

◆

"What counts is not necessarily the size of
the dog in the fight—it's the size of the
fight in the dog."

DWIGHT D. EISENHOWER

MURPHY AWOKE TO a splitting headache. He thought at first that
he'd lost the use of his hands and was only mildly relieved to recall
that they were secured behind him with wire.

He was sitting on a wooden chair in a pine-paneled room. The
floor consisted of a wood grating. When he'd been brought to the
room, he'd been told that it was a malfunctioning sauna, and
though its steaming days were apparently over, it served his cap-
tives' purposes quite well since it was soundproof.

He was not alone in the sauna. The tanned blond man who had
knocked him out was standing by the door, arguing with Larry
Newfield. Newfield called the man a "screw-up," and Murphy
smiled. "Don't mind Larry, son. He tends to blame the troops
when things go sour."

Newfield turned from the blond man and strolled over to Murphy. He stood in front of the detective, and removed a service
pistol from his belt. It had a gold filigreed frame and mother-of-
pearl grips.

Newfield used its squat, ornate barrel to lift Murphy's chin.

"Awake again, eh, Murph?" Newfield said, sounding bored.
"This time try to stay with the program. I know about the Laura
Christen letters that went out to Mike Roberts and that *National
Examiner* scumbag, Dunbar. What others are there?"

"You're asking the wrong boy, Larry old sod. No reason not to tell you a little thing like that. If I knew."

"You don't expect me to take I-don't-know for an answer." Larry yawned. "Before it's over, you'll tell me what I want. And you'll help me lure Margaret out here, too."

"Meg doesn't exactly come running when I call, Larry."

"She'll come. She's loyal, like her old man. But until she arrives, let's use the time. What do you know about Intercom?"

"I was asking my broker that very same question only yesterday."

Newfield smiled. "And what did he say?"

"Not a promising investment. Too much deadwood at the top."

Newfield drew back his gun and whacked the side of Murphy's head with it. "We've been through too many campaigns, Murph. You know the wise-guy act won't play in this room. I want you to tell me everything you and Margaret found out about the people trying to smear Congresswoman Christen."

The blow had caused Murph's right eye to blink uncontrollably. He said, "So far, Larry, you're our main suspect."

"Me? Don't be an asshole. Whoever's been spreading tales about Christen has also jeopardized my little operation. I just got rid of a couple of blackmailers who were the likely culprits. But I want to make sure."

"Gee, boyo, but a passel of bodies have floated over the dam on this one."

"Don't tell me you're crying over a couple of drug peddlers, goddamn blackmailers, the both of them?"

Murphy shrugged. "Those are new ones on me. I'm thinking more about a private detective named Stuart Wayland who left a nice wife and kid." He paused and added, "And maybe the hotel guy, Hamilton. And Charlie Stern."

"Charlie's not dead, merely resting," Newfield said with a nasty laugh. "Maybe we should bring him down here."

Newfield turned to the other men. "Kerry, go up to the Rose Room and get Stern for us." The tanned blond's face remained sullen, but he headed for the door. "And send the woman down, too," Newfield added.

Murphy squeezed both eyes shut, then opened them. The nerve

that had been affected by the last blow seemed to be quieting down. He watched Newfield as he strutted up and down the room. He said, "Sit down, Larry. You're making me tired, man."

"Wait'll you see Charlie, Murph. He's never felt better. Getting three squares a day, naps in the afternoon."

Murphy yawned and let his head fall to his chest.

In about ten minutes Niles returned with two people. One was Charles Stern, looking hale and hearty as advertised. The other was Murphy's secretary, Nina.

The detective blinked and looked at her. He put as much sadness into his voice as he could and said, "Morning, Nina. Doin' a little moonlighting, I gather."

Nina looked away. "You can take this as official notice of her leaving your firm, Murph," Newfield said.

"I don't imagine she was ever really there," Murphy said with a tinge of wistfulness.

"It was a matter of money, Murph," she said. "Nothing personal."

"Oh, hell no, Nina. Nothing personal at all. Try telling that to all the folks who went on the big sleep this go-round. Nothing personal at all."

Murphy glanced at Charles Stern, who hadn't moved from the center of the room. He was dressed in jogging clothes—matching sweatshirt and pants, dark blue in color with a bright yellow stripe down the arms and legs.

"Well, Charlie, what do you think about all this shop talk?" Murphy asked. Stern held his head at a strange tilt, staring at a spot where the wall met the ceiling as if it were the most fascinating thing he'd ever seen. He said, "I ran five miles today and wasn't even winded."

"Well, that's something," Murphy said. He turned to Newfield and asked, "What's he on, Larry?"

Newfield grinned wolfishly. "Something we're playing with a Lady Amber. Wipes the old memory slate clean. No more stress. No cares of the day. No mental problems of any kind. Just physical gratification. Eat. Sleep. Screw. What a life!"

"I ran five miles today and wasn't even winded," Stern said.

"Your wonder drug does seem to limit conversation, Larry," Murphy said.

"Another of its positive benefits."

"So that's how the folks at Lady Amber spend their time, coming up with magic potions and the like?"

Newfield nodded. "It was beautiful, Murph. About twelve years ago, before I was elected the head of Intercom, the company decided to make a grab on Hamilton Resorts, a reasonable acquisition. We had a nice sharp sword to hold over Ivor Hamilton's head—we found out his son was guilty of vehicular homicide, and the lad seemed inordinately fond of little girls. Some piece of work, our Tommy was. So Ivor caves in without a fight and we're patting ourselves on the back and none of us even realized the true value of HRI —it controlled Lady Amber. A completely respectable cosmetics firm."

"Excuse me," Nina cut in. "If you're through with me, Larry, I'd like to get some sleep."

"Sure, honey," Newfield said. "I just wanted you to say hello to Murph."

Nina looked at Murphy, scowled, and left the room.

"I swear, Murph," Newfield said. "The way you train your people is pathetic. That little lady has been spoiled rotten. She is gonna have to shape up or ship out. Anyway, where were we before we were so rudely interrupted?"

"The respectability of Lady Amber."

"Exactly. It was respectable when we took it over. It's still respectable, only now the company spends a lot of time developing new and better products. Take this stuff we market under the name Maintain. Men our age have a quick pop and suddenly it's like being back in Saigon with a little yellow gal on each knee. But that's not the beauty part. Increase the dose with a little bit of this and a little bit of that and . . . whammo. Even a dour, uptight Russian, come to town to win hearts and minds to the benefits of unrestricted international trade, can wind up in the kip with jailbait. Result: a protectionist bill. We control the whole goddamn show, Murph. If we want a bill passed, it gets passed. If we want it to bomb, its proponents are going to find themselves in the juiciest sex scandals brains even more demented than mine can conceive.

Hookers on houseboats in the Potomac. Teenage boys being molested in the Senate elevator. A congressman's wife being schtupped on the Capitol steps by Ralph, their loyal German shepherd. You name it, we can arrange it. As a former president was once heard to say, progress is our most important product.''

Murphy groaned. "It's so disillusionin'. Haven't we got enough bad boy politicos with overdeveloped libidos without you lobbyists slipping aphrodisiacs into the Perrier?''

Newfield chuckled. "Never underestimate the power of love, Murph.''

Murphy took a deep breath and let it out slowly. He was sorry that Newfield was being so candid with him. It meant that he probably wouldn't be passing any of the information along.

"Maybe I won't put you away, Murph,'' Newfield said, as though reading his thoughts. "Maybe I'll just dust off that devious mind of yours. In any case, I don't plan on doing anything to you just yet.'' He cast a dark glance at Kerry Niles. "My formerly faithful right hand seems unable to get Margaret out here. So you're going to have to do it, Murph.''

"I don't think so.''

Newfield grabbed Murphy's hair, yanked his head up off his chest, and pushed his face close to Murphy's. "You definitely have a warm spot for the girl, don't you, Murph? Can't say I blame you—she is a hot little bitch. I think she's sorta sweet on me.''

"Then maybe you're the one should give her a call, Larry.''

Newfield released Murphy's hair and wiped his hand with disgust on the detective's shoulder. "No. You're gonna bring her here for me.''

"You know, Larry,'' Murphy said, "since we all left Uncle Sam's employ, we've shifted careers a bit. But you're the only one of us who's made the move from mercenary to business executive seem like a step down.''

Suddenly there was the sound of a fire alarm blasted through the room. Newfield shouted to Niles to check it out.

Niles opened the door to distant panic shouts and the faint smell of smoke. "It's a fire,'' he said dumbly.

"Take a look. If it's serious, come back here. Fast,'' Newfield growled, moving to the screaming alarm and pulling the switch that silenced it. The door closing behind Niles left the room in total silence.

"There was a time when I would have wanted a backup to handle you," Newfield said to Murphy. "But you've been eating too many candy bars, honey."

"My partner handles the physical demands of the business," Murphy said. "She was trained by experts." Then, for no reason Newfield could discern, the Irishman gave him a wide grin.

60

◆

Airborne

◆

"Our problems are man-made, therefore
they may be solved by man."

JOHN F. KENNEDY

AFTER JAKE HAD dozed off in the darkened first-class cabin, Laura
remained awake, thinking, trying to sort out her priorities. She got
as far as the first two—her increasing affection for Jake and the
fact that someone had a contract out on both of them. Then she fell
asleep.

She was awakened by Jake's arm brushing across her to pick up
a copy of *Newsweek*. He turned to the Newsmakers page. She saw
her own picture, taken during a session arranged by Catsy, staring
back at her.

Jake, seeing that she was awake, began softly reading the squib,
something about "the specter of House sexism rears its head
. . . and she's a knockout!"

"Please," Laura said. "No politics. I'd rather hear more about
Intercom. If it's as enormous an organization as you and Theo
seem to think, the fellow across the aisle may have some buddies
waiting at Dulles."

Jake nodded. "Maybe we should call ahead and have the police
standing by when we land."

"Really? And what exactly do I tell them?"

"Theo Koriallis said that—"

"I hate to tell you this, Jake, but Theo is not exactly the voice of truth and honesty."

"At least we could show them our friend the crew cut across the aisle."

"What about him?" Laura asked, annoyed. "He's guilty of purchasing a first-class ticket and having a bad haircut. You have to understand my position, Jake. In spite of everything, I haven't abandoned my plan to give Lew Ronkowski a fight. And I can't do that if the word gets out that I've suddenly turned into a raving paranoid."

"Then," Jake replied with a sickly smile, "we have only three hours and forty-five minutes to figure out how to deal with the rest of the Intercom team."

61

◆

Washington

◆

"I'm not afraid to die. I just don't want to
be there when it happens."

WOODY ALLEN

THE DRAPES IN the large living room gave Margaret the idea. They
were thick and smelled of cleaning solvent. It took only two
wooden matches from the box she'd lifted from the kitchen's
larder to start a small fire. Actually the drapes smoldered more than
burned, which was fine with her. She wasn't trying to kill anyone,
just clear the building. Along with the matches she had helped
herself to a maid's long cotton smock that concealed her black
combat outfit and her gun.

The sweepers and dusters were the first to react. Then the
banshee-like alarms kicked in. The halls began to fill with spa
guests, looking anything but bright and cheery in their robes and
slippers as they scuttled for fresh air.

Margaret left her place of hiding and darted in and out against
the flow of human traffic—just one of the hired help. Pausing just
inside a room that tried to look like an English study, with wall-to-
wall books, a fireplace, and sturdy leather furniture, she watched
the staff frantically trying to bring the guests to order. An old
woman had fainted; others, men and women alike, were running
about and screaming. Some had, against orders, returned to their
rooms for valuables.

She saw Kerry Niles entering the hallway from a stairwell near the rear of the building. She ducked back into the room and waited for him to go by, then went out and mixed with the crowd, moving against the rear stairwell.

She followed it down to a wide, deserted hallway with a gleaming tile floor and a series of doors labeled ADMIN. OFFICE, ACCOUNTING, SOCIAL DIRECTOR, MASSEUSE. She paused at the first, ADMIN. OFFICE, pressed her ear to the door, and heard nothing.

But she noticed something. Marring the polished corridor were two dark streaks—the kind that might be made from the rubber soles of a man's shoes if he were being dragged. The streaks led past the offices and turned in at a door at the very end of the hall marked SAUNA. There was a wooden sign hanging on a hook at the center of the door. It read, UNDER RENOVATION. USE SAUNA, BUILDING A.

Margaret bent close to the door. She removed her maid's smock, took out her gun and started to place her hand on the knob.

Someone standing behind her said in a soft, whispery voice, "Hi, lady. Can I have my little gun back now?"

She turned around very cautiously. Kerry Niles was pointing a .357 Magnum at her face. "This is its big brother," he said, twisting her weapon from her hand. He pushed the muzzle of the Magnum an inch from her nose and cocked the hammer. "Now, let's go in, OK?"

Inside the sauna, Margaret first saw her partner, in a chair. His head and collar were covered with blood, but he seemed to be alive. Charlie Stern was standing nearby, humming happily to himself and looking at the ceiling. Newfield was seated on a sauna bench, neatly attired in a gray business suit. He stood up and said politely, "Margaret—I can't tell you how happy I am to see you again."

She took a deep breath. "I'm happy to see you again, too, Lawrence. Because now I can tell you to your face what a fever-brained weasel you are."

"Oh dear—and I thought we were so close."

"Do you always use drugs on your women, Larry? Is that the only way you can get any?"

Newfield's smile vanished. He studied Margaret carefully, weighing some sort of decision.

"Fire trucks coming, sir," Niles interrupted. "We've got maybe five-ten minutes."

"No time for anything fancy," Newfield told him. "Prepare a couple of hits."

Niles took out a black leather case from his pocket. When Margaret had searched him, she'd made a big mistake in assuming it was a cigar case. But Kerry Niles used it to store several small vials and two devices that looked like sawed-off hypodermics.

"I ran five miles today and I wasn't even winded!" Charles Stern proudly informed them yet again.

"What's wrong with him?" Margaret asked.

"Some of that . . . special Lady Amber medicine," Murphy told her. His voice was slurred and hesitant. "They're gonna market it . . . as Instant Alzheimer's, the Balm for Overactive Minds. . . . I think Larry's cute boyfriend is fixing us with a potion."

"No," Newfield said. "This is some good old reliable Maintain Maximum. The diagnosis will be heart attack, in this case prompted by asphyxiation."

Margaret turned to Murphy. "Blondie's got a twin sister, Murph," she said. "That's how I made him at the airport. They look alike."

Newfield shot an angry glance at Niles.

"At least they *used* to look so much alike," Margaret said.

"What's that supposed to mean?" Niles asked.

"Don't pay her any mind, Kerry," Newfield said. "Just do the goddamn job."

The sauna door opened and a familiar face appeared. A sudden flutter of hope rose in Margaret's breast. But it died when Nina turned to Newfield and said, "Larry, the whole front of this goddamn building is like a smokehouse. What's happening?"

"Ask Margaret," Newfield said. "I suspect she's the firebug."

Margaret looked at Nina sadly. She'd always liked the woman.

"This is for you," Newfield said, handing Nina the Magnum.

Nina was surprised by the gun's weight. It took both hands to position it. "This isn't something I do," she said, pouting.

"She doesn't do windows or guns," Murphy said.

"You're paid to do what I tell you," Newfield told her. He moved toward the door. "Now keep an eye on Margaret and Murph while Kerry gets ready."

"Where are *you* going?" Nina asked.

"If you must know, since the people I pay can't seem to accomplish it, I'm going to put the lid on this nonsense myself by getting rid of the source of our concern."

He paused at the door for a final look at Margaret, saluted, grinned, and made his exit.

Margaret turned to Murphy, gave him an imperceptible nod, and began to shuffle away from him.

"Stop right there!" Niles shouted at her. "Nina, if either of them moves, shoot that bitch. Don't worry about the old mick."

"It would be hard to shoot old Murph," Nina said, "but I've never much cared for you, Margaret."

So much for friendship, Margaret thought.

Niles held up a syringe. Instead of flanges, the barrel of it was smooth, tapering out to a hollow top. Inside it was the plunger. The whole thing was designed to fit like a cap on a finger, needle pointing out. With one poke of the finger, the needle would prick the skin and at the same time the plunger would be depressed.

It reminded Margaret of something that Boris Karloff might have used in one of those old horror movies her father used to love. She was so fascinated by the design of the thing that she had to force herself to look away from it.

"Well, I guess Larry has saved his own skin," Murphy said.

"Shut up," Niles ordered.

"It was like that in Vietnam, too," Murphy went on. "Last in and first out . . . Our man Larry . . . Nobody you'd want to share a foxhole with. Or a prison cell. Isn't that right, Charlie?"

"Five miles today and I wasn't even winded," Charlie told him.

Nina licked her lips nervously. "Kerry—can't you step on it a little?"

"Is that fire trucks I hear?" Murphy asked. The noise was loud enough now to enter the thick-walled room.

"The police," Margaret added. "I called them too."

Niles didn't react. The needle was in place, capped on the index finger of his right hand.

Nina suddenly panicked and shoved the Magnum at him, butt-first. "Here. Take this. I'm out of here."

Niles grabbed the Magnum with his left hand. "Unreliable skank," he grumbled. He turned to Murphy. "You first, gramps." He was only inches away from the chair, needle held close, point upward.

"I broke her face," Margaret said loudly.

"Huh?" Niles shifted his gaze to her.

"I smashed in your sister's face," Margaret said matter of factly. "Broke her nose. Put a nice deep gash right across her forehead. It'll take more than Lady Amber to make her look like a human being again."

Niles, trembling with rage, raised the gun. "You're dead."

Murphy seemed to shrink down in the chair, then suddenly he pushed his shoulder up under Niles' wrist. The blow was not forceful, but it was enough to set off the hair trigger of the Magnum. The report was tremendous in the small room, and shattered a portion of the wall not far from Charlie's head. He didn't even flinch.

Margaret took a step and then kicked out, catching Niles' right elbow with her toe. Following the elbow, up went the hand and the finger and the needle, which entered the underside of Niles' chin. Screaming, he jerked it out and whirled on Margaret.

He tried to bring his gun around and aim it at her, but his arm refused to obey him. He sighed as the gun dropped to the floor. With a last burst of strength he made an ineffectual swipe at Margaret's shoulder with the needle, missing by a foot.

His back was to Murphy, who had drawn up his knees with the idea of trying to kick Niles in the spine, but it wasn't necessary. Niles stiffened and began to pant. His tanned face was now a bright purple.

Howling, he threw himself onto a sauna bench and began to grind his pelvis against it.

Charlie gave up his contemplation of the ceiling to calmly observe Niles' gyrations.

Margaret helped her partner out of the chair and began to undo the wire around his wrists. Murphy weaved, but managed to stay upright. Like Charlie, he was fascinated by Niles, who was now flopping like a flounder against the bench.

"Isn't that something," Murphy said.

"I ran—" Charlie started to say.

Margaret was standing by the open door. Smoke was pouring into the hall and into the sauna room. "Are you guys coming?" she called to them.

Murphy took a last look at Niles, whose body gave a final, galvanic jerk and was still. He said, "Show's over. Time to go, Charlie."

"Do you need help?" Margaret asked Murphy, who nodded.

She let him drape his arm over her shoulder. They were about to start out when he said, "Wait." Holding her arm, he bent down and retrieved the black leather case that still contained an unused hypodermic device and several vials of fluid.

"What do you want with that?" Margaret asked disgustedly as she helped him and Stern from the room.

"I was thinking the office could use a display case full of stuff like this. Souvenirs from a life on the edge."

"Idiot! We're running out of fresh air and you're still playing the fool." They were in the smoky hall now.

"On the other hand, Christmas is just around the corner. This could be the perfect gift for the gal who has everything." He wiggled his eyebrows at her.

"That's it," she said, shaking loose of his arm. "Find your own goddamned way out. Charlie and I are going to run. Come on, Charlie."

"Five miles?" Charlie asked.

62

◆

"The efforts which we make to escape
from our destiny only serve to lead us into
it."

RALPH WALDO EMERSON

"I DON'T THINK we want to hang around for your luggage," Jake
told Laura as they moved through the terminal.

"My car isn't far," she said.

"Let's catch a cab," he said. "It's quicker and we don't have
to worry about wandering around in isolated parking structures."
As he spoke, he searched the crowd, trying to catch sight of the
man with the crew cut, but failing.

Outside the terminal they brushed past an elderly man and
entered a just-arrived taxi that he had been waiting for. The old
man looked at them through the window of the cab. He was
wrapped in a thick dark blue overcoat, a yellow muffler, and a soft
brown hat. "I was here first," his reedy voice complained.

"I'm sorry, sir, but this is a matter of life and death," Jake said.

"But I was here first!"

"There'll be another cab in a minute, sir," the driver told him.
It in no way appeased the old man. The driver was a thin black man
with glasses that had been taped at one joint. His freshly pressed
white collar under his bulky sweater suggested that he'd just come
on duty. He asked their destination and as Laura gave him her
address, he rolled up the side window, cutting off the old man's
mutterings.

"God, I hate people who do what we just did," Laura said. She sighed, took a deep breath, and smelled the coffee in a paper cup that was held in a plastic ring on the driver's dash. She grimaced and asked Jake, "How many cups of that stuff did I have on the plane?"

"I lost track at nine."

As his cab moved out into traffic, the driver noticed Jake looking intently at the terminal's exit doors. "Everything all right back there, folks?" he asked.

"I think so," Jake told him. "I think things are fine." Then he smiled at Laura and leaned against the cab's worn seat and relaxed.

THE man with a crew cut moved beside the old codger at the cab stand and watched Laura and Jake as they drove away. The man turned to him. "I'm next!" he said defiantly. "I already had one goddamned cab stolen right out from under me."

"Relax, pops. The next one's all yours. I don't suppose you heard that couple say where they were headed?" the newcomer asked.

"Just because I'm eighty-two doesn't mean I'm deaf," the old man answered testily. Then he proved just how acute his hearing was.

Shivering in the Washington chill, the man with the crew cut ran back inside the terminal. He found the nearest bank of pay phones and dialed a number that connected him with a machine. He repeated the address the old man had given him, then said it again, slowly. He did not know or care why his boss, Lawrence Newfield, wanted to know Laura Christen's destination. He only knew that his job was now completed and he could catch the next flight back to L.A. He hadn't had time to grab either topcoat or sweater. And now he wouldn't need them. Every so often things worked out the way they were supposed to.

63

•

> "Plans get you into things, but you got to
> work your own way out."
>
> WILL ROGERS

"WE SHOULDN'T HAVE just left Charlie there, wandering around
boasting about his long-distance running," Margaret said to Murphy, who was fiddling with his car phone. They were parked just
outside the spa area. The slate-gray morning sky was clotted with
dense black smoke.

"The crowd was very impressed with his achievement," Murphy said. "Besides, we'd have been stuck till Christ got back up
on the cross if we let that bunch start askin' us questions. There are
times to stay, Meg, and times to—" He shifted his attention to the
phone. "Hello, who's this? Well, Miss Halloran, you'd better
wake up your duty man and tell him that Charles Stern of your
office is in crucial four condition at Brookeville Spa out in Rollingwood, Maryland. It's by the— Yeah, that's right: where the big fire
is. Make sure you tell the duty man that Stern has been fed some
kind of chemical . . . No, Miss Halloran, I don't think I'd like to
leave my name."

He hung up.

Margaret stared out the window at the smoke and the fire engines roaring past. "I feel lousy about Nina," she said.

"Not as lousy as she's gonna feel," Murphy said. "But first
things first. Is Laura Christen still in Los Angeles?"

"Last I heard."

"I don't suppose you heard where she was staying?"

Margaret shrugged. "Her office here might know."

A few minutes later he replaced the receiver and told Margaret, "She's supposed to be coming into the office in the afternoon. Maybe she's back in town already."

"So?" Margaret said.

"When Larry took his powder, he mentioned something about cutting off his whole problem at the source. I think the Congresswoman *is* the aforementioned source."

"So what's our plan?" she asked.

"My God, woman," Murphy said. "Don't you know that plans never work. That's why we're gonna rely on good old-fashioned blind luck."

64

◆

"I captured some of the people who tried to assassinate me. I ate them before they ate me."

IDI AMIN

HEADING FOR LAURA's house in Georgetown, Jake and Laura's taxi found itself in the midst of the morning rush hour. The twenty-six-mile trip from Dulles into the Capital took over an hour, and it was 10:15 when Laura finally used her key to let herself and Jake into the nearly two-hundred-year-old building.

Jake checked the street a final time before entering, but the area seemed peaceful enough, filled with the usual morning sights.

Still, he felt safer once they were inside Laura's home. He was even relaxed enough to appreciate the tasteful furnishings and decor of the spacious living room. While Laura headed for the kitchen to seek out the rudiments of a light breakfast, his eyes naturally moved to one book-lined wall—reading material was as good as a psychoanalytic evaluation of its owner.

He studied the titles on the shelves. They were mainly nonfiction—biographies, a few historical studies, a smattering of essays. He couldn't stop himself from looking for his own books. He found one of his better "as-told-tos," devoted to the life and times of a former secretary of state. Beside it was his Vietnam book, *Distant Echoes,* which had been issued as quietly as a whisper and shortly went out of print. He knew now that he definitely was in love.

Almost childishly, he pulled the volume from the shelf and

started to carry it to the kitchen to show Laura. Before he could get there he heard her scream, *"Jake—run! Get out!"*

Then she was being shoved through the kitchen door, stumbling, hitting the doorframe with her shoulder. Behind her was Lawrence Newfield. The president of Intercom held a beautifully ornate pistol in his right hand.

"Laura didn't really mean that, Jake," he said. "What she really wants is for the two of you to die here in each other's arms—like Romeo and Juliet. So stay where you are."

It was the light reflected off the fancy gun that caused Jake's mind to take an irrational backward spin away from the present threat and back to past dangers. Another pistol, in the fist of an evil-smelling, unshaven D.C. mugger, pushed into his neck. He started to tremble.

Then it became a sputtering Uzi in the hand of a Nicaraguan, his face covered with a red scarf. Jake reached out for the gun, but it faded away and the scene changed. There was a blinding bright light. A woman was screaming, "Don't hurt him!" Laura and Danielle were there. They looked at him and smiled, but the chandelier tinkled, exploded, and went out.

". . . a rather feeble response," a voice was saying.

Jake opened his eyes. Laura was looking down at him.

Newfield seized her by the back of the neck and held her at arm's length, his gun pointed at her head.

"There's no need to harm her," Jake said.

"Jake, I wish that were the case," Newfield said. "Congresswoman, I'd love to see you rub the nose of that gimpy bastard Ronkowski in the dirt. He's been a thorn in my side for years. But the sad fact is that I have to get the children off the street. Intercom's use of Lady Amber must stay hidden."

"Don't you think that Laura's violent death will make people all the more curious about her past?" Jake asked.

"Possibly," Newfield said thoughtfully, still holding Laura tightly. "But if she's murdered by some demented, burnt-out writer she picked up in an L.A. hotel, they'll be thinking more about that than about her past. What's your professional opinion, Jake?"

"Does the burnt-out case kill himself out of remorse?" Jake asked.

"As good a reason as any," Newfield said. He released his grip on Laura, reached inside his coat, and removed a little Beretta automatic. "I found this in your bedroom, Congresswoman. Under your lingerie. Handguns in the home—a national scandal!"

Jake threw his book at his head. Newfield ducked and the book brushed his scalp, slamming ineffectually into the wall behind him. He shifted his weight just as Jake grabbed his right ankle.

Suddenly Jake felt an explosion in the pit of his stomach where a foot had been driven. He let go of Newfield's ankle and the foot battered him again. He felt bile rise in his throat, then, from the corner of his eye, he saw the thick barrel of the Llama swinging down at him. He dodged it but the pistol connected painfully with his shoulder instead of his head.

Then he was leaning forward and Newfield's foot was rising toward his face. It collided with his chin, and his head snapped back. He fell hard onto his back.

Through blurred eyes he looked up to see Laura strike out at Newfield, but the powerfully built man merely dodged the blow and knocked her halfway across the room.

He returned his attentions to Jake, and the reporter felt a sharp pain in his side, followed by another. Newfield was kicking him in the ribs.

Jake saw a shoetip flash past his eyes. A final jolt. He saw the chandelier explode once more. This time it didn't fill him with fear. Only peace. Danielle looked at him through a red haze and said, "Goodbye."

Newfield, breathing hard now, bent down and studied the unconscious newsman. "A little slow on the reflexes to be playing the hero." He shrugged. "Laura—you can be quite the tiger when you work at it. Just look at the way you defended yourself against this poor deranged madman when he tried to attack you. I guess that's why he shot you with your own gun before he killed himself."

He aimed the Beretta at her chest. She closed her eyes.

And the door buzzer sounded. Newfield froze.

The buzzer rasped again.

"Send them away," Newfield whispered into Laura's ear. "If you don't, I'll kill them, too."

She glared at him.

"And pull yourself together, dammit. Now move!"

She straightened her hair and her dress while he dragged Jake to a spot where he couldn't be seen from the front door.

The buzzer echoed again through the house.

Newfield nodded to Laura.

She went to the door and opened it.

Standing there was a man she'd never seen before. He was large and his clothes were askew. His hair was wet and sticking up at odd angles and there was dried blood on his neck. He said, "My name is J. B. Murphy, Congresswoman, and you have no idea how happy I am to see you all glowing and alive."

Laura opened her mouth, at a loss for something to say.

Newfield stepped out of the shadows and moved behind her, aiming both guns at the newcomer. "Come on in, Murph, old friend," he said. "You're just in time for the party."

Murphy stepped reluctantly into the room. Newfield gestured to the open door. "Did you grow up in a barn?"

"In a rose garden," Murphy replied, shutting it.

"You look like hell, by the way," Newfield told him.

"You should see the other guy." Murphy was pale and breathing heavily. "It's about your junior execs, Larry. This one fell so madly in love with a sauna bench, he sorta forgot about us . . . Who's that on the floor?"

"A reporter named Jake Alban. He'd never have made it in our club, Murph. Doesn't have that competitive edge."

"He's the guy working for Penny Krim?"

"Not anymore," Laura said defensively.

"How bad off is he?" Murphy asked.

"A few taps. Nothing serious—so far." Newfield dug his toe into Jake's side. Jake moaned and opened his eyes. "Sit tight, soldier," Newfield told him, "a new recruit has joined the regiment. And that reminds me—we seem to be missing somebody. Where's your better half, Murph?"

"Well, that's the thing," Murphy said. "You see, Larry, at this exact moment Meg's chatting up some folks from the FBI about you and Intercom and Lady Amber and all those sour little secrets you've been trying so hard to keep to yourself. So the toothpaste is out of the tube and you have no reason now to kill the Congresswoman or that poor sod on the floor or anybody else. Not that you ever need a reason.''

Newfield reflected for a moment. Then he grinned. ''That's bullshit about the Feds, Murph. As long as I've known you, you've never liked or trusted those donkeys. So where's my little Margie?''

''I tried,'' Murphy said dejectedly.

''Maybe I'd better just take care of you now, Murph, and figure out later what to do with your mortal remains. You just aren't part of this scenario.''

Newfield pointed the Colt at Murphy's head, then hesitated. Murphy shouted *''No!''* at the top of his voice. Then he collapsed backward to the floor, rolled over, and appeared to pass out. Simultaneously the kitchen door swung open with such force that it smashed against the wall.

Newfield wheeled, stumbled, and fired the Colt awkwardly, without aiming.

The bullet sailed way high, into the kitchen and out the opened back door. Margaret Stafford had somersaulted into the room and was squatting near the kitchen door, aiming her Nova with both hands up at Newfield's face.

''Margaret,'' he said with a sickly smile. ''That was one hell of an entrance.''

''Drop both guns,'' she ordered.

Newfield froze. ''You know, darling,'' he said in a relaxed tone, ''I've worked with lots of women . . . and I must say that I never knew one of them who had the guts—''

She shot him just as the knuckle of his right trigger finger began to whiten.

Newfield's head jerked back so hard that his neck snapped. He fell to the carpet, his ruined face inches from Murphy's nose.

Murphy staggered to his feet as Margaret kicked both weapons from Newfield's lifeless hands. She stared so long and so hard at the dead man that Murphy was afraid she was going to be sick.

''Championship shooting, Meg,'' he said. ''You know—I tried

to do that some twenty-odd years ago, but your father stopped me. If he hadn't, think of all the hassle it would have saved.''

Jake groaned and Laura rushed to him, sat down on the carpet, and cradled his head in her lap. He opened his eyes, winced, and smiled up at her. "Laura . . . ?" She leaned down and brushed her lips across his.

"Ahem!" Murphy cleared his throat loudly and broke the mood. Laura frowned at him. "It's not that I'm ungrateful," she said, "but just who *are* you people?"

"We're just a couple of hired hands, Congresswoman," Murphy said. "Hey, Meg—catch the back door, will you? I'm freezing." Margaret stood with her hands at her sides, swaying, looking more and more pale.

"Meg!" Murphy shouted at her. "Please shut that goddamned door."

She ran into the kitchen.

"Congresswoman," Murphy said, "you'd better go get me a mop or something before the entire contents of this reprobate's skull end up on your carpet."

Ashen-faced, Laura said, "Don't worry about my carpet. I'll be getting rid of it anyway."

"Are you gonna hold up?"

She nodded weakly.

"Meg—you OK?" he shouted.

"I'll . . . be fine," she replied, walking back into the room. She took the 9 millimeter Nova from her pocket and handed it to Murphy, butt forward. "I'm sure the police will want this," she said.

"You'd better put it away for now," he said.

"The *police,*" Laura said, ruefully. "I'm very happy to be alive, but I wish I could have extended my political life a little longer, too. That doesn't seem to be in the cards."

"You never know," Murphy said. "It's cold outside—means closed windows. If your neighbors are at home, maybe they heard the shots. Maybe not. People will often talk themselves out of getting involved." He reached inside his coat and removed the leather case with the chemicals and the syringe that he'd taken from the spa. He wiped it carefully with his display handkerchief.

Then he bent down and slipped the case into Newfield's coat pocket.

He stood and addressed Jake. "There are a couple ways we can play this. We can leave poor Larry where he is and bring in some law. That might become rather troublesome for the Congresswoman and her plans to change the future of U.S. politics. Or we can deliver him somewhere it might do some good and let events take care of themselves. It's up to you."

"Me? Why me?"

"You're the newshound," Murphy said with a smile. "Which story would you rather write?"

65

◆

"I consider that women who are authors,
lawyers, and politicians are monsters."
PIERRE AUGUSTE RENOIR

PENELOPE KRIM DID not usually arrive at the office before ten, but
that morning she stormed into the Empire Building in a fury. While
she'd been on a wretchedly uncomfortable plane, nursing a painful
case of sunburn, an international banner-headline story had been
taking place without her.

And it was her goddamned story!

The papers on the desks of the weekend staff said it all, their
front pages yelling of murder and political blackmail.

The events had unfolded in stages. First was the startling revela-
tion that Lawrence P. Newfield, highly decorated Green Beret,
soldier of fortune, and CEO of the influential Intercom, Inc., had
been found murdered in his car in the Intercom garage.

No one saw the car drive in. Every executive at Intercom had his
own dark Mercedes, and the garage attendant admitted that he was
unable to tell one from the other. The slugs had passed through
Newfield's head and were nowhere to be found, making identification of the weapon impossible.

The second stage involved Intercom itself. Certain unusual articles found on Newfield's body led the police to look into the
services performed by Intercom, and this in turn opened the door
for the Federal Bureau of Investigation to enter the case.

Wild tales of drugs, sexual enslavement, blackmail, and murder
began to surface. The race to keep tabs on unfolding developments

had been so swift that, by the end of the day on Friday, the evening news reporters, including anchorman John Kilmer (who himself had broken the story of the tie-in between Intercom and the murder of local columnist Jeremy Dunbar) looked as if they'd been wrung dry.

Much of this had happened while Penelope Krim, still in Los Angeles, had fallen victim to too many piña coladas on the sunroof of the Casa Bel Air. And the goddamned Latin waiter with his dark skin and white teeth and sexy droopy moustache who'd been so attentive the whole day had turned out to be a would-be actor, a guy named Max Steinman who thought that she was a power agent.

Adding to Penelope's rage was the fact that Jake Alban's byline had appeared on a number of syndicated articles about "The Intergate Scandal."

Further, the Washington buzz had it that Alban and Congresswoman Laura Christen were spending a great deal of time together. Penelope's comment when she heard that was, "When does the son of a bitch have time to write?"

She shoved her way into Horace Marsten's office. The little man's silver hair had fallen to both sides of his nearly bald dome, and his usually dapper clothes were in dire need of a dry cleaner. He'd been working nonstop since the Intercom story surfaced and had little time for Penelope and her complaints.

In the middle of her tirade the phone rang and he picked it up. It was a proofer asking a question. Horace listened for a beat, then he stared at Penelope. "You can help with this, Penny. How cool does it get at night out there in L.A.?"

"Cool? Do I look like a goddamn barometer?"

"Would you say 'chilly' or 'frosty'?"

"Given that choice, 'chilly.' "

"Great," the little man told her and said into the phone, "Make that read, 'under the bright stars, the Lavery home burst into a glowing fireball, heating the chilly Hollywood night . . .' "

"Oh, shit!" Penelope said.

"Something the matter?" Horace Marsten looked concerned.

"Goddamn 'glowing fireball'?" she shouted. "Did that two-faced bastard Jake Alban actually use 'glowing fireball' in his article?''

"Sure did. Very visual. It's being picked up by four hundred and thirty-two papers. By the way, honey, you're gonna need a new assistant. Louise is working with Jake for a while."

"Well, hell, Horace, why don't you just give him my office while you're at it?"

Horace Marsten stared at her, his silence offering her little assurance and no satisfaction. When he did finally speak it was to ask, "What in the world's the matter with your face, Penny? Is that sunburn or hives?"

Her response was to storm out, slamming the door behind her.

Back in her office, she flopped behind her desk, opened her briefcase, and removed the folder containing the Lavery drug receipts. Her tiny eyes glittered like marbles on her lobster-red face. She lifted the phone and dialed a number.

She had to go through two secretaries before she reached Catsy Braden. "I want to meet with your mother," she said.

"I'm not sure—"

"Just tell her I've got the receipts for the deliveries she made for Gordon Lavery back in 1972. We can discuss them in her office on Monday at two o'clock."

66

◆

"Any fool can tell the truth, but it requires
a man of some sense to know how to lie
well."

SAMUEL BUTLER

MURPHY LIKED THE food at Maison Blanche but was less than thrilled by the restaurant's lunchtime atmosphere. The table for two he was sharing with Margaret was an oasis of serenity in a sandstorm of cross talk, wheeling-and-dealing, lobbying, politicking, schmoozing, and seducing.

"My God," Murphy said, surveying the roomful of TV reporters, journalists, politicians, and a sprinkling of movie stars, "it's a wonder their stomachs haven't turned to cheesecloth, trying to eat with all this going on."

"Try some more bisque. It's calming," Margaret told him.

"Earplugs would help."

"I see where even without Intercom's interference, the restrictive trade bill still was voted down," she said.

"Go figure," he said, staring at her. "On the plus side, they've added Tommy Hamilton, the Laverys, and Stuart Wayland to Larry's account. The other Intercom execs, Theo Koriallis included, have flown the country."

"What do you suppose will happen to Amber McNeil and her husband?"

Murphy shrugged. "They've hired that guy from Texas to represent them, the one who thinks he's Andy Griffith or something. My guess is they'll wind up free and broke. American justice. And before I forget, would you mind telling me whatever it is you think you know about that fatal car accident near Aspen?''

She gave him a sweet smile. "They call it deduction, Murph. In Tommy Hamilton's fictionalized account of the accident, which I lifted from the ranch, he was steering a boat so that his pal could water-ski. Larry Newfield told you that Tommy was guilty of vehicular homicide.''

"And you surmise from this—"

"That Tommy was drunk and driving Robert Christen's car when it crashed into Buddy Radin's truck. The broken whiskey bottle on the highway was Tommy's, not Buddy's.''

"And Tommy moved his good friend's body into the driver's seat?''

Meg replied, "Or someone simply changed the accident report.''

"Then why did Buddy take off?''

"Maybe he was scared. Maybe he was paid off by the Hamiltons. Probably a combination of both.''

"They would have had to work fast.''

"When there's big money involved, speed is not a problem," she said.

Murphy frowned. "I don't like our political friend knowing about all this.''

"I don't think she does," Margaret said. "In the manuscript, the Tommy figure clams up about his guilt.''

"It's a fascinatin' theory, but does it cause a blip on the big screen?''

"Sure it does," she said, leaning forward, eyes flashing, into the story now. "I think that when Theo Koriallis tried to help our . . . political friend sue the company everybody assumed was culpable, he learned the truth.''

"I suppose his lawyer could have unearthed Buddy Radin," Murphy said.

"Probably. Anyway, Koriallis got the real story. He used the threat of exposure to force Tommy's father to sell out to Intercom, a company Koriallis controlled at the time.''

"I'll buy every word of it," Murphy said. He hoped he hadn't sounded patronizing. He knew how much she hated that. But he was proud of her. She probably hated that, too. He asked her, "Do you have a theory about Tommy's other alleged problem, according to the late Larry?"

"The child-molestation stuff?" She shook her head. "Well, that's in the manuscript, too. But I don't see that it's had any impact on our investigation."

Murphy was about to say something when he caught a movement in the corner of the room and forced his eyes away from her. Across the mass of noisy lunchers, Minority Leader Mike Roberts stood up from his table and headed toward the exit doors at the rear of the room.

"Here goes," Murphy mumbled, standing up and moving in that direction.

Feeling more than slightly foolish, he entered the men's room and stepped up to the empty urinal next to Roberts. He waited for the other two occupants to leave and for the Minority Leader to zip up, then handed him an envelope. Roberts folded it and slipped it into his coat pocket. "Is it complete?" he asked.

"As much as anything in life is," Murphy replied.

"And the bottom line?"

"The subject is as clean as the proverbial hound's tooth, except for a short flirtation with a married man now under investigation—"

"What?"

"It happened way back when," Murphy said. "And if the married fella is as shrewd as I think he is, there's no chance they'll be getting him back in this country to talk about her or anything else."

A senator they both knew entered and they waited for him to leave. When he did, Murphy grumbled, "Swell meetin' spot you picked, Mike."

"It's as good as your goddamned bakery," Mike Roberts said. "Look, the main question is: Will she get dragged into this Intercom thing with Lady Amber Cosmetics?"

"She was out of the company years before Intercom went in. It's all in there." He pointed to the spot where the folded envelope rested. "They'd be wastin' their time dragging her into it, but if they do, she'll walk away clean, so help me."

Mike Roberts nodded and the two men went to wash their hands. "Thanks for handling this one, Murph," he said.

"Our pleasure, Mike. How's Charlie coming along?"

Roberts shook his head. "They're putting him through tests at Bethesda. Physically, he's like an oak. But his memory is gone with the wind. What a mess, huh?"

"The courts are gonna be filled," Murphy said. "Every bill that's passed or failed with Intercom in the picture is gonna be given close scrutiny. And every sod who's been busted in the kip is gonna claim he was the victim of Larry's love potion."

"I wonder if they'll ever find out who killed Newfield?"

"It doesn't look like they're makin' much progress," Murphy said. "That's one medal they may not be handing out."

"We were damn lucky that tip got the Metro police there before somebody at Intercom found the body."

"It renews your faith in law and order," Murphy said.

"Did you find out who sent me that goddamned letter that started all this?"

"It's in there," Murphy told him. "A couple named Lavery, who had it in for the honorable lady."

The Minority Leader made a noise that sounded like "Mhrumph," nodded, and left Murphy alone in the restroom.

Murphy checked his facial abrasions in the mirror. They seemed to be healing nicely. He was sure he'd done the right thing, telling Mike Roberts the one little lie about the Laverys.

67

♦

"Slander, like coal, will either dirty your hand or burn it."

RUSSIAN PROVERB

WHEN LAURA AWOKE that morning in her big, tufted bed, she was aware of a weight pressing against her stomach. She smiled when she realized that it was a man's hand. She looked over at Jake, lying on his side, still asleep. The bruises on his face were turning colors, but his skin had lost its pallor. And the dark circles that had ringed his eyes had faded completely.

He was a man at rest. No nightmares.

As she watched him, Jake stirred. He made a little sound halfway between a hum and a grunt and opened his eyes. His smiling gray eyes. He said, "Well, here we are again."

They met each other halfway in a "full body press," as Laura called it. Then, in spite of a moment's apprehension about morning mouth, they kissed. Passion stirred. Then flared.

She could barely stand it. Love. Romance. Exquisite sex. All wrapped up in the same wonderful package.

When they had exhausted themselves and lay back against the pillows, Jake said, "I don't think I'll ever be satisfied again with just a cup of black coffee in the morning."

"All part of my scheme," she told him.

"Let's go out to dinner tonight," he said. "Someplace expensive. If anybody asks, you can tell them I'm your bodyguard."

The reference was to an ongoing discussion they'd been having about going public with their relationship. Jake wanted to tell the world. Laura, agreeing with the advice of both Jim Prosser and her daughter, thought that they should keep their love a secret until after the election. Now was not the time to present herself as a starry-eyed romantic to her fellow members of Congress.

"Let's eat in for a few more weeks," she said.

He smiled and nodded, but she knew he was not happy with her answer.

AT precisely two o'clock that afternoon, Laura was in her office, standing behind her desk and asking her visitor, Penelope Krim, to take the chair nearest her. Penelope squinted at Catsy, who had led her from the reception area to Laura's office, and announced airily, "I don't think we'll need you, *dear*."

Catsy flushed and turned to Laura. Laura rewarded her with a smile and said to Penelope, "I'd like my daughter to hear whatever you're going to say."

Penelope shrugged. It probably wouldn't be anything her dope-head daughter didn't know. If only the police had found drugs in Catsy's apartment, Penelope could make it a like-mother-like-daughter piece. She flounced onto a chair facing Laura. Catsy sat on the couch, perched forward with her hands on her knees. Penelope unsnapped her briefcase and withdrew several photocopied sheets, passing them to Laura. They were copies of the drug receipts. Laura's were circled in red ink.

"Any comment?" she asked.

"About these?"

"You deny that you made deliveries of drugs on those dates?"

"All I can say is that I never knowingly delivered any drugs on any date. Nor have I ever sold any drugs or used any drugs. And you may quote me."

Catsy smiled sweetly and said, "Penelope, what is it about narcotics that thrills you so?"

The columnist responded with a sneer and turned back to Laura. "Perhaps you can tell me what these abbreviations and dates mean?"

Laura shrugged. "You'll have to ask the person who wrote them."

"I understand that the writer is dead. Killed in a car crash," Penelope growled.

Laura paused for a moment and said, "Then I don't understand what you're doing with the property of some deceased person. But that's your business, not mine. Is that all, Ms. Krim?"

"Doctor Krim."

"Forgive me, *Doctor* Krim."

Penelope rose to her feet, a mighty figure of a woman. "Just one more thing. I hear you've been sleeping with Jake Alban. Has he bothered to inform you that he has genital herpes?"

Jake had told Laura of his escape from Penelope at the Casa Bel Air. She stared up at the triumphant look on Penelope's puffy red face and said, "Jake? Herpes? Oh, *Doctor,* I'm afraid somebody's sold you some bad information. I can personally attest to the fact that Jake is as healthy as a weed. And, though this is not for publication, he is as virile as a stallion."

Penelope stopped at the door, turned, and said, "Have your fun while you can, Congresswoman. Columnists are the worst enemies a politician can make."

68

♦

"Everything comes, if a man will only wait."

BENJAMIN DISRAELI

THE NEXT DAY Penelope Krim's column was devoted to Laura Christen and the "improprieties" in her past. The newswoman was not specific in delineating them, but she hinted at everything from adultery to bestiality, and the Congresswoman's early connection to a "famous cosmetics company currently under criminal investigation" was mentioned.

Several copycat journalists followed Penelope's lead, conjuring up a salacious squib or two. Within a week the tabloids were filled with pictures of Laura. Mainly, they were unflattering candids—Laura with her eyes closed, Laura making a disgusted face, Laura at the end of a long jog, perspiring, hair in strings, dressed in an old Fila warm-up suit and looking as if she were on relief.

As the rest of the world began its celebration of Christmas, the supermarket newspapers continued a mini-crusade against Christen. Nothing much was said in these articles, but it was said in bold type. LAURA: CONGRESS'S MILLION-DOLLAR BABE, SEX-GODDESS TO SPEAKER? LAURA'S LIVE-IN LOVER, and MOM TAUGHT HER HOW. This last was a reference to a photo of Catsy Braden drinking champagne from her shoe at a party while still in her teens. Curiously, the article ignored Catsy's reputation to focus on one the newspaper created for Laura.

● ● ●

303

Two nights before Christmas, Laura and Jake were relaxing in front of a television set in Laura's den. They had been living together in her Georgetown home, but not openly. This meant the blinds remained drawn day and night. Laura used the front entrance, where at least three or four photographers congregated at any time of the day and night, while Jake entered via a circuitous back-door route. It was annoying and demeaning, but they both understood enough about the situation Laura was in to put up with it, at least until after Congress had chosen its next Speaker.

As they watched a television talk show, its host launched into a monologue that began, "Hey, how about that Congresswoman Laura Christen? First the President says she's his pick for Speaker of the House. Then we find out a lot about the lady's lifestyle that makes you wonder what kind of repute that House is gonna have. Whatever they say about her, she's gotta be the sexiest politician ever. How sexy is she? Well, she's so sexy that Jesse Helms is saying that kids under eighteen shouldn't be allowed to look at her."

Jake zapped off the set. "If we'd gone out to a movie, like I suggested, you wouldn't have heard any of this dreck."

"If we'd gone out to a movie, he would have had more material for his monologue. Oh, Jake, I hate not being able to live the way we want to. But it won't last forever."

"No, it won't."

She tried to lighten the mood. "I made the cover of the *National Tattler* today," she told him. "With nearly all of my clothes on."

"Then the *National Tattler* really missed the boat," he said, pulling her toward him.

69

•

"Christmas won't be Christmas without any presents."

LOUISA MAY ALCOTT, *LITTLE WOMEN*

THE NEXT DAY there was a very subdued Christmas Eve party in Laura's office. Presents were exchanged, hot cider and egg nog and cookies were consumed. The fruitcake was left untouched, as fruitcakes have always been.

Laura approached her adviser, Jim Prosser, who was sitting before the Christmas tree, his back to the party, gazing at the blinking lights with a singular lack of enthusiasm for the happy season.

"Well, Jim," she said, "you've been walking around like a zombie the past few weeks. I was hoping the tie I gave you would rate at least a tiny smile." It was a bow tie, patterned after one that Harry Truman, Prosser's favorite president, often wore.

"It's a splendid tie," he said.

"What's the matter, Jim?"

Just past her shoulder he could see Catsy looking their way nervously. He said, "In nine days, the 106th Congress is going to meet. And according to everything my sources tell me, the Democrats have been doing a hell of a job getting their pigeons to return to the fold."

"The tabloid press has been annoying," she said. "But surely my fellow members can see that nothing of substance is being said. I'm not even sure what it is I'm being accused of."

"You're speaking out against sexism and careerism in the

305

House. That's a worse crime than anything the tabloids can hang on you."

"How do I stand?" she asked, not sure she wanted to hear.

"The President's backing helped. But I wouldn't be at all surprised if this bad press isn't giving him second thoughts."

"He wouldn't change his mind?"

Prosser shook his head. "No. That'd make him look even worse. But it may cause him to give the Republicans a little leeway in how they vote."

"Then what do we do?"

Behind his thick glasses, Prosser's eyes looked sad and moist. "Nearly all of Congress has gone home for the holidays," he said. "So unless there's a lot of phoning and faxing going on, the big push will take place on the day before Congress meets. We've got to be ready with something to undercut the bad publicity. I've set up a meeting with Blaine and McKesson on the 26th," he said. The reference was to the public relations firm that had handled her reelection. "Gat McKesson has a few ideas he wants to run past us."

"I hope they're brilliant," she said.

He started to say something, but thought better of it. She bent down and kissed him on the cheek. "Merry Christmas, Jim."

"Merry Christmas, Laura," he replied. What he had to tell her could wait. This was not the time or place.

FIVE miles to the west, on the seventh floor of the Paradine Building, J. B. Murphy lifted the white beard from his face and filled his mouth with the contents of a shotglass of ten-year-old Glenfiddich. He savored the smoky malt flavor, sighed, and popped the fake beard back into place, more or less.

"That's a fine present, Meg," he said, holding up the nearly full bottle of scotch. They were in his office, with the door open to a remarkably lively party.

"You surprised me," Margaret Stafford said. "I wasn't expecting anything so personal." Her present lay in a box on her lap. A soft-pink shoulder holster.

"Well," Murphy said, pouring them each a shot of Glenfiddich, "it was a toss-up between that and one of those new body-armor vests. If you don't like the color, it comes in black, baby blue, and a sort of purple."

"Pink's fine," she said.

In the outer office the rest of the staff were singing carols with a rock and roll beat. "It's very festive out there," he said, "all things considered."

"That kid Pat Arthur almost attacked me as I was leaving the ladies' room," she said. "When I elbowed him in the stomach, he pointed to the mistletoe some pervert had tacked over the door to the lav."

"The kid, who's about three years younger than you, has a crush on you," Murphy told her. "I was feeling guilty about suspecting him of being our spy, so I showed him where all the mistletoe was."

"You're a great father figure, Murph," she said. Then, altering her mood downward, she added, "Speaking of spies, I understand Nina got away."

He nodded.

"Too bad," Margaret said. "She caused a lot of damage."

"Somebody else has caused even more damage," he said. "And I'm not sure what to do about it."

"Somebody in this office?"

He shook his head and the Santa's cap fell to the floor. "Forget I mentioned it."

"Impossible, with my memory," she said.

"Then ignore it."

"What's bothering you?" she asked.

He pulled the beard from his face. "This last mess."

"The Christen case? I thought we did pretty well."

"We give poor Mike Roberts the go-ahead on Christen, and suddenly her mug, and a bit more of her anatomy, is spread all over the papers."

"That's not our fault. And it isn't even *her* fault. She *is* clean."

"Maybe," Murphy said.

"You don't think so?"

"I dunno," he replied. "I'm still working on it."

"Working how?"

"I haven't figured that out yet."

"When you do," she said, standing up, "let me know. I suppose you're seeing your widow friend later."

He nodded. "Midnight mass at St. Matthew's." He noticed that she was standing under a sprig of mistletoe attached to his doorframe. "What about you?" he asked her.

"My new neighbor's having a little thing. Dinner. Something. Well, Noël and all that, Murph."

"You have yourself a merry one, Meg. I'm sorry. *Margaret.*"

She waved a hand at him. "Call me what you want, Murph. For the New Year I'm giving up trying to teach old dogs new tricks." She looked up at the mistletoe, shrugged, did an abrupt about-face, and was gone.

70

◆

"The man who raises new issues has always been distasteful to politicians. He musses up what had been so tidily arranged."

WALTER LIPPMANN

GAT MCKESSON, OF the public relations firm of Blaine and McKesson, arrived at Laura's offices five minutes early for their meeting. He was a short, thickset man with thinning hair, a nose too large for his face, and the confident smile of a born winner. He followed Laura, Catsy, and Jim Prosser into the small conference room, removed his topcoat and, once coffee had been poured for all, quickly laid out his plan of attack.

He saw the tabloid stories and the bad press as a secondary problem. His firm knew how to turn that sort of thing around. Readers of supermarket scandal sheets were not going to be voting for Speaker in just eight days. Where they had to focus their energies was on the members of Congress. Commitment was the key. They had to hang on to the Republican votes and erode the hold that Ronkowski had on the Democrats. He suggested they go completely on the offense.

On one hand, they would point out Laura's qualifications: her success as a businesswoman, her productive years in the public sector, her work with committees. As for her twelve years in Congress, they would note that in times gone by, the average length of congressional service before election to the chair was seven years. In fact, there was nothing that stated specifically that the Speaker even had to be a member of the House.

On the other hand, they would make her Independent status stand for fairness and loyalty to Congress rather than to party. They would make her gender stand for equality and democracy.

"And," Gat McKesson added, "we'll shake every goddamned political skeleton out of Lew Ronkowski's closet and pile them up on the Capitol steps like sculptures for all to gaze upon."

As McKesson was about to leave, he handed Jim Prosser an envelope and whispered something in the Professor's ear. Laura followed Prosser back to his office and asked him about the envelope.

"It's material one of your Republican brethren received this morning," Prosser told her. "Gat photocopied it for me."

He opened the envelope and withdrew a piece of art. It was a caricature of Laura in a parody of the Lady Amber advertisements. She was dressed in a tiny bra and panties, walking toward the Speaker's stand of the House. The caption: "I dreamt I was two heartbeats away from the Presidency in my Lady Amber underwear."

"Who sent this?" she asked.

Prosser shook his head. "Ronkowski or one of his cronies. Gat doesn't think it'll have any real effect."

"But it was sent to everyone?"

Prosser nodded. "Except to you, of course."

"The next eight days are going to be long ones," she said.

ACTUALLY they passed very quickly. While the combined forces of Lew Ronkowski and Penelope Krim and the media in general did their damnedest to destroy her reputation, Jake did his best to make her evenings romantic and carefree. But the strain of keeping their relationship a secret was wearing on him, and Laura knew it.

On New Year's Eve, instead of attending any number of parties to which she'd been invited, at her request they'd celebrated at her home. Throughout the quiet dinner, their conversation was easygoing and facile.

Finally Jake removed a small box from his pocket and pushed

it across the tablecloth. It was a delicate, very lovely engagement ring.

She took it from the box and slipped it onto her finger. There were tears in her eyes.

"I don't believe in long engagements," he said.

"No," she agreed. "The sooner the better."

"We can do the blood tests next week and apply for the license."

The license, yes. Though it made her feel guilty, she could not help the question that flitted through her mind: How would an impending marriage affect the vote in the House?

She looked across the table and she knew at once that Jake had sensed her hesitation. He smiled. "The license can wait a few weeks," he said.

Was that sorrow or disappointment, or both, in his eyes, she wondered. She reached across the table to clasp his hand. "I love you," she said.

He did not ask her if she would wear the ring in public. Instead, he said, "I love you, too."

Later, in her big chintz-covered bed, as Washington welcomed the future, they enjoyed the present.

On January 2, the day before the members of Congress were scheduled to convene, Jim Prosser came to Laura's office carrying a large envelope.

As she took it from him, he spotted the ring.

"Is that what I think it is?" he asked.

She nodded. "Jake and I are going to be married."

"When?"

"As soon as the Speaker is elected."

"Shall I send out a press release?" he asked glumly.

"What do you think?"

"I've told you what I think," he said a bit waspishly. "What we need to do is call attention to your abilities as a politician, not to your domestic situation."

"Then," she said coldly, "I don't suppose we should send out a press release, Jim."

"Wearing the ring isn't a good idea, either," he said.

"I'm not taking it off," she said. "I'm proud of it. And if anyone mentions it, I want no equivocation: I am engaged to be married. In other words, we won't make a big thing of it, but we will definitely not deny it."

Jim Prosser nodded his head like a chastised little boy. He waited while she opened the envelope and removed two photocopied sheets. One was the reproduction of several drug receipts, labeled *Convicted Dope Dealer's Messenger Receipts*. A circle was drawn where "Laura" appeared on the receipts. The other sheet was a copy of the note that had been sent to Ronkowski labeling Laura a drug dealer.

"Esther Cooper made these copies for us," the Professor informed her.

"It means that Ronkowski and Penelope Krim are working together. I wonder which one is responsible for the mailing."

"Esther can't believe that Ronkowski would stoop so low. But she is incensed at the thought that he might have been a party to it."

"Incensed enough to back me?" Laura asked hopefully.

Prosser took a deep breath and let it out like a sigh. "No. She's a Democrat, first and last. But she's planning on abstaining from the vote."

"What about Roberts and the President?" she asked.

"I've been afraid to call. I suppose they've got a copy of this trash, too."

"What can we do?" she asked.

"I don't know. I've asked Gat to join us for lunch."

"Fine," she replied, heading toward his door. "That'll give me enough time to make a call."

"To whom?"

"To a private investigator I met recently," she said. "I have something I'd like him to do for me."

71

◆

"Politicians, after all, are not more than a
year behind Public Opinion."

WILL ROGERS

ON THE MORNING of what was thought to be the crucial meeting of
the 106th Congress, Jake did one of his favorite things: He watched
Laura getting dressed.

He was still in bed. Around him were scattered the morning
papers in which the Intercom Scandal had begun to take second
billing to the continuing story of Laura's challenge.

The general consensus was that the congressional vote was too
close to call. Lew Ronkowski was confident that his position was
secure. He had said so the previous night to Ted Koppel. Laura had
also been invited to be on the show, but had declined on the advice
of Gat McKesson, who felt that her being seen on the defensive on
national television would not serve the cause.

"I think I'll visit the Capitol at noon," Jake said. "If you feel
you can spare a visitor's pass."

"It'll probably be a waste of your time," she said. "I doubt
there will be a vote today."

Jake arrived precisely at the noon hour to discover that she'd
been right. The Democrats, fearing Laura still might have enough
backing to win, were noticeably absent. The longer the vote could
be postponed, the less chance she had of winning.

The House adjourned without a quorum.

• • •

313

THE absenteeism continued on a daily basis, and with it, Laura's chances waned. On the evening of the fourth day of no-quorum, she departed her offices feeling glum and beaten down. Her spirits picked up only slightly when she arrived at the apartment to find that Jake had prepared a candlelit dinner.

She could hear him clattering around the kitchen while she unloaded her homework and slipped into slacks and a loose-fitting blouse. "How was your day?" she called out as she sipped the glass of wine he'd poured for her.

"Another day, another dollar, another byline," he said, entering the dining room wearing an apron that read, KISS THE COOK. He pointed to it and said, "I found this in the kitchen. I thought it might make an interesting story: 'Laura Christen's Sexy Tips for Homemakers. Tip Number One: Kiss the Cook.' "

Smiling wanly, she rose to kiss him, holding him tightly, letting the kiss linger.

He drew back suddenly and said, "I almost forgot." He went back into the kitchen and returned with two hands behind his back. "You pick: the right hand or the left?"

"The right."

"OK," he said, obviously exchanging the contents of both hands. When he brought the right hand up, it was holding a *National Examiner*.

"This is my choice for the best Laura Christen cover of them all. Ta-da." Spread across nearly the full front page was a photo of Laura's ice-princess face topping the voluptuous body of a nude mud wrestler. The headline read: WHO'S THROWING MUD ON LAURA CHRISTEN?

"See," he said, "they're in your corner. The article claims that radicals are trying to destroy your political career. They've tied it in somehow with the impending Japanese takeover of America. I sense Gat McKesson's fine Italian hand in it somewhere."

"I bet he even provided that photo," she said sarcastically. "What's in the other hand?"

"Something that should make us both very happy," he said, holding out a sheet of Thermo-Fax paper. On it was an announcement informing the Empire Syndicate that because of the continued Democratic absenteeism, the Clerk of the House of Representatives had felt compelled to call upon the Sergeant at Arms to arrest members who fail to report for a quorum. One way or the other, the House was going to convene on Monday.

72

◆

"Self-knowledge is a dangerous thing,
tending to make man shallow or insane."

KARL SHAPIRO

"THANKS FOR DINNER," Catsy Braden said to Jim Prosser, who
was occupying her Volvo's passenger seat, "but I'm still not sure
what prompted it." They had eaten at an excellent Georgetown
restaurant and were now parked in front of his brownstone apartment building.

Prosser slipped his fingers under his glasses, pressed the bridge
of his nose and told her, "There's something I want you to give
your mother."

He reached under his topcoat and withdrew a sealed envelope.
"Hand this to her tomorrow, after . . . whatever happens at the
meeting."

"What is it?" she asked, looking at the long white envelope
with her mother's name typed in its center.

"My resignation." He reached for the car door and opened it,
letting in a blast of cold air.

"Wait a minute!" Catsy said. But he was out of the car with the
door slammed shut behind him.

She got out, too, letter still in hand, and followed him to the
building. "Wait a minute, Jim," she repeated. He didn't stop and
she rushed to catch him.

They entered the brownstone.

"You think she's going to lose, don't you?" Catsy asked as
Prosser keyed open the hall door.

"Probably," he said, continuing on. "Please don't misplace that letter."

She looked at the envelope in her hand, shoved it into a pocket, and followed him. "So you're quitting," she said.

"Not because she's going to lose," he said. "I made that clear in the letter."

She frowned. "Then what? Because she's shacked up with Jake Alban?"

Prosser paused before his apartment door. "That's part of it," he admitted.

"It's not going to last," Catsy said.

Prosser made an odd forced chuckle and turned to her. He said, "You don't know anything about her, do you?"

She followed him into a dingy apartment, so annoyed by the tenor of his question that she barely noticed the dreary furniture and dull yellow walls. "Know her? I'm her goddamned daughter!"

"Now that you're here, would you care for something to drink?" he asked, tossing his coat onto a chair and moving to an old stereo console on which rested several dusty bottles.

"What've you got?" she asked, slipping out of her coat.

"Sherry and . . . Rock and Rye."

"Sherry, then." She watched him pour the fluid into two tiny delicate glasses. Then she surveyed the room. She'd never been there before. God, what a dump. She tried to imagine her mother there, lying on the threadbare chocolate sofa, getting it on with the Professor.

She took the offered glass and sat on the sofa. "If you think Alban is some sort of passing infatuation," he said, joining her, "then you really don't know Laura."

"OK," she agreed. "She does seem to have really gone off the deep end for the guy. But that's no reason for you to quit."

"It's not just that," he said. "Think about what we've done, the horrible things we've caused."

"You're talking like a crazy man, Jim. I hope to God there's nothing like that in the letter."

"No." He shook his head. "Just a simple resignation. No reason given."

"Once the press find out, they'll say your quitting is another sign that she's through in politics."

He sipped his sherry and thought about that. Finally he said, "No. I'm not that important to her career. Or to her."

They sat in silence for a few minutes. Then Catsy said, "There's still the chance that our plan will work."

"That doesn't matter anymore," he said. "It wouldn't justify what we did."

"That's crap. If she becomes Speaker, anything is justified."

"That's where we disagree," he said. Then he asked, "Why is it so important to you that she win?"

"Voters don't like losers. If she's beaten by Ronkowski, she probably won't be reelected. And I don't want this to end. Not for her. Not for me. I actually love working with her," Catsy said. "It's the only time in my life when we've ever connected."

"You should tell her that."

Catsy shrugged. "If I did, maybe that would ruin it."

He looked at her and for the first time that night he smiled. "Maybe it wouldn't."

"Do you like me, Jim?"

He shrugged. "I'm not sure how you mean that."

"When I asked you if you and Mother had made love, I suppose I was wondering if that would be another way of connecting with her, by sharing a man with her. Maybe that would give me a better fix on what she's about."

"What makes you think that sleeping with somebody lets you understand them any better?"

"It couldn't hurt," she said, moving closer to him.

"Do you love your mother?"

She cocked her head to one side. "The only thing I'm sure of on that score is that I love her more than she loves me. Which may not be saying much."

"What makes you think she doesn't love you?"

"Oh, Professor, let me count the ways."

"Give me one."

"I could tell you how I lost my virginity. I was twelve years old at the time. Probably a very backward twelve by California standards." She paused. "But I'm not twelve any longer, and I don't like thinking about it. Wouldn't you rather do something constructive—like making love?''

He shook his head. "I don't think so.''

"Ohhh, but you'd like it.''

"I'd probably like it very much,'' he said. "Then where would I be?''

"Poor, poor, Jim. You're bummed out because Mother's found some other guy. Well, I can make you feel good again. Because I'm better than she is.''

Jim Prosser looked at her a bit awed. "You really should get yourself straightened out,'' he told her.

She moved beside him until her thigh pressed against his. When he didn't pull away, she took that as a positive sign. She lifted the glass from his hand and placed it on the ugliest coffee table she'd ever seen.

Then she guided his hand to her breast.

He said, "This won't prove anything.'' And he let his hand fall away from her body.

"I can make you happy, Jim,'' she said. She put her hand on his thigh and moved it until it was on his crotch.

He stared at her. She leaned forward and kissed him. He did not respond. But his body was reacting and she smiled. "You see,'' she said.

"That's just biology. I can look at a picture in a book and get the same reaction.''

She stared at him. This aging, desiccated scarecrow was turning her down. She couldn't work up either anger or indignation.

She stood, picked up her coat, and went to the door. "So long, Jim. I guess we won't be hearing from you again.''

"No,'' he said. "I guess you won't.''

She nodded and walked out of his apartment.

He returned to the sofa, gathered the two dirty glasses, and was walking with them to the kitchen when there was a knock at the door.

So it wasn't going to be that easy to rid himself of Catsy, he thought. He put the glasses down and went to the door. He hesitated before unlocking it, trying to get it straight in his mind what he'd say to her.

That accomplished, he opened the door.

It wasn't Catsy Braden. A tall, sturdy, middle-aged man in a well-cut black overcoat was smiling at him. There were several not-quite-healed scratches on his face. The man said, "Professor Prosser, my name is J. B. Murphy. You don't know me, but there are a couple of things we have to talk about."

73

◆

"I suddenly realized . . . I'd been around congressmen and senators—or, as we on the Hill liked to call them, '535 high-school class presidents with a few prom queens thrown in'—for too long."

WILLIAM "FISHBAIT" MILLER, CONGRESSIONAL

DOORKEEPER

APPROXIMATELY TWO HOURS before noon, at which time Congress convenes, Penelope Krim sat at her desk in her semidarkened office, munching a hot toasted bagel piled high with cream cheese and imported salmon, which though not authentic lox, was doing a fine job of substitution. She didn't often eat breakfast. Actually, she was not often awake for breakfast. But this was a special day—one that would turn Laura Christen not only into yesterday's news but yesterday's political hopeful. And she, Penelope, was applying the coup de grâce.

The previous evening she had met with Lew Ronkowski at a Filipino restaurant on L Street. The curious Chinese-Spanish cuisine had certainly not been to her liking. Nor to his. But, as he explained, a Filipino restaurant would be the least likely place for their meeting to be observed by anyone who mattered.

She had, while devouring some sort of pickled squid that later gave her severe indigestion, handed him the letter she had taken from Jeremy Dunbar's body accusing Laura Christen of giving birth to an illegitimate child. Ronkowski's face positively beamed as he scanned the note. Uttering the word "bastard," he allowed one of his hands to carelessly slip from the table and rest on he thigh. *So the food is lousy,* she'd thought. *Big deal! This is th goddamn Speaker of the House feeling me up.*

"What happened to the bastard?" he asked, slipping the lette into his coat pocket.

She frowned. "I don't know. That son of a bitch Jake Alba probably found out before he began porking the slut. Does i matter? Either the little nipper's dead, aborted probably, or it' alive somewhere. The point is: *She never acknowledged it.* It wil embarrass the shit out of her."

"Indeed it will."

"Too bad the police have already decided that the head o Intercom ordered Jeremy's murder. This would tie Laura to tha too."

Ronkowski mulled that over. Then his face broke into his fa mous monkey grin. "There are many ways to skin a she-cat," h said. He looked over the assortment of dishes in front of them "Would you like to try the stuffed shrimp, Penny?"

"No, Lew," she'd replied, "but another double vodka toni would do me just fine."

In her office, reviewing the night, she leaned back in her cha and focused on Laura Christen. Jake had obviously told Laura tha the letter existed and that she, Penny, had it. When it surface Laura would know precisely who had been responsible. She like that. She liked it so much that when her boss, Horace Marste passed her office he was surprised to hear her humming a tune l recognized as "I Feel Pretty."

At fifteen minutes to noon, Penelope emerged from the Empi Building, flagged a cab, and headed for the Capitol. On the wa she skimmed the *Post* and paused at the "Today in Congress listing. There it was in black and white: "The election of tl Speaker of the House." If the *Post* said it, it must be so.

The traffic slowed to a crawl as they passed Third, approachir the Capitol. The cabdriver turned and said, "If you're in a hurr you'd do better walking."

She didn't mind. It was a beautiful day for a walk. The sun w shining. Who cared if it was forty-five degrees? As she paid tl driver, he asked, "What's the big deal today? All the traffic. Somebody getting a medal?"

"Nope," she replied. "Somebody's getting the ax."

SHE was not the only member of the press heading toward the day's big show, she noticed. Usually the election of the Speaker was a pro forma occurrence. The Democratic caucus would have made its choice and that would have been that. The others were there because they were curious about who the next Speaker would be. She was there because she knew.

She entered the main building and headed up an elaborate marble stairway to the gallery along with the herd of other reporters and visitors. As she neared a door, she spotted the same young woman with bright red hair that she'd seen at Laura Christen's press conference so many weeks before.

She glared at the redhead, who was presenting her credentials at the gallery door, and wondered, as she often did, why she felt an instant dislike for people she hadn't even met. Suddenly, as if by a sixth sense, the redhead turned and saw her staring. Then the impudent bitch raised her hand and gave Penelope the finger. Who the hell did she think she was?

When Penelope reached the security guard, she asked him the slut's name. "Margaret Stafford," the guard told her. "She's a guest of Congresswoman Christen's."

MARGARET was annoyed with Murphy. He'd been up to something the whole week, arriving at the office early, staying late, making phone calls to the West Coast. When she'd asked him about it, he'd told her that he was putting the finishing touches to the Christen case, but refused to be more specific.

She did not appreciate his keeping her in the dark. The Christen case had been her responsibility, after all. If more work was required, she should be involved.

In a somewhat petulant mood, she had busied herself with several new clients. A senator's secretary, an American, had hired the agency to try to find out where her ex-husband, a Saudi diplomat, had illegally sequestered their child. The owner-CEO of a D.C. corporation wanted to know how its main competitor was learning of events at his board meetings. A local judge, a friend of Murphy's, had asked the agency to locate his beloved Rolls-Royce Silver Wraith, which had been stolen from his garage.

The Rolls had been the easiest. A boyfriend of the judge's teenaged mistress had taken it. Unfortunately its major parts were now adorning Rolls autos all across America. Margaret had put an electronics expert to work in the boardroom. And she had traced the Saudi to Manhattan, where she planned to be the following day.

But that noon she had set time aside to attend the congressional session to witness Laura Christen's fate and, not coincidentally, to see if she could figure out what had been keeping Murphy so busy.

She found a single seat near the front of the gallery and then searched the crowd for a sign of the big Irishman. Failing that, she looked down to the floor, where the members of Congress had begun to take their seats. Several of them were carrying white slips of paper which they showed to one another.

She spotted Lew Ronkowski limping gingerly down an aisle, shaking hands and chatting merrily on his way to his seat on the top dais. She did not see Laura Christen.

LAURA awoke that day with butterflies in her stomach and a vague sense of unease. She and Jake had a very light breakfast and very little conversation. He was still in his bathrobe at 10:30 when she decided to leave for her office.

He put his arms around her and pulled her to him. "You're going to be fine," he said.

She wasn't so sure, but she refused to admit it.

She knew he was working on a long piece about preteen street gangs for the syndicate, and she asked if he thought he'd be able to get to the Capitol to see the election.

"Even if I have to bring the chief warlord of the Tomacks with me," he said.

"Maybe we should have asked your warlord's advice on how to handle Lew Ronkowski," she said.

"I think you can handle him on your own."

She smiled. "With a little help from my friends," she said. "Murphy's meeting me at the office."

"Did he get the depositions?"

"He was expecting them late last night," she said. "It's that time difference from the West Coast."

He took her hands and kissed them. "Hey," she said. "What about the lips?"

"You just put on your lipstick."

"There's more where that came from," she told him, moving into his arms.

CATSY's day began at seven. She groaned, opened her eyes, and stared at the flaccid member of John Kilmer's hand puppet resting on her pillow. Kilmer was one pillow over, mouth open, snoring loudly. It had been his snores that had wakened her.

She slipped from the roiled bed, the early morning chill covering her with goosebumps. She felt logy, sinuses clogged, but these were not cold symptoms. Instead they were becoming her normal morning conditions.

She drew her robe around her and made her way to the bathroom, where she stared at herself in the mirror. Her eyes were dull and she saw the beginning of crow's-feet. Were her features coarsening? Maybe she'd take a week off and visit a spa. Then she could join a health club and . . . but why go on? She knew she would do neither of those things.

Jim Prosser's refusal to have sex with her had bothered her more than she'd let on. Other men, not many, had turned her down. But none of them had been as wimpy as the Professor. It had been a mistake to even try to seduce him.

In any case, she'd arrived home, feeling sorry for herself. She'd drunk half a bottle of Chardonnay and, slightly tipsy, had called John Kilmer, the eternal stud who she knew would help her regain her confidence.

Kilmer had arrived, puppet in hand, ready for anything. But she had continued drinking, finishing one bottle and seriously denting another. And by the time they'd gone to bed, she barely knew what was happening until it had happened. And in the cold light of morning she had remembered one thing—he had fallen asleep unsatisfied.

A shower, a cup of strong, black coffee, a brushing of teeth, and her spirits began a long uphill climb. By the time she was dressed and walking out the door, Kilmer's snores still rattling the bedroom windows, they were almost to a height where she could face life with some of her old verve. This was the day her mother would be elected Speaker of the House. Or would not be.

She arrived at Laura's darkened offices, unlocked the door, and went straight to the coffeemaker, which she plugged in.

Then she walked to her own desk, consulted her schedule, and tried to plot her day.

Within an hour the offices began to come alive. There was a definite crackle in the air. All of the staff knew the importance of the upcoming election.

At a little after eleven, her mother arrived. A stocky man, no longer young, had been waiting for her. They both entered her private office and closed the door.

The man seemed familiar to Catsy, but for some reason she couldn't remember where she'd seen him before. He looked rather interesting. Some scratches on his face made him resemble a thug, a not-unhandsome thug, who had polished a few of his rough edges.

At twenty to twelve, her mother's door opened and the man left, nodding to her on the way out. Idly, she nodded back.

She asked Laura about him and discovered his name was Murphy. "He's trying to locate some material I need, but we may have missed the deadline. Are you coming over with me?"

Catsy threw on her coat and mother and daughter caught the congressional subway. They didn't talk. Laura seemed preoccupied, breaking her concentration only to be polite to other members of Congress taking the short ride.

Inside the Capitol, Catsy watched her mother enter the main door, then she headed up to the gallery.

Jake Alban was there on the front row, looking down on the floor. When they'd first met, his face had been bruised and his chest had been taped because of a cracked rib, causing him to move like an old man. Since then she hadn't seen much of him. He and her mother had been maintaining a very low profile as a couple. And Catsy had not been invited to Laura's home ever since Jake moved in. Once again she was the outsider.

She wondered if Laura might not be afraid to let her spend too much time with Jake. She smiled at the thought and headed toward him. "Is this seat occupied?" she asked.

Jake looked up at her. "Oh, hi, Catsy. No. Sit down, please."

She could see what had drawn her mother to him. He seemed like a nice guy, but there was a tension under the surface. "Is Mother taking good care of you?"

There was something about the way she said it. Jake studied her before replying. "Very good care," he said.

"She's the best," Catsy said, leaning forward and watching Laura, down below, moving toward her seat. "At almost everything," she added.

"You mean there's something she can't do?" Was he just keeping it light, Catsy wondered, or was he starting to play?

"Oh, she can do it," she said. "It's just that she's not the best at it."

No reply this time. Just a brief smile.

"I am," Catsy said. "But you shouldn't just take my word for it."

"I think I'll have to," he said, standing up. "If you'll excuse me, there's someone I have to see."

He moved off through the crowd of spectators and reporters and stopped before the same man who'd been in her mother's office earlier. What was his name? Murphy. They both stopped speaking suddenly and looked at her. The Murphy character nodded at her again.

Then they continued talking. Murphy removed an envelope from his coat pocket and handed it to Jake, who headed out through the gallery doors. Murphy walked toward her.

"Good day, Mrs. Braden. Jake said I could take his seat."

"Where's he going?"

"To give something to your mom. My name's J. B. Murphy, by the way. Please call me Murph if you're so inclined."

"What is it you do, Murph?"

"Scuffle here and there for a buck," he said. "But on good days it brings me a lot of satisfaction."

"And is this a good day?"

"It's shapin' up that way."

Catsy became aware of something just over Murphy's shoulder.

She said to him, "There's a woman right behind you who's scowling at us."

Murphy turned to see a young, pretty woman with short, bright
red hair staring at him. Once she had his attention, she shook her
head sadly, as if to say she found him disappointing in every way.

He shrugged and faced forward again.

"Who was that?" Catsy asked.

"My cleaning lady."

74

◆

"The world is round and the place which
may seem like the end may also be only
the beginning."

IVY BAKER PRIEST

AT 11:55, BELLS were rung to summon dawdling members to the
Floor of the House.

Laura watched the Democratic side of the House begin to fill.
There would definitely be a quorum. A quorum and a vote.

The Clerk of the House of Representatives, a spindly man with
glasses the thickness of jelly jars, approached the Speaker's podium on what appeared to be arthritic limbs. He banged the gavel
several times and as the chatter diminished to a mild rumble, added
one last rap.

He then nodded to the Chaplain, whose red melon of a face
quivered with solemnity as he cleared his throat and began in
a loud, sonorous voice, "Let us pray, dear God, as we assemble
here . . ."

"Amens" filled the chamber.

Laura felt as if she were in one of those dreams in which you
were trying desperately to accomplish some task but for some
reason time had shifted into slow motion. Then she noticed a paper
at her feet. She scooped it up as the Clerk called for those present
to stand for the Pledge of Allegiance. She glanced at it as her lips
mouthed the Pledge. And her heart sank.

She barely remembered to sit as the Clerk pounded his gavel for
silence once again and began the organization of the 106th Con-

gress. Her despair turned to anger as the Democratic caucus nominated Lewis Ronkowski as Speaker of the House.

Applause for Ronkowski filled the chamber. On Laura's lap was a copy of the letter a "fan" had written to Jeremy Dunbar accusing her of having had a baby out of wedlock. Someone (popular nominee Ronkowski, probably) had added the line, "Was this letter the motive for murder?"

Laura looked up at the visitors' gallery. Jake was there somewhere. She wanted to see him, to see his comforting smile. Instead she spotted Penelope Krim, in the front row, leaning forward, staring at her, grinning like a gargoyle. With her wide shoulders and small head, she resembled a football player getting ready for a tackle . . .

A football player! Where had she heard a woman described as a linebacker? In her office? The evening after Jeremy Dunbar's murder?

Frantically, she searched for her notebook, then scribbled something on a sheet of paper. She folded it and signaled for a page. She handed the boy the note and asked him to carry out the instructions on it.

As he hurried up the aisle to the exit, she heard her own name being placed into nomination. The resulting round of applause was considerably more restrained than Lew Ronkowski's cheers and huzzahs. But, she told herself, the shouting wasn't over yet.

THE Clerk's call for a Roll vote was interrupted by a fragile, distinguished-looking congressman, a Democrat from Illinois, who rose for a point of order and, with no small display of eloquence, opened the floor to discussion.

One by one members rose to pontificate on general issues such as free trade, the family, voter turnout, and the sacred duties of American motherhood. Eventually this led up to the more immediate and far more interesting topic of Laura's nomination. A fat, perspiring congressman from a farm state asked with heavy humor if "Lady Christen's election would not find her to be a mentor of Republicans and a tormentor of Democrats." Another man hinted darkly that the election of an Independent could drag the House of Representatives back to "the perils and chaos of pre–Civil War times" if not worse. The inevitable phrase "two heartbeats away from the presidency" was used not by Ronkowski but by one of his cronies, a dwarflike, whey-faced congressman from the Far West who wore what appeared to be a red fright wig.

After considerably more of this, Congresswoman Esther Cooper stood up. She turned slowly, gray-haired and slightly stooped, and let her bright blue eyes, behind rimless glasses, sweep across her audience. Then, facing the daises, she began to speak.

In a strong, unwavering voice she informed those assembled that Laura Christen had at one point tried to convince *her* to run for Speaker. "I told her I was too old," Congresswoman Cooper said, enunciating every word. "But I agreed with her that changes were needed. I told her I realized how responsible she has been in bringing more women to this great institution. She is young and she is able. And she is the one who should seek the position."

She paused, and the members began to mutter yeas and nays.

"I'm not finished," Congresswoman Cooper said firmly, and the chatter ceased. "I told Congresswoman Christen that I would not support her. How could I and remain faithful to my leadership position in the House and in my party? But that was then."

Suddenly, Lew Ronkowski rose from his seat and called out, "Will the gentlewoman from New Jersey please yield the floor for a question?"

Cooper looked over at him and in an annoyed tone snapped, "Sit down, Lewis."

The House burst into laughter.

When order was restored, she continued. "As I said, I had decided *not* to support Laura Christen. But then I began receiving these"—and she held up the familiar photocopied sheets—"these tawdry bits of trash that I am given to understand emanated from the offices of a public relations firm employed by the present Speaker of the House."

She looked again at Ronkowski and said, "Don't put on that innocent look, Lewis. Only this morning I received a sworn state-ment from the young fellow who actually manned the photocopy machine. In a vainglorious attempt to hold on to your precious position, Lewis, you have sent each of us this supposed *evidence* that Congresswoman Christen once worked as a dealer in illegal narcotics. Then you have followed with more of your *proof* that she had an illegitimate child and abandoned it.''

She faced the assembly. ''Some of you out there may have accepted this nonsense as fact. Much the same as the poor misguided people of America have believed the filthy nonsense spewed out by those supermarket scandal sheets and certain so-called *columnists*.

''I doubt that there is one among us who has not felt the sting of the Big Lie. I can only hope that none of us has accepted these Big Lies without question. Anyone who knows the Congresswoman, anyone who has worked side by side with her in this august body, will recognize the charges for what they are—scurrilous untruths.

''But there is a time for faith and a time for hard proof. And for that we should thank the man who investigated the claim.'' She shaded her eyes and looked up at the gallery. ''I hope you're up there, J. B. Murphy.''

Murphy's face was a bright blushing red.

Congresswoman Cooper raised a manila envelope and drew from it a sheet of paper. ''What Mr. Murphy was able to secure is a signed statement from Senator William D. Yeagan, Democrat, Wyoming. Twenty-one years ago, as a young district attorney in the City of Los Angeles, he successfully prosecuted a couple, Darla and Gordon Lavery, on counts of drug possession and distribution. According to Senator Yeagan, far from being implicated in that prosecution, Laura Christen was largely responsible for the apprehension of the Laverys and assisted him greatly in building a case against them.

''Since then, the Laverys have borne Congresswoman Christen an ill-will that has manifested itself in vicious falsehoods such as this fictional garbage, which our illustrious Speaker has so generously passed along to us.'' She held up the photocopied sheets once again. Then she crumpled them into a ball and tossed them away dismissively. There was total silence.

Suddenly the stillness of the chamber was broken by Laura's voice, calling, ''Will the gentlewoman yield the floor?''

Esther Cooper looked at Laura with the kindest of smiles. ''With the utmost pleasure," she said, "I shall yield the floor to the gentlewoman from California."

Esther returned to her seat as Laura thanked her and paused with just a hint of uncertainty, staring into the alert faces of her fellow members, some friendly, some scowling in open animosity. "I appear before you not to discuss my qualifications for the post to which I aspire. My qualifications are a matter of record. I have made no secrets of my political views.

"The main reason I have chosen to speak at this time has nothing to do with the business of politics. Simply stated, I wish to correct some of the things that have been written about me and said about me here today. As the gentlewoman from New Jersey has just told you, the stories about my dealing in drugs are blatant lies. She is incorrect, however, when she says that the most recently circulated rumor, the one you received this morning, is equally false. It is not."

THERE were murmurs now. And the clicks of cameras from the press gallery. Laura continued and as she did, her eyes began to tear. "On the morning of December 12, 1972, I gave birth to a male baby in a private hospital in the state of Nevada. My son died . . . less than twenty-four hours later . . . of natural causes. I was unmarried at the time. I had done nothing wrong except to fall in love and then to enjoy every moment of my child growing inside of me. I felt no guilt then, only sorrow over the loss of my beautiful baby. I feel no guilt today, only confusion as to why this very personal tragedy has been brought to your attention at this time"— she raised the page and waved it—"in a manner so uncommonly cruel and heartless. I thank you for your attention and, Congresswoman Cooper, I thank you for yielding the floor."

As Laura took her seat, Congresswoman Cooper stood and began the applause. It was picked up by people in the visitors' gallery and then floated softly down to the members of Congress, where it became a roar.

Laura stood and looked at her fellow members as they rose in her honor, continuing to applaud her.

As order was restored, Esther Cooper once again addressed the assembly. "I shall not prolong this discussion," she said. "If

Laura Christen is guilty of anything it is of refusing to accept the status quo, of deciding to stop criminals like the Laverys who ply a trade built on the destruction of the human will and spirit, of standing up against hardheads like Lewis Ronkowski who treat the hallowed Congress of the United States as if it were a men's club, where women are only allowed by special dispensation.

"I urge every woman in this chamber who has felt the scorn of her masculine associates, and every man who has allowed his narrow prejudices to lead him to eagerly accept lies against women, to vote their conscience. Mr. Clerk, I move the previous question and call for a vote on the nominations for Speaker. And I ask my colleagues to join me in voting for the honorable lady."

Once more applause filled the chamber.

Twenty-four minutes later, the vote was announced by the Clerk. Christen: 334, Ronkowski: 99, both nominees abstaining.

With the sound of clapping and yells filling her ears, Laura was ushered to the chair by the Committee of Escort. It was then that, by tradition, the outgoing Speaker was given the floor. Lewis Ronkowski had not risen to his position in his party by swimming against the political tide. Exaggerating his limp outrageously, he stood and began an eloquent farewell to the "old, dark days of cronyism and sexism" and a welcome to "the refreshing sea wind of equality and uncompromising professionalism that would carry our ship swiftly to our goals."

But as he limped past Laura on his way from the upper dais, he whispered, "Enjoy it while you can, sweetiepants."

Her swearing in was swift and solemn. She then addressed the chamber. "I will try to make this brief," she said. "I'd like to close this session not with my plans for the future but with an apology for something I've done. It's nothing that has been mentioned here. As unprofessional and, I suppose, even scandalous, as have been these most recent revelations, I feel no shame for them. I have lived my life as well as I was able.

"I disclaim any responsibility for the fact that someone—and I won't speculate on his or her identity—has spread stories about me. That person will have to answer not to me but to a considerably less benign authority. The original letter that so carelessly discussed the tragedy of my lost child was evidence illegally removed from the scene of a crime. That crime is part of a much larger investigation that involves both the Washington Metropolitan Police and the Federal Bureau of Investigation. I am confident that these organizations will be quick to trace the recent history of that letter.''

She paused. ''But to return to my apology . . . It involves a man named Jacob Alban, whom I will be marrying next week. Because I wanted so badly to receive the honor you have bestowed on me today, I made the decision to keep our relationship a secret. I forced him to do the same, against his better judgment. I felt that a public display of my private life at this time, with everything that was being written about me, might in some way have diminished my capability in your eyes. I was mistaken. I apologize to him and I apologize to you for not believing enough in your ability to separate love from cynical slander.''

She backed away from the platform and once again was greeted by a standing ovation. Through the open door at the rear of the chamber she saw Jake waiting for her.

She was scarcely aware of the handshakes and the words of encouragement as she floated down the aisle. Then she was in Jake's arms and the doorman was chuckling behind a gloved hand.

''Kiss me, Jake,'' she said.

''In front of all these assembled?''

The doorman winked and closed the door on the smiling faces of the members of Congress, keeping his back turned to the couple.

They kissed then. And when they parted Laura cried, ''OK, now let's go tell the rest of the world.''

He hugged her tighter and said, ''There's something else we have to do first.''

75

◆

"Truth is tough."

OLIVER WENDELL HOLMES

As THE CROWD vacated the visitors' gallery, Murphy leaned over and said to Catsy Braden, "Sit down for a minute, Catsy. I'd like to talk with you."

With a mischievous smile, she complied, certain that at the very least she was about to be asked to dinner. "Well," she said brightly, "what's on your mind, Murph?"

"It's about the way you and Jim Prosser tried to red-dog Ronkowski."

"What's that supposed to mean?" she snapped, starting to stand.

He put his hand on her arm. "C'mon now, hear me out."

"Why should I?"

"Because if you humor me, I probably won't go to the police."

She sat down, looking around the gallery. The area near them was almost deserted. The redhead was taking her time leaving. She was looking at them.

Murphy said, "At the party for the Ford Theater, I sort of overheard you and Prosser chatting about something you were both keeping from the Congresswoman."

She said nothing.

"I know what it was. The Laverys sent a blackmail threat to your mom and you intercepted it and took it to the Professor. He wanted to confront the Congresswoman with it, but you had a better idea. Why not defuse the threat by spreading a bunch of wild rumors that wouldn't pan out? Then, even if the Laverys began telling tales about your mom, the thing about the baby, for example, everybody would assume it was the boy crying wolf again.

"Using the Laverys' blackmail note as a guide, you and the Professor sent a couple of nasty little letters you created out of thin air. The Ronkowski note about drugs produced a lovely effect. He was so hungry for that sort of thing, he didn't bother to check it out. And we just saw it bounce back on him hard."

"I'm not sure what you're trying to prove."

"I don't have to try and prove anything," Murphy told her. "I've got a full statement signed by the Professor. He was just looking for a father confessor."

"Good old reliable Jim," she said. "Okay, suppose we did send a few letters. The plan worked. Mother is the new Speaker of the House."

"You sent Mike Roberts a note about your mom's money being tainted. You took a chance. Suppose he didn't bother to check it out? Suppose he just withdrew his support?"

"Then we would have sent him another letter with an even more outrageous lie," she said. "If one was untrue, they all would be in doubt."

"The problem was, Roberts sent some poor sod of a detective to check out your mom's past and that rattled the cage of a real mean fella named Newfield. Your little trick cost that detective his life. And that gossip guy. And some poor truckdriver who it turns out didn't run over your father after all. And Tom Hamilton."

Her eyes started to tear. "I'm sorry about the others, but I'm glad Tommy's dead. I'd like to think I did have something to do with that."

"Why, Catsy? What was Tommy to you?"

She closed down. "Nothing. I don't know why I'm sitting here, listening to your nonsense."

"Did Tommy hurt you when you were young?" he asked. "You told Jim Prosser you lost your virginity when you were twelve. They say Tommy liked very young girls."

The tears were flowing now. Murphy stared at her uncomfortably, then put his arm around her. She replied between sobs, "I tried to tell my mother, but I couldn't. She was so close to him. I was afraid she'd think I was lying. Or, worse, that she'd blame me.''

"Did you ever tell her?"

She shook her head.

"Why not, girl?"

"Because later I began to think it was all *her* fault. He was *her* friend, not mine. She had all the money in the world, but we wound up living in *his* house that summer. She flew back to Washington leaving me in *his* care.''

Murphy realized with a shock that she had reverted to a childish singsong. "She didn't know she couldn't trust him," he told her softly. "But if you'd said something, she would have believed you. She'd believe you now.''

Catsy pulled away from him, leaving the little girl behind. He handed her a handkerchief and she used it to dab at her eyes and face. "This is very foolish," she said. "It was so long ago.''

"This stuff doesn't just go away," he told her. "You've got to do something about it. There's somebody you should talk to.''

"A shrink?"

"Well, yeah, that, too. But I had someone else in mind.''

He stood up and led her from the gallery.

LAURA'S Seville was parked at the curb, precisely where Murph had asked Jake to put it. Jake was leaning against the back fender, his overcoat tight around him, trying not to look their way as they descended the Capitol steps. Murphy was conscious of Margaret on the periphery of his vision, standing to their right, watching them.

When Catsy saw the car, saw her mother in the passenger seat, she stopped. "What have you told her?" she asked Murphy.

"Not a thing. That's up to you.''

"This isn't going to work," she said. "I wouldn't know where to start.''

"Start with Tommy Hamilton and see how it goes from there.''

"I don't think I can.''

"Think of it as a test," he said. "If you pass, you get to move on with your life. If you fail, you stay where you are, unhappy, screwing around, hurting people and hurting yourself.''

"It's too hard. I don't—"

She stopped. Laura had seen them and was getting out of the car. She waved at them. Then, apparently puzzled, she called out, "Catsy? Is something the matter?"

"There's your opening," Murphy told Catsy. "You're never gonna have it easier."

She gave him one fleeting, vaguely troubled nod, and went to meet her mother. She walked slowly, hesitatingly, at first, then rushed into Laura's open arms.

The two women, pressed close together, daughter speaking, mother listening, began walking toward Independence Avenue. Jake looked up at Murphy, saluted, and got into the Seville to follow them.

Murphy felt Margaret's presence beside him before he actually saw her. "What in the world have you been up to?" she asked. "With that stupid grin, you look just like an overgrown leprechaun."

He turned to her, assuming his most serious demeanor. "I've been saving souls, like the priest my sainted mother prayed I would become."

She raised a skeptical eyebrow. "I can never tell when you're lying," she said. "It's what I like most about you."

"Then why don't we go close up the office and find a nice restaurant where we can see which of us tells the biggest lies."

She raised an eyebrow. "You'll win," she said. "It's the only game you're sure to win."

The combination of the cold and the afternoon sun brought a glow to her face. Her hair was like fire. Her green eyes were sparkling.

God, but she reminded him of her mother.